THREE DEADLY TWINS

David A. Thyfault

ISBN 978-1-937862-86-1

Library of Congress Control Number 2015909204

This book was published by BookCrafters,
Parker, Colorado.

This book may be ordered from
www.bookcrafters.net
and other online bookstores.

DEDICATION

To my lifelong pal, Eddie Marquiss.

I wish you were still with us so you could read the book that you inspired.

WITH GRATITUDE

Many people contribute to a book like this so thanks to you all. Special thanks go out to:

George Andrews
Robert Arnold
Caroline Byers
Kristin Feldkamp
Heather Rhode Hughes
Liz Netzel
Mary Ann Rhode
Jason Thyfault
John Walker
The gang at Fire Station 28, Denver, Colorado
BookCrafters

CHAPTER 1

If it weren't for the bars on the windows and the glaring lack of walls around the stool, Don's cell would have resembled a dorm room in a struggling junior college. Breakfast was over and it would be a couple of hours before he'd be allowed in the common area, which was one of the token rewards for being less bad than most of the others.

At five-foot ten, early thirties, and white, Don ought to be doing something more productive. Instead, the ever-boring routine of minimum security dragged on while the well-trained wisp of brown hair that dangled above his baby face added to the collegiate effect. But prison wasn't a place for no college boys.

One of the worst parts of living in this particular ten-by-twelve chunk of real estate was the bathroom arrangement —or the lack thereof. Don had pooped in worse places, especially during the brief period he spent on the frontlines in the early part of the Iraq war.

At least those sons-a-bitches had a good excuse. Port-a-Potties would have been easy targets. This was different. The state could have built some walls around his friggin' stool if they had wanted to. He shook his head, unbuckled his belt and parked his butt. About all he could do for the next few minutes was read a recycled mag and think about Miranda.

With the paperwork finished, Don washed up better than

he needed to just to kill a few extra minutes before returning to his bunk, where he laid down. As always, his flattened foam pillow smelled stuffy. So did everything else around there. No wonder. Fifty miles inland, Lancaster California was nearly always dry and hot in spite of the air conditioning.

Bored beyond bored, he sighed. At least this was better than living among the general prisoner population where he could easily get stuck with a know-it-all tough-guy cellmate. For now, maybe he could sleep some time away. Horny, he wondered what Miranda was up to.

Slow minutes crept past before he heard a familiar clinking coming in his direction. It had to be Jingle Keys, as Don thought of the huge black guard with the perfect smile—except for the gold tooth on the lower right. His official name was Officer Jackson. Something was up. This wasn't part of the routine. Probably had something to do with somebody else in one of the nearby cells. A moment later Jingle Keys stopped just outside Don's extra-thick hardwood door. Don opened one eye. A large key invaded the deadbolt.

"Evans," Jingle Keys said with more authority than the drill sergeants Don once knew. "I brought you a present."

Huh? Don rolled over and sat on the edge of his bunk as a wide-eyed fellow about his age, with a folder-sized envelope in one hand and a blanket and coffee cup in the other, eased his way into Don's not-so-private hideout. A goddamn cellmate. He glared at the new guy, who was both taller and thinner than he, then back to Jingle Keys. "Couldn't you stick him with somebody else?"

"Nope," Jingle Keys said. "It's your turn. He's a first-timer."

The newbie's anxious eyes scanned the boxy cell as if they were getting used to a dark room. Then he extended his shaking hand. "I'm Thomas. Sorry to invade your space."

Invade. He got that right. Don preferred to be alone, especially at night when he was free to think about Miranda. But what the hell could he do? This wasn't no damn hotel and any boisterous protests would be perceived as making trouble. Like it or not, Don had a new cellmate. "Don't worry about it," he said, taking the dude's hand. "Ain't your fault. I'm Don Evans."

Jingle Keys stepped backwards into the doorframe. "You girls play nice," he said, his golden tooth accenting a mischievous grin. "I don't want to hear no banging on the walls, if you get my drift."

"Cute," Don said just before the heavy door clanked shut and the auto-lock clicked. He turned to his new cellmate, would have liked to say what he thought of smart-ass guards, but opted instead to ask the usual question. "What you in for?" He'd best not be no chi-mo 'cause Don didn't have no sympathy for child molesters.

Thomas carefully placed his coffee cup and blanket onto the counter, but clung to his folder as he slowly eased onto the remaining bunk as if it were a nest for Amazon-sized bedbugs. Don resisted the urge to laugh.

"I fell off a ladder, broke my collarbone and over-dosed on pain meds," Thomas said. "Doctor cut me off but I met a guy who said the stuff was basically just heroin and he could get me some on the cheap. So I stockpiled a couple dozen decks. Then I got busted. Cops said I intended to sell it, which was bullshit." He shrugged. "Since I wouldn't rat out my source, the bastards sent me here."

There was probably more to this guy's misfortune than that, but Don had learned a long time ago that most of the greeners fluffed up their stories—at least until they understood that they weren't getting out early. At least the guy wasn't no stooly. Don respected guys who knew how to hold their mud. "We all got screwed in one way or the other," he said. He flashed his arm around the cell as if he were a magician introducing a beautiful assistant. "Now we're both stuck in the Shithole Motel."

Thomas pulled his folder close to his chest. "What about you? Get caught in the arms of some other dude's wife?"

Don snickered. "Not me. There's enough women out there without doing that crap."

"But it had something to do with a woman, didn't it?"

Don sat up tall. "How the hell'd you know that?"

"Simple. You're more focused on getting out of here than making waves. You must have something going on."

Good observation. This guy didn't seem so bad, especially for a newbie. If nothing else, his fresh ears lent Don an opportunity to burn a half-hour or so. "Her name's Miranda. We met over a keg of beer at a twins convention."

Thomas grinned for the first time since he'd arrived. "Twins convention?"

"Twinsburg, Ohio. Not far from where I grew up. They do it every year. I just went for kicks."

"So you're a twin?"

"An identical. But me and Mac ain't like normal twins. We hate each other. Ain't spoken in years."

"Mac and Donald? Like hamburgers?"

Don smirked. "Worse than that. When we were one damn day old, our old man was drunk, as usual, and named us after that goddamn fairytale."

"Old McDonald had a farm?" Thomas said, grinning even bigger than before. "Didn't your mom say something?"

Don waved his hand dismissively. "Couldn't. That bastard beat her up when she argued with him."

Thomas tilted his head. "Well, neither name is that bad —until you hear them both together and in the right order. What did your brother do to piss you off?"

"Everything. Asshole always thought he was better than me. When our old man beat us, Mac cried like a damn girl, so I got the worst of it. After high school, he got a motorcycle and rode around the country, but I had to go in the goddamn Army. When I got back I tried to look him up, but he had a girlfriend and wouldn't let me crash with him. He was always screwing me over so screw him back." Don suddenly realized he cussed a lot more when he talked about his brother.

"What about Miranda? She got an identical too? Maybe you could hook me up when I get outta here?"

"She's fraternal. Got a mentally challenged brother named Mickey. He acts like a ten-year-old. Lives in a group home. Gets mad as hell sometimes. She brought him to the convention for a change of pace. All she wants is to take care of her brother."

"So you hit it off pretty good, but something must have gone wrong."

"You got that right." Don checked the clock again. Time moved faster when the bullshit was flying. "We hooked up and I came back here to California. We was getting along pretty good when we went to a bar where some half-drunk asshole tried to pick her up. You know the type. Big son-of-a-bitch. I told him to leave her alone, but he didn't like me butting in, so later him and two friends with billy clubs was waiting for me. I coulda handled that one dude, but not all three with weapons. They got me on the ground and banged on my head and face pretty good." Don proudly pointed to a scar on his eyebrow. "Took eight stitches. I hung in there as best I could, then that first bastard grabbed Miranda. I thought he was going to rape her. I got back to my knees but one of the other pricks treated my head like a goddamn golf ball and took a full swing. I woke up in the hospital with my eye swollen shut, and damn near lost my ear. Good news was enough other people was standing around by that time that Miranda didn't get hurt."

Thomas shook his head. "But it wasn't over, was it?"

"Hell, no. I wasn't going to let that chicken shit get away with his crap. He didn't know I'm a bad ass with cutters, knives. Grew up with 'em. Trained with 'em as a Green Beret. Even became a butcher when I got out of the service. I can split a toothpick with a machete. Coulda slit that son-of-a bitch from ear to ear too, but Miranda stopped me."

"Really? If she stopped you, how'd you end up in here?"

"She talked me out of killing the bastard, but I wasn't

gonna let him off that easy, so me and her compromised. One morning, after he went to work, I jimmied his door with a Bowie knife. I wanted to cut up everything he owned, furniture, kitchen cabinets, all of it. But when I got into his bedroom, I was attacked by a big old boxer that was hiding from the noise until I got too close. Damn thing was lightning-fast."

Thomas's head snapped back. "You stabbed a dog?"

"Sliced. It was an accident, cause of my reflexes—how was I supposed to know that dude was watching somebody else's pet? Anyway, the damage was done and I had a ton of blood on me when I got back to the parking lot. Trouble was I had parked in a reserved spot and the woman it belonged to just come home and already got my plate number to have my car towed." He shrugged. "I got a three-year bit in this shithole for destruction of property and cruelty to an animal —although I never would have hurt that dog if he didn't catch me off-guard."

"Three years, huh?"

"Only got four months left. Miranda thinks I'm some Prince Charming 'cause I stood up for her, but she's the one who's got her shit together. In addition to taking care of her brother, she comes to see me every week, and once a month we get to go to the bone yard."

"Bone yard?"

"Love cabins, Dude. For conjugal visits. The main reason I keep my nose clean. Don't want them to take that away."

"Now you're making me wish I had a girlfriend."

"Just wait a while. It gets worse." Don pointed at Thomas's folder. "That's enough about me. What you got in there?"

Thomas lifted the file. "This?" He glanced inside. "Papers from my attorney. We were just talking about filing an appeal with the court." He frowned and tugged a few pages out. "Hey. This can't be mine. My dumbshit attorney musta—oh, I see what happened. These people have the same last name as me. He got some of their papers mixed up with mine."

"Interesting. Mind if I take a look?" Don asked, reaching for the misplaced papers. Practically anything was better than reading the same magazines over and over. He glanced through the pages. "This stuff was written back in the 'eighties. Looks like some old farts left a bunch of money to their granddaughter." He scanned further. "Says she don't get the money 'til she gets married."

"That's strange. How much money we talking about?"

Don flipped the papers over and back. "Can't tell. Some of the pages are missing. Gotta be a lot, though. Nobody would spend money on legal fees to do something like this over peanuts."

"That girl's probably filthy rich by now."

"Not if she ain't married yet. You got any more pages in that folder?"

Thomas thumbed through his file. "Nope. Looks like we just got part of it. Why don't guys like us ever catch a break like that girl did?"

Don tossed the papers aside. "'Cause we're a couple a losers in the Shithole Motel, that's why."

CHAPTER 2

Miranda pressed her blonde hair aside and delicately spritzed some *Euphoria* behind her ears. She climbed out of her black SUV and into the relatively cool ninety-nine degree desert heat. At thirty-five years old, the heat bothered her a little more than it used to. She brushed her hand down the front of her blue polyester pantsuit and heard the clickety-click of her sandals as she strode toward the building. She wondered if it were possible to overdress for a conjugal visit.

Her visits with Don had nothing to do with pity sex. She genuinely loved him. He'd always treated her differently than most men she'd met—including the married ones—who all seemed to have one thing in mind.

In fact that was the problem with nearly everybody she'd gotten close to in her life. They'd exploit nearly anybody if they could get ahead in some other way. Her parents were like that.

Back in Chicago, where she grew up, her daddy was an attorney and her mother enjoyed the relative comfort that his success afforded them. But Daddy had immoral dealings. For instance he once convinced an elderly couple to sell their long-held family deli to a friend of his at half its value when he could have just as easily helped them get a loan and keep their store. Miranda never forgot how proud he was for his so-called *accomplishment*.

Her mom had moral problems too. At the time, Miranda was too young to understand that when Mommy dropped her off at a midday baby sitter's, from time to time, she was actually sneaking off with a lover. It wasn't until Miranda was in sixth grade that she saw the guy waiting in a car for her mom and was later told he was *Uncle Larry*, but there were never any other references to this mysterious relative. What else could it have been?

Then there was the worst part—how they both treated Miranda's sweet twin brother, Mickey. They were the ones who failed to put locks on the kitchen cabinets. Then, when he was three, he found some cleaning products under the sink. Nobody knows exactly how much he drank but the brain damage was serious and permanent. From that time on her parents kept him in institutions where he had always been grouped in with other mentally challenged people. They looked upon him as an inconvenience. A lost cause. She concluded they treated him like that because there wasn't anything for them to gain by investing additional time, effort or money in him. Nonetheless, Miranda always loved her brother and had to plead with her parents to take her to visit him.

Her parents weren't the only people she'd known who mistreated others. Most of the bosses she'd had manipulated people for their own gain if they could. One potential employer came right out and made sex a condition of her employment. She'd turned in her resume to secure an assistant manager's job at one of the well-known printing companies she now referred to as Stinkos. The very next day she was invited in for an interview where crooked-toothed Kenny took her in his office and said matter-of-factly, "If you'll go to bed with me, I'll give you the job." Somebody else might find a situation like that to be erotic, but not Miranda. She simply walked out.

Then there was her ex. They dated a couple of years before they got married. But almost instantly he lost interest in intimacy with her yet he forever flirted with the help, especially the barely-legal group. At first she wondered how he could be so interested in those relatively naïve young women while she had more sensuality in one finger than they had in their entire wrinkle-free bodies. But it didn't take her long to figure out it was a numbers game to him. Notches on the bedpost. The thrill of the chase. His self-esteem was at its highest when the young bimbos flirted back. Then when she had evidence he'd taken the next step, that being into bedrooms, at least two or three times, she divorced him.

The ultimate life-lesson she derived from these relationships was many successful people would turn their backs on people with whom they had relationships if it meant they could get something better from somebody else.

All of this was why she liked Don right from the beginning. He may not have had a college education or his own business or a big-time job or even a nice car. But there was one thing he had that none of them did: loyalty. Don was always more concerned for the relationship than he was for himself.

When they first met at the twins convention, instead of treating her like an outlet for lust, Don took some time off of his meat-cutting job and flew to California where they had several dates without ever discussing intimacy. Even though he was a little rough around the edges, he was both interesting and fun to be with. He cared about her and was nice to Mickey. All of that made the physical part of their relationship more natural and meaningful when it finally happened.

Several months later, after Don moved to California and got a new job, he took on three thugs at a bar because one of them wouldn't leave her alone. Nobody else, including her ex, had ever done anything that chivalrous for her. That cemented it. Don deserved the same loyalty from her, even if it was awkward sometimes, like on conjugal visit day.

As she drew closer to the building she popped a TicTac in her mouth. As badly as she wanted to see Don, she wished it wasn't so obvious why she was there. But, they were only allowed one visit per week and only one of those each month was in private—and all were limited to an hour. She simply had to draw on her high school days, when she had had a minor role in the annual play, and *pretend* it didn't bother her. She scoffed at the magazine articles she'd read in which women complained that their sex lives had become dull.

She made her way through the main gate and toward the check-in area. If she was fortunate, Don might have some ideas about how she could work things out for Mickey's newest problems. She fought off a shiver. Mickey never adapted well to moving.

Once inside, Miranda turned off her cellphone and checked in her belongings before a female guard, Maxine Montoya, patted her down and escorted her to the waiting area. After she spent a few minutes of pretending to be invisible, the heavy clinking of keys in a nearby doorknob indicated that Officer Jackson and Don had arrived.

Without a hint of discretion the guard looked her over as if she were already naked. She wished she were a lot smaller. An inch tall would be about right. She hurried toward Don, who was wearing the usual orange jumpsuit, and wrapped her arms around his neck. "How you doing, Donnie?" she said as tenderly as possible.

"Hold off there, you two," Jackson said while pointing toward the yard. "Save that kissy-face stuff for the cabin."

"No problem," Don said with enthusiasm. He snatched Miranda's hand and together they led Jackson into the yard, which was surrounded by a tall chain-link fence with barbed wire rolled on top. A wide, straight sidewalk led through a nicely kept xeriscaped area of lava rock, Joshua trees, cacti and desert flowers. To their left, the whir of window-mounted air conditioners on four identical modular homes disturbed the peace.

"Number four," Jackson said from behind Miranda. "But don't go too fast. I don't want to work any harder than I have to in this heat." She dragged her feet along like a man so that her rear-end wouldn't sway and attract his sleazy eyes, but she assumed it was a waste of virtue.

At Cabin Two, behind the purr of the air conditioner, Miranda heard some thumping and an overly loud moan of pleasure from another woman. Don squeezed Miranda's hand as if to signal they would be doing the same thing in mere minutes. She squeezed back.

"Stop right there," Jackson said as they reached the final cabin. He stepped around them and unlocked the door like a bouncer in a low-priced brothel might do. "One hour. That's it," he said, helping himself to another lustful gaze at Miranda's breasts. "Be ready when your time is up. I ain't in no mood for messing around. Got it?"

"Yeah, yeah. We got it," Don said.

Inside, the main room was cool, clean and simple. Like the other cabins, it had a walled-in bathroom sans tub, which Don liked. In addition, there were a couple of metal folding chairs and a double bed on which the mattress sagged.

Ordinarily Miranda preferred some hugging and cuddling before making love, but this particular time she hoped a "wham-bam-thank-you-ma'am" arrangement would leave them with some time to discuss Mickey's anger issues. She removed her jacket and wrapped her arms around Don's neck. "I've been looking forward to this, Donnie," she whispered.

"First, I've got something to talk to you about," he said, nudging her away. He scooted to the curtains, looked up the sidewalk. "He's gone." Don flopped onto one of the chairs and patted the other. "Sit down. This is important."

He hadn't been this animated in the thirty-one months he'd been there. "What's the matter?"

His eyes razored through her. She pulled at the top button of her blouse. "You're not going to try to escape are you, 'cause that would be foolish since you're getting out in a few months anyway?"

"No, no. Nothing like that. I need you to listen to what I have to say—the whole thing. We don't have time to argue over details or ask a bunch of questions. So let me get everything I want to say on the table; then we can discuss the most important items one by one if we have time. Okay?"

She sighed. "But I want—"

"Don't worry. It'll be worth it." He rose, checked out the window again then slipped his chair directly in front of hers. "The other day, I got a new cellmate. A first-timer. His name is Thomas. He accidentally got hold of some documents about somebody else who had the same last name as his."

"So what?"

"The papers were about a trust for a woman named Rachel who lives somewhere around here. Apparently she doesn't know that she'll inherit a lot of money just for getting married."

Miranda sighed. "Why are we wasting time?"

"You promised not to ask questions. Remember?"

Miranda mockingly touched her forefinger to her lips. "Oops. My bad. But hurry."

Don grinned. "That night, after lights out, I realized I'd found a once-in-a-lifetime goldmine." He touched her cheek with the back of a knuckle. "You and me are going to be filthy rich."

A get-rich-quick scheme? Yeah, right. Those always work. Miranda primped his collar. "You're wasting our time, Donnie. I need to talk to you about-"

He twisted his head down and away. "This is more important. We're talking about the big leagues here, and I want to see what you think. But this ain't for no good girls, so if you don't want in, that's okay."

"Let me guess. You want me to tell that woman about her trust and she'll be so grateful she'll run right out and get married to a handsome prince and give us a big reward. Right? 'Cause if that's it—"

Don scoffed. "Nah. That's small ball." He lowered his voice. "I know how we can get it all."

Miranda leapt to her feet. "It sounds like you're talking about something dishonest and I wouldn't want to steal somebody else's money." She jammed her hands onto her hips. "Do I have to remind you that we won't be alone like this again for another month?"

"I know that, Baby. I want to do it too, but that ought to tell you how important this is. Now, you promised me that you'd listen to the whole thing, so please just stick with me until you've heard me out."

Miranda folded her arms across her chest. "Alright, but you're wasting our time if you think I'm going to cheat somebody out of her inheritance."

"I don't think she'll miss it." He inched his chair even closer, placed his knees against hers. "It's a double con, double murder."

Miranda rolled her eyes and shook her head. "I can't believe this."

"It's beautiful," Don went on. "The first step involves that asshole brother of mine. You'll have to trick him into falling in love with you, which should be easy 'cause he's a sucker for good-looking blondes."

"Oh, please tell me more," she said with all the mockery she could generate.

"Then it gets trickier. You'll have to tell him about the trust and persuade him to meet that Rachel woman. Then he'll date her and figure out what he has to do to get her to marry him."

"Uh-huh. That ought to take fifteen minutes or so."

Don ignored her. "When they get married, the trust money becomes hers. A few months later, she has a horrible accident and my brother miraculously inherits her money."

"A horrible accident? No sweat. The God of Accidents is always standing by in case we need him."

Don put his hand on Miranda's knee. "By that time, I should be out of this shithole and all we got to do is get rid of Mac once and for all. Since I look just like him and nobody knows either of us around here, I'll become him and nobody will suspect a thing. Then you and me slip off somewhere and live like royalty." Don sat back and locked his hands behind his head. "Okay. That's the gist of it. Now it's your turn. What do you think?"

"Is that all?" she said thrusting her hands skywards. "Just a couple murders? And I thought you were going to say something crazy. I have an idea. Maybe Jackson will loan us a gun. When do we start?"

Don shook his head. "C'mon. Cut the sarcasm. I need you to be open-minded. Give me some legitimate feedback."

Miranda sighed. "Legitimate feedback? Okay. How's this for legitimate feedback? That has to be one of the dumbest things I've ever heard from anybody, ever, especially you." She checked the clock and wrapped her arms around his shoulders. "We only have twenty minutes left. I don't want to waste them. I have something to talk to you about."

Don removed her hands. "I thought you'd say something like that, but this is doable and it'll change everything for us. Now what's the first thing about it that bothers you?"

She would have screamed out loud if she weren't afraid somebody would think she was having a record–setting orgasm. Instead she lowered her voice. "You're kidding. Right? All I wanted to do was make love and discuss Mickey, but you're too stoked to care."

"No, Baby. It's the opposite. You're the one who doesn't understand. We need this. Let me try again."

Second verse, same as the first. Don launched into the same litany, ignoring her rolled eyes, folded arms and sighs of frustration until finally, a shadow darkened the curtain. Miranda's heart jumped as the combination black guard and white knight waggled his key into the lock. Thank God. She bolted to the door.

On the way back to the holding area Don tried to grasp her hand, but she pulled back, disgusted and unsure if she wanted to see him again. She rushed straight to the check-in area, retrieved her belongings and got the hell out of there.

Outside, she marched briskly and breathed deeply. Shaking her head, she yanked her cellphone out of her purse, checked the read-out. There were a half-dozen new text messages from the director of Mickey's group home; the first one was painfully simple: *EMERGENCY!*

CHAPTER 3

An unanticipated honk sent Miranda, red eyes and all, swerving back into her lane. Damn it. Stay focused. A difficult objective considering all the unwelcome turmoil that had jammed its way into her life. Another tear dripped into her lap.

No more than a long hour had elapsed since Don exhibited a lack of ethics that she never would have imagined. Then Dr. Fenn, the female director of Mickey's group home, summoned her.

She should have anticipated the call. After all, she'd had several face-to-face conversations with Fenn about Mickey's outbursts. And of course there were Miranda's very own eyes. She'd seen Mickey's heightened impatience and the anger when he lashed out at others. Why did she kid herself into thinking he'd magically get better on his own? It appeared that her days as an ostrich were over. What a dope. She pulled into the group home parking lot and speed-walked to her appointment.

After checking in, she slouched into the lounge chair in the corner of the combination living room/lobby. The whole place boasted of organization, much like Fenn's own office, where the walls were packed with certificates and awards, and photographs with her colleagues and other photos of her cats. Missing were pictures of kids or a husband or any other indication of a core family.

Miranda clicked her tongue against her teeth. That was another reason she should have seen what was coming. Fenn was married to her job. A pro like that went to all the conferences, took all the continuing education classes, read all the new books on the subject at hand. When a person of that ilk warned her of Mickey's escalating problems, she should have taken the message more seriously. But as usual, she put more emphasis on hope and prayers than studies and science.

"Miranda, come on in," Dr. Fenn said from the corner.

Miranda rose and followed the ever-proper fortyish doctor into her private office. "Your work area always looks so nice," Miranda said, knowing from previous conversations that they both had to keep their surroundings extra tidy around certain clients, such as Mickey, or the clients got nervous and easily aggravated.

"Thank you. I'm sorry to have been so persistent this morning, but I really needed to speak with you."

"I'm the one who should apologize, but I was in an important meeting where cellphones weren't allowed."

"Nonetheless," Fenn said, tapping one of her desk drawers, "I want to thank you for coming as quickly as possible." She hesitated a moment then leaned forward. "You know we love Mickey, but I'm afraid I don't have very good news."

Miranda raised her hand to her mouth. "Is he okay?"

Fenn nodded. "For now, but this morning at breakfast, something set him off. He became very aggressive. I thought he was going to hurt another client and we couldn't allow that. We could lose our license."

"Of course not. I'm sorry. Where is he now? Would you like me to talk with him?"

"He should be awake soon, but it took Blaine and three others to restrain him." She tapped her drawer again. "I'm afraid we had to inject him with haloperidol again."

Miranda pressed her foot to the floor to stop her nervous knee from bouncing up and down. "His doctor said it's okay —when you have to do it."

"I'm afraid it's not that easy. The crux is that we're not in a position to give that much special attention to any one client. It's not that we don't want to help Mickey, because we do. If we had a bigger staff, it would be different. The truth is, we need to focus on the lower-maintenance clients."

Miranda's hands shot to her mouth. "Oh, my God. You're throwing him out?"

Fenn tilted her head to the side. "I wouldn't think of it like that. It's just that we all want to do what's best for Mickey. That's why he needs to be somewhere that's better equipped to help him. He's very strong when he gets like that, you know."

That was one of the reasons he didn't stay with Miranda. She simply couldn't take care of him by herself. "But where?" she asked, eyes tearing up again. "You've said that there are very few facilities for mentally challenged children, let alone full-grown adults."

"True. There aren't many options for people like Mickey." She reached into the same drawer and retrieved an envelope-sized brochure and handed it to Miranda. "I called the manager of this facility. I think it would be a great place for him."

The colorful cover contained a picture of about twenty people, half being medical types, the others apparently their clients. "The Broadhouse? Aren't they private?"

Fenn nodded. "They're the only community for mentally challenged adults that has enough of the right resources to take care of Mickey. They just opened a new community in San Clemente—but they're filling up fast. If you want to—"

"But that's two hours away and they must be expensive."

"They get an occasional grant and a few donations, but most of their money comes from a monthly fee they charge the clients' families."

Miranda tried to swallow, but her throat was too dry. "I don't think I can afford them. What about the county? They must have some other group homes like yours. Maybe one of them can take him?"

Fenn shook her head. "There are a couple institutions, but they're in the same predicament we are. So are the state facilities. We're all overcrowded and underfunded. I'm afraid Mickey wouldn't get the kind of care he really needs or deserves in any of the government-run facilities. It could make him worse or even shorten his life."

Shorten his life? Miranda lowered her head and uncrumpled a tissue then dabbed her eye. "How much does it cost?"

"Based on his condition, between four and five thousand dollars a month, maybe a little more."

"But I can't afford that. I only have enough from my divorce settlement to last me a few more months. I'm getting a loan against my home, but that will run out, too. And I could never get a job that would pay me that much money."

"I understand," Fenn said while handing Miranda a fresh box of tissues. "I really do. What about your parents and other family members? Isn't there anybody else who can help?"

"Not really. Our folks never could deal with Mickey. They were mean to him. Never visited him. As if his disease was his fault. That's why I brought him out here, to California, where the facilities are better. Now they don't like me either."

"Maybe you could approach them again. They might change their minds if they know the urgency."

Miranda shook her head. "The last time I asked them for money, they just hung up on me. We're on our own."

Fenn nodded. "Unfortunately, I've seen that same situation too many times before. Some people just can't handle having special people like Mickey in their lives. I know how much he means to you. We love him too. Maybe I can keep him another few weeks, but then I've got to move him."

Miranda lifted her tissued hand to her eye. "But every time we move him it just confuses him."

"That's why we should consider The Broadhouse. I'm convinced that he'll get better if he gets the regular personal attention they can give him. If you can handle it, he'll never have to move again." She rose. "We can go see him now if you want to."

*   *   *

Miranda and Fenn entered the Safety Room, the place they put the clients who might hurt themselves or others. Mickey was in bed, under a sheet and a light green blanket and stirring. "Hi, Baby. It's Miranda."

Given his shorter-than-average height and wavy, sandy hair, nearly anybody could see the family resemblance between Mickey and Miranda, although the greying of his temples and the gentle crow's feet in the corners of his eyes and mouth along with established wrinkles in his brow and jowls made it appear as if he were at least ten years older. Miranda clicked her tongue against her teeth. He was only thirty-five and already wearing out. Mickey scratched the top of his head with both hands. "I don't feel good, Miranda," he said slowly.

Miranda placed her hand on her brother's slightly reddened forehead. Just as she thought. He was very warm. "I know you don't, Baby," she said pulling the blanket down, "but you'll get better when the medicine wears off."

"I want my sunglasses and my hat."

"I'll have somebody get them," Fenn said before she left the room.

There was a small private bathroom in the corner. "I'm going to get you a cool wash cloth," Miranda said. "Would you like that?"

"Uh huh, and my sunglasses." Miranda grinned as she moved toward the sink. Mickey always thought sunglasses made him look like Elvis. The trouble was the other clients liked his sunglasses too. Sometimes they'd take them away. It wasn't that they were thieves, they just didn't know any better. Fortunately, none of them could tell one pair of sunglasses from another so Miranda bought them by the dozen at the dollar store so Mickey would always have a pair. She bought baseball hats by the dozen too. She rinsed a washcloth in cool water, dabbed it across his forehead and tilted her head. "Does that feel better, Baby?"

"I love you, Miranda."

Her lower lip puckered. She never felt more appreciated than when Mickey was loving and tender like that, as he was most of the time. To her, those oft-said three words had more meaning coming from him than when somebody with a high status might say them. There was no ulterior motive with Mickey. Not even an expectation that she would say it back. It was just a simple gesture of true love that she cherished more than any other love she'd ever felt. How could her parents have abandoned such a gentle and loving man? "I love you too, Baby. I love you too."

One of the other staff members, Jennifer, entered the room. "Here's your hat and sunglasses, Mickey."

His face lit up like a kid who just got a brand new skateboard for his birthday. He sat up and reached for the items as if they were the only things in the world that mattered. "Thank you, Jennifer. I love you."

Miranda and Jennifer exchanged glances as Mickey smiled with an enthusiasm that everybody always said was contagious. The happy Mickey was back, at least for a while. He was the only person Miranda knew who could make everybody else happy too. She could never forgive herself if she allowed him to languish in some underfunded facility that would deal with his problems by injecting him with dangerous drugs and ultimately lead him to an early death. She had to do whatever she could to prevent that.

CHAPTER 4

Immediately after Miranda's meeting with Dr. Fenn, she made calls in search of any options that Fenn may have overlooked, but not surprisingly, it was as the doctor said. Miranda had either to keep Mickey in underfunded and crowded government facilities that could never give him the care he'd need or find a way to get him into The Broadhouse —and there was only one possible way she knew of to pull that off.

By the time Thursday rolled around she'd become so concerned for Mickey that she considered thoughts she never would have imagined. She recalled Don saying the lady with the trust wouldn't miss her money. Miranda gulped back her reservations and returned to the prison on the regular visiting day. This time she'd pay better attention to what he had to say.

They were brought together in the main visiting room. A large desk was at the front of the room for a guard, and several smaller tables were scattered around for the prisoners and their callers. Officer Jackson was on duty. As always, he gawked at Miranda, but based on the unholy thoughts she'd been harboring lately she knew she had no right to judge anybody else.

She and Don got a table near the back of the room with Don's back to the wall. After she told him about Mickey, he placed his finger to his lips. "We gotta play this smart. If Jingle Keys comes around, I'll scratch my nose. Got it?"

"Got it," she whispered, already coming to grips with what she was contemplating. "But before I agree to anything, I need to ask a lot of questions."

"Of course, but we don't have much time."

They never did. She leaned as close as she dared without drawing Jackson's wrath. "You have to tell me everything again," she whispered. "Exactly how much do you know about that Rachel woman? Are you sure she lives in this area? What does she do? How do you know she's not married already? Are you sure that the trust is activated when she gets married?"

"Hold it," Don whispered and raising his index finger. "One question at a time. I don't know much of that stuff. Thomas only got a few pages."

"That's not good enough, Donnie. It's too vague. I need to know a lot more."

He rolled his eyes. "You didn't expect somebody to write all of the background info out for us did you?"

"No, but you said you figured out all the details."

"I meant the basics, but how am I going to do any serious snooping around for specifics? They don't exactly let me come and go as I please around here. We just have to fly in the dark on a couple of these things."

Her eyes popped wide open. "Fly in the dark? We can't do that! We don't want to stick our necks out if we don't know it's safe."

"I assumed all of that would be among your duties."

"My duties? Great. Now I've got to—"

Don's eyes leaped past her. He scratched his nose and winked.

"I'm thinking about painting my house," she said while winking back. "What do you think of yellow with light blue trim?"

Don grinned. "I dunno. Whatever you think."

"That retired guy across the street has some tall ladders."

She waited for Jackson to walk past them, and toward the other tables. Then, "What about your brother?" she asked, picking up where she left off. "Why can't we just bypass him and wait until you get out of here? Then you can schmooze Rachel yourself. If you can persuade her to marry you, we've got what we want without complicating the whole thing with Mac."

Don shook his head. "First off, we gotta get that chick off the market before somebody else wiggles in on our money. Second, if things don't go as we plan, the cops will bust my son-of-a-bitch brother, not me. That way you and me can still dance in the moonlight even if things go wrong."

Go wrong? "But nothing is going to go wrong, right?"

"You just told me that you've only got enough money to pay for Mickey's new place for a few months. If we're gonna do this, we can't afford to drag our feet."

She riveted on Don's eyes. "If I do this, Mickey gets at least half the money. Maybe all of it."

"Alright, already. Your brother gets half of our cut, no matter how much that is. There. Are you happy?"

"Just making sure, Donnie, because without that I wouldn't even think about stealing somebody else's money."

He tapped her hand. "Me neither, Baby. From here on out, it's all about Mickey."

As disgusting as Don's plan was, this single issue made it almost, barely, sort of, remotely bearable, but that wasn't the only thing she wanted to resolve.

Just then, Don tweaked his nose again.

CHAPTER 5

After Miranda set her anxiety aside, she agreed to do some homework regarding the mysterious trust. Some of her questions had answers and some of the answers led to more questions. Regardless, Don would want to know what she discovered. This time Maxine Montoya was the presiding guard in the visiting room.

"What'd you find out?" Don whispered almost immediately.

Miranda stuffed her fingers under her thighs to hide the shaking. "Mickey got accepted at The Broadhouse," she said, faking a grin, "but I'm a nervous wreck. I haven't eaten much and I keep getting diarrhea."

"Gross."

"I had to give them a huge deposit and it doesn't look like I'm going to get as big of a line of credit out of my home as I thought."

"Don't worry about that. I already figured you'll have more than enough to cover all our costs. It's what they call venture capital."

"We have to be very careful, Donnie. I can't afford to lose that money."

He tapped her hand. "Relax. You have way more than we'll need. Now, what about that Rachel chick? What'd you find out?"

She pursed her lips. She would have appreciated a little sympathy about her situation, but if she whined about it he'd probably remind her how little time they had. Best just to get to the point. "Before I answer that, I want to clarify a few things."

Don shook his head. "The rules again? Okay, but hurry."

"You've got to agree one more time that there's not going to be any killing—either of Rachel Johnson or Mac or anybody else. That's very important. Right?"

He rubbed his face with both hands, then said, "Look. I agreed to spare Rachel, but if my brother screws us over I ain't cutting him no breaks. He's an asshole. Deserves what he gets for all the bullshit he's done to me and everybody else over the years."

A chill flushed across Miranda's shoulders. "No, Donnie. That's not good enough. I don't care what he's done. If you want to kill him, you can count me out. It's not negotiable."

He hesitated but Miranda stared in his face and waited him out. Finally, Don examined his nails. "Okay. Okay. Don't get your panties all scrunched up. I'll figure out some way to make him want to leave town on his own."

Until that moment Miranda hadn't realized that her heart had been pulsating like a cruise ship's engines. "That's better," she said. "Now, about Rachel's money. I don't want to steal more than we need, just enough for Mickey to get by."

"Like I said. I ain't greedy. We'll wait to see how much she has. If she don't have all that much, we'll let her keep some."

"At least half?"

"Okay. Okay. We'll let her keep half of her money if we find out she ain't got a lot, but I'm betting she's got a couple mil."

"If that's the case. She keeps half and we'll split the other half with Mickey?"

"Yeah, yeah, yeah. Half for her. Half for him. Half for everybody. By the time we're done splitting our pie into all them halves, there ain't gonna be nothing left for you and me 'cept crumbs."

"Well this isn't about us. It's about Mickey. Now there's something else and it's very, very, very important, Donnie. It's about your brother."

"For Chrissake, Baby," he said, while shifting in his chair. "We just went over that. We're never going to get nowhere if we keep plowing the same damn ground."

"This is different. The last big thing. If we get this straightened out, you've got yourself a partner."

"Hurry, before I die of old age."

"I will, but I want you to look me in the eyes and listen to me, cause I think you've got so many dollar signs floating around in your head that you've overlooked a major problem."

Don plopped his elbows on the table and laid his chin in his palms. "I ain't forgot nothing," he said with too much confidence for her liking.

She floated a peek over to the guard's table and back. "If I have to trick Mac into thinking we're boyfriend and girlfriend I'll probably have to make love with him and I don't want to do that. It's cheating. That's what my husband did to me and I hated him for it. It was why we got divorced."

Don sat back and waved a dismissive hand in the air. "Is that all? This ain't cheating. We both know what's going on here. It's about setting us up forever."

"You mean setting Mickey up."

"Whatever."

"I'd rather just tell Mac the truth. Then we can share the money with him too."

Don pounded his hands onto the table. "I ain't doing that. Haven't you ever known a really rotten person? There are lots of guys like that in this shithole. They're scum and deserve what they get. You gotta make him think he's in love and then break his damn heart. That's the only way this works."

"But, I don't want to make love to anybody else, Donnie, especially somebody like that."

Don shook his head. "You're looking at it all wrong, Baby.

It's like a job. We go to work, do what we have to for a few hours so we can get other things we want out of life. That's all this is, a job with a great big payday at the end. It's no big deal unless you make it into one."

"Look, we both know I'm no angel, but it could take months for me to win him over, not to mention he has to win over Rachel. I might have to make love to him a whole bunch of times. Doesn't that bother you? Because it sure as hell bothers me."

He squeezed her hands. "How many times do I have to tell you there's no *love* to it? There ain't no emotions in it. It's just a necessary step to get what we want. Like dates or marriages. You give up some things to get other things."

She leaned way forward. "But if he's as callous as you say he is, I'm not sure I can get intimate with him even once. You gotta promise me that if I can't stand him, I can call this whole thing off before we get in too deep."

She heard papers rustle from the area of the guard's table. "Twenty more minutes, everybody," Officer Montoya said.

Miranda glared into Don's eyes. "If Mac gives me the creeps, I get to call the whole thing off? Right?"

"Okay, but remember: If you walk away, Mickey's the one who gets screwed and I don't mean in a fun way."

"I won't forget," she said. "but I don't want to make love to somebody I hate. I already feel like a damn whore."

"You ain't no whore, Baby. You're just on a mission." Don grinned. "But if you was a whore, you'd be damn good at it. Now if that's all, what'd you find out?"

With the most distasteful issues mitigated, Miranda sighed. "Okay then. I guess we understand each other. I just wanted to clear those things up." She looked both ways as if she were a schoolgirl about to cross the street. "Rachel's an assistant principal at the high school in Palmdale."

Don smiled and made a large check mark in the air. "And she's still single," he said, making a second imaginary mark.

"How'd you know that?"

"Simple. If she was married, she'd already have her money and probably wouldn't be working, and you wouldn't have grilled me on all those other issues."

Comments like that reminded Miranda that Don was a lot smarter than he usually sounded. She took an imperceptible moment to savor the renewed confidence she had in him. "The school year is coming up so I called her under the pretense of doing a survey for an article in the district's newsletter. I figured I'd just ask her some basic questions—get her talking about her job, what she likes and dislikes, before I asked her about her marital status.

Don's lower lip curled while his head bobbed up and down.

"Not even a boyfriend," Miranda said proudly. "But it wouldn't do any good to hook her up with your brother if she's not psychologically ready for a relationship, so I asked her about her views on families."

"That worked out too, didn't it?"

The word *astute* occurred to Miranda but she plowed on. "We talked about how kids usually do better in school if they have two parents in the home."

"So why isn't she married? What's my brother got to do to break the ice?"

"That's what I wanted to know, so I staked her out. I felt like a damn criminal."

"Yeah, yeah, and you didn't like it, but we're still here, so what's the skinny?"

Miranda's eyes narrowed. She would have liked some understanding, but Don was right. She was on the verge of being a full-fledged criminal. It might be time to quit whining. "She's not very attractive. Looks kinda bossy."

"A Moped, huh?"

"Those little motorbikes? What do they have to do with anything?"

Don grinned. "A jail term. A guy wouldn't mind taking her for a ride as long as his buddies don't know about it."

"Whatever," Miranda said, shaking her head. "She's a Plain Jane. You know. Low on make-up and jewelry, bland clothes, hair could use a perm."

"Now she sounds like a lesbo."

"I was thinking that too, but she spoke well of men, so I went by her house several times. She stayed home on Friday and Saturday nights plus all day on Sunday. No men. No women either. To tell you truth, she seemed like a nice lady who is simply content with her life."

Don lifted his chin. "Don't be thinking that *nice lady* bullshit. You'll feel sorry for her and that'll make it harder to do what you got to do."

Miranda bit lightly at her lip. She'd already told herself that she couldn't afford to care about Rachel. She had to keep her feelings out of it.

"Five minutes," Montoya warned.

Miranda glared at Don. "I have to get that money for my brother. What's next?"

"Finally." Don looked over at Montoya. He leaned closer, lowering his voice. "You gotta go to Rochester, New York in two weeks. They're having their annual auto show and Mac never misses it. All you gotta do is volunteer to work at one of the booths or hang around the entry door until he shows up. Then turn on that good-girl charm of yours. He never could resist a good-looking blonde."

Miranda smiled at the compliment. "Shouldn't be difficult to recognize him."

"Naw. People always got us mixed up. Have a drink with him, then go on a date. Stay with him a week or so if you have to, but get him to come to California, just like you did with me. In the meantime I'll figure out how to hook him up with Rachel."

"Time's up."

Already?

Minutes later Miranda was outside, on her way to her SUV. This was it, the end of the beginning. If things went as planned she'd be on her own for a week or so and this role wasn't going to be anywhere near as simple as the one she had in high school.

CHAPTER 6

Jean drowned some cubes with a double shot of vodka, then added a like amount of pulp-free O.J. to her glass. Screwdriver in hand and having already donned her best dress and the only decent necklace she owned (neither one of which could possibly match the attire that Clifford Clifton's other dates must have worn), she meandered into her tiny living room. There, she anxiously peered through the narrow crack she'd left between her frayed curtains. Finally, the tardy Mercedes rounded the corner. If she were lucky, Clifford wouldn't come in. She closed the curtains and returned to the kitchen to finish off her drink.

A few moments later the anticipated thumps came from outside her door. Jean paused before opening it, then said, "Hi. You musta been busy?"

"Always am," Clifford said from the porch, "but our reservation isn't for over an hour yet so no big deal."

An hour? Her shoulder-length brunette hair swished like a ballerina's tutu toward the digital clock by the TV. That would mean nine o'clock. "Oh. I guess I misunderstood. I thought we said eight?"

Clifford shook his head. "You said to *come by* around eight and we could have a drink first, remember?"

It didn't sound familiar, but she couldn't make him stand on her porch for another hour. Besides, she wasn't about to argue with a man of Clifford's import. In addition to being ten years his junior, she was just a lowly receptionist at a Palmdale law firm, where he was one of their best clients. She had to let him in. She shrugged and stepped aside. He probably didn't expect much from her home anyway. "Sorry. My mistake. Come on in. I can make us a couple of screwdrivers."

Jean watched Clifford's eyes as he entered. Based on what she'd heard, his local home resembled a palace with lush grounds, an Olympic-size pool and all the luxuries. Her eighty-year-old cracker box wouldn't even match his guesthouse. "Nice place," he said.

She closed the door behind him. "We're going to fix things up next spring. At least get a coat of paint on it." She pointed a few feet away to the bedspread-covered sofa that she'd vacuumed a little earlier. "Have a seat while I mix our drinks." Thankfully, she'd gotten most of the dog hair off.

After taking a few short steps into the kitchen, Jean grabbed some glasses and then the orange juice from her magnet-covered refrigerator and took a position behind the table so that Clifford would have to look at her instead of her home.

"Back at the office," he said from the sofa, "you mentioned you have a son. Is he around?"

"Stump? Oh, no. He usually stays with his cousin at my sister's when I have things to do."

"Stump?"

She nodded and grinned as she finished pouring the vodka. "A nickname. My sister gave it to him when he was learning to walk. His real name is Neal."

"I take it he's short and pudgy?"

She curled her lip for a second, and added some O.J. to his glass. "Not really. He's a little shorter than some of his classmates, but he's not as chubby as he used to be."

Clifford crossed his leg and draped his arm across the back of the sofa. "Tell me a little about him."

Strange. "Why would you want to know about him?"

"Simple. Most moms love to talk about their kids. It gives me good insight into both of them."

He was right. It would be a lot easier for her to discuss her son than her home, or any of the important things that Clifford had going on. She grinned. "Well, okay. You asked for it. He's thirteen, a bit more independent than most kids and pretty interesting, actually."

"Interesting?" Clifford rose and moved toward the kitchen. "How so?"

Jean slid a couple steps to her right, so Clifford wouldn't be facing her embarrassingly dirty kitchen window. "I dunno. Lots of ways, I guess." She handed Clifford his drink.

He raised the glass. "Here's to an enjoyable evening." As nice as he was, he had to feel out of place.

After they tapped their glasses Clifford tasted his cocktail. His tongue rimmed his lips as he looked at the drink more closely. "You like it?" Jean asked. "I use cucumber-flavored vodka."

He nodded approvingly. "I'll have to remember that."

Just then, in the backyard, the neighbor's cat bolted across the top of the privacy fence. Right behind it, Stump's aging long-haired mutt, Dogg, chased after it the best he could. Jean's eyes and thoughts shot in Clifford's direction. If he'd seen the ruckus, he had to see the dirty windows too—and the security bars. If she had to, she'd explain that the former owner had installed the non-releasing type, which made the windows nearly impossible to clean.

"He must be one of these perfect kids I hear about. A mama's boy. Straight A's. President of his class. Things like that?"

Jean nearly laughed out loud. "Hardly." Fortunately, Clifford seemed unaware, or at least unconcerned, about her windows.

"Well then, what makes him so *interesting*? Has he ever been in any trouble?"

Another strange question. He must've had a special reason for that one, too. "Not anything major. But there was one time when I nearly killed him." She put one hand on her hip. "You sure you want to hear this?"

"Why not? I'm not going anywhere for a while."

"Okay then," she said as they returned to the living room and shared the almost-hairless sofa. "It was four years ago, during the holidays, when Stump was just nine. We'd already lived in Palmdale for a couple years. I tried to explain that I didn't make enough money to buy all the things the rich people had, like Christmas trees, but he'd heard enough of my old-people excuses and he was determined to do something about it."

"Oh, yeah? Like what?"

Jean shifted her feet and looked straight in Clifford's eyes. "Before I answer that, would you mind if I ask you a question of my own?"

"Guess not."

"This place must make you uncomfortable," she said while waving her hand toward the kitchen. "I mean, from what I hear, you own several nice homes in addition to your three car dealerships. You even drive a Mercedes. Why would an important person like you ask me out in the first place?"

Clifford swigged at his glass. Then, "Don't you sell yourself short. There's something genuine about you. I like that, so I asked one of the attorney's about you and he said that you're a lot of fun, too." Clifford held out his glassless hand, palm up. "Who wouldn't want to know a woman like that?"

Jean raised her glass in a mock toast. "How nice. What about your TV commercials? Why do you hire somebody else to act like you when you could just do them yourself?"

"Good question. Our studies indicated that people would rather buy cars from a younger guy like Chris because his blonde hair and suntan reek of California."

Jean nodded and sipped at her drink. Now that she thought about it, Clifford's thinning dark hair, tiny crow's

feet and turned down mustache did make him look a little
like an aging con man. Oh, well. At least he seemed to be
a little more comfortable with the simple people than she
expected. Her home didn't seem so bad after all.

"Now tell me more about Stump and the Christmas tree.
What did he do?"

"Well," she said with a new calmness, "there was one
of those temporary tree lots up on the corner. Stump had
figured out that they weren't very crowded right after
school let out, so he hid behind a hedge until the sales guy
took his only customer to the back of the lot to inspect some
trees." Jean snickered. "I still can't believe he did this. That
ornery little monster of mine snagged a six-footer from the
front of the lot and dragged that big old tree all the way
back to our house."

"No kidding. That must have been a challenge."

"Three blocks," Jean said proudly, "but Stump's never
been a quitter. By the time he got home he had sap all over
his hands." She giggled. "You should have seen the mess on
the door frame from his sticky fingers."

Clifford grinned, shook his head.

"Well anyway, he got an apple box from our laundry
room and covered it with an old sheet. Then he crammed
this sofa next to the chair in the corner over there and stood
the tree on top of the box to make it look even taller."

"Clever kid," Clifford said, bobbing his head. "He'd make
a good car salesman."

Maybe the owner of the dealership or the credit manager,
but never a salesman. They talk people into doing things
they don't want to do. "Somewhere, he'd seen popcorn on a
string used as a garland, but we only had the buttery kind,
so he threw a bag in the microwave." She threw her arms in
the air like she always did at that point. "Oh my God, what
a mess." Both she and Cliff giggled. "He tried to tie some
sewing thread around it. But was only able to get about
twenty pieces to stick on his string. As far as he knew, that

was good enough. So he drooped it across the front of the tree the best he could."

Cliff rubbed his knee against Jean. He was smiling now, obviously enjoying her story.

"Then he made a picture frame from some wood scraps he found out in the yard. He got some glass and added a picture of me and him that my sister took on his first birthday." She pointed across the room. "That's it over there. We gave him his very own chocolate cake, with extra icing, and let him have it." She grinned, "You know how kids are. He became a chocolate disaster so my sister wanted to get a picture. I stuck my fat head in there, just as he smeared a big gob of icing on my eyes and nose. You never heard so much laughter."

Cliff glanced to the wall and back, apparently eager to hear more.

"Then he wrapped the picture with some birthday paper because that's all we had and he proudly leaned what would become my favorite Christmas present of all time up against the sheet-covered box."

Cliff placed his hand on Jean's knee. "I already like this kid."

Jean beamed. "Everybody does. But by that time this place looked like a battlefield." She glanced around the room. "It was even worse than it is now."

"But you must have known he didn't buy that tree?"

"When I got home, all I wanted to do was decompress. You know, kick my shoes off, maybe take a hot bath, but Stump was sitting in the corner with the biggest grin you could imagine. He gave me this bit about how he worked at the lot for an hour after school for a few afternoons and they gave him the tree for free."

"But you knew otherwise?"

"Not yet, but the guy from the tree lot banged on the door. He said he saw Stump walking off with the tree and the neighbors knew where we lived."

"Uh-oh."

Jean grinned. "I was so mad I could have spit fire. I'm sure Stump would have loved to hide, but where's he going to go in this tiny place?" She sipped at her drink and enjoyed the warmth that always engulfed her when she got to this part. "He said he did it all for me. He wanted me to have a tree and my very own present for a change, just like everybody else. It was so unselfish, I wanted to cry."

"You let him keep it, didn't you?"

"Oh, no. I couldn't do that. I told him that even though we both knew what he did was wrong-headed, just knowing that he cared enough about me to do something so stupid made that my all-time favorite Christmas."

"So you paid the guy for the tree?"

"Oh, no. Couldn't afford it, and I sure wasn't going to approve of stealing. I made him apologize and take it back. Then I told him he was grounded until the day after hell froze over."

"Cute story, but I think I would have worked something out with the guy from the lot."

"Then he'd think he could break rules and laws and expect me to cover for him. That wouldn't have been right."

"I guess not." Cliff finished his drink and held up his glass. "You were right. He is *interesting*. Very interesting." He checked his gold watch. "Looks like we still have some time. Mind if I make us another round?"

CHAPTER 7

Upstairs and away from Aunt Gerry, "I call bullshit," Stump said. He sprawled on his cousin's brand new bed. "If my mom was arrested again she would've told me about it."

"She's been hiding it from you, cuz." A year younger than Stump, Willie was sorta cool most of the time, especially when he let Stump play with his video games. "It was yesterday. My mom and dad picked her up from the jail again. They made me come up here so they could talk, but I heard them say she called in sick and got caught driving when she went out for some cigarettes. My dad said it was her third DUI. One more and she's going to jail for a long time."

"Ain't no way, Willie. I know her better than any of you. She's learned her lesson. She never drinks and drives anymore."

"My mom told me not to say anything to you, but I thought you'd want to know."

"Nope, nope, nope. I don't care what you guys think. My mom ain't no alcoholic. She told me she hardly ever drinks anymore, and I believe her."

Willie's head bounced back and forth. "We're talking about a couple sisters here, cuz. They know each other pretty well. Ask yourself which one has a reason to lie.

Think about it. How many times have you found your mom passed out?"

Willie might as well have scratched off one of Stump's biggest scabs. Truth was, if he had to make a flip-the-bird guarantee that she'd cleaned up her act he couldn't do it. She said she'd straightened up before only to have more problems. "I dunno. A few times I guess."

Willie threw an old chunk of a carrot at Stump. "Now I'm the one calling *bullshit*. I've been with you at least four times when we found her zonked out at your house. I bet you've found her other times, too."

Stump grabbed at the bed covers. "Alright, I guess that's true, but what the hell am I supposed to do about it? I'm not lucky like you. You have a whole family. You live in a better house and a better neighborhood. You've got video games, an iPad and your own phone." He rubbed the top of his fuzzy head. "Hell, I don't even know who my friggin' dad is."

"Yeah, I know. Have you asked her about him?"

"All she says is he was some guy she used to date. And once he knocked her up, he split. Nobody's heard from him since."

"Maybe if you found him, he'd help out? He might throw in some money. You guys could sure use it."

"No shit." Stump sat up, draping his scuffed-up tennis shoes over the edge of the bed. "It'd be cool if he was rich like you guys. I might even get an allowance." He looked at Willie's carrot, wishing it were a cookie.

"We could ask my mom who he was."

"I doubt she'd tell us anything. If my mom doesn't want me to know who my old man is, you can bet her little sister has been sworn to secrecy."

"Guess so. What about your birth certificate? His name would be on there."

"Never seen it." Stump hesitated, and then quickly stood. "But there's a locked metal box in our laundry room. It might be in there."

Willie grinned. "Are you thinking what I'm thinking?"

"I think so, Dude. My mom's on a date, won't be home for at least a couple hours. We might be able to find the key to that box."

"It'd just take us twenty minutes to get there if we use our trick. We could be back in an hour."

"I'd like to check on Dogg too. He ain't been getting around too good lately."

Willie jumped to his feet. "I'm in," he said, as he grabbed three bucks off his dresser and then his new tennis shoes with the flashing red lights built into the soles. "I'll tell my mom we're going to the gas station for some beef jerky."

CHAPTER 8

After a couple of drinks and Clifford's considerate questions, Jean only had another half hour to kill before their luxury ride to one of the plushest restaurants in all of California. "You know something," she said, massaging her jaw. "I thought that tonight would be awkward, but you're a lot easier to talk to than I'd expected."

Clifford placed his hand on her knee. "What can I say? I like all people. Rich. Poor. Black. White. Everybody has good qualities, including you. You're a fascinating woman." He gently rubbed her lower thigh.

She smoothly added her palm to the back of his hand, mostly to prevent it from wandering further north. It wasn't that she was prudish. She'd long ago shed the silly "wait until the third date" notion. But she and Clifford were peas from different pods. He'd tasted wild meat in caves and drunk award-winning wine in castles, all with some very interesting people. There was so much more to discuss that any intimacy they might share could wait.

A familiar and well-timed whimper came from the back door. Good. Dogg could provide a final topic of conversation before they embarked on the evening's activities.

"Sounds like somebody wants in," Clifford said, pointing his chin toward the noise.

"He wants to be with us, but it's not a good idea." She

scrunched up her nose. "His ears are smelly because I can't afford his meds until my next payday. Do you have a dog?"

"Oh, yeah. Two fine red-haired Irish Setters. Well trained. Good hunters."

Dogg persisted and Jean rubbed her jaw, wishing she'd slept a little better the night before. "The only way he'll quiet down," she said, hoping Clifford didn't notice her near-yawn, "is to let him in for a few minutes. He'll get bored and want to go back outside."

"Well, if that's the only thing that'll quiet him down, I say let him in for a few minutes."

Her drink running low, Jean washed down a cold perk-me-up swallow, then looked over the rim. "Are you sure, cause his ears aren't very pleasant."

"Like you said, it'll make him feel better and quiet him down."

"How impressive," she said, nodding her head and raising her glass in the air. "The all-powerful Clifford Clifton has a soft spot for dogs." She rose and turned toward the back door. "Just a few minutes. I promise." Jean blinked hard, plucked an ice cube from her glass and flipped it in her mouth. A moment later Dogg, tail flopping from side to side and whimpering from excitement, said his happy hellos to both Jean and the new guy.

"I see what you mean," Clifford said, waving his hand in front of his nose. "It's stronger than I expected."

Jean's tongue shifted what was left of her ice cube to the side of her mouth. "I'm so sorry. I'll put him back out in a minute."

"What did you do, before you went to work at the law firm?" Cliff asked, while scratching Dogg's back.

Nice of him to tolerate both the doggie stench and her fast-blinking eyes. "Oh, not much. I grew up in Wisconsin. Hated it. Too cold. Then I accidentally got pregnant and was forced to grow up real fast."

"Accidentally? Why not get an abortion?"

Jean didn't like to lie to people, but she had developed

an alternate story to that part of her life. "The father wanted me to, but I couldn't imagine such a thing. After that, he quickly disappeared and I didn't have the funds to find him or the desire to fight him for child support, so Stump and I hung around near my family until he was almost eight." She rubbed her eyes. "Sorry."

Dogg took another sniff between Cliff's legs and Cliff pinched his knees together.

"Damn it, Dogg. Leave him alone." She clenched her jaw to fight off another sudden urge to yawn. "I'll let him out and finish my story in a minute."

After Dogg was out, the door slammed shut and Jean heard something fall off the crowded shelves in the laundry room. Later, she'd remind Stump he was supposed to clean out the mess. She rejoined Clifford. "Now, where was I?"

Clifford smiled and raised his eyebrows. "Stump was about eight."

"Oh yeah. By then, my sister got married and moved to the next subdivision over. The nice one."

"Must be comforting to have her so close by."

"Comfortable. Yeah that's what it is." Her words were coming slower. "Comfortable."

"A lot of women in your situation would be stressed out, maybe eat too much from nerves, but you're looking real nice. In good shape."

Jean felt a strong urge to lie down and close her eyes. "Whoa. I must not have gotten enough sleep last night," she murmured.

"No problem," Clifford said calmly, while lightly placing his hand on one of her breasts. She would have pushed him away, but she was too weak, and limp. She realized she'd been drugged as her head eased backwards and settled on the back of the couch.

"I know you can still hear me, you stupid bitch."

True. Her body was nonresponsive, but her mind remained vaguely aware of what was going on.

Clifford slid one hand behind her back and the other under her legs, lifting her up. "Pity you won't be able to move, because we're going to get extremely familiar with each other. Don't worry, it won't hurt much and it'll all be over before you know it."

A few steps and his foot pushed open the bedroom door. "This will do just fine. Oh yes, there's another thing you'll want to know," he said as he laid her gently on her back. "It would be most imprudent of you to say anything to anybody about our little get together, tonight. I can get to that tree-stealing son of yours anytime I want to." As he laid her on her back, Jean knew that she should be horrified, but she really wasn't, or was she? Her mind felt so muddled she couldn't really tell.

Clifford undid the top button of her blouse. "By the way, you don't deserve a dog."

CHAPTER 9

"**R**un or walk?" Willie asked.

With the swiftness of someone who just got bit in the butt, Stump leapt from Aunt Gerry's front step to the grass. "Last one to the corner eats donkey turds."

As expected, the head start was enough. Even though Stump was fifteen pounds heavier, he reached the first intersection before Willie. He turned. "I hope you like that, donkey turd," he said, pretending he wasn't winded.

"You cheated, asshole," Willie said, sucking slightly at the air. "I'll get you after the next block 'cause I'm in better shape than you."

"No way. I'll outfox you."

Neither of them could recall how they came up with the run-a-block, walk-a-block idea, but it came in pretty handy around the neighborhood. "I gotta admit one thing," Stump said, huffing. "This idea about finding my dad is exciting. I've thought about it before, but you've got me to thinking I deserve a dad too."

"'Course you do, Dude. Dads can be cool. If you had to guess, what do you suppose happened to him?"

Stump shrugged. "Don't know. Could be anything. Maybe he's a spy, or in the witness protection program, or building hospitals in Africa."

"Yeah, but he might be a loser. Maybe a doper or a drunk.

Your mom knows guys who drink. He could have picked her up in a bar, screwed her and disappeared without ever knowing you were born."

If some other guy had spoken of his mom in that way Stump would have jumped in his face, but Stump and Willie could talk to each other in ways that strangers couldn't. "Naw, my mom wouldn't have done that. I think he's doing something important."

"If nothing else, we might be able to find out his last name," Willie said.

"I'll bet it's not 'slowpoke,'" Stump said with a shit-eating grin on his face as he took off running again.

"You buttlicker. Wait for me."

Two more cycles of the run-and-walk method brought them to the elevated highway that separated their subdivisions. They were both breathing more heavily but not completely out of wind. On the lower level, where the sidewalk was and the traffic noise was reduced, a group of cars was backed up behind a stalled Toyota. "Check that out," Stump said between breaths and pointing to the license plate: 1TZA383.

"Huh? That again? I'm too lazy to figure it out."

"Dude. Just look at your cell and change the last three numbers to the letters on a phone pad."

Willie had observed dozens of Stump's number conversions. He looked again and thought about it. "Oh, yeah. I get it. 'Itz a dud.'"

"C'mon, Dude. You gotta admit that's pretty ironic. The car that breaks down has plates that say 'itz a dud.'"

"I guess so, but that's not exactly what it says."

"Sure it is." Stump turned to double check the characters and explain why that particular grouping of numerals and letters represented exactly what he had claimed.

"Sucker."

Dammit. Willie already had an insurmountable lead.

After several more run/walk cycles the boys made it well into the less-desirable neighborhood, where Stump lived and where the foliage was mature, and the homes were smaller, older and much more likely to have been neglected. With a half-mile to go, it was time to walk another block.

"You know something?" Stump said, breathing harder and with sweat beads forming on his forehead. "If I don't find out who my dad is today, I think I'm gonna get firm with Mom, force her to tell me about him. I deserve the same rights as everybody else."

"Makes sense to me," Willie said as they passed a massive trellis full of red roses. "Your luck, he'll turn out to be on a chain gang, or a sex slave to a tribe of pygmy women."

Stump smiled. "That wouldn't be so bad. But I still think he's something cool like a submarine commander or a brain surgeon. Why else would he avoid Mom and me?"

"Who knows, but either way you still deserve to find out what the story is."

Willie won the last run session and they could walk the final block and a half. They rounded the last corner where Stump's house came into view. "Hey, look at that," Stump said, trying hard not to sound too winded. "A Mercedes in our driveway. It looks like Mom's still home."

"Good. We can ask her if your birth certificate is in that box."

"Nah. Might cause another fight. I'd rather wait until they leave, then we can find the key and figure it out on our own."

They'd nearly regained their breath by the time they came to the next-door neighbor's home. Dogg was in Stump's backyard barking, probably at a squirrel. "It's a Mercedes, alright." Stump said as they walked up his driveway. "A nice one, too."

"Maybe it's your dad," Willie said, sarcastically.

Stump smirked and opened the front door to see an unfamiliar, half-naked man, shirt draped over his arm, shoes and socks in hand, come from the hallway into the living room. The man appeared to be somewhat startled, but not overly concerned. He stuffed what looked like a pair of red lace panties into his pocket, then reached for his zipper. Stump was old enough to know that his mom sometimes did adult things, but he'd never walked in on her. "I'm Stump. Who are you?"

"None of your business. You're not supposed to be here." The guy shot a glance at Willie and then back in Stump's direction. "You fellows better go outside and play with your toys or whatever you do."

"Where's my mom?"

The man dropped his shoes, cramming his socks in his pants pocket. "Right where she belongs. On her back, in the bedroom." He jammed his bare feet into his shoes.

Stump's widened eyes shot a glance at the closed bedroom door. "She better be okay."

The guy quickly threw his arms in his shirt and wrapped it around him. "You tell her to keep her mouth shut or I'll see to it that she ends up worse off than she is now." He reached for the front door. "If that's even possible."

Freaked out, the boys bolted toward Jean's bedroom where Stump slapped at the door. "Mom? You okay?" No answer. The knob was locked. He made a fist and tomahawked the damn door again. "Mom? Mom? You okay?" Desperate, he backed up, yelling, "I'm breaking down the door." He lowered his shoulder and thrust himself past the latch and the now-shattered frame.

The room was a mess. His eyes raced toward the bed. Just like the guy said, his mom was naked on her back and apparently passed out. Her face and stomach were smeared with bright red lipstick. Her underwear drawer had been pulled from the dresser, and the contents strewn on the bed and floor.

Instinctively, he pulled the sheet over her body. "Mom? Mom? Talk to me. Are you okay?" He thought he heard her moan.

"Dude," Willie said, nervously, "I'm gonna call 911."

"Get an ambulance. Hurry."

Outside, the Mercedes screeched away.

Stump grabbed his mother's hand and dropped his head to her belly. "Hang on, Mom," he begged, fighting off a sob. "Please hang on."

CHAPTER 10

Two weeks had passed and Miranda was escorted to a table in the visitor's room where Officer Jackson delivered Don to her. She smiled at Don, sending him a clue that she had good news. As usual, they held hands above the table. "Did you find him?" Don anxiously probed the second Jackson was out of range.

Miranda leaned toward him and whispered. "Except for his mustache and a large scar on his knuckles I could've sworn he was you." Mac was also slightly more chiseled, probably because Don didn't get much exercise. "I hung around a booth with some guys who did custom paint jobs. I recognized him instantly. All I had to do was smile. Within minutes, we were yakking about his Harley."

Don squeezed her hand. "Named Annie, I bet?"

Miranda's eyebrows bumped upwards. "How'd you know that?"

"He's always been obsessed with Annie Oakley. Dork even named a Big-Wheel after her. His first bicycle too—and two big bikes that I know of."

"This one is number five. It's indigo. He was impressed because I knew it was one of the colors in the rainbow."

Don made a gagging gesture with his finger. "Our mother taught us that. ROY G. BIV. Red, Orange, Yellow, Green, Blue, Indigo and Violet. Always in the exact order. Blah. Blah Blah."

"I learned it in art class," Miranda said, wrinkling her nose. "I saw what you meant, though. He's a charmer at first. We had a hotdog and talked about the irony of each of us having a twin brother. I told him about Mickey, but he was more interested in talking about his bike than anything else."

"Trust me, that 'nice guy' bit won't last forever."

"He asked me if I'd like to meet her. It took me a moment to realize he was speaking about his bike, like it was a real person."

"See what I mean? He's a moron."

"He was right about the paint job though. It was stunning. He even had 'Annie' painted on the tank."

"D'you go for a ride?"

She shook her head. "I still wasn't sure about him, so I said I'd do it later, when I had more time. Then he suggested dinner."

"You agreed, didn't you?"

She sighed. "Yes. It's tonight. When I leave here, I'm taking a friggin' four-hour flight back to New York. I lose another three hours for the time zones. He's supposed to pick me up at my hotel around eight, but I'm not sure I want to go anywhere with that guy."

Don squeezed her hands. "You got to, Baby. I know he's disgusting, but you gotta do whatever is necessary to get him back here."

"Are you sure we can't just tell him what we're up to and split the money with him? That would be a lot easier."

"No way. That's *our money*. I'd rather kill the SOB." He glanced at the guard's table, then lowered his voice. "Look, we need him — for Mickey."

"I'd call this whole deal off if it weren't for Mickey. But right now, I can't even imagine going for a ride on that bike, let alone going to bed with him."

"Just take it one step at a time."

"I don't know, Donnie. He creeps me out."

"That's why we should wipe him out when we're done with him. The prick deserves it."

"I can't do that either," she said, rubbing her temples. "I'm no good at any of this."

"Trust me on this one. For now, all you gotta do is get him out here. Okay?"

She took a deep breath. "I'll try."

Don's head bobbed up and down. "That's what I wanted to hear." His eyes flashed over her shoulders. "I gotta go. You know what you have to do. Right?"

She sighed. "And you remember that I get the last word. Right?"

*　*　*

Following a tedious, doubt-filled flight, Miranda landed in New York. At best, she was confused as hell. She loved Don, and remained intrigued by his blueprint for Mickey. If it could be pulled off, and still leave Rachel with plenty of other money, all three of them would escape the perpetual financial problems that always hovered over them. At worst, she'd use her "get out of jail free" card to call off the whole con.

For the time being, all she had to do was meet Mac for dinner and determine if she could stomach the idea of developing a relationship with him. Like Don said, there would be no real emotions in it.

Her tight red slacks, dressy pink sweater and new white tennis shoes made a sexier impression than she would have ordinarily liked. As she reached for a dainty gold chain with a single pearl on it, the phone by her bed rang. Exactly eight o'clock.

Mac wore a classic black leather jacket, a light-blue button-down shirt and tasteful dress slacks. "I'm not surprised," he said, "but you look spectacular."

She reminded herself not to get side-tracked by his glitter and b.s. "Thank you. You look nice, too."

"You ready?"

Miranda swallowed hard. "You'll take it easy, won't you? I've only been on a couple bikes."

He showed her the scar on his knuckles again. "This taught me not to drive like a crazy person."

Two matching indigo helmets were attached to Annie's roll bar. Miranda pulled hers in place and assumed she'd look pretty cool in the bitch seat.

Mac mounted the bike and she wiggled between him and the roll bar. She mouthed a silent prayer and grabbed his belt. After a click of his foot, they headed toward the harbor.

Thankfully Mac drove sensibly, not like some of the guys she'd seen weave in and out of traffic. The bike was big and powerful and too loud for much conversation, so she mostly just held on, enjoyed the moment and rehearsed questions she'd ask him later.

Finally, they rolled into a steak and lobster place where Mac ordered them each a glass of red wine. "Just one," he said. "Can't afford to get tipsy."

Miranda thought the same thing. "I'm surprised we've hit it off so well," she said, only half-lying. "I feel like I've known you longer."

"I hate to think it's all going to come to an end. Maybe we could meet in Sturgis next summer."

"What's Sturgis?"

"South Dakota. There's a big motorcycle rally every year."

"I don't know. All those bikers might be intimidating."

He grinned. "You'd be surprised. Most of those guys are businessmen, lawyers. Guys like that. Besides, if you're with me, nobody will hassle you."

"I'll think about it."

"A couple years ago, a daughter of one of the bikers came down with cancer so we filled a beer keg with money for the medical bills."

She tilted her head to the side. "Touching."

"I thought you'd appreciate it, considering your brother's situation. How is he, anyhow?"

"Not very good. I had to move him to a new facility. It takes a while to adjust."

"I hope it works out."

He sounded more compassionate than she expected. If she hadn't been warned, she could actually like Mac. "What about your childhood? Where were you raised?" she asked, partly wondering how his version would compare to Don's.

"Ohio. Out in the sticks. My old man was a drunk. Abusive. Mom was a little better, but she coulda used a backbone. She wouldn't stand up to him."

"Sometimes mothers take the abuse so their kids don't have to."

"That might be it. All I know is, he had a scary cellar. Wouldn't let any of us go down there unless we were going to get the belt. When we were born he wasn't even around to take our mother to the hospital. Later, the nurses said she was the only woman they ever heard of who self-delivered twins."

Miranda lifted her hand to her lips. "Really? How'd you all get there?"

"We nearly died. It was the middle of the winter. The next day the sheriff drove by and noticed that she'd left the front door open. He checked it out and saved all of us."

"Wow. That must have been really tough." Miranda enjoyed hearing information Don had never mentioned.

"The old man got his comeuppance when we were in high school. They hauled him to jail because he'd robbed a jewelry store some twenty years earlier and ended up killing a night guard. We were all shocked."

"No wonder you don't like him. What happened then?"

"We moved into town. I graduated the next year and haven't spoken with any of them since. Don't want to either."

Miranda folded her hands in her lap. "I would have guessed that you and your brother would have been closer. What happened between you?"

Mac smirked. "Things started going downhill after he flunked the fifth grade."

Miranda's tummy tightened. "Oh, really?" Don had never said anything about flunking.

"Yeah. I always got better grades. One time we killed a rat in the school library. He dissected it and put the guts in the librarian's desk. Then he got caught and tried to get me to share in the blame. But why would I take the blame for something I didn't do?"

This too was news. Miranda raised her shoulders as if to reply to the rhetorical question.

"Another time he killed a dog just because it wandered in our yard."

Miranda's jaw about dropped. "He killed a dog?"

"Oh yeah. He was always good with knives. Better than me. He made spears, killed small animals. He might have made a decent taxidermist, but he never had the attention span."

Miranda's foot shook. The only dead dog Don had ever mentioned was the one he killed before being sent to prison.

"I'll admit I helped kill the rat, but Donald was too sadistic for me. I lost interest. But Laura Leigh was the final straw. She was his girlfriend before she decided she liked me better because I had a van and was in a band. I kept my drums in there. Then one day they were all slashed up. I knew damn well Don did it, so I called the cops."

"On your own brother?"

"I thought they'd just have a talk with him, but they charged him with a low-level felony. I guess they wanted to teach him a lesson. Later they offered to erase his record if he'd go to college or join the service right after high school. They left his case open for a little over a year. Then he went in the Army. By that time I'd already left home and been on the road for a long time." Mac tilted his head. "Let's talk about something else—like Mickey? Why'd you have to move him?"

Miranda forced herself to stay focused on the conversation at hand rather than jumping to conclusions about either

Don or Mac. "He's gentle as a lamb most of the time. But sometimes he has emotional problems and he's pretty strong. They wanted him to go to a place where he could get more attention."

Mac nodded. "Sounds like he could use a little help." He pulled out a large wallet and withdrew a piece of paper. "That's why I made out this check." He grinned. "I didn't know your last name so it just says Miranda. I want you to use it for Mickey."

Miranda couldn't believe her ears. "I can't take your money."

"Baloney. I can get more money. This is important. I want you to take it. It'll make me feel good."

She looked at it more closely. Six hundred dollars. "This is really sweet. Are you sure?"

"Sure I'm sure. It's not that big of a deal."

She wrapped her hand around her glass. "Well, okay then. Thanks a lot—from the Munchaks."

Regardless of Mac's motives, his kindness and generosity made Miranda's other decision a little easier. Good thing she hadn't messed up the king-size bed in her hotel room.

CHAPTER 11

The ambulance took forever to get Stump and his mom to the emergency room. Aunt Gerry was already there. Now, some forty minutes later, the double doors flung open. "Neal Randolph?" asked a white-coated doctor with glasses.

Stump's heart jumped. He hustled toward the man. "Is she going to be okay?"

"I'm her sister," Aunt Gerry said, with Willie at her side. "How serious is it?"

"It's not good news. She still hasn't come to."

"Oh, no." Aunt Gerry's hands shot to her mouth.

"She's definitely been drugged. We just don't know which one. We're running more tests."

"Ecstasy?" Aunt Gerry asked.

"Don't think so. This is stronger. Could be Rohypnol, called *roofies* on the street. Victims are in a dream-like state, semi-aware of what's going on, but can't do anything about it."

Stump rose to his toes, tugged on the doctor's arm. "She's going to be okay, isn't she?"

"We're doing all we can."

"You're going to arrest the guy who did this, aren't you?" Willie asked.

"That's not up to me. We've got DNA. It can tell us who did this."

"We don't need no DNA," Stump said, shaking his head. "The guy's license plate is *KARS 4U*."

"I didn't see that," Willie said.

The doctor made a note.

Aunt Gerry placed her hand on Stump's shoulder and then turned toward the doctor. "When will you know more?"

"When the tests come back from the lab. We'll let you know."

* * *

Some ninety minutes later Stump's mother came to and had been taken to a room. After the nurse took her vitals, she was told of the date-rape drug.

"I can't believe this," she said. "All I wanted to do was have a good time. Enjoy a classy evening for once in my life. But instead I get doped up by some damn pervert."

"If it makes you feel any better, Honey, Stump got his plates," Aunt Gerry said.

"We already called the cops," Stump added. "They'll be coming by later."

"No. No. No." His mom rolled her head from side to side. "We can't do that. That's the worst thing to do. I might get fired."

Aunt Gerry patted Stump's mom on the hand. "We can talk about that later, Honey. Right now you need more rest."

"You have to tell them we made a mistake, Gerry. I don't want to turn him in. He can get even."

Stump took his mother's hand. "I'm glad you're okay, Mom, but you have to quit drinking."

She thrashed her head back and forth. "Don't you people get it? This wasn't my fault."

"I know that you didn't take the drug on purpose, Mom, but if you didn't drink so much, you wouldn't get in these situations. You had lipstick all over you."

Her eyes widened. Then she pursed her lips. Finally, "I remember him smearing it on me. But I couldn't say anything or stop him."

"See. That's what I mean, Mom. You get into these tight spots and barely know what you're doing. I had to wrap you in a sheet so the ambulance guys wouldn't peek at you. It's embarrassing."

"I'm sorry I embarrass you," she said sarcastically, while rolling her head back and forth.

"But this isn't the only time. You remember last month when I found you on the floor?"

Aunt Gerry patted her sister's arm. "And we all know you've missed some work, Honey."

"And you might lose your driver's license," Willie added.

Stump's mom looked scornfully at Willie, and then turned to her sister. "Lydia said I'll be okay if Stump vouches for me and says I'm doing better."

"I know, but you don't want to use up your last chance in court. And, the same thing goes at your job. You can't keep asking Lydia to bail you out. She can't work on cases that pay their bills if she's in court doing favors for you. Neither one of you is getting your work done."

There was a gentle tap at the door and the same doctor Stump had seen in the waiting room walked in. Stump clenched his jaw as the doctor stepped right next to his mom's side. "How's our patient feeling?"

"I'm angry as hell, and a little groggy, but I think I'll be okay."

"That's good. I was worried about you for a while there." He glanced at the others in the room and then back to Stump's mom. "Would it be okay with you if I talk openly with you and your family about some of this?"

"Of course. They know what happened."

"Not just that. I want to have a broader conversation about your drinking."

"Go ahead. I've heard it all already."

"Okay, then. Have you told your family about your last trip in here?"

Stump's eyes bounced from the doctor down to his

mother. He hadn't known that. His mom rolled her head to the side without replying.

The doctor looked at Aunt Gerry, then at Stump. "We had tests run then, too. Her liver has sustained a great deal of damage. I'm afraid she can't go on like this much longer."

Stump dug his fingers into his palm. It sounded as if the doctor was saying she might die. How could he live without his mom?

"On the other hand," the doctor continued, "the liver has remarkable self-healing qualities. If she stops drinking she'll have a much better chance. I'm sorry to be so dramatic, but she could really use the family's help."

Stump's mom closed her eyes for a few seconds. Then she sighed. "You're right about the drinkin—and all the rest. I'm going to quit, or at least cut way back."

Stump hugged her. Hopefully, this time she really meant it.

The doctor patted her arm. "I can tell you've got an awful lot to live for. Now, if you'll excuse me, I have some other people waiting."

"Everybody is right," Stump's mom said to her family as the doctor walked out. She turned toward Stump. "I get stressed out about not having enough money to get by."

"Couldn't we find Dad? He might be able to help."

She shook her head. "I've told you before, I don't know where he is."

"Just tell me his name and I can see if I can find him on the Internet."

She rolled her head again. "We have to make it on our own, so stop asking."

"But it might solve everything."

"I said, *no*. If you want to help me, straighten up the house and clean up the back yard. It's disgusting back there. You do that and I'll worry about my driver's license and my job. They're all I have left."

"You've still got all of us," Stump said.

CHAPTER 12

Miranda wallowed in an inner conflict. She felt guilty for cheating on Don and reminded herself that Mac was not to be trusted. At the same time, she actually liked Mac. After she verified that he had no significant employment commitments, the invitation for him to stay with her in California for a while rolled naturally off her lips. Now, he and Annie were somewhere in the middle of the country and on their way to meet her.

Meanwhile, it had been two weeks since she'd last seen or spoken with Don and another conjugal visit day had arrived. As before, they followed Officer Jackson toward the make-out cabins. On the way, she thought about some things Mac had said about Don. She wondered how much of it was true.

Officer Jackson opened the cabin door. "You know the routine," he said. "I'll be back in an hour. If you're not ready to go, you won't be able to come back next month. Got it?"

Don watched Jackson walk off, before turning to Miranda. "What about Mac? Is he here?"

In the past, Miranda overlooked Don's tendency to rush things. After all, they only had so much time, but this time she'd hoped he'd ask her how she was doing, be more sensitive to all she'd been through. "He's on his way," she said matter-of-factly, "but I haven't had a chance to approach him about Rachel. We're still just getting to know each other."

Don stepped away from the window and toward her. "You don't understand the urgency. We have to get her off the market before somebody else gets to her."

"I know," she said, while pulling out of his grasp. "I'm trying, but I can't just ask a stranger to help me cheat a woman out of her money."

Don waved his arm in the air. "Those people are rich. They can afford to share their money, but this is the only way we can help your brother." He placed his hands on her shoulders. "Where do things stand now?"

"He should be here tonight. He's riding his motorcycle."

"Okay, then. At least we're making some progress. Just keep doing what you have to do, but remember to keep the emotions out of it. That will make it easier."

Easier? None of this was easy, let alone *easier*.

"We can talk about it more in a few minutes." His tone had softened. He reached for the top button on her blouse. "It's been two months."

Miranda pushed his hand aside and backed away. "I need to ask you something first."

"Well, hurry up. We've already wasted nearly ten minutes."

"I will, but this is important to me. Your brother said that when you were kids, you killed a rat. Is that true?"

"Why were you talking about that?"

"Because I was getting to know him and asked him about his childhood. Was he right? Did you kill a rat?"

Don shrugged. "It was in the library. We did them a favor."

"But he said you cut up the rat and put it in the librarian's desk. That's nauseating, Donnie."

Don smiled. "Well, sometimes boys do silly things just for kicks. What's the big deal? Nobody needed that rat."

"He said you killed a dog, too. Just because it came into your yard?"

Don grabbed the chair and dragged it across the floor.

"He's the one who killed that dog, not me. This is the kind of thing I was telling you about. The man can't be trusted."

"Are you sure about this, Donnie? 'Cause you killed that other guy's dog, too."

He pulled her closer. "Of course I'm sure. You've got to believe me on this, Baby. He's lying to you just to make himself look better."

She sighed. Her shoulders slumped forward. "I don't know what to think." Or who to believe.

"You've got to get those negative thoughts out of your mind. We're running out of time and I need your body."

Within a couple of minutes he was on top of her. She felt sorry for his limited opportunities and accommodated his aggressive urges. Then, as quickly as it started, he let out a loud grunt and it was over. "Wow. That was fantastic," he said and plopped on his back.

Miranda rolled to his side, unfulfilled, and wished she felt the same way. She laid her hand on his chest. His heart pounded hard and steady like the bass drum of a marching band. She couldn't help but think of how different things were when she was in bed with Mac.

*　*　*

The next afternoon Mac glided into Miranda's driveway and that night they made love. She told herself she was just doing what she had to do and that his evil side would show up sooner or later, but down deep she liked him more than she wanted to admit. He spent the night.

Now another day had come and they were returning from a trip to San Clemente where they went to lunch with Mickey at a restaurant that overlooked the Pacific.

Still some twenty minutes from her home, Mac looked at the brochure they'd picked up at The Broadhouse. "I can see why you liked that place. It's clean and those people obviously love what they do. Mickey seemed to like them a lot."

"So you don't think he's weird?"

"Weird? Hell, no. He may not have to worry about paying the bills, or making dinner like most of us do, but his problems are just as real to him as ours are to us. I think that makes him as normal as anybody else."

She moved her hand to his side. "That's so nice. Can I ask you something? Would you mind if I call you 'Sweets' from now on?"

Mac smirked. "Sweets? Where'd you get that?"

"I don't know. It just seems to fit. You're always so sweet. It makes me glad I invited you to come out here."

"That's interesting because I wasn't certain that you meant it, but I'm really glad you suggested the idea."

Sometimes their conversations flowed so well he led her to the exact things she wanted to talk about. "That's not all I've thought of."

"What's that supposed to mean?"

"I've got a really crazy idea, but I'm not sure you can handle it. Are you open to something really bizarre?"

"Handle what?"

"Can you keep a secret? A really, really big super secret?"

"I don't know," he said smiling. "A really, really big super secret sounds way too important for somebody known as Sweets."

By that time her home was just a mile away. She hit the blinker and took the right lane. "It's so big it'll surprise the hell out of you. So do you want to hear it or not?"

"You're not going to tell me that you've had a sex change operation, are you? I don't think I could handle that after some of the things we've done."

She tilted her head and lowered her voice. "Does my voice sound like I'm really a man?"

"No, but it's delightfully sexy."

"What if I told you I know how we can both become millionaires?"

He smiled. "Let me guess. You've got a system to beat the lottery?"

She waved her hand in his direction. "I mean it. It might take six months or so but I know where we can get a whole lot of money."

He smirked. "Who do I have to kill?"

She looked right at him. If only she could tell him that she'd already covered that precise issue with his brother. "Nobody. There's this really rich old woman who's got so much money she wouldn't even miss a million or two."

"If I didn't know better," Mac said while she pulled into her driveway, "I'd think you were drunk. How'd you learn of this scam?"

"If you must know, my ex's attorney told me about it during the divorce, even though they're not supposed to talk about other people like that." It wasn't exactly the truth, but it was close enough.

"The grandma used the same firm to set up a large trust for her granddaughter and we can get some of that money."

"Steal money from some little girl? I can't believe you'd do that."

"First off," Miranda said as they pulled into the garage, "That 'little girl,' as you called her, is in her thirties. Second, she doesn't even know the money's been set aside for her. And third, they have so much money they'll never need it all. So what's the difference if she inherits seven million or nine? Either way, it's not going to change anything for her." They reached her living room and Miranda wrapped her arms around his neck. "Meanwhile, a million or so could really change our lives, especially Mickey's."

"Mickey? What does he have to do with this?"

"Everything. Today he was doing pretty well, but he's not always like that. Little things send him into fits."

"Oh."

"One time he liked a baseball hat that another patient was wearing. Mickey wanted to wear it too. The caregiver tried to explain that it wasn't his but he couldn't understand. He got real angry and it took several men to restrain him."

Mac nodded. "Must be awful to be wrestled to the ground and not understand why."

"The only way to calm him down is with injections of haloperidol. By the time he wakes up, he's forgotten about whatever made him angry."

"How often does this happen?"

"It's been happening more lately. That's why I had to move him to The Broadhouse. They think they can help him without all of the violence."

"Well, that's great. So what's all this got to do with the grandma and granddaughter?"

"Money. The government facilities don't have enough resources to work with Mickey. When something goes wrong, about all they can do is gang up on him and drug him. But it's dangerous. The only alternative was The Broadhouse. I have to pay almost five thousand a month. I only have enough for a few more months. Then what am I going to do? I have to do something now or they'll move him again and he'll never get better."

Mac walked slowly into the living room, picked up a picture of Miranda and Mickey that was sitting on her end table. "So this idea of yours is all about Mickey's care, huh?"

"MediCal will only cover basic treatments, but that's not enough." She squared her shoulders to his. "Don't get me wrong, Sweets. I don't like taking somebody else's money, even if they won't miss it, but Mickey has been getting worse. He's having bad dreams. He's afraid and doesn't understand. It's wrong to be mauled and drugged up and denied access to the only care that can make him better." Miranda kissed Mac's cheek. "I need some help."

Mac stared back into the picture. "What made you think I'd consider something like this?"

"Are you kidding? I asked you a bunch of questions. You're a big-hearted guy who cares about underprivileged people and you think outside of the box. I love those things about you."

Mac nodded. "I know how much you love your brother," he said. "And you and I seem to have something special going on. I guess it wouldn't hurt to find out more about what you have in mind." He sat on the couch, looking at the photograph.

CHAPTER 13

Jean was back into her regular routine with no apparent residual effects from the drug. She had just made it home from work. Fortunately, Stump was spending the night with Cousin Willie.

As often was the case at the end of the workday, Jean's aching feet begged for attention, but first, she needed a drink. In the kitchen, she set down the sack she'd just gotten from the liquor store and pulled out one of two large vodka bottles. After she hid the bag and the other bottle in the laundry room, she splashed a few ounces of orange juice over a half-glass of vodka and invited the first swig to wash away the dryness. Next stop, her bedroom.

There, she drank down a hold-me-over gulp and set her half-empty glass on the dresser. She exhaled and sagged into her dressing chair where she kicked off her heels. Her left foot nearly leapt onto her lap for a ten-second massage. Not to be ignored, her right foot received equal attention before she slipped out of her work clothes and chugged down the rest of her screwdriver.

After she donned a comfortable pink velour bathrobe she visited the private bathroom off her bedroom and began an extra-hot bath. She inserted a new CD into her player and welcomed the soothing voice of Michael Bublé while she reached underneath the sink for a bottle of lilac-scented bubble bath that she'd bought at Nordstrom's. Two full caps was the correct amount. She lit a dozen lilac-scented votive candles and placed them in their usual spots around the tub and the room.

While the bubbles multiplied, and her preferred fragrance was engulfing the room, she returned to the kitchen and secured a follow-up screwdriver, stiffer than the first. That done, she fed Dogg and then returned to her private paradise. With the flick of a switch, the transformation was complete. The candles danced in the darkness, and an unremarkable room had become no less than a suburb of heaven itself. She hung up her robe on the back of the door and lit a cigarette.

With a Marlboro in one hand and her favorite cocktail in the other, Jean melted down, past six inches of dancing bubbles, into the steamy hot water. She sucked in two lungfuls of glorious bliss. She may not have done many of the things that rich women did, but she could teach anybody how to take an incredible bath.

After fifteen magnificent minutes it was time to settle in for a quiet evening. Functional white panties, a faded pair of blue jeans and a bulky grey sweatshirt found their rightful places.

She returned to the kitchen and tossed a bag of popcorn into the microwave. While waiting for her low-cal dinner she made herself another screwdriver. A few minutes later, she settled into her black leather recliner to watch some TV. It wasn't long before the usually reliable receptionist passed out, like she had done so many times before. Fortunately, this time, nobody would know.

*　*　*

The following Saturday morning, Jean woke early, curled in the fetal position. The sheets felt cold and stiffer than usual. She opened her eyes. Shocked, she was in an unfamiliar bedroom, facing a grey-haired stranger who seemed much older than she. Her eyes widened, Her brows lifted. Who was this man? How did she get there? Oh, yeah. She remembered going to Kelly's, a neighborhood bar. She looked at her bed partner. That's right, he'd bought her a few drinks.

Her head throbbed and she needed some water, but she remained motionless. She was wearing panties, but nothing more. Her stomach tightened as she began a well-deserved self-interrogation. *What the hell have you done? How're you going to get out of here? What if you're in danger?*

Still immobile, she scanned the room with crusty eyes.

A cluttered dresser was behind him, topped by a photo of the man and a woman who appeared to be his wife. Jean tried to remember if he was a widower. Couldn't recall. Couldn't see his ring finger. She should find her clothes.

She slid her foot backwards to the edge of the bed and tried to slither imperceptibly away, but her bedmate must have detected her movement. He opened his eyes. She gritted her teeth and her stomach tightened. "Good morning," he said in a friendly tone. "That was a wild evening!"

At least he didn't sound like a mad man. "Yeah," she replied, half-smiling and trying not to reveal her trepidation. "What time is it, anyway? I have to get to an appointment."

He checked the digital clock on his night table. "8:20. Don't you want some breakfast first? I make a good omelet."

"No thank you. I'm late and I need to get going." Her heart pounded harder as she searched the room for any clues that might reveal where she was. She glanced at her mystery partner for a better look. Still didn't recognize him. She grabbed a pillow, pulled it close.

"You don't really need to hide those," he said, pointing his jaw toward her breasts, "after last night."

"Someone is waiting for me," she lied. "He gets nervous when I'm late." She grabbed her clothes off the bench at the end of the bed. "I gotta go."

"Okay then," the grey-headed stranger responded. He rolled naked out of bed. "If that's how you want it, that's how it'll be."

Jean yanked on her clothes and sucked down three successive cigs while she nervously waited for her unknown acquaintance to wash up, shave, and get dressed.

Eventually, he finished and they found their way to his garage. Within ten minutes they were on a street she recognized. Another few miles and she'd be in her own neighborhood. Finally they reached Kelly's and she saw her car. "Can I get your number?" her date quizzed. "My wife is going out of town again next week."

Jean felt sick for having spent the night with a married man. "I don't want to see you again," she said as she jack-in-the-boxed herself sideways out the door.

CHAPTER 14

Stump was pissed off. His mom had told him they were going to spend Saturday morning cleaning up Dogg's yard and catching up on other chores, but it appeared he was the only one who took the commitment seriously. The night before he used his run-and-walk technique to get home from Cousin Willie's by nine as requested, but when he arrived he found a note from his mom that assured him she'd be home at a reasonable time. Yeah, right. Didn't call either.

She'd undoubtedly gone drinking again. What the hell's the matter with her? She heard what the doctor said. Her selfish attitude pissed him off.

He probably should have straightened up his room, but instead he looked out back and saw Dogg curled up under a large bush. He poured kibbles into a bowl and whistled for his four-legged pal to come eat but it took a couple similar attempts before Dogg heard him and came, tail wagging, for breakfast. Stump's nostrils caught the ghastly ear-stench. "Whew!" A peek reveled that a thick yellow pus had taken up a lot of Dogg's ear canal. Stump sat with his buddy and petted him while he ate. Hopefully his mom would have some money for meds very soon.

It was past nine when his mom finally walked in. Her unkempt hair, smeared makeup and wrinkled clothes confirmed his suspicions. "You did it again, didn't you, Mom?" he snapped.

She plopped her purse on the counter. "None of your business."

"Who was it this time, Mom? Do you even know?"

She pointed at him. "Don't you talk to me like that. I'm not in the mood for your sarcasm." She sniffed at the air. "Did you clean up the yard like I told you?"

"I'm not dumb, Mom. I know what you did. Everybody else knows about you, too."

"Everybody?" she said plopping her hands on her hips. "Who's everybody?"

"Everybody. Everybody. Everybody, Mom. Don't you get it? Aunt Gerry, Willie, the neighbors, even the kids at school. Everybody knows."

"And just what do these geniuses say?"

Stump shook his head and folded his arms across his chest. "I don't want to talk about it."

"You opened your big mouth, Buster, so back it up. Exactly what do these backstabbers say? Come on tell me. I want to hear it."

"I'm not sure I want to tell you, Mom. It might hurt your feelings."

"Well, you've been beating around the bush so stop playing games and tell me what they say."

He hung his head. "They say that you're a drunk and easy. That you're going to jail." He raised his head and opened his eyes widely. "What would I do then?"

"And just how did they know about that?"

"I don't know. Maybe Willie told them. It doesn't really matter. I just want you to stop drinking. I want a normal mother, that's all."

"You can tell those brainiacs for me to mind their own damn business."

"I do, Mom, but you embarrass both of us. This just proves you should help me find my dad. Maybe he can help us."

"For Christ's sake, Stump. Not that again. I told you we don't want him in our lives."

"Speak for yourself. He might have changed since the last time you saw him. We could go on vacations. You wouldn't have to date other men. We'd both be better off. How are we going to know if we don't even try to find him?"

She paused and touched his shoulder. "Look, I know that most boys your age want to know their dads, but you have to believe me. Nothing good could come out of your meeting him. All that matters is we love each other, regardless of what anybody else says or does, and we've got to stick together. You have to trust me on this. I'm the adult and you have to respect that."

"But this is about both of us, not just you. You have to respect me, too. That includes my wishes to know my dad and how you deal with your drinking. Don't you remember what the doctor said? And another thing. We never have enough money for the basics like clothes and a cell phone. Have you smelled Dogg's ears lately? When you drink away your paychecks, you're not respecting him either."

"Look who's talking. I've asked you to clean up dog poop at least a hundred times, but you act like you don't know what I'm talking about. Now the back yard is so gross, I'm surprised Dogg even goes out there."

Stump hated to admit it but when he was alone he could do more chores, but there was always a more entertaining alternative, even if it was just watching TV. "And what about that laundry room?" she went on. "You keep saying you're going to clean it out, but you never do. And your room. Have you changed your sheets like I asked you? I doubt it."

"Wrong, Mom," he said smugly. "I did a load of my laundry last week."

"I saw that, but when it was done, you just threw everything in a pile on the floor by your bed. Now everything is wrinkled. Just look at the shirt you're wearing. If you would have put it away when the time was right, it wouldn't look like crap."

"Wait a minute here, Mom. I know what you're doing. The best defense is a good offense, right? You're the one who comes home after being out all night. But rather than admitting you drink too much and working on it, you're trying to deflect the blame from you to me—but we have to focus on you, Mom. Not me. If you don't do something different, you're going to kill yourself. That's a lot more important than wrinkled clothes."

She paused for a long moment, then sighed and drew him toward her. "I can't believe you sometimes. When you say things like that you make me ashamed and proud at the same time. I'm sorry I let you down again. I promise to try harder."

"But you always say that."

"I know, Honey, but you just have to give me one more chance. I'll show you." She lifted his chin. "Okay?"

"I worry about you."

She wrapped her arms around him. "I love you and don't want to hurt you. You know that, don't you?"

"I'm worried about Dogg's ears, too. Can we take him to the vet?"

She looked at poor Dogg and nodded. "You're right. He's a member of Team Randolph, too. I'll see if Aunt Gerry will lend me the money."

CHAPTER 15

Mac and Annie had only been in Palmdale for ten days but they already loved the multi-lane highways. When the traffic bogged down, such as now, they straddled the lines between lanes and bypassed the idiots in the bumper-to-bumper chain. There's our exit," he said as if she could hear him. They worked their way up the ramp and negotiated a couple of side streets before dipping into the high school parking lot. Mac scanned the area. "Good news, Annie. There's a spot right next to her car."

"*Perfect,*" he imagined her saying.

They coasted into the open spot on the shotgun side of Rachel Johnson's car. He already knew a lot about her. He scanned the lot one more time. The coast was clear. "This is it, Annie. Time to shit or get off the pot."

"*Are you sure you want to do this?*"

"Oh yeah. Mickey really needs this and Miranda has done her homework. If this lady is as rich as we think she is, we can help Mickey without even hurting her."

"*But we've never done anything like this before. I think you might be falling in love.*"

Mac scoffed. "Me? In love? You must be sniffing your high-octane gas fumes."

"*Push the button. I'll try to lower the kickstand.*"

"No problem." He held the bike steady and performed

the kickstand ritual that he figured out after they'd hit a large pothole on a back road in Wyoming and knocked it out of alignment. It took a few yanks and a twist before it jiggled into place. "There we go."

"You must really want to impress Miranda."

"I admit that's part of it, Annie, but I've never really made a difference in anybody's life and this is a chance to do something special." He opened one of the leather saddlebags, snatched a screwdriver and quick-scanned the area. Near the other end of the field there were some guys in shorts and another group wore football helmets, but no other pads. Track and spring practice, he assumed.

He squatted next to Rachel Johnson's front tire, removed the valve cap and pushed the pin to let out the air. That done, he drove a scratched-up screw into the tire before he returned to the saddlebag to exchange the screwdriver for some polish and a rag. "All we can do now, Annie, is wait."

Not long thereafter, the final bell announced the end of the school day, and a parade of students fled as if they were escaping a sniper. Before long, a few more athletes gathered by the football field and a spattering of teachers and administrators meandered toward Mac and Annie.

Eventually, Rachel Johnson stepped out. He recognized her from Miranda's description—mid to late thirties, short dark hair and glasses. "Here she comes," Mac whispered. Fortunately, she was alone.

Mac watched her out of the corner of his eye. As she drew closer he was surprised by how tall she was—nearly six feet, he guessed. He poured a couple drops of polish onto Annie's tank and spread it around. When Rachel Johnson reached the driver's side of her car Mac had his opening. "Hi, there. It's none of my business, but I noticed you have a flat." He aimed his jaw toward the damaged tire.

She looked at Mac, sucked in a deep breath and blew it right back out. "Great." She threw her belongings on the driver's seat before slipping around to check it out.

"You don't look like you're dressed to fix a tire," Mac said, smiling. "Would you like me to do it for you?"

She sighed and shook her head. "You don't have to do that. I can call somebody."

He dismounted. "By the time they get here, I can have it fixed for you. It's no big deal, and I don't have anything else I need to do."

She hesitated. "Well, if you really don't mind, I guess that would be nice."

Mac dipped his head approvingly toward the back of her car. "You'll need to open your trunk."

A couple moments later Mac had secured a wimpy looking spare and the lug wrench. "This is one of those temporary spares. Are you familiar with them?"

"No, not really."

"I can explain how they work, if you'd like. You never know when it might happen to you again."

She shrugged. "I guess so."

He squatted down. "You know something," he said while turning his head, "this might be easier if we knew each other's names. Mine's Mac."

She looked out over the field. "Most everybody around here refers to me as Ms. Johnson, but you can call me Rachel. I'm one of the assistant principals."

"Okay then, Rachel it is." He plugged the wrench onto one of the nuts.

"Are you a parent to one of the students?" she asked as he twisted the wrench.

Mac snickered. "Nah, I was just driving by and noticed the football field. It brought back some old memories, so I pulled over to polish my bike." He inserted the jack into the pinch flange and pumped the handle a few times. Moments later the front corner of her car, including the tire, was suspended above ground. He spun the tire so she could see the screw. "There's your troublemaker. Any tire shop can plug it for you."

"That's good to know. How did you come to learn so much about cars and tires?"

"I was raised out in the country," he said while he replaced the bad tire. "We had to fix things ourselves, because the conveniences of the city were too far away."

Rachel smiled. "For a while there I thought you might work in a tire store or something."

"Not me. I'm an in-house electrician at NASA's Research Center across town. I just got the job a couple weeks ago."

"An electrical engineer?"

"Not an engineer. A regular electrician. The guy who runs wires, builds circuits. Stuff like that. Those people are always changing things around and it's up to me to get them set up and work with the building inspectors."

"Sounds important."

Mac shrugged. "If the lights don't work, neither does anybody else."

He put the damaged tire away and grabbed a rag and some sanitizer from Annie's saddlebag. "That ought to do it," he said as he wiped off his hands.

"This was awfully nice of you, Mac. What do I owe you?"

"I couldn't charge a friend who I know on a first name basis just for changing a tire." He hesitated. "But there is something you could do for me—to return the favor, I mean. To tell you the truth, I don't really know anybody around here, and I've enjoyed talking with you." He aimed a finger over her shoulder. "What would you say to a quick walk around the football field? Perhaps you could tell me about Palmdale."

Rachel looked toward the field where all athletes were going through their workouts. "Why not? It's a beautiful day."

As they strolled around the field Rachel told Mac a little about her career and mentioned being an only child of an only child. By that time their pace slowed and they'd reached the bleachers on the other side of the field. She raised her eyebrows. "Do you mind if I ask you a question?"

"By all means," Mac replied. "That's what friends do." The small talk seemed to appeal to her.

"I noticed the name Annie on your motorcycle. Is that your girlfriend's name?"

Mac smiled. "We'd better have a seat," he said, pointing to the front row. "When I was a kid my mom got me a book about Annie Oakley." He shook his head. "I must have made her read that book to me a hundred times."

Rachel grinned.

"Mom and I both liked how Annie could outshoot the men. It was a great lesson—anybody can be successful if he or she wants it badly enough."

"I wish more of our students understood that."

"I named my bicycles after her and then did the same thing with all my big bikes. That Harley is the fifth one." He paused and looked into Rachel's eyes. "But that's not all. I even got a tattoo of her on my chest—stupidity and too many beers."

Rachel laughed. "At least you realize it wasn't the smartest thing to do."

"Anyway, there's something Annie and I do that's pretty strange."

"Oh really? What's that?"

He looked around as if he was about to reveal one of NASA's national secrets. "Do you remember that movie from about ten years ago called *Cast Away*?"

"With Tom Hanks?"

"That's it. Annie and I are like Hanks and Wilson—the volley ball." Mac paused again looked around the field. "I'm almost embarrassed to tell you."

"Go ahead. You'd be surprised by some of the stories I hear in my job."

"Alright then, but you're going to think I'm nuts." He glanced at the scar on the back of his knuckles. "About a year after high school I got my first Harley. Naturally I named it Annie. Our first long drive was down to Florida for spring break. Before I knew it we were going all over the place. Once in a while we rode with other bikers, but mostly I preferred to travel as a single. All of that alone-time enabled me to think through things, have internal debates to develop my philosophies and conscience." Rachel nodded.

"Sometimes I talked out loud," Mac continued, "but eventually I just imagined I was literally speaking to Annie. Before long, I could make her respond by giving her the throttle or by downshifting or swaying. Then I started imagining she was talking back—just like Hanks and Wilson."

"I can understand that," she said smiling. "When I was a little girl, I used to play house with Barbie and Ken. I'd sit them around a little dinner table and we'd all have lengthy conversations about the day's activities."

"Yeah, but I bet you outgrew it?"

She shrugged. "I don't play with dolls anymore, but I talk to my cat and talk back to the TV occasionally. Talk to myself when I drive too. You're just like anybody else. Only most men wouldn't admit it."

"Whew." Mac pretended to wipe some sweat off his brow. "I was beginning to think I'm nuts." He pointed to her hand. "I see you're not married. Is there a real-life Ken somewhere?"

Her hair swayed from side to side as she shook her head. "Not at the moment. Most of the men I've met drink too much, so I just quit looking."

From off to the side a football bounced in front of them and settled at their feet. Mac rose and snagged it off the ground before motioning for the youngster who was coming for it to run to his left. Then he lofted a tight spiral right over the boy's shoulder as if they'd been rehearsing the exact same move for years.

"Impressive," Rachel said as they resumed their walk. "Did you play?"

"It's been a long time."

"Ever been married?" she asked. "Had kids?"

"No to both, but I like older kids and they seem to like Annie. We get in all sorts of conversations about traveling."

"Oh, really?" she said as they found their way back to the parking lot. "We're looking for some summer activities for some of the students. Would you have any interest in discussing some of your motorcycle travels with them? They might like that."

"Might be interesting," Mac pointed his jaw toward her Toyota. "What would you say to meeting me same time tomorrow? Then we can take your broken tire somewhere and discuss it."

* * *

After Rachel drove off Mac and Annie pulled away, too. *"How'd it go?"* Annie nearly asked.

"Good news, bad news, Annie. Miranda's going to be very happy, and that's what counts the most—for her brother's sake—but it was harder than I expected."

"Something go wrong?"

"A couple small things. She seems like a decent person. That might make it harder to cheat her out of the money."

"I thought you said her family wouldn't miss it?"

"That's what Miranda tells me, but it's harder when you attach a face to the plan."

They swung around the corner. *"What's the other thing?"*

"I'm almost ashamed to say it, but she's not very attractive, especially compared to Miranda. It's going to take time to get that money, maybe six months or longer. Until then every time I touch her, I'll be thinking of Miranda. Same thing if I should see her naked. How am I supposed to ignore that?"

"Maybe you should just call the whole thing off. We can return to New York."

"Can't do that, Annie. It would disappoint Miranda and I think we've got something special going on."

"*Well then, it appears you're like a piece of lumber. Sooner or later, you're going to get nailed or screwed.*"

"That old line, huh?" Mac eased off the throttle, tapped the breaks. "Pull into that driveway, Annie." Up ahead, a Budweiser truck was jammed up close to the back of the bowling alley. "I could use a cold beer."

CHAPTER 16

"You wouldn't believe how much better Dogg smells," Jean said to her sister. "I don't know what I would have done if you hadn't lent me the money."

Gerry had just dropped Cousin Willie off before going to her beauty parlor. "Glad to do it, Honey. But next time don't wait so long. The poor thing must have been scared half to death."

"At least he got most of his hearing back. I don't know how I'm ever going to repay you and Dirk. Not just for the loan, but for everything you do for us."

Gerry smiled. "That's what sisters are for. Are you prepared for your court date tomorrow?"

Jean nodded. "Lydia tells me that it usually takes four DUIs before they send you to jail. This is only my third and Stump will be there to tell them he needs me."

"You're cutting it awfully close. Wouldn't it be a lot easier to stop drinking or at least to stop driving after you've had a drink?"

"I've already done that," Jean said, while reaching for a cigarette. "In fact you'll be surprised by what I threw away last night. Stump even saw me."

Gerry glanced at her watch. "Oops. I'm sorry, but I'm running late for my appointment. Why don't you tell me about it while you walk me to my car."

* * *

"C'mon, Dude," Willie said to Stump, who was scooping up dog poop. "Let's go to the mall. I gotta get a new backpack."

"Not right now, man." Stump replied as he added full-sized dog turds to one of the bags. "I promised my mom I'd clean up the dog shit and then clean the outside of the windows. It'll only take me an hour or so."

"Windows? Doesn't your mom clean the windows?"

"Just the inside. I do the outside. It's part of a deal we cut. She agreed to throw out the last of her vodka if I'd do a couple things to help out. All I gotta do is get the stepstool, reach between the bars and wipe them down."

"Don't the bars have a release of some kind? That would make it a lot easier."

Stump shook his head. "New ones do, but these were on here when we bought the house. She likes them because they make her feel safer."

"So she threw out her vodka, huh? She must have meant it this time."

"Yep. Right in front of me. I finally got through to her." He plunged a few more doggie leavings into a sack. "I think it was also because of her court date. She wanted me to be certain that she'd straightened up so I could toot my horn for her."

"I hope so, man, but my dad thinks they might throw her in jail."

"Not according to her attorney. Especially after I get done telling them how well she's doing."

Willie gazed around the yard, let out an exaggerated sigh. "If I help you with the damn windows, will you go to the mall when we're done? You can have my old backpack. It's still in pretty good shape."

Stump hesitated a second, then grinned. "But that leaves all the dog shit for me, and I've already picked up my share.

Why don't I clean the windows and you be the poop dude for a while?" He held out the shovel and grinned again.

"I can't believe I'm doing this."

A moment later, the back door swung open. "I'm going to the grocery store, Honey," Stump's mom said. "You boys want anything?"

"How about some chocolate ice cream for later?"

"Okay. Anything else?"

"No, but we're going to the mall when we get done. Okay?"

"That's fine, as long as you have your work done. I should only be about an hour or so."

The door closed and Willie whispered to Stump. "Hey, Dude. Did you ever find your birth certificate?"

Stump stopped and looked his cousin in the eye. They both knew what they were going to do as soon as Jean drove off.

The laundry room, or catchall room, as they sometimes referred to it, was in the center of the house. It contained the hot water heater, the washer and dryer, a broom and mop plus a collection of over-stuffed shelves. "She doesn't throw anything away," Stump said as they entered the room. "There's boxes in boxes, stacks of sacks and enough junk for a garage sale."

"God, what a mess." Willie mumbled. "Where's the metal box?"

Stump's eyes turned skyward. "Used to be on the top shelf, but I don't see it. I'll hop up on the washing machine." An endless collection of boxes and paper products, including his old puzzle books, surrounded him.

To his side, additional shelves were stuffed with tax records, wrapping paper, old toys, and boxes of things that they no longer used. "I don't know why we keep all this crap," he said. He shuffled a few items around. Then, "Here it is." As he stretched for the box, his hand scraped across some bags, thereby creating a miniature paper avalanche.

"Holy crap," Willie said as he took the box from Stump and bounced backwards.

"Damn it!" Stump hollered out. "Look at this." He grabbed an unopened gallon of vodka and showed Willie a quart-sized canning jar that also contained clear liquid.

CHAPTER 17

Stump couldn't confront his mom about the vodka for fear she'd want to know why he was messing around on the shelves in the first place. On a more selfish level, about all he knew for sure was the metal box was locked so he needed to locate the key. Sidetracked on both counts, he and Willie returned the laundry room to its previous condition and bolted to the mall, for which Stump got a better used backpack out of the deal.

Now it was a new day and Aunt Gerry had just pulled into the driveway to take him and his mom to her hearing.

In the courthouse corridor, Jean's attorney, Lydia, hurried toward Jean. "Good news. We got Judge Vaughn. I've known her forever. She never breaks up families. All we have to do is play this the way we rehearsed and you're guaranteed that extra chance you need."

Fifteen minutes later a similar case was underway. The defendant, a Mr. Paxton, got busted for drunk driving and injuring a young girl in his neighborhood. The girl was in attendance, in a wheelchair, with her parents, who happened to be friends of Paxton. They said they were certain it was just an accident, and they hoped the court would forgive him. Then, when Judge Vaughn asked Mr. Paxton to step forward, Stump got a closer look at the injured girl. Both of her legs were in casts and she wore a neck brace.

"You darn near killed your friend's daughter," Judge Vaughn said to Paxton. "The court has elected to sentence you to one year in the county jail." Mr. Paxton shifted his feet as the judge turned a page in her file. "Fortunately for you," she continued, "there is some additional evidence to consider. The doctor's report shows the victim is expected to have a complete recovery after a little more physical therapy." She turned another page. "I see you've also gone to some AA meetings and seem to be working on the matter. Additionally, you're the primary breadwinner in your family, and you've only had two DUIs. In view of these added circumstances, I'm electing to temporarily suspend your sentence."

The defendant blew out a deep breath. "Thank you, judge. I really appreciate it."

"Next time you'll not only serve time for whatever else you do, but I'll also reinstate the sentence I just suspended. Do we understand each other?"

"Yes, ma'am. I get it." He turned and hugged his attorney.

The judge tapped her gavel. "Next case. Jean Randolph."

Stump's mom and her lawyer moved toward the center of the room. "I'm Lydia Schwartz, judge. Attorney for Ms. Randolph."

The judge glanced at her file jacket. "Your client is also here for sentencing. Is that correct?"

"Yes, Your Honor. Ms. Randolph admitted what she did and apologized. It's only her third DUI."

"Do you want to call any witnesses before I pass sentence?"

"Yes, judge. We'd like to call the defendant's sister and her son."

For the next ten minutes Aunt Gerry prattled through a touching story about how tough her sister's life had been. But Stump couldn't forget the girl in the wheelchair. It was pure luck that his mom hadn't hurt somebody too. Abruptly, Aunt Gerry stepped back and Stump was called upon.

"Good morning, Mr. Randolph," the judge said. "I

understand you want to say a few words on your mother's behalf?"

Stump hesitated and looked at his mom. Lydia pointed her jaw toward the microphone and mouthed the words, "Go ahead." He sighed and leaned forward.

"Nobody would want to rat out their own mother, but I don't want anybody else to end up like that girl who was just in here."

"Go ahead; tell me more," the judge said.

Tears came to Stump's eyes. He took another breath. "A couple weeks ago Mom got in trouble because of her drinking and had to go to the hospital."

Jean whispered something in Lydia's ear, probably something about the rape not being her fault. "The doctor warned her to quit or she could die. She promised she would stop, but she's been drunk more times since then. Each time, she promises she'll stop or at least slow down. But she never does. Yesterday she told me she quit and poured out an opened bottle of vodka right in front of me. Then she made a big deal out of throwing the bottle away." He heard movement from the direction of his mom and her attorney.

"What happened next?" the judge asked.

Stump sniffled. "I was cleaning up the yard and needed a bag so I went to our catch-all room. That's when I found out she lied again. Some bags fell off the shelf and I found two bottles of vodka—a full one and a pickle jar with some in it."

The judge glared at Jean then returned her attention to Stump. "Are you saying she had two bottles on hand after just telling you that she threw everything away?"

He nodded and wiped away a tear. "Yes ma'am. I figured out that she had emptied her other bottle into the pickle jar and then put some water in the empty vodka bottle so that it looked like she was throwing away vodka, but it was really just water."

"Your Honor," Lydia butted in. "I'm sure Neal is confused.

He couldn't know what was in the bottle that Ms. Randolph threw out."

"He's your witness, counselor. If you didn't know what he was going to say, you shouldn't have called upon him. I'll hear him out." To Stump, she said, "What makes you think she threw out water instead of vodka?"

"I smelled the liquid in the pickle jar. It was definitely alcohol. And then she hid it. Why would she do that? It was just so she could put on a big show and make me think she threw the stuff out."

Lydia rose again. "Your Honor. That's just Neal's opinion. He's no expert on alcoholic beverages."

The judge held up her hand. "I said I want to hear him out." Back to Stump. "Go ahead, Mr. Randolph. You were saying?"

Stump finally got enough nerve to face his mother. "I'm sorry, Mom."

She turned her head away, disgusted.

"She lies over and over again. Her lawyer gets her extra chances, but she never changes. I don't want her to hurt anybody like that girl. The doctor said if she doesn't quit drinking, she might die. But she doesn't listen to anybody. In a few weeks we go back to school and I won't be around to help her as much. I think you should throw the book at her, or whatever it is you can do. I love my mom, but she won't fix her problem so I want you to do something drastic to help her." His head felt like it weighed a hundred pounds.

The judge turned to Lydia. "Counselor?"

"Ms. Randolph loves her son, Your Honor. She's a good mom. They need each other and I think you should give her one more chance. I'm sure they can work through all of this. They've been survivors all their lives."

The judge addressed Jean. "What about you, Ms. Randolph? Can you tell me any reason I shouldn't put you in jail?"

"Because youngsters need their parents," she said meekly.

The judge went quiet and turned a couple of pages in her

file. Finally she lifted her head. "The court agrees with Ms. Randolph. Our children do indeed need their parents to watch over them and keep them safe." She turned to Lydia. "However, the evidence shows that Ms. Randolph can't control herself. In this family it appears as if the roles have been reversed. Neal is the one who acts like an adult and she's the one who acts like a reckless child. They need each other alright, but he seems to be the only one who gets that."

Judge Vaughn motioned to Jean. "For starters, the court orders you to immediately surrender your driver's license to the state for a period of time to be determined at a later date, but not less than one year."

Jean covered her mouth and the judge resumed, "I'm tempted to separate you from Neal for at least a year. Then maybe you'd have time to think about the damage you're doing to your son."

Jean's hands shook. "Please judge, don't do that. He needs me. He can't even do his laundry correctly or cook a good meal."

The judge raised a halting hand. "From what I've heard today, Ms. Randolph, it's the other way around. You're the one who acts like an irresponsible child."

Jean's attorney held up her hand. "Judge, may I say something?"

The judge nodded.

Lydia took Jean's hand. "I know how important drinking and driving is to you and our society. Like you, I've seen the problems first-hand. But breaking up this family would not be good for Neal. He needs his mother just as much as any other child needs his or her mom. I'm asking that you reconsider. Give her one final chance to straighten up. For both of their sakes."

Judge Vaughn removed her glasses. "You may be correct, counselor. But she's the one who doesn't understand consequences." She retuned her glasses to their rightful place. "I'm sentencing Ms. Randolph to thirty days in the county jail." Stump's mom gasped and her attorney shook her head. "And just to show you what life would be like without your son, I'm restricting you to one hour of visiting rights each week. Maybe if you find out how lonely you get when you're not together, you'll finally modify your behavior." She turned to Stump. "Do you have somebody you can stay with for the next month? If not, I can make arrangements for you to live in a court-approved facility."

Stump wiped his cheek with his sleeve. "My Aunt Gerry might take me."

Aunt Gerry stood. "Of course I will, Your Honor. I'll take care of him."

The judge turned back to Stump. "What you did today took incredible courage. I don't see much of that around here. I want you to know that I personally respect you for doing something so difficult. Your mother is going through a very tough time in her life. She needs you. And I know she loves you. Never forget that, no matter how difficult things become between you."

"Yes, ma'am."

The judge returned to Jean. "One more arrest and I'm going to split you guys up for a year. Understand?"

"But this isn't fair. The previous guy got off."

"I'm very serious, Ms. Randolph. Hopefully you'll get serious too." She turned her head toward an armed man at the side of the room. "Deputy, escort Ms. Randolph to the Sheriff's office for processing." She tapped her gavel on her desk. "Next case."

CHAPTER 18

Following Mac and Rachel's meeting on the football field, Miranda noted that there was still a lot more to find out and to do, but it appeared as if Don's plan had genuine promise. She picked up two disposable cell phones—"burners," as the sales clerk called them—and gave one to Mac; then she completed his image as a NASA electrician by scraping together some work clothes and a fake picture ID to clip to his shirt. Thereafter, Mac wore his "uniform" and visited Rachel nearly every day.

About ten days after the original meeting, Miranda began slipping him money from her recently approved line of credit so it always appeared as if he had the kind of spending money an electrician might carry around. He also followed up on one of Miranda's suggestions and rented a van in which he and Rachel took six students to a Dodger's game. A few days later, Rachel offered to let him move into her guest room—strictly as a roommate.

At first, Mac's new housing arrangement represented a step closer to the trust money, but he quickly complained about spending the nights at Rachel's place instead of at Miranda's home as had been the previous norm. When he speculated that it would take so many similar nights to complete the plan that it might not be worth it, Miranda pleaded with him not to quit. "I know it's difficult, Sweets, but Mickey and I would really appreciate it if you'd hang in there until we know for certain whether or not we can escalate your relationship into a marriage."

That day she "appreciated" him more than any woman had ever "appreciated" him before. He agreed to keep going as long as they continued to make progress.

One night Mac called her and said he was taking Rachel to dinner. "I'll let you know how it goes," he said, "when I see you in the morning."

Now, that time had come. Mac parked in Miranda's garage and let himself into her kitchen. He grinned. "It happened," he said before they even said good morning.

Miranda tilted her head. "I'll be damned," she said holding her arms out for a hug. "Tell me about it."

"After dinner, we had some wine. Then when we got home we got right to it—didn't even talk about protection."

"That's it? Simple as that?" She squinted her eyes nearly closed. "It's almost as if she *wants* to get pregnant. Why else would she be so cavalier?"

"That's fine with us, right? 'Cause if she thinks she's pregnant, she'd probably agree to get married."

"It's intriguing, all right."

"As far as I'm concerned, the sooner the better. Either that or kill the whole deal."

"It could have been the liquor," she suggested. "You know something, Sweets? You may have found the quickest way to get her to marry you. I think you should ask her if you can move your things out of the guestroom and into her room."

"But that would mean I'd have to literally sleep with her every night."

"You've got to try, Sweets. It will tell us if she was just tipsy, or if she secretly wants to have a baby."

* * *

The next morning, Mac donned his uniform a little earlier than usual. He jumped on Annie and they darted out of the driveway without warming her up. Annie sputtered as if she needed a cup of morning coffee. "Bad news, Annie. We gotta get to Miranda's ASAP."

"I thought you seemed anxious," he imagined her saying.

"Can't help it," he said, shifting. "Two nights ago everything was going perfectly. Rachel and I got it on for the first time. I asked Rachel if I could move into her room but we ended up getting it on again without her answering the question."

"Did you raw dog her, again?"

"She didn't even hesitate," he replied while twisting the throttle, "so this morning I asked her why she didn't make an issue of it and her answer damn near knocked the wind out of me." Ahead, a yellow light ahead urged them to hurry up. "Now it looks like a medical issue has ruined Mickey's best shot at a decent life."

"Maybe this will give you a reason to back out."

"I'm okay with that if Miranda is, but if we keep going, I gotta get some sleeping pills for Rachel at night."

"Good plan. That way, you can sneak out and spend more time with Miranda."

"It's not just that, but I need a break from her. I'm tired of the morning charade, dressing up like a damn electrician before we bolt over to Miranda's place. I'm always worn out when I get there."

"I never thought you could get too much action."

Mac smirked. "Our assistant principal isn't as proper as she'd like people to believe."

"You think you might have problems getting it up? 'Cause they've got pills for that, you know."

"Not so far, Annie, but I'm supposed to make Rachel think we're in love. I can't expect her to marry me if I can't pull that off and it's difficult to get aroused by her when Miranda is so close by."

"Sounds like you're all going to get screwed one way or the other."

CHAPTER 19

Miranda hadn't slept well since Rachel had told Mac about her medical issue. Now Miranda had to tell Don there was genuine doubt it they could ever get to the trust money.

After taking their positions in the visiting room, Don verified that the guard was out of earshot before he leaned forward. "I hope you've got good news for me."

Miranda turned her hands palms up. "We've got a couple big problems, Donnie. If we can't come up with an answer, Mickey isn't—"

"What kind of problems?"

"For one thing, I almost didn't get to come today. Mac is spending so much time with Rachel that when he finally gets away, he clings to me like tape. I had to lie to him just so I could see you."

"What's the big deal? You've been coming here every week without him knowing about us."

"Like I said, the more time he spends with Rachel, the more he clings to me when he's free. I told him I have to have Thursday mornings off—for 'girl things,' like the beauty parlor, shopping, cleaning house."

"Sounds good. Did he buy it?"

"Not at first. He said I could use nights and weekends for those things, but I told him that wasn't enough. I think he'll be okay with it for a while."

"Good. Now what's the other problem? The last I heard, he'd just moved in with that Rachel chick and you were going to get some pictures of his hair style and tattoos so I can match them when I get out."

"That's the least of our worries right now." She looked over her shoulder to the guard's desk where Officer Jackson was skimming through a magazine. "Everything was going great until yesterday. They'd made love a few times and Rachel didn't make an issue of birth control. We figured that she secretly wants to have a baby, so Mac started talking about kids and families."

"Yeah? Sounds fantastic. So what's the snag?"

"Yesterday she said she never let herself get her hopes up, after the surgery."

"Surgery? What surgery?"

"When she was younger. She had a cancer-like growth on her ovaries. After her surgeon removed it he said there was substantial doubt whether she could ever get pregnant. But he also said he'd seen crazier things. Anyway, now her periods are irregular, sometimes several months apart, and it appears she's not capable."

Don's jaw tightened. "Damn. Now we'll have to stick with the earlier plan. Mac's got to charm her into marrying him."

Miranda shook her head. "That isn't going to work, Donnie. They'd have to live together longer. There'd be an engagement period, then a wedding. That could take a year or longer. Mac isn't going to hold up that long. Besides that, she might figure out that he's not really employed or she might just say no."

Don smacked his hand on the table. "You got any other bright ideas?"

She shrugged. "I wish we did, for Mickey's sake, but we needed her to think she was pregnant."

Don pursed his lips. Then, "Wait a minute. You just said we needed her to think she was pregnant, right?"

"Yeah. But we can't count on that now."

Don wagged his index finger. "You're looking at it all wrong, Baby. It doesn't matter if she's pregnant or not. All she has to do is *think* she is. All we gotta do is convince her she's pregnant, even if she isn't."

Miranda blew out a breath of frustration. "I don't follow."

Don grinned. "Don't you see? Her surgeon's comment —that he'd seen crazier things—left the door open to the possibility and it's obvious that down deep she really does want to have a baby. Otherwise, she would have made Mac use a condom to eliminate all doubt, but she didn't do that. It's clear as a bell. She'll want to believe us."

Miranda shook her head. "Even if that's true, she's not stupid. How are we going to make her think she's pregnant in the first place?"

"I can think of a couple of ways. First, you need my dipshit brother to get into her cell phone."

Miranda's heart sped up. Once again she was convinced that Don was smarter than most people would think. She was excited again. Maybe there was still hope for Mickey.

CHAPTER 20

Stump slid a plastic bag across the seat. "Can I turn the radio on?" he asked Aunt Gerry as he buckled his seat belt.

"I guess so, but not too loud."

It had been a week since Stump's mom went straight to jail, without passing Go. He'd never seen her as disappointed in him as when they handcuffed her and led her out of the courtroom. She may have forgiven him countless times for lesser failings, but this was a new level. He chewed at his thumbnail. Then, "Do you think they put her in with any murderers?"

"She's in county jail, Honey," Aunt Gerry said, "not a state prison or federal penitentiary. It's not very plush but most people are in for lesser crimes. They usually get out in a year or less."

"I hope she's not too scared."

"What's in your sack?"

"I brought the picture of mom and me with our chocolate faces. She likes that one."

"She sure does, but I'm not sure they'll let you bring that in. The website said all she could accept is reading material."

"I know, but she was really mad at me when they took her away, and this is her favorite one."

Gerry shrugged her shoulders. "We'll try it, but I wouldn't get your hopes up."

A weird siren interrupted a song on the radio and a deep-voiced announcer butted in. *"K.R.A.B. has just learned that local automobile dealer, Clifford Clifton, was arrested minutes ago. Our on-the-spot reporter, Lacey Abeytos, has more."*

"Oh, my God," Gerry said as she raised a hand to her mouth. Stump leaned forward and turned the volume up.

"That's right, Andrew," the reporter said with a matter-of-fact tone. *"I'm at Clifton GMC, where L.A. police have just loaded Mr. Clifton into the back of a squad car. The K.R.A.B. news team has learned that Mr. Clifton was charged with several crimes involving a date rape drug, including aggravated sexual assault on a woman who had to be taken to the hospital. Officers tell us the victim's son, a student, walked in on Clifton and the victim. More amazingly, the student had the wherewithal to memorize the license plate number of the now infamous dealer's car. Clifton proclaimed innocence to this reporter, but if convicted as charged, he faces up to twenty years in prison."*

"Thank God for that," the guy at the studio said.

"We should tell all our listeners," the reporter continued, *"that the man we all see on TV doing Clifton's commercials is really an actor by the name of Christopher Flossel. As far as we know, Mr. Flossel had nothing to do with the alleged crimes. Stay tuned to K.R.A.B for more information as we get it. Back to you, Andrew."*

Stump jumped with such force his seatbelt seized and nailed him to his seat. He slapped at the radio knob to silence it. "Ha! That'll teach you not to mess with the Stumpster's mother, you bastard." Oops.

"I know you're happy, Honey. So am I, but when you talk like that it makes you sound uneducated."

"Sorry."

"The Stumpster?" she asked. "Where'd that endearing term come from?"

"I dunno," he beamed while shrugging his shoulders, "But I hope they hang the bast—oops—I almost did it again. I hope they hang that *animal*."

She tapped his knee. "See? You boys can control your tongues when you want to."

Stump could have told her that Cousin Willie had the foulest mouth Stump knew of but he had more important things to think about. There was good news to tell his mom.

His enthusiasm must have been contagious because a little later a deputy allowed him to give the picture to his mother, provided he removed it from the frame.

While he did as he was told, he wondered if they thought his mom was going to break the pane into a collection of weapons and organize a mass jailbreak.

After a brief pat-down, they were led to a small conference room where his mom was already sitting behind a stout oak table with her back against the far wall. Her hair was straight, she wore no makeup or jewelry and her shapeless jumpsuit made her look like a partially crumpled sack of oranges.

Her nonchalant glance in his direction made one thing perfectly clear: She was nowhere near as happy to see him as he was to see her. Aunt Gerry dropped her magazines on the table and hugged her sister; then it was Stump's turn.

He reached his arms out. His mom allowed the embrace, but showed no matching affection.

"I don't suppose you brought me any cigarettes," she said. "Or are you trying to teach me another lesson?"

Stump and Aunt Gerry looked at one another. Why hadn't they thought of that? "We'll see if we can't drop some off with the guards later," Aunt Gerry said.

Jean turned away.

"Guess what?" Stump said in his most excited outside voice. "They arrested that car dealer. We just heard it on the news."

Jean turned her head his way. "Great," she said, sarcastically. "Now, I'll lose my job on top of everything else."

"I don't think so, Honey," Aunt Gerry added. "I called Lydia yesterday. She said they're holding it open for you."

"Is that the genius who said I had a lenient judge who never breaks up families?"

"Look what I brought," Stump said, still trying to be cheerful. He slid the frameless picture her way. "I can leave it here if you want me to."

"Everybody else gets four chances. I only got three."

If Stump had been a balloon, all the air would have just escaped. "This is your fault, too," he painfully shot back.

"Thanks for the support."

"Look, you two," Aunt Gerry offered. "Right now it doesn't really matter whose fault this is. Let's not play the blame game."

There was an awkward silence, and then Stump said, "Dogg is doing better."

There was no reply.

Although Stump desperately loved his mother and genuinely regretted his role in putting her where she was, the word "bitch" came to mind. So did the idea of bringing up his dad again, but even he had enough sense to bite his tongue once in a while. It probably wasn't a good time to say he wished he had a cell phone either.

"We've gone back to your house a couple times," Aunt Gerry said. "Stump watered the plants and we aired it out."

Jean nodded.

"Five minutes, everybody," the guard said.

"Is there anything I can do, Mom, to make you feel better?"

She didn't reply. A few additional benign topics were similarly dismissed. Finally, the guard spoke again. "Wrap it up folks. We've got other people who need this room."

If only Stump could have said something brilliant, but brilliancy was not within his grasp. Only regret. "I'm sorry I did this to you, Mom."

His mom lifted her eyes toward him but said nothing until the last possible second. Then, "I love you both," she said to their backs.

Stump spun around and grabbed and hugged her. "We love you too, Mom."

CHAPTER 21

"**W**hy was she like that?" Stump asked when they got near Aunt Gerry's house. "Mad the whole time, except at the end."

"She's desperate, Honey," Aunt Gerry said as they pulled up. Dogg was standing on the couch and looking out the living room window. "She knows we're right, but it's hard to accept. Change and jail are scary. But she loves you more than you can ever know."

Sounded reasonable enough. Stump blew out a gentle breath. "I'm glad she doesn't hate me."

Inside, Stump and Dogg went upstairs to Willie's room and Stump told him about the jail, Clifton's arrest, and Aunt Gerry's mistaken implication that only appropriate words ever come out of Willie's mouth. "Screw that," Willie said, with a mischievous grin.

"My mom wouldn't talk to me most of the time but your mom said she was just scared. I hope this court stuff does her some good."

"Rules suck."

"Yeah. Like having to go to bed at ten o'clock," Stump said, referring to one of the house rules. He patted Dogg on the head. "I know what we can do. We can go to my place and see if we can find the key to that box."

Willie agreed and made up a plausible excuse to tell Aunt

Gerry. "Mom, Stump wants to go to his house to get a video game."

"Can't you just play with one of yours?"

"But he has a new one that he borrowed from somebody else. We haven't played this one yet."

"I don't have time to take you. I've got to finish making dinner."

"You don't have to take us. We can use our hurry-up trick and be back in less than an hour."

"I want to take Dogg too," Stump added. "He could use the exercise."

Aunt Gerry's head twisted toward the clock on her stove. "Alright then," she said as she grabbed a potato peeler. "But be careful and get home by five."

It took sixteen minutes to make the nearly two-mile trip. Dogg got to check out the backyard, while the humans looked everywhere they could think of for a key that might fit. Finally, Willie asked, "How long has it been since your mom used that box?"

"I don't know, Dude. Maybe a year or so."

"If it's been that long, she might not look at it again for a long time. I say we pry it open."

"I don't want to piss her off."

"You just said she might not see it for years and even if she does, she'll probably think it fell off the shelf or she broke it herself when she was drinking or something."

Stump lifted his head. If there really was a birth certificate in there, or anything else that could provide a clue as to who his dad was, he wanted to find it. "Good point. I'll get a chisel and a screwdriver from the garage."

"And a hammer," Willie said.

Within minutes, they sprang the latch. The first glance inside revealed a second-place ribbon that Stump won on field day and an award he got for perfect attendance in second grade at his old school. Beneath that there was an old nametag that Jean must have gotten from a convention. It had her current last name on it, offering no hint if she'd ever used a different last name. Still deeper in the pile, there was a small stack of greeting cards along with some funeral schedules and wedding announcements. "I don't know most of these people," Stump said.

"Take them. Your dad could be one of them. We can do Google searches."

Stump shoved them in his pocket and shuffled through the remaining items in the metal box. At the very bottom he nudged aside a very tiny red envelope, about the size of a business card. "There's nothing else," he said.

"What about that little red packet?" Willie asked.

"Don't know." On the back, it was stamped Palmdale Bank and contained its address. "Main Street. I think I know that building," Stump said. He opened it, found an odd-looking key.

"I know what that is, Dude," Willie said. "My parents have a key like that for their safe deposit box. I went with my mom once to get a car title."

"Would the bank let us in this box?" Stump wondered out loud.

"They might. After all, we've got the key."

"Doesn't sound right. If it was that easy then anybody with a key could get into anybody else's box."

A wrinkled brow indicated that Willie's mind was churning. "Come to think of it," he said, "I think we had to sign some papers to get in."

Stump crossed his arms. "Nothing is ever easy, is it?" He looked at the busted-up latch on the metal box. "I hope we didn't do this for nothing."

"I still think we should go to that bank and see if they'll let you in that box. You can tell them your mom sent you."

"I can take them a note, like we do at school. I know her penmanship well enough."

Suddenly, in the back yard, Dogg burst into aggressive barking, which he usually reserved for stray dogs or other yard invaders of all types. Stump eased down the hall and gazed through his mom's bedroom window. A uniformed cop was checking out the back yard. Uh-oh. Did they know about the metal box?

He gulped and quickly tiptoed back to the kitchen where he shoved the now–damaged metal box in a lower cabinet just as someone banged on the front door. "Police. Open the door; we know you're in there."

Stump's heart pounded as if he'd just run a half-mile. He slowly cracked the door inward. "Can I help you?" he said, pretending to be innocent.

The officer's hand was near his holster as if ready to draw his gun. "What are you guys doing in there?"

"Nothing," Stump said, lifting his arms. "Just getting a video game."

"Do you live here?"

"Of course he does," Willie said, from behind.

The cop spoke to Stump. "Mind if I come in and look around?"

"I guess so." He couldn't remember if he put away the things in the box. Could they know about those things?

Two officers stepped in. One pointed. "You guys sit on the couch while we have a look around." The other cop disappeared into the hall. Dogg growled and whined at the back door.

A few minutes later the policeman returned from his inspection with a pill bottle in hand, and asked Stump, "What brand of toothpaste do you use?"

"Colgate. You can borrow some."

"No, thanks." The officer held up the pill bottle. "What's your doctor's name?"

"Doctor Stuart. Why?"

The cop looked at his partner, nodded. "They're good." He addressed Stump. "Last week we got a call to keep an eye on this house for the next month. Somebody said that you and your mother were out of town for a while so when we saw the lights on, we had to check it out."

"His mom's in jail," Willie blurted out before Stump could stop him.

"Oh, yeah?" the cop said, twisting his head Willie's way. "For what?"

"It's my fault," Stump said. Then he proceeded to tell the police about his mom and the court.

Finally the cop butted in. "Alright, then. You guys be careful." After they left it was too late to do anything but grab the little red envelope and return to Willie's as they'd promised Aunt Gerry.

CHAPTER 22

When Miranda told Mac that she had figured out a couple of different ways to make Rachel *think* she was pregnant, he accused her of watching too many Looney Tunes, but she parroted Don's rebuttals and emphasized that this new idea could be carried out in just a few months.

Fortunately for her, Mac admired her devotion so he reluctantly agreed to stick with her, provided the sham was risk-free and wouldn't take too long. That resolved, he sneaked into Rachel's cell phone and secured the number for one of Rachel's doctors. Now Miranda had arrived at the doctor's office for an appointment of her own and under a false name.

She was certainly uncomfortable about taking her clothes off for a gynecologist she didn't already know, but she reassured herself that he'd neither care nor know who she really was. Besides, after all she'd been through at the prison, modesty simply didn't matter as much as it once did. She pursed her lips, entered the waiting room and approached the receptionist desk. "Hello, I'm Vivian Sanders. I have an appointment with Dr. Gravely."

The young pony-tailed receptionist checked her computer, and handed her a clipboard and a cup. "After you fill out the new patient information, we'll need a urine sample." Vivian sat in the corner and filled in the form: her name, Vivian

Sanders; new in town; one of her friends referred her; she planned to pay with cash; she waived the opportunity to have a nurse present during examinations; she was having stomach cramps.

After she turned in the paperwork and provided a urine sample, Vivian was escorted into an exam room and instructed to put on a white paper gown.

Alone, she could see herself in a small mirror by the sink. Was Mickey's well-being really worth all the problems? Of course it was. Besides, it would all be over within a few months one way or the other. After that she and Don could move on—but what about Mac? Maybe she'd rather . . . No. Don't think about Mac like that.

A gentle knock was followed by the entrance of a white-coated doctor with a stethoscope dangling at the ready. As he quick-scanned his clipboard and sat on a stool, Vivian Sanders quick-scanned him: not bad looking; in his early fifties; a touch of grey in otherwise sandy hair. "Hello, Vivian," he said. "Says here you're having cramps?"

Vivian extended one hand and tapped her tummy with the other. "Not real bad, but I thought I should check it out."

"I see," he said as he rubbed his fingers. "You'll have to excuse me. My hand tingles today."

She nodded. "I was thinking I might be pregnant."

"What about other symptoms? Are you late?"

"A week or so, but that's happened before."

"How about nausea or cramps?"

"I've felt a little queasy in the mornings, lately."

He made a note on his clipboard.

As Gravely progressed through the basic list of questions and then the examination, Vivian looked for opportunities to ask questions of her own, to draw him out. To seem nonthreatening. She remained calm, serious and deliberate and took special care not to rush him so as to eliminate any impression of careless haste on her part.

Then, near the very end, as Gravely grabbed his clipboard

and was making his final notes, she had her chance. "Can I ask your opinion on something unrelated before I leave?" she asked in a very serious tone.

"Of course," he said, looking up.

"You're going to think this is silly, but I'm writing a book in which a gynecologist is having a hard time making ends meet. He wants to get his new religious girlfriend to marry him by making her think she's pregnant. Then, right after they get married, he plans to kill her for the insurance money. Does that sound believable to you?"

He smiled. "The financial part sure does. With the high cost of insurance and rent and everything else." He glanced back at his clipboard.

"What about making her think she's pregnant? How hard would that be to carry off?"

He raised his head again. "I suppose he might be able to rig some test results for a while, but obviously, the ruse would be over as soon as she has a period."

"Yeah, but this particular woman goes months in between periods, so that might not happen for a while, just long enough to get married."

"Well then, I guess it's possible, depending on the woman. Some of them take those do-it-yourself pregnancy tests from time to time, just to reassure themselves they're still pregnant."

"So you're saying it's possible?"

"I suppose so," he said looking at his clipboard, yet again.

Vivian hesitated for a moment. Then, "What kind of payday would make it worthwhile for this doctor?"

Dr. Gravely raised his head. "Payday? I thought you said he wanted insurance money?"

Vivian smiled, stared straight in his eyes and lowered her voice. "What if I told you there was no book but the whole thing was really possible in real life, only the doctor doesn't have to do anything we talked about except tell her she's pregnant and everything else would be taken care of for him?"

He stared right back at her. "Are you saying what I think you're saying?"

"What if you were that doctor?"

He rose and set the clipboard on the counter. "I sure wouldn't do anything like that, and I can't imagine anybody else doing anything like that either."

Vivian also rose. "But you just told me it was possible. What if you had a half million reasons and nobody could tie you to any of it?"

"Yeah. Right. Good luck with that. I've got to go see some other patients now."

Vivian handed him a slip of paper. "If you change your mind, here's my number. No need to go to the police. It's a disposable phone."

Dr. Gravely wadded the paper and threw it in the trash. He mumbled something inaudible as he left the room.

Alone again, Vivian looked at the not-so-clever woman in the mirror. Then she hurried to get dressed and let herself out without paying her bill.

CHAPTER 23

Paradoxically, Mac was both too busy and too lonely at the same time. Originally, he'd reasoned that he could withstand a few months poking Rachel by night as long as he could be with Miranda by day. But he hadn't thought it through well enough. Rachel also had the weekends off and he had to spend them with her. Then Miranda made things more difficult when she demanded to have all Thursday mornings off so she could do "girly stuff," as she'd put it.

About all Mac could do while he waited for Thursday afternoon to roll around was hang out with Annie, like in the good old days. "I guess he damn near threw her out," Mac said, referring to the gynecologist.

"So what are you going to do, now?" Annie almost asked.

Mac grinned. "One thing I can say for Miranda. She's a thorough thinker. Doesn't give up easily either. She's planning on setting up a midwife's office."

"Does she know a midwife?"

"She knows what they do, at least she says she does. She rented some space and has a lead for some used equipment and furniture from a chiropractor."

"You have to admire somebody who would do all of that for her disabled brother."

Mac nodded. "That's another reason I lo—" He caught himself in mid-sentence and scooted down an alley. "When

I'm with Rachel time seems to stop. With Miranda, it's the opposite. Can't get enough of her."

"I'd marry Rachel myself if I could get high-riser handlebars with some sexy pink tassels out of the deal."

Max laughed, pulled into the bowling alley. "Cecil will have the bar area operating by now."

"Beer for breakfast?"

"Gotta kill a couple hours, Annie."

Inside, there was more activity and chaos than on previous Thursdays. A quick scan of the lanes revealed a white cane with a red tip leaning against a bench and others just like it near the lanes on the far end. Sighted people were helping blind people, mostly teens. Some of them were smiling and laughing. It was the kind of reminder Mac needed.

While he was buzzing around in the sunshine, juggling two women and in the process of snagging a mill or two, other people had to deal with real challenges. Permanent ones. He made his way to the bar area and grabbed a stool where he could watch the group. The bartender automatically plopped a draft beer in front of him. "Must be Thursday," he said.

"You got me figured out, Cecil," Mac said. "What's going on?"

"The bosses cut a deal with a School for the Blind. Twelve weeks at half-price."

"Oh, really? That's nice." Mac washed down a slug of beer just as one of the blind guys sent a ball flying rather quickly down the lane before several pins plunked into each other. "Ooh, yeah!" he yelled out.

"That one's a marine," Cecil said." Got blinded in Iraq."

Mac nodded. "Gotta admire guys like that. You say they're going to be regulars?"

"For a few months anyway. After that, who knows?"

Mac sipped at his beer and watched one of the girls throw a gutter ball. "Do you think they could use some help?"

* * *

"Hi, Sweets," Miranda said as she wrapped her arms around Mac's neck. She'd just gotten back from her weekly visit with Don. Mac's arms felt more natural than part of her would have liked. "Sleep well last night?"

"Not really," he said as he glanced around her living room. "I prefer to be with you."

Miranda smiled, lifted his chin. "Me, too. But we still get together every day while she thinks you're at work. That's the important thing."

"Every day except weekends and Thursday mornings and holidays and whenever you want to vacuum."

The regret and tenderness in his tone was the kind of thing that made her doubt Don's repeated warnings about Mac. Either Don misread his brother or made it all up so she wouldn't fall for Mac. "You always know what to say to make a girl feel good."

Her eyes widened. She reached in her pocket and pulled out an envelope. "Here's your allowance."

"I hate taking money from you."

"I know, but it has to appear like you have some spending money." She reached out and touched his nose. "Besides, you're going to help me get it all back. If we're lucky there might even be some left over for us to go on one of those long bike rides you talk about."

He pinched the envelope. "It's thicker than usual."

She tapped his arm. "There's a car show coming up. I got you some tickets so you can take Rachel and some of her students. We gotta keep her happy and hanging in there." Miranda brushed a strand of hair from her eye. "Speaking of Rachel, did you change her cell phone like we talked about?"

"Yep. I substituted your burner number for her gynecologist's. I just hope she doesn't notice the difference."

"Not likely. It's not a call she'd make very often. While we're on the topic, I bought those exam tables we talked about. Movers are loading them into our new medical space as we speak. Can you help me straighten everything up tomorrow?"

"Glad to have something to do." He shook his head. "I don't know how you remember all these details."

"That's what I do with my time when you're not here, Sweets. She tugged on the bottom of his shirt. "I've been looking forward to seeing you all day." She nudged him toward her bedroom.

Mac grinned and followed her. "You'll never guess what happened at the bowling alley today. There were a bunch of blind people having a good time. They're going to be back on Thursdays for a while so I volunteered to help out. We should take Mickey bowling sometime."

There was that tenderness again.

CHAPTER 24

There were just a couple weeks of summer break left. Uncle Dirk was at work and Aunt Gerry was doing volunteer work at her church. That left Stump and Willie free to get to the bank in search of a birth certificate.

With the little red envelope and its weird key tucked in Stump's pocket, they were out the door by eight-thirty. Their run/walk technique was needed because the bank was several miles away along the canal where there were only a few cross-streets.

They were into their third cycle when they came to a home with a moving van out front. As they approached the back of the big truck a young fellow, about their age, emerged carrying dumbbells. The guy yelled back into the storage compartment, "Hey Dad, some neighbors came by to help us." He turned toward Stump and Willie. "That's why you're here, right?"

Stump smiled. "Not really, but we thought we'd welcome you to the neighborhood. I'm Stump." He flipped a thumb his cousin's way. "This is Willie."

The kid set his dumbbells down. "My name's Richard Dick," he said with an extra-wide grin that begged for a comeback.

"A double Dick?" Willie said, falling for it.

The guy smiled just as his dad came forward and joined the fray. "You'll never guess his brother's name."

Stump wasn't sure if they were serious, but it seemed okay to go along with the momentum. "Is it Peter?"

"Right-o," Richard said. "Have you ever pricked your finger?"

"Or fingered your prick," both Richard and his dad said in unison. It was obvious they'd used that line before. Stump realized the *potty-mouth* was a means of bonding with them. All sorts of guys talked like that, but he'd never heard a dad get into it. It was sorta cool though. Instead of the old dude bossing his kid around, he played harmless word games with him. Stump would gladly accept a dad like that. "I bet you have a wiener dog and a pussy cat," he added.

"Did you know that a titmouse is actually a bird?" Willie said.

Stump shook his head. "That one's pretty lame, Dude."

"Why? It has double meaning too."

"We were sniffing around crotches, not boobies."

They all laughed at Stump's spontaneous crotch pun. "My real name is Richard Barnes. You can imagine how many times I've heard the word *dick*."

Stump nodded. "How old are you?" he asked, already considering Richard to be his new friend.

"Almost fourteen. You?"

"Same." Stump flipped the thumb toward Willie. "He's only twelve. Are you going to be in 9th grade?"

"Yeah. You want to show me around?"

"Rad. Maybe we'll be in the same class. Just don't get Mrs. Swalling. We call her *Swallow*."

"Wicked," Richard said with the same ornery grin as before.

Stump liked Richard and his father immediately. "Hey, we're going to Palmdale Bank. It's a few miles away but we run a block then walk a block to get there faster. You want to come with us?"

Both Richard and Stump looked at Richard's dad, who was already shaking his head slowly back and forth. Apparently he still had some adult qualities inside him.

"Better not," Richard said, "but I'd like to get together after our things are unloaded. Like tomorrow. You can tell me more about the teachers. You got a cell phone?"

"I got one," Willie said, excited to be of value again.

They traded numbers and then Stump had another idea. "We could probably help you guys for a half-hour." He glanced at Willie, who seemed disappointed but agreed anyway.

"That'd be wicked cool," Richard replied.

A little over an hour later Stump and Willie ran/walked their tired butts all the way into the lobby of Palmdale Bank. "We need to get into our safe deposit box," Stump told the receptionist as he tried to regain his wind.

"Is your mother or father with you?"

Stump was ready for the roadblock. "No, but it's in my mom's name. Here's the key. And a note. She asked me to get something out of it for her."

The lady looked over the key and the note. "You guys have a seat over there by the windows. I'll tell Mr. Osborne you're waiting."

"See, Dude," Willie said as they waddled to the waiting area. "Those keys are important. You might own a bunch of cool things you never even knew about."

"I dunno, Dude. That lady didn't act right. Besides, I'd settle for a birth certificate or anything else that tells me who my dad is."

"Hello, gentlemen," a friendly voice came from off to their left. "I'm Bob Osborne, vice president. I can help you in my office."

Stump and Willie nudged each other as they followed 'the vice-president' whose wrinkled white shirt contrasted with his near-perfect haircut. Probably single, Stump thought. In the office, Stump and Willie sat in twin chairs across from Mr. Osborne's desk. "So let me see if I understand," Osborne said. "Can I see that key of yours?" Stump nodded and handed it over.

Mr. Osborne pointed his jaw toward his computer monitor. "First off, I don't see your mother's name in our data base. Are you sure she's one of our customers?"

"She might have used her other name," Stump offered.

"That's possible. What is it?"

This wasn't going well. "I'm not really sure."

"Not sure?"

"I hoped you might have it."

Osborne looked down his nose. "We wouldn't have any way of knowing that unless she told us."

"Well, what are we supposed to do?" Willie asked. "We need to get into that box."

The banker hesitated a moment. Then, "Okay, guys. I'm going to level with you. We haven't used this type of key in four years, before we remodeled and got a new system. Everybody got new boxes and new keys."

"What about the things that were in his mother's box?" Willie asked. "Did you save them?"

Osborne's brows packed down to the top of his nose. "I'm afraid not. Banks operate under strict rules. We gave everybody written notice that we were changing systems. There were only a few people who didn't exchange keys. They were notified by certified letter." He leaned forward as if he was going to share a secret. "If you want to know my best guess, I'd say your mom once had one of our boxes, but lost this key. Somewhere along the way she cleared out the box and let her lease expire. Happens all the time." He slid the key back into the red envelope. "There's something else," he said, setting the envelope down. "You're lucky we don't call the cops."

The boys' heads bounced back and forth as if they were riding bumper cars. The banker held up the note that Stump said his mom wrote. "No adult would expect us to accept a note like this. Forgery is a serious crime, you know."

Stump's stomach felt like he'd just swallowed a large ice cube.

"That's not all. You were also about to commit wrongful entry and fraud. You ever heard of a felony?"

Stump turned his head toward the exit doors. He wasn't sure about Willie, but he could get there in a few seconds.

CHAPTER 25

Don had always told Miranda that Mac was not to be trusted, but she'd experienced the exact opposite. He'd already made some incredible sacrifices to help Mickey. He also did nice things for the kids at Rachel's school and volunteered to help blind people at the bowling alley. It didn't add up.

She already knew what Mac thought of her, but today would be an excellent opportunity to turn the page over and find out how she really felt about Mac, down deep where her long-trusted instincts took over. She'd be ugly. Would he still appreciate her without the glitter? She donned some blue jeans and an old blouse, pulled her hair back, and skipped the bulk of her makeup.

At eight-thirty, Mac coasted into her garage and parked. Almost immediately she joined him. "Morning, Sweets. You're punctual today."

Mac looked her over and pulled her close. His kiss was passionate and sincere. She wanted to moan, but she restrained herself. "You even look hot in work clothes," he said softly.

Hence his nickname. She smiled. "Thank you, Sweets." She held out her keys. "You drive."

"Did the movers finish up?" he asked, hitting the garage remote.

"They said they did. Apparently the chiropractor even threw in some decorations and supplies. All we have to do is move everything around so the place looks genuine."

Mac hit the blinker and exited the highway. "Are you sure chiropractor tables will work? That's a different specialty."

"Two are no good for us, but the other one is perfect. I had to buy them all to get the one I wanted."

Mac swung the SUV around a corner. "You think of everything."

After they arrived, they walked hand-in-hand toward the entrance. "Medical buildings are so formal," he said, massaging the scars on his knuckles. "I'm amazed you were able to get a three-month lease."

"It's the economy, Sweets. They have lots of vacancies." She snickered. "It wouldn't surprise me if the manager stuffed my cash in his own pocket and never sent it to his home office."

Inside the lobby, granite walls and brass trim created an atmosphere that any good midwife would be proud of. Miranda's nostrils instantly caught the potent scents of medicine and cleaning products.

They made their way to the building directory. "Cool," Mac said, looking near the bottom. "They got your name in there: *Vivian Sanders, Midwife*."

An elevator ride was followed by brief walk down a classy hallway. Then a twist of a key and a flick of a brass door handle allowed access to Suite 303. "Wow, this furniture looks great in here," Mac said. "You can barely tell it's used."

Miranda smiled. "I told you it would all work out, Sweets."

They strolled around, looking in boxes of supplies and decorations as well as file cabinets. Ultimately Mac entered one of the exam rooms. "Crap," he yelped, "This isn't going to work."

Miranda's eyes widened. "Why not?" she asked, hurrying toward the room.

He pointed at the end of the exam table. "This damn table

doesn't have those stirrup things." His arms flailed as he spun halfway around. "I knew it was a mistake to buy out a chiropractor. They don't use stirrups. What the hell are we going to do without those stirrup things?"

Miranda rolled her eyes, laughing. "Fear not, my friend." She nudged him out of the way, reached down to the side of the table and grabbed a jumbled collection of chrome parts that were tucked neatly into a built-in cubbyhole. Two quick tugs and a gentle twist brought the stirrups into position. She grinned right at him. "Do you want to try them out yourself, just to be certain?"

A flush of red washed across Mac's face. "How the hell was I supposed to know?"

"You know something?" Miranda chuckled, kissed him on the cheek. "You're a lot of fun, sometimes."

He pretended to wipe sweat off his forehead, and blew out an exaggerated breath of relief. "Now it looks like all we have to do is organize the place a little bit."

"Before we do that," Miranda said, holding up a syringe, "I've got to practice drawing your blood."

Mac curled his lip. "I gotta build up my nerves for that one. Mind if we straighten up first?"

"What's the matter? I told you I used to give my mom injections for her diabetes. This won't be much different."

"I'm going to do it—for Mickey's sake—but I need to build up a little courage first."

Several hours faded away as they moved furniture, hung pictures, stacked files in strategic places and placed a non-functioning but genuine-looking phone at the receptionist's desk. Eventually the common areas and one exam room evolved into what looked like a credible office for the imaginary Vivian Sanders and the only patient she'd ever have.

Finally, Mac stuffed some trash in one of the empty boxes by the door. "I guess all that's left to do is vacuum and clean up. That bathroom is pretty gross. You want me to work on that?"

Miranda grinned. "I've never heard a man offer to clean a bathroom," she said. "But I can do that tomorrow." She held up the syringe and some alcohol. "We've got some unfinished business."

"Damn. I thought you might forget that."

"I know this is no fun," she said, then projected a pouty lip, "but I still need a little practice. I promise to be as gentle as possible."

Mac let out an exaggerated sigh. "Okay, but if I'm going to be your pincushion, can we try to keep it to just one arm?"

A flush of pleasant warmth filled her. On top of everything else Mac had done for her and Mickey, he was really going to let her practice drawing blood. This proved in yet another way that he sincerely cared about her and her brother. "I'll wash up while you gather the last few boxes."

In the bathroom, Miranda looked at herself in the dirty mirror and shook her head. She couldn't look much worse, yet Mac didn't seem to notice. She knew now that she loved both brothers, but that was way too dangerous. Sooner or later she'd have to pick one or the other. For the time being she returned to the waiting area.

"My turn," Mac said as soon as she opened the door.

She grinned at his apparent nervousness. "I'll get everything ready," she said, moving toward the exam room. A few minutes later, the bathroom door opened. Apparently he'd stalled about as much as he was going to. "In here, Sweets," she called out.

When Mac opened the door she was completely naked, on the table with her feet in the stirrups. "I figured if I'm going to poke you in the arm, it's only fair that you get to play doctor and poke me too."

Mac laughed. "I love you," he said as he leaned over and his lips found hers.

CHAPTER 26

Rather than call the cops, Mr. Osborne encouraged Stump and Willie to come back when they got older and could open an account of their own.

After that, their run/walk return trip was exhausting but they did manage to come up with a new idea. If they could discover where Stump's mom worked back when Stump was born, they might find somebody who knew his dad.

Now, Stump and Aunt Gerry were on their way to see his mother for the second time in two weeks. Stump brought one of his old puzzle books and several magazines from the laundry room. As he slid into Aunt Gerry's car he pushed aside a wimpy plastic sack. "I got some magazines."

"Well done, Honey. I'm sure she'll like them. I brought her some underwear."

Hmm. Up to that point Stump hadn't thought about his mom's underwear situation. Why would he? He sometimes had to be reminded to change his own shorts. But a woman who loved her baths as much as she did must certainly appreciate new underwear too. He was glad Aunt Gerry thought of it. "Can I ask you something?" he probed.

"Of course, Honey. We're family—we can talk about anything."

"Do you think Mom will still be pissed off?"

Her head snapped his way, then back to the road. "An

intelligent person, such as yourself, ought to be able to say what he means without being so vulgar."

He missed his mom. She wasn't so obsessed with his word choices. "Okay. Do you think she'll still be cranky?"

"That's better. It's difficult to say. We're just going to have to find out when we get there."

This time, when they arrived, his mom had a huge grin on her face. "There are my favorite people," she said, touching each of them on one hand because that was all of the body contact that was allowed without making the guards nervous.

She aimed a giant smile Stump's way. "I showed the picture to everybody. They think you're cute."

He lifted his hands to his throat, pretending to adjust an invisible necktie. "They're right."

His mom turned to Aunt Gerry. "You look like you've lost a couple pounds." Stump wondered if women really noticed small changes like that in each other.

Aunt Gerry shrugged. "Been better, been worse."

What could she possibly complain about? As far as he could tell, she had life by the balls, er, testicles.

"Why? What's wrong?" his mom asked.

"It's no big deal, but Dirk's having a rough time with all the extra activity at the house. He's allergic to dog hair and it makes other situations difficult—if you know what I mean."

"I met a new friend," Stump said. "His name is Richard."

His mom looked at Aunt Gerry then back to him. "Oh really? Tell me about him."

"He moved into a house by Willie's. He'll be in my class. He wants me to come over and lift weights."

"Be sure to include Willie."

Stump lifted both hands, palms up. "He doesn't want to go."

"That's another thing," Aunt Gerry said. "It's a good thing school is starting next week."

Jean's forehead wrinkled. "Why. What's wrong?"

His aunt glanced at her watch. "You two could use a few

minutes alone." To Stump, "I'll wait for you in the car." Stump couldn't tell if she was sad or angry.

"Don't go," Jean pleaded, but it was too late. Her sister was gone. She turned to Stump. "What was that all about? Is everything okay?"

"To tell you the truth, Mom, we're not getting along all that well. I don't want to be ungrateful, but we snap at each other and they're boring. Aunt Gerry corrects my language and makes me go to bed at ten. Uncle Dirk just reads and hangs around in his garage. Doesn't let Dogg in the house. Aren't dads supposed to take their kids to places like Disneyland once in a while? He won't even go get an ice-cream cone."

She patted his hand. "This isn't easy for anybody. Just do the best you can for two more weeks. Then it'll be you and me and Dogg again. That's all anybody can ask."

"I'll try, but it's not easy," he said.

"I know. Now listen. I need to talk with you about next week. I don't want you to miss school so I'm going to ask if they'll let us meet at night."

"But what if they don't?"

"I'm not taking you out of school just because I did some dumb things."

"Can I ask you something before I have to leave?"

"Sure, Honey. Anything."

"Where did you work before we moved to Palmdale?"

"Huh? What brought that up? If it's about this obsession of yours about your dad, just forget it, okay?"

How did she know? Oh well, he could still ask Aunt Gerry the same question in a few minutes. After his time was over, he joined his aunt at her car. Her eyes were red. "Did I do something wrong?" he asked. "You ran out of there awfully fast."

She sniffled. "It's not you, Honey. It's between Uncle Dirk and me, but I don't want to talk about it." She tapped his arm. "We'll both feel better if we have some hot chocolate."

Maybe this was the opening he needed. "I was hoping to ask mom about her past but we ran out of time."

"Her past? What about it?"

"I know she grew up in Michigan and Wisconsin, but I don't know what she was like as a little girl, who her friends were, where she used to work, how she met my dad. Things like that."

"What do you want to know? I might be able to help."

Finally. "What did she do for work before we moved to Palmdale?"

"She was a secretary in a textile plant."

"What kind of tiles?"

His aunt grinned. "Not tiles, Honey. Textiles. Fabrics for draperies and tablecloths."

"See? That's what I mean. I never knew that. Do you know what the company was called or at least where it was located?"

"It's been a long time. I don't remember the name but it was in Milwaukee. That's about all I remember about it."

At least it was a clue. For the moment, his aunt seemed content to talk about anything other than her own life. This might be his chance to make progress on another issue. "Can I ask a favor? There are only a few more days until school starts. Can Willie and I stay up later at night until then?"

"We'll have to ask Uncle Dirk," she said and then turned her head to the side and cried.

CHAPTER 27

Miranda had just driven several miles without remembering any of it. It had been a few days since she and Mac set up the midwife's office. Now, she was on her way to see Don for their monthly conjugal visit. Aside from the humbling ritual to get to the love cabins, there was the inconvenient fact that they never had enough time, especially now that there was so much going on.

Exactly what was she going to tell Don? The day-to-day workings of the plan would be easy enough, but it was the other things, the internal things, her feelings, that ate at her.

She couldn't tell Don he was wrong about Mac, let alone that she'd grown to love him. She couldn't explain away her guilt by saying she still loved Don too. That would be high schoolish.

Worst of all, she and Don had agreed she'd keep her feelings out of it and she had failed. It was bad enough to sleep with Mac when Don knew about it, encouraged it even, but hiding what those meetings meant to her was deceptive and the same as cheating. She hated that part of what she was doing. She was cheating on both of them. Don didn't know about her real feelings for Mac and Mac didn't know about Don at all. She recalled how she had felt when her ex cheated on her. She shook her head. She hated him for cheating. What a hypocrite.

Regardless of any of this, it wasn't fair to hold Mac in such high regard while Don was stuck behind bars and incapable of lighting her fire to the same extent. The fair thing to do was let Don know how much she appreciated his slowing down and whispers and touching and smiles. She nodded at her idea, just as her burner rang and broke her thoughts. It had to be Mac. "Hi, Sweets," she said.

"Hello, Vivian? This is Coleen at Dr. Gravely's office. The doctor would like to see you for a follow-up visit. Are you available tomorrow?"

* * *

Across town, Mac had donned his work shirt and nametag as usual. After he wrestled with Annie's kickstand he had a couple of hours before the blind group would be at the bowling alley. "Hey, Annie. You up for a little road trip?"

"You bet. I'm always up for some fresh air."

"Miranda told me about a huge park in Antelope Valley, called The Devil's Punchbowl. It's supposed to have some good winding roads."

"Hell, yeah. Let's check it out."

Mac downshifted and gave Annie the throttle. She completely approved. They slipped through the last stoplight at the edge of town where the speed limit bumped up to fifty-five. "You know something, Annie," he said into the morning air. "Lady problems can be awfully complicated. As soon as Rachel's cycle is right, I'm supposed to make her think she's pregnant so she'll want to call her doctor."

"Isn't she too smart for that?"

"Miranda's got it all figured out. She's going to intercept the call and refer Rachel to the midwife's office." They leaned into a banked curve that preceded a gradual incline. "Miranda thinks of everything. I just wish I could be with her more. If we're lucky we'll wrap this up in a few months." He smiled. "I feel like a kid looking forward to Christmas or the last day of school."

The speed limit dropped to forty and a yellow sign indicated an S-shaped curve would follow. Annie loved those challenges. She dug down into third gear. They moved through well-banked curves that seemed built strictly for them. As they progressed, the trees and tall grasses slowly yielded to canyon walls and sparse greenery.

Deeper into the canyon, the warm midmorning sun played peek-a-boo behind the overhead ridge. After more turns and hills they had ascended to the rim of the canyon. The view was astounding. Mac nodded his approval. "Nobody up here," he said, before Annie gracefully guided him around the final few bends.

They pulled into a small parking area, near a viewing platform. As usual, Annie's kickstand needed a little coaxing before it settled into its rightful spot. Mac turned off the engine and followed a groomed gravel path to the platform.

He enjoyed several deep breaths as he walked across the platform and stood behind the railing. There, he gazed in awe at a thousand treetops gently swaying in unison below him. Several birds drifted gracefully in the warm updraft at the canyon wall. It was the kind of place where men would propose to their sweethearts. He grinned. Miranda must have known that, too.

He gazed into the valley again and felt sorry for the blind people he'd met who could never really see anything like this. His heart jumped. But they sure as hell could bowl. He looked at his watch. He was going to be late.

CHAPTER 28

By the time Friday afternoon arrived, Stump was disgusted with his aunt's entire family. Aunt Gerry picked on his word choices, Willie was disrespectful, Uncle Dirk made him go to bed by ten, and everybody treated Dogg like a curse. Stump called Richard who agreed to get together to lift weights.

"My mom's out shopping," Richard said as they entered the garage-turned-exercise-room. "Just two more days 'til school starts. You ready?"

Stump removed his tee-shirt and tossed an old towel on the handlebar of the treadmill. "Some of the girls need bras."

Richard laughed and casually waved his arm before the equipment. "Help yourself," he said, while he picked up his cell phone. Stump grabbed a medium-sized pair of barbells, and pulled them upwards.

"Stand in front of the mirror," Richard said. "Let's take pictures so we can see our progress." Stump eased into position and slowly raised his weights.

"Right there."

Stump checked out his biceps. "How's that?"

"Good, Dude," Richard said as he clicked. "Have you ever played rugby? You've got the right body for it. Strong legs. Stocky."

"Rugby?" Stump watched his arm as he allowed the

weights to slowly descend to his sides, then brought them back up again.

"It's just as tough as football, but doesn't have as many injuries. I bet you'd be good at it." Richard snapped a couple more pictures. "My turn." They traded the phone for the weights and Richard took the position of honor before the mirror. "Down the road we can get some of Mama's little helpers."

"Helpers. Why would we need any help?"

Richard grinned as he raised his arms and flexed his muscles. "PEDs, Dude. You know. Steroids."

"Steroids? I always heard they were dangerous."

"Not if you don't overdo it. Helps you grow facial hair too."

Stump rubbed his bare chin. Nothing.

Twenty minutes later they had a bunch of pictures and the sweat in Stump's pits suggested he'd expended plenty of energy.

"We ought to take a break before we do the last set," Richard said. "I'll get us a couple of Red Bulls."

Stump tilted his head as Richard headed for the kitchen. "Those are expensive. Won't your dad get pissed?"

"Are you kidding? He buys 'em by the case." Richard grabbed the cans from the fridge and handed one to Stump. "A couple of these babies and you'll be throwing weights around like a Tasmanian devil."

"A couple? I shared a can with Willie once. Made me nervous."

"That means it was working, Dude." They each slammed down a few slugs.

"Why do you live with your cousin?" Richard asked. "Are your folks out of town or something?"

"Strange you should ask that. I've never met my dad, but I've been trying to figure out who he is."

"Won't your mom tell you?"

"She says she didn't want to spend her whole life fighting with the guy so she left the state without even telling him she was pregnant."

"Dirty pool, eh? You've gotten by without your old man this long. Why fight it?"

"That's what she keeps saying, but I want answers. I've been trying to find a birth certificate or something else that will help me figure out who he is."

Richard nodded. "Must be a pisser to not know something like that. Got any leads?"

"My aunt said my mom worked at a textile company in Milwaukee a long time ago. As soon as I get a chance, I want to see if anybody back there remembers her and my dad."

"I doubt if people keep records that long."

"That's not the worst of it. I don't even know the company's name."

"Sounds like a long shot," Richard said before letting out a powerful belch. "But we can use my computer to Google it. Why don't I do the search and you make the calls on your cell phone."

It was a fingernail on chalkboard moment. "I don't have a cell phone, remember?"

"Oh yeah, I forgot. Dude, you gotta get one. Everybody needs a phone."

"No shit. That's one of the reasons I want to find my old man. Maybe he can send us a few bucks. It's only right."

"True that. Is Milwaukee in Michigan?"

Stump grinned. "Wisconsin." After a quick search, Stump's new buddy found a handful of textile plants in Milwaukee. The first one didn't answer, probably because it was out of business. "Good one," Stump said after Richard read out the next number.

"Good one? What?" Richard asked.

"You had 2-6-4-6-5 in that order."

"Yeah, that's what it says. So what?"

Stump pointed to his phone pad. "It spells out 'boink.' Their phone number has a boink in it," he said, grinning.

"Let me see that."

After the brief giggle-a-thon, Stump was able to leave some voicemail messages. That done, Richard popped his second Red Bull. "The hospitals in the area might be able to search their records for the day you were born and come up with some useful information," he said.

"Why didn't I think of that?" Stump wondered out loud. He glugged down the rest of his first can and popped his second one to stay up with his pal.

With all the calls made, and enough time for a small buzz, Richard grabbed some weights and returned to the front of the mirror. "I hear the high school football team is pretty good. We should go to a game sometime."

"I guess we could, but I don't have much money."

Richard flexed his muscle in the mirror. "No sweat. I can always find a way to sneak in. You want to know what's a kick in the pants at games?"

"No, what?" said Stump.

"I like to sit on the opponents' side of the stadium and talk trash. Say they suck or were lucky when they scored, just to see what they'll do."

Stump's stomach was full but he gulped at his Red Bull anyway. "I've seen people like that at baseball games and on TV. Sometimes they get in fights." He lay on the floor to do a few sit-ups.

"I never let it get that far," Richard assured him. "They know I'm just messing around. Besides, I lift weights. I can kick most of their asses if I have to."

That was probably true. Even though Richard was younger than the high school crowd, he was about their size and probably could take on a lot of them.

All of a sudden, an insanely loud NASCAR ringtone came from Richard's cell. He glanced at the read out. "See, Dude, I told you. It's one of those textile places." He turned on the speaker and handed the phone to Stump.

"Hello, this is Elizabeth. I work in the office at R & B Textile. I understand you want to know about Jean Randolph."

Stump covered his mouth so she couldn't hear him belch. Then, "Yes, ma'am. She's my mom." Fortunately, he and Richard had already worked out what to say. "Actually, I'm trying to find my dad. I've never met him, but there's been an accident and my mom's in the hospital. She wants to talk to him. Do you know who he might be or where I can reach him?"

"I'm sorry to hear that. I've been working here for over thirty years and I definitely remember your mother."

Stump's heart pounded harder. "What about my dad? Do you know who he is or where I can find him?"

The woman hesitated. Then she said, *"I don't mean to be indelicate, but she dated several men, including Robert, who worked on the loading dock."*

Stump sat down and wiped some sweat from his forehead. This could be the lead he'd been searching for. "What do you know about Robert? Where can I find him?"

After another stall, she said, *"Well, this is awkward, but do you have dark skin or curly hair?"*

"No. Why?"

Richard dropped to the floor and laughed so hard he made Stump smile, too. "I don't think that's him," Stump assured her. "Is there anybody else?"

"Not that I can think of, but if I come up with anything new, I'll give you a call. I'm sure your mother would appreciate it."

"Thanks anyway," he said. After they finished the call, Stump turned to Richard. "Don't know if it's the Red Bull or the call, but I'm stoked."

"Probably a little of each. Hey, you want to stay the night?"

"Sure. I'd better call my aunt."

CHAPTER 29

Stump's mom hugged him so hard she squeezed a silent fart out of him. "I'm so grateful that's over," she said. Given that the jail had made no allowance for Stump to visit her at night, it had been two weeks since they last saw each other and one week since Uncle Dirk's allergies had gotten the best of him. Instead of allowing Stump to spend the night at Richard's, he insisted that Dogg be taken to a kennel.

"Can we go get Dogg now?" Stump pleaded as he buckled up. He's been in jail, too."

"We're on our way, Honey," Aunt Gerry said.

"That's another thing I regret," Stump's mom said. "We leave Dogg alone too much. Poor thing has nothing to do. He needs exercise and to be with other dogs."

"He likes to sniff their butts," Stump said, relieved that he could squeeze in a little potty talk again.

Aunt Gerry shook her head in mock disgust, turned to her sister. "So, how you doing, Honey?"

"It wasn't all bad," Jean said. "I read the Bible and *Chicken Soup for the Soul*."

"That's a good one," Aunt Gerry confirmed as she braked for a stoplight.

"That judge was right. All the loneliness made me understand how lucky I am to have a good family like you guys in my life. I don't want to end up like some of the other women in there." She spun her head toward the back seat. "I've learned my lesson for real this time, and I have you two to thank for it."

"No more drinking?" he asked, wanting to hear her say it again.

"Nope. No drinking. Don't need it now. Thanks to you."

"That's wonderful, Honey."

An inner peace washed over Stump. There was strong conviction in his mother's voice. Aunt Gerry sounded like she sensed it, too.

"Another thing I learned," his mom continued. "There's no love stronger than that which a mother feels for her children."

Stump reached forward and rested his hand on her shoulder. "Me too, Mom. I love you, too."

"I'm going to help you with your schoolwork and you can help me with the housework. That way, we'll both do better."

"Hey. Look at that," Stump said pointing to the car in the next lane and slightly in front of them. "That license plate."

"Oh, yeah. It says, MOM in it," Aunt Gerry said.

Jean looked at the plate. "I'm also thankful to be with the only person I know who sees messages in license plates."

Stump grinned.

"So how's school so far? You got any new teachers or girlfriends?"

"He's a dreamboat, alright."

Stump snorted at his aunt's snide comment. "I can bench press a hundred and twenty pounds."

"Oh? With your new friend? How's that working out?"

"I didn't get to go over there very much," he said.

"Well, Honey, Aunt Gerry has a lot on her mind and didn't want you to get into any trouble."

"How we going to get in trouble lifting weights and drinking Red Bulls?"

"Red Bulls? Where'd you get money for those?"

"Richard's dad buys them by the case. Richard thinks I should join the rugby team."

"That'd be nice, but we don't have any money for sports right now. I'm lucky I have a job. It'll be a couple weeks until I get a paycheck—then we've got to catch up on all our dumb bills."

"Richard said the coach could get somebody else to pay for my uniform, but I turned them down anyway. I know how you always say when I start something—"

"Right. You have to finish it. You have to do well in school. It's the only way you can get into college."

"Here we go," Aunt Gerry said as she pulled into the kennel.

After some paper shuffling and another small loan from Aunt Gerry, Team Randolph was back home and together for the first time in weeks. The mood was right. "I'm glad you're feeling so much better, Mom, because I have a confession."

She lit a cigarette and pinched his cheek. "You? A confession?"

"Uh-huh. While you were gone I wanted to find out who Dad was, and you always said I was born in Milwaukee, so I called the big hospitals back there. I had them check their records but nobody ever heard about me. Why not?"

The grin on her face melted. "I wish you hadn't done that, Stump. It means you don't trust me."

"But we agreed that we're going to be honest with each other, and withholding information is the same as lying. Everybody says I deserve to know who my dad is. Why doesn't anybody have records of me being born?"

"I don't want to argue about that now."

"What happened to being honest with each other?"

"I already told you. I didn't want to be entangled with him or anybody else from that era, so I left there and ended up here. That was my choice and I don't have to say any more."

"C'mon Mom, 'fess up. Richard says I deserve to know."

"Then go live with Richard. As long as you live under my roof, you need to respect my decisions."

"Decisions? That's a laugh. How can a drunk make good

decisions?" Whoops. Her head pivoted his way. "Sorry, Mom. I know you're doing the best you can."

She pursed her lips. Then, "Look, it's my first day back and I'm exhausted. I have to work tomorrow and I've got enough drama on my plate without arguing about the past. I just want to take a nice hot bath and enjoy being home for now. If you'll respect that, and not bring this up again for a while, you can invite Richard over for barbequed hamburgers tomorrow night and I'll rethink your request."

CHAPTER 30

Miranda sat across from Dr. Gravely's desk, which was cluttered with files, journals and boring medical items in random piles. One of his pictures included him and three women. Based on their ages, it was probably his wife and daughters.

Fifteen minutes slipped by while Miranda contemplated Gravely's motives. It was most likely one of two things. Either he had more interest in her previously veiled proposal than he first indicated, or it was some sort of set up; She'd just have to ease into the situation and make him play his cards first.

Finally, he entered and took a seat behind his desk. His hand jittered. "Hello Vivian—or whatever your name is," he said in a monotone. "Sorry to keep you waiting."

"I had the day off," she said, trying to sound nonchalant. "Is something wrong?"

He swiveled in his chair and lifted a slightly quivering finger. "I'd like to talk to you about that book of yours."

Why was his hand shaking? Was he as nervous as she was? She raised her eyebrows to urge him on.

Neither of them spoke for a moment, then he leaned back in his chair. "After you left the other day I got a call from my neurologist. It was like others I'd been getting. After we hung up I got to thinking you and I might be able to scratch each other's backs."

As long as he was willing to do the talking she was willing to listen.

"I don't know if you've noticed my hands shaking, but I've been diagnosed with ALS, or Lou Gehrig's disease. The brain stops communicating with the muscles."

She'd heard of it. "I'm sorry to hear that."

"So far, I've hid it the best I could, but now people are asking questions. They tell me I've only got another year or so."

If this was true, the poor guy was screwed. But it could still be a scam. "Isn't there anything they can do?"

He shook his head and leaned forward. "It gets worse. I'm flat broke. About all I've done for my family is put my girls through medical school."

"That sounds like a lot to me," she said.

"It's extremely expensive. So is my practice and my bank won't make me any more loans." He took a long slow breath and held it a moment before letting it out. "I must have thought I'd live forever, because I never bought any life insurance."

As tragic as the doctor's situation was, if he was on the up-and-up, he needed money and that meant he was reconsidering joining her.

"On top of everything else," he went on, "my wife and I haven't been close in years. She says I work too much, but that's how I've hidden some of my symptoms from her." He glanced at the photo on the bookcase. "The bottom line is, I still love her and can't leave her with all my debt. She'd never make it on her own. I want her to know she always mattered to me a lot more than she ever knew."

Miranda noticed his eyes tearing up. She nodded slowly. "I thought it was something like that."

"I need some big money and apparently you've stumbled upon an opportunity to get it. But you obviously need me too, so I've decided to listen to what you've got in mind. If I like your idea I might join you."

Wow. This may have been the best news since Mac agreed to come out to California. But discretion remained in order.

"Before I say anything I want to know how I can be sure you're being straight with me."

The doctor nodded. "Fair enough. I have reports from my own doctor about my disease and letters from my banks indicating my situation." He handed her a short stack of papers. "See for yourself."

She took it. "What about you? You don't seem worried about me. How do you know I won't double-cross you?"

He shrugged. "I've got nothing to lose. But if you hurt my wife, I'll find a way to make you wish you hadn't. So, how about it? You give me the details. If I like what I hear, I'm in, and you can tell me your real name." She looked him in the eye. He sounded sincere and his papers confirmed his story, but there was still a possibility that she was being set up.

"If I think you're nuts," he continued, "you can walk out that door and nobody knows who you really are or what we talked about." A faint smile stretched his lips. "You can win but you can't lose."

Miranda had always been good at reading people. The sadness in Gravely's watery eyes, coupled with the shaky fingers, were very convincing, but there was one hell of a lot at stake. He could be taping everything she said. "I'd rather we go for a walk and I'll tell you outside."

"Why? Nobody can hear us in here."

"Bugs. I want to see inside your shirt, too."

He grinned. "Smart. I'll tell my staff we'll be back in fifteen minutes. Will that do it?"

"Better make it twenty."

A little later she'd spilled most of the details about the plan, her partners, her brother, and his patient, Rachel Johnson. "All we need you to do is help us make her think she's pregnant," she said. "And keep it up until we get the money."

He stopped, faced her. "Alright, you've convinced me that you're a clever bunch. Three twins, helping a fourth one. All without really hurting anybody. I'm not really sure how you can do all that and skip out on that woman without the cops knowing who you are, but that's your problem. Just don't drag my family's name into it."

Miranda twisted a strand of her hair. "There's no benefit in doing that, unless you double-cross us."

"Okay, then let's talk numbers. Just how big is this trust and what's my cut?"

"That's one of the difficult things. We don't quite know how much is in it, but my partner thinks it's at least a million. The best I can tell you is we should know within six weeks."

"Okay then. I want the first million and you guys get the second one. We split the rest."

"We can't do that. The whole reason I'm doing this is for my brother. As I said, he needs the money for medical reasons. You can understand that, can't you?"

"You're breaking my heart," Gravely said sarcastically. "I'm struggling too, you know—or did you forget that already?"

Miranda paused and sighed. "If I don't take care of my brother first, the whole deal is off. That means you don't get a dime and your wife is on her own with no way to support herself."

Gravely nodded. "What's your counter offer?"

Miranda recalled how they once said they'd leave some money in the trust for Rachel but that seemed unlikely now. "The best we can do is split the first million between my brother and you. Then you get a third of everything else."

"I want half of everything."

She shook her head. "Can't. There has to be some money in there for my partner and me, too."

Gravely's shaking fingers scratched at his ear. "Okay, I'll accept your proposal under one condition. Given the possibility that the trust is insignificant, I want fifty thousand, up front—let's call it a good faith deposit."

CHAPTER 31

Miranda took a bite of her doughnut and threw it back in the sack. Comfort food didn't help. The good news was, Don was getting out in three weeks. The bad news was, Don was getting out in three weeks. Today would be their final conjugal visit.

In a way she missed the days when Don was originally locked up. Before conjugal visits, before Mickey declined, before stealing and cheating became justified.

There was a relative innocence in those days. They held hands above the table and talked away the whole hour, mostly about how great it would be when Don got out and their lives would magically return to what they had previously been. Now that day was near and nothing was like she thought it would be.

Some of it was Mac's fault. He had been spiking Rachel's late-night wine with sleeping pills so he could spend more time with Miranda and that was straining everything, including her relationship with Don, who deserved a lot more loyalty than she'd been exhibiting.

Hog wash. Miranda crumpled the doughnut bag and threw it on the floor of the rider's side. Who was she trying to kid? Why was she blaming it on Mac? She loved his company and how he made her feel during those late-night stay-overs. But all that would have to change when Don was released. He'd want to stay with her, too. How was she going to cut Mac off?

At least her intimate moments with Don might improve. Lately the rare sessions in the love cabins had become pressure-packed brainstorming conferences after which she was expected to carry out the con's intricate requirements. The few minutes of meaningless intercourse that followed might have impressed a prostitute in search of a fast buck, but it didn't do a damn thing for Miranda.

As the prison came into view, her heart was cluttered with hope, guilt and confusion. She couldn't deny there was a certain excitement to being entangled in the middle of a love-quadrangle, but a crisis point was fast approaching.

At the moment, all of Cupid's arrows were pointing her in Mac's direction, but under the surface where common decency resides, she knew that wasn't even remotely fair. Don didn't have a chance in the game of love if he was behind bars 24/7—all for protecting her. She'd always hated people who turned their backs on somebody they'd once loved, but there she was right in the middle of a big kettle of betrayal stew. How the hell did she let that happen? She had to regroup. Get her head out of her rear-end and remember all Don had done for her and Mickey.

This particular day she would have liked to disregard all the newfound complications and devote herself entirely to Don like he deserved, but there were other more pressing priorities. She sighed as she pulled into the prison parking lot. For now, she still wanted to get that money for Mickey, but there were fifty thousand reasons the con could be dead.

After Officer Jackson locked them in cabin three, they wrapped their arms around each other for an initial hug, but Don quickly patted her on the shoulder, just like she used to do with her grandmother when she wanted the hug to be over. She wanted desperately to hold him, to love him to prove to herself she was determined to control her stupid lustful heart. He pulled away. "Is the doctor on board?" he asked without any idea how tormented she was.

What could she expect? He had one stinking hour per week, while everybody else had 168 hours. "I'm sorry, Donnie. He's willing to help us," she said, bypassing the temptation to complain about all she had done and the money she lost trying to get a midwife's office up and running, "but I think I lost him."

"Why? What happened?"

"He's sick and has financial troubles. He needs money as badly as we do."

"Great, so what's wrong?"

"I had to tell him everything. It was the only way to get him to trust me." She released a deep sigh. "He wants fifty thousand dollars, Donnie—to prove we're real. I told him we don't have any money. But he insisted."

Don shook his head. "Wrong answer. You should have told him about your line of credit."

"But I don't like to use that money. It's all I've got and I'm already slipping cash to Mac so it looks like he's really got a job and money of his own. What would happen to Mickey if I lost the rest of it before we get Rachel's money?"

Don lifted her chin. "Look. We all got to do whatever we can, or it's not going to work. Then Mickey's out of luck anyway."

She bit her lip. "But it's still not enough. I can only get about thirty-five thousand. Mac doesn't have money either."

Don sat next to her. "You've got to do whatever it takes to bring that doctor on board."

Her head shot his way. "You don't expect me to screw him too, like you made me do with Mac, do you? He's old enough to be my father."

"Don't be ridiculous. He sees so much pussy it wouldn't mean anything to him."

"Including mine, during our first appointment. Why the hell did I do that?"

"Don't be so hard on yourself. You had to. That's all.

Get over it." Don rested his hand on her thigh. "That guy is desperate. He has no other options or he wouldn't have called you back. You've got to get the thirty K—in cash. Tell him it's all you have. He'll be forced to take it."

She smirked. "But what if I lose it all?"

"That's my whole point, Baby. This is the only way Mickey has a chance. If we don't do this he's toast."

For the next twenty minutes Don asked her question after question and listened intently to her answers, guiding and coaching her as they went. Just as importantly, they held hands like the old days. When was she going to learn?

Every time the chips were down, Donnie was the one who came through. He may not have been the lover that Mac was but he was like a hidden foundation beneath a home with Christmas lights on the roof. Those lights wouldn't even be there to shine without the foundation holding everything up. Same went for Mickey's future. Don was the one who made that happen, nobody else, not even her. Most importantly, he'd proved that he would never turn his back on her like she almost did to him. And the kicker was he did all of that in one hour a week. It would be pure idiocy to let love lust cancel all of that out.

Then, near the end of their hour he said, "Ultimately this is about you and me and Mickey. We can't let anybody else get in the way of that. If we have to deviate from any of our plans along the way, then that's what we do. Adapt to the new situation. Go with the flow. However you want to say it. But we gotta stay true to each other."

It was as if she'd just gotten a well-deserved mind-spanking. Her eyes darted to the clock. If only she had the time to show him how much she appreciated him after all, but Officer Jackson would be back in minutes.

Then, as if Don read her mind, he drew her to him and kissed her, then nudged her backwards. "Relax, Baby. I got Jackson to give us an extra half-hour."

She hadn't seen that gleam in his eye for months.

CHAPTER 32

"**W**ell?" Stump cornered his mother in the kitchen.

"Not now," Jean said, brushing him off and stepping around him.

"But you promised." She grabbed a paper towel, walked briskly into the living room, but Stump wasn't going to let her get away again. He followed in line like a baby duck follows its mother. She wiped a bunch of artful Dogg saliva off the window above the coach. "I've only been home a few days. I'm way behind on everything and still trying to get acclimated to a life without a driver's license. This isn't a good time."

"But whenever I bring up the topic, you make excuses."

"I'm sorry it seems like that, but I've got more important things to do right now." Her hair danced from side to side as she shook her head. "I don't even have enough time to wash the windows properly." She returned to the kitchen. Stump followed and watched her discard the paper towel. What was so hard about that?

Outside, Dogg made an ugly hacking sound. His mom pointed out the window. "For instance, Dogg still has that damn kennel cough and I've got to get somebody to take me to get new meds—which I can't afford. You don't want him to suffer, do you?"

"Aw, come on, Mom. You're just using that as an excuse to change the subject."

"I'm glad you think that's all it is," she said as she removed some dishes from the sink, mostly his, and added them to a stack of others on the counter, also mostly his, before rinsing it out. She grabbed some dish soap from down below and poured some into the sink, turned on the water and began yet another chore. "Regardless, I don't want to dredge up painful memories."

He frowned. "Painful? You never said that before. Did my dad hurt you or something?"

"Stop saying that," she insisted as she scrubbed glass after glass and dish after dish. "You had a biological father, but no dad." She dunked several pots in the water, swished a dishrag around each one.

Stump grabbed a drying towel. "How can a person be a dad if you won't let him try?"

She glanced at his towel and nodded her approval. She let out the water and wiped off the counter while he finished drying one of the small glasses he had left in the sink with milk in the bottom. "I realize this is important to you," she said hurriedly, "but I've got so much else on my mind, like right now I get to go vacuum the entire house. Then, it's change the sheets, do the laundry and mop the kitchen."

"But that's what you always say. It can't be that traumatic, can it?"

"It is to me, especially now that I can't drive and Aunt Gerry and Uncle Dirk are talking about divorce."

Divorce? She might as well have crashed a tank into his head. "What are you talking about? Nobody ever said anything about a divorce."

She finally slowed down for a moment and faced him. "That's because it's painful, just like this dad-thing of yours is to me. I wasn't supposed to say anything until they know more, but Uncle Dirk's company has been laying people off. They've already warned him to look for something else. Stress like that spills into personal lives. That's all I'm going to tell you about it. You have to promise me that you'll keep this quiet. Nobody wants to hurt Willie." She buzzed into the living room again.

Stump followed and half-heartedly plucked some dog hairs off the couch. He was beginning to get it. His own problems seemed rather petty compared to everything his mom had to do, and compared to what could happen to his cousin. "But they shouldn't be having problems. They have lots of money."

"Not any more. If they lose their income all they get is unemployment money. That's not enough. If Uncle Dirk doesn't take some other job they'll be in the same boat we're in. Barely getting by."

"Will they have to move?"

"I don't know, son. That's among the things they have to work out. But when people have stress like that it affects everything they do. People worry and argue with each other. You just can't turn problems like that on and off when you don't like them."

"Like your drinking?"

"God knows that's been tough too," she said, nodding. "It affects the whole family and it's difficult to reverse. Now do you understand what I mean when I say I have too much on my plate right now?"

Wow. He kinda did. Being an adult wasn't as easy as it usually looked.

She walked across the room, picked up some mail that needed discarded. "All I want to do right now is finish some housework and get ready for the office party tonight."

Office party? A loud warning siren went off in Stump's head.

CHAPTER 33

Mac released the button on his jacket, yanked his helmet over his ears and jiggled Annie's kickstand into place. He glimpsed at the tired man looking back at him in his left mirror. He needed a lift. "You up for a fast trip to the drugstore, Annie?" he asked after starting her up.

"Sure am."

He grinned and revved her engine a little more than necessary. It was equivalent to telling a world-class track star to, "Get on your mark."

His left hand clamped the clutch handle and his left foot jammed the shifter into low gear. He might as well have held up a starter's pistol and said, "Get set."

His anxious right hand cranked the throttle while his left hand simultaneously popped the clutch. "GO!!!"

Annie's front wheel jumped into the air, like the hooves of a bucking bronco as she bolted forward with all of her might. They leaned ever so slightly to the left, so they could blow through a small pile of leaves. God, how Mac loved that bike!

After calming down, Annie began a conversation. *"There's still time to bail out, you know."*

"I was thinking about that, Annie. Rachel might feel a little depressed for getting dumped but she'd probably get over it fairly quickly."

"But, what about Miranda? Would she handle it?"

"That's the real issue, Annie. I like her a lot—maybe even love her and she needs me."

They quickly zigzagged through a half-mile of light traffic. "And I can't let Mickey down."

"The fringe benefits don't hurt either, do they?"

Mac smirked. "That's for sure. It's almost like we're of one body and one mind."

"Seems to me you've got to shit or get off the pot. Either get in with both feet or get out."

"I think that's a mixed metaphor, Annie, but I get your drift. Only trouble is, I'm not sure how much longer I can keep this up." They dipped hard to the right and pulled into the parking lot of a drug store, where three boys, about fourteen, were hanging around outside. One of them, presumably the leader, was smoking something.

Annie glided into a spot in front of the ice machine where Mac engaged the clutch and goosed the throttle. She roared, causing the boys to turn their heads. Annie was cool.

Without making eye contact Mac removed his helmet and dismounted. He jiggled the kickstand and helped his pal stand up before he unbuttoned his jacket and strutted a few steps to the entrance.

Once inside he glanced furtively at the overhead signs. He would have liked to abandon his objective, but Miranda had given him an assignment. He headed down the aisle where the feminine products were kept. He was the only one there, but it was embarrassing nevertheless. His confidence had evaporated. In spite of his apprehension, he studied the shelves before he quickly grabbed a box of pregnancy tests, *the ones in the orange-colored box*. Dr. Gravely said it should be the kind with the cup and litmus strips as opposed to the applicator type.

Like a fullback with a single objective, Mac lowered his head and rushed to the checkout lane. He paid the bill, hurried out the door and breathed a sigh of relief. Outside, the youngsters had predictably gathered around Annie.

*   *   *

A few more days had passed before Stump's life returned to something resembling normal. He was proud of his mom and hadn't mentioned his dad for a while. On Saturday, he and Richard and Willie took a run/walk trip to the drugstore. Once there, Richard lit a cigarette-size cigar that he got from his grandpa. Then a biker and a cool-colored bike pulled in. When the biker disappeared into the store Richard wanted to check out the bike.

Shortly thereafter the dude returned and wiggled in between them. He opened one of the black-leather saddlebags and quickly tucked away a paper bag. "Hey fellas, how's it going?" he said.

Richard pointed at the gas tank. "Hey mister. Who's Annie?"

The guy patted the gas tank as if it was a baby's head. "A very old friend."

Richard blew a smoke ring and nodded, as if he understood, but Stump was stumped.

The biker pulled a helmet over his head. "I'm Mac. Who are you guys?"

Stump began to speak but, "I'm Richard. This is Stump and Willie. They're cousins."

"It's nice to meet you fellas," Mac said as he pointed with a knuckle-scarred hand at Stump. "Don't you smoke?"

Stump wrinkled his nose. "Tried it, but—"

"He's a wimp," Richard said. "Do you smoke, Mac?"

"Me? Nah? My mom told me that most of the girls don't like it. Besides, it's too expensive."

Stump nodded as Richard gently eased his cigar hand behind his back.

"You fellas go to the high school?"

"Stump and I do," Richard said, "but Willie's too young."

"You know Ms. Johnson?"

"The tall assistant principal?" Stump asked.

"That's her. She's a good friend of mine. She wants me to have a talk with some of the guys about motorcycles and life on the highways. There'll be pictures and refreshments. You should come."

All three nodded. "When is it?" Stump asked.

"Not sure yet. When we know more, she'll put it in a newsletter or on a bulletin board or something." He threw a leg over his bike's seat, twisted his key and cut a tight circle. "Catch you guys later," he said just before he and the purplish motorcycle danced over a small pile of whirling leaves.

"I'm going to get a bike like that someday," Richard said.

CHAPTER 34

The early-morning fog misted Mac's face. "It's chilly today," he said to Annie.

"How was that party last night?"

Mac grinned. "You would have been proud of me, Annie. I turned on the old Mac charm, and before the evening was over Granny and her friends were eating out of my hands."

"That must've made Rachel happy."

"No shit. She raved about how Granny practically adopted me." Mac paused. "On the way home she kept saying she loved me and expecting me to say it back."

"Did you?"

"I pretty much had to. When we got home she took it up another notch, wanted to make love. She really got into it this time. Sorta fun for a change. Sometimes she can be alright." He arched his back. "Want to go to Malibu Beach?"

"It's Thursday. What about the bowling alley?"

"I like those kids, but they've got plenty of volunteers. They can get by without me. I was thinking of doing something more peaceful."

They slowed down for a couple seconds. *"We could check in on Miranda first, to see if she really spends her Thursday mornings doing what she says she does."*

"Believe me. I've thought about that, but if she suspected

that I don't trust her it would probably ruin everything. I just need to roll with it."

"Then we're going to the beach."

"Let's do it." Mac throttled her hard and speed-shifted into the next gear. They blew through a yellow light and merged onto the Sierra Highway. "Granny and her husband owned a big ranch in Silicon Valley," he said, repeating something he had heard at the party. "Then when all the high-tech companies showed up, they sold out."

"That's primo land. It must be where the inheritance comes from."

"That's what I was thinking too, Annie. I didn't hear how much they got, but it had to be a pretty penny as my old man used to say. A few years later Pappy died from a heart attack and Rachel's parents died in a boating accident. Granny and Rachel were the only heirs to all that money."

"And you and Miranda and Mickey."

"Miranda and I might move to the Dominican Republic or someplace like that after all this is over." Mac checked Annie's left mirror and slipped over into the fast lane.

Later, when they got to the coast they went north for a long drive, grabbed lunch and eventually pulled onto a ridge that overlooked the ocean and a colorful hillside. He found a well-placed bench and enjoyed the soothing mumble of waves crashing beneath them. He dozed.

When he awoke, the clouds had darkened and moved closer. He peeked at his watch. Nearly three. He quickly scooted toward Annie. "We're late. Rachel's gonna be pissed. I've gotta call Miranda, too. I won't be able to see her this afternoon either."

Back on the highway, he and Annie took their place on the white lines, in between lanes. They moved better than the bumper-to-bumper slowpokes but it still took until five-thirty before they coasted into Annie's favorite corner of Rachel's garage—the one to the right, away from the bright light of the window.

Mac glanced at his watch. Rachel wouldn't be impressed by how quickly they made it back. He hustled into the kitchen where she jumped in his face, saying, "Well, it's about time. You're almost an hour late."

"Thirty-three minutes," he snapped back.

She placed her hand on her waist. "You should have called."

That growl of hers reminded him of a rich person talking down to a worker and he was tired from his ride. He moved closer and lowered his voice. "Let's get something straight. I'm not one of your bad students, and I don't like being treated like one. Got it?"

As the words left his lips, he realized he had risked everything that he and Miranda had been working for. What if Rachel told him to move out? Then she blinked and dropped her arms. "I'm sorry, Mac, I'm a little stressed out. I had no right to talk to you like that." She shot him a small smile. "Maybe I can make it up to you after dinner—like yesterday."

Whew! He grabbed her hand. "I'm sorry too, but I had to work late." He kissed her cheek. "Why don't you go upstairs and finish getting ready. I'll be right there. I have to get something first."

A few minutes later, he joined Rachel in the bedroom where she was buttoning up her blouse. He held up an orange box. "Before we head out, you ought to take one of these tests!"

Rachel eyed the box and shook her head. "I already told you that things like that are a waste of time."

"I know," he said in his most gentle voice, "but I love you and if you were pregnant, it would be like hitting the lottery to me."

She turned to him. "I didn't realize you were that serious about it. Even so, I'm not sure I would ever want to have a baby." She raised a limp hand. "Doesn't matter though. The doctor said I'd probably never conceive. That's why we don't use birth control."

"I know, but stranger things have happened."

She rolled her eyes. "Not really. I don't have any symptoms and I don't even keep track of the days."

Mac shoved a hand in this front pocket. "Aren't you at least curious? Can't you just humor me?" he asked.

Rachel sighed and reached for the box. "Alright, if it means that much to you. Then can we go out to that dinner we talked about?"

He grinned. "I promise."

She headed for the restroom and Mac followed along like a puppy dog. When she turned to close the door, he was already in the doorway. Her eyes widened as she raised her eyebrows. "You don't expect to watch me, do you?"

"Why not?" he said. "I've seen you pee before."

"Yeah, but this is strange."

Mac shifted his feet and smiled. "There you go again, making a mountain out of a molehill."

She sighed, shook her head and opened the box. "No applicator? Why'd you buy this kind?"

"The salesclerk at the store said that it's the most accurate and more dignified," he lied.

Rachel clicked her tongue, shook her head and began the task while Mac helicoptered over her head. "It sure as hell isn't very dignified when you have an audience." A moment later she placed the full cup on the vanity. Mac smiled and held out the dipping strip.

"You do the rest," she said while putting her clothes back together. "I'm going downstairs. After you realize we wasted our time, we can go to dinner like we agreed."

"How long does it take?"

"You can read the box, can't you?"

When done, Mac headed downstairs. Rachel turned her head in his direction. He focused on her face and stuck out his lower lip. "Negative."

In that split second, before she had a chance to say I told you so, he saw both a glimmer of hope and veiled disappointment in her eyes. In spite of her words to the contrary, Rachel definitely longed for a baby of her own.

CHAPTER 35

Stump was asleep at cousin Willie's. On the other side of town, several of his schoolmates, all older than him, had just returned from the movies.

The Lexus in the driveway indicated that Bradley's old man, Brad Senior, was home from his date. At first the boys were a little noisy but when Bradley opened the back door, all was dark and quiet inside. "Shh," Bradley said to his pals, "My old man must be asleep."

"I gotta take a leak," Michael said.

Bradley pointed to a doorway that led to the main part of the house. "Back there," he said softly as he and one of the others, Phillip, eased into the back room.

Almost instantly Michael rejoined them, grinning. "You guys won't believe this," he whispered. Turning to Bradley, "Your old man and some woman are asleep and naked in front of your fireplace."

"No shit?" Phillip said.

"There's some booze and a couple glasses on the table," Michael added.

"Completely naked?" Phillip asked.

"Yessss, Dude. You can see everything."

Six eyes traded glances before three heads, all of one mind, pivoted. Save for the Internet and an occasional peek at family members, none of them had seen a real-life full-grown naked woman before. The opportunity was too fortuitous to ignore.

Like a pod of sharks stalking a wounded tuna, the youngsters slipped through the darkness toward their prey. A minute later they were just outside the room where the nude bodies were. Michael stuck his head in first and confirmed what he'd seen before. He signaled for the others to follow.

At first they were dead silent. Brad Sr.'s bare butt faced them. It would have been both disgusting and humorous if that was their primary focus, but it wasn't. There was a stark-naked woman lying on her back, head toward them and one leg leaning up against a glass-topped coffee table. One breast was visible, but if they could get to the other side of the room, her most private area would be on full display. They tiptoed their way around the room.

A used condom was on the floor, near the couch. Neither of the naked adults moved. Somebody whispered that they must have been passed out. Shhh.

Finally, they arrived at the best vantage point and crowded together. Wide eyes and pointing fingers zeroed in. There it was. Hairy and glorious. A real woman's vagina. As clear as any book or video they'd ever seen. For a few wonderful minutes, there was dead silence as their faces gang-gawked at the view of all views.

When the initial shock had worn off Phillip instinctively grabbed his cell phone to take pictures while the others smiled their approval.

At first Phillip captured a half dozen wide shots. Then he squatted and took a position at the woman's feet for the ultimate close-ups. He got it all.

Then Michael tried to take it one step further. He whispered, "Phil, get one of me touching her boob."

Suddenly, Bradley grabbed Michael's arm, "No, you idiot," he whispered. "She'll wake up."

"She's not gonna know," Michael insisted as he reached out his hand toward the woman.

Bradley yanked him harder just as Brad Sr. squirmed.

In an instant the circling sharks transformed into a school of clownfish and scurried for the back room where they remained deathly quiet for several more minutes. Finally Michael broke the silence. "Let's go back."

"No, Dude," Bradley said, "There's nothing left to see and we already have a shitload of pictures. We should quit while we're ahead."

"I agree," Phillip added.

With nothing left to gain, three happy erections pointed three happy adolescents out the back door. They'd just witnessed the greatest show in Palmdale since Barnum and Bailey had left town many decades earlier.

CHAPTER 36

On Monday morning before the first bell, Stump saw Richard and about ten other guys buzzing around excitedly. Richard hustled over to Stump. "Dude. Bad news. That tall guy over there has a bunch of dirty pictures. You can see everything."

"So? Porn ain't hard to get."

Richard shook his head. "I think it's your mom."

Stump's head swirled to the tall guy and the others encircling him, then back. Richard had only met Stump's mom once. "No way, man. My mom ain't like that."

"Dude. She was passed out. I'm really sorry. I wouldn't have looked if I knew it was her."

"Can't be." On the other hand, Stump's mom had disappointed him before. Every muscle from his jaw to his butt cheeks tightened.

"I don't think anybody else knows who she is. He said he got the pictures a couple nights ago."

That was the night Stump had stayed with Willie. But after jail she'd said she'd quit doing bad things. "It must be somebody else."

"Dude. It's her."

Stump had to check it out, so he made his way toward the "oohs" and childish giggles. Twenty feet away, somebody in the group said, "Forward it to me." Others made similar comments. Idiots. Then Norman, one of the guys Stump knew, broke away from the group and was checking out his cell's screen.

"Did you get the pictures, Dude?" asked Stump.

"Yeah. They're awesome."

"Can I see?"

The first picture was a full body shot—toe to head. Somebody might as well have hit him in the stomach with a baseball bat. Pissed like he'd never been pissed before, Stump glared at all the guys who were ogling at dirty pictures of his mom. He knew there was no way he could get everybody to delete the pictures or stop forwarding them to anybody else, but he wasn't going to walk away either. Like a sharp shooter in a video game he zeroed in on the originator.

It didn't matter that Phillip was older and bigger. Stump pushed his way past a couple of peer pervs and slammed his fist just below Phillip's ribcage. He grunted violently, folded over and dropped his cell phone.

Nearly everybody else stopped gawking at pictures and rubbernecked to the action. "Who the hell are you?" Phillip choked out.

"You're gonna regret what you did, asshole." Stump landed another smashing blow, then swung again. This time Phillip saw it coming. He avoided some of the impact but Stump still landed a stinger to his neck. Phillip's head twisted from the power of the punch.

Phillip projected his longer arms, holding Stump off for a second before Stump sent another wild swing his way. This time the blow landed in Phillip's chest. His face red, Phillip regained his stability. "Alright, you little prick," he said. "You want me, you got me."

A tightened fist rammed into Stump's left cheek, ripping the shit out of his upper lip. "Oohs" of approval echoed through the now growing crowd. It hurt like hell but Stump didn't care. He was pumped with adrenalin. He swung again, harder and more determined. He got the ribcage and another grotesque grunt roared from Phillip's core. Phillip might get the best of him but Stump wasn't going to quit until everybody saw that there was a price to pay for messing with him.

With renewed determination in his own squinting eyes, Phillip sent a head-high swing to Stump's left side, but Stump saw it and ducked. Then another punch came from the other side. This one caught Stump on the ear and knocked him sideways, almost felling him. He tried to shake it off but then Phillip buried a powerful guided-missile of his own deep into the softest pit of Stump's gut. An ugly guttural grunt indicated he'd had the wind knocked out of him. Then another punch landed square on his nose, busting the cartilage and sending a blood-shower out his nostrils. He couldn't see or breathe. He fell to the ground, gasping for air. But Phillip wasn't done. He drove a fist into the top of Stump's head. Just then Richard jumped between Stump and Phillip. "That's enough. Let him alone."

"Get out of there, before you get the same thing," some other guy said.

Richard faced the guy directly. "I ain't afraid of you, but it was a fair fight and Phillip won. That's the end of it."

"Cool it," somebody said from the crowd. "Stears is coming." Stears, the bad-ass J.V. football coach, was jogging toward them. Everybody knew it was over.

Stump sucked in his first breath in a while as Richard helped him to his feet.

Phillip hurried toward Stears, raising both hands in feigned innocence. "That little bastard attacked me."

With Stump's hands, face and clothes all awash in a flood of blood, he finally caught his breath. He faced the amazed spectators, then looked at Stears and Richard, who slipped him a blood-splattered cell. "Here, it's Phillip's. I got it off him."

Stump nodded at his pal and stuffed the phone in the front pocket of his blood-soaked shorts before he took off running.

Stears yelled at Stump as he hurried off the school grounds, but he wasn't going back.

It took him several minutes before he could breathe better. In addition to basic bruises, his ribs throbbed, his upper lip was torn from the inside and his nostrils were plugged. None of it mattered though. At least not for now. He spit out a big wad of blood and saliva, then paused by a parked car to check himself out in the side mirror. Looked like shit. Didn't care.

He ran and walked nearly two miles before he reached the parking lot where his mom worked.

*　*　*

Jean was rifling through her desk when the entry door burst open. She raised her head and gasped at the heavily battered and gory face of her son. "Oh, my God," she cried out. "What—"

Stump plunked a blood-stained cell phone on her desk. "Pictures," was all he said. Then in a blur, he pivoted and sprinted out the door.

"Wait," she said, scared. She slammed her desk drawer closed and ran after him but he was too fast. He was already halfway to the street and still going. Stunned, she gave up.

She quickly returned to her workstation and seized the bloody device he'd plopped on her desk. Gross, thick blood had congealed in the corners. She moved past the reception area to Lydia's office. "Would you mind watching the front? She asked hurriedly. "I have to go down the hall."

In the ladies room, Jean stood shivering behind a stall door. She flicked on the ugly phone and found the pictures. She scanned a few benign ones before she shrieked so loudly the whole office could hear her.

CHAPTER 37

In the middle of town there was a wide riverbed with tall cement walls topped by a wrought-iron fence, designed to keep the kids out. But Stump had seen kids messing around down there. He climbed over the fence and made his way down among the sand and weeds.

The water flow was just a weak trickle, as usual, except during the rainy season. He went for one of the walls under a traffic bridge where it would be difficult for anybody to see him. He tucked himself among bushes and a few hot, wet weeds and a bazillion mosquitos. Who cared? Sometimes the scabs of the flesh paled compared to the wounds of the heart.

He held back a sob. It didn't matter what the doctors told his mom. Jail didn't make any difference. Countless promises were all lies. So what if her naked body titillated the troops? Spread 'em, Mom, spread 'em. Let anybody see. Just so you get a free drink out of it, right?

If it didn't matter to her why should it matter to him? Why care at all if he was just going to get his heart ripped out?

Who was he pissed off at anyway? His mom for being an irresponsible drunk or himself for always being so anxious to believe anything she said, just so long as it didn't bring shame or embarrassment on him? In some ways he was just as bad as she was, worse even, for being so effing gullible. What a dumb shit. He threw a pebble toward a puddle. Missed that, too. Figured.

Even though he got Phillip's cell, everybody was spreading the pictures around. Even Phillip could get them back—although he'd have to get a new phone. He hesitated a second. Wasn't that the shits? The bad guy was probably gonna get a brand new phone out of the deal while Stump would be expelled on top of getting his ass kicked.

Damn it, Mom, this is your fault. Not mine. You're the one who should be paying the price. You're the one who said you learned your lesson, but you didn't learn a damn thing, did you, Mom, did you?

Is this why you won't tell me who my dad is? He knows you're a drunk. He trusted you too, but you dumped on him, didn't you? That's it, isn't it?

If I knew who or where he was, I'd take my chances with him. Anything would be better than living at the end of your yoyo.

You don't care who you hurt. All you have to do is say you're sorry and everybody else has to forgive you. Right? Well, not the Stumpster. Not this time.

Why, Mom? Why?

He folded his knees under his chin, laid his arms on his knees and cried.

CHAPTER 38

Grossly bloodshot eyes weren't going to stop Jean from what she had to do. She couldn't blame Stump for being furious. She'd lied to him again, gotten drunk again, passed out again, and embarrassed them both again. She didn't deserve to be forgiven again.

Over a year had lapsed since the last time she visited an Alcoholics Anonymous meeting. Back then, she lacked commitment, but on this particular Monday night she meant business. The meeting was held in a small neighborhood retail center. A discreet side entrance with no sign on the door was consistent with the organization's name: Anonymous.

Inside, there were a couple dozen folding chairs scattered around eight long tables. About eight people were already there when Jean entered the room. A couple of them looked familiar. She took a seat near the back, next to the only other woman in the room. The woman introduced herself as Emily.

Before long a handful of others straggled in and a tall, thin man stepped to the front of the room. "Everybody please take a seat. It's seven o'clock and time to get started," he said. He took a quick glance around the room. "I can see we have a couple of new faces tonight so allow me to introduce myself. My name is Ernie Evers. I am the owner of this building and a member of the group."

"The crazy people's group," a bald-headed Hispanic guy said. Others chuckled.

"Don't confuse them," Ernie said with a feigned reprimand. "It's hard enough to get up the nerve to come to these meetings. As I was saying, let me explain how things work around here."

"Ah gee, do we have to?" somebody said sarcastically from the side of the room. The comment seemed to lighten the mood.

Ernie held up a rattan basket and handed it to the fellow in the front of the room. "The collection plate is to cover our expenses, including the ten dollar fee that I pay somebody to make coffee and clean up the room for us each week. While that goes around, each person will have a chance to speak. Sometimes we just say our names. Other times we might expose our souls. Whatever you choose. Either way, we've all been there, as the saying goes. So no matter what happens to you outside these walls, remember we are the people who understand you best. We know first-hand what you're going through."

While the attendees finished seating themselves and passed the basket around, Ernie continued. "We'll start up here tonight, with the youngest member of our group."

The young man rose. He looked too young to be wrestling with alcoholism. "Hello, my name is Bob," he said, "and I am an alcoholic."

"Hi, Bob," the other members responded in unison.

"As most of you know, I got drunk on my twenty-first birthday and drove into a street light. They had to amputate one of my girlfriend's legs and she has very little feeling in the other. At first I was pissed off at the court for sending me here, but after six months of sobriety, I realize how screwed up I was." He sat down.

"Thank you, Bob," Ernie said. He nodded to a pudgy woman in her mid-fifties. She stood.

"Hello, everybody. My name's Irma. As you know, I am an alcoholic."

"Hi, Irma."

"Since we've got guests, I'll spare you my whining so they might have a little extra time if they need it."

"Thank goodness," somebody mumbled, just as the collection plate arrived at Jean. It appeared as if most attendees had dropped in a buck or two. She reached in her purse and found her only two bills: a five spot and a one. Her financial condition was such that she couldn't afford anything, but her psychological condition was such that her self-imposed price was everything she had. She plunked in the full six bucks.

Then, it was the turn of the fellow next to her, a middle-aged gentleman with a nice mustache. "Hello, my name is Myles," he said. He spoke more softly than the others. "And I'm an alcoholic."

"Hi, Myles."

Myles held up what looked like a large token. "I'm pleased to say I've finally made the six-year plateau. Just got my chip this morning." The crowd applauded and actually cheered.

Ernie looked right at Jean. "Myles is one of our stars. He coaches anybody who needs it and helps wherever he can. He's even pulled a couple all-nighters when some of us fell off the wagon."

"Speak for yourself," the Hispanic guy said.

Ernie chuckled, nodded. "Especially me," he said. "Anyway, Myles is a good friend to us all."

Jean smiled at the man. He had dark hair, was just a smidgen under six feet tall and seemed to be in fairly good shape. He wore no wedding ring.

Myles took his seat and it was Jean's turn to stand. Public speaking wasn't her strength, but Stump's wounds lent her courage. "Hello, my name is Jean and I'm-" She paused as her mind chewed on what she was supposed to say next. She'd always avoided ascribing the "A" word to herself. Seconds passed as Jean scanned the room of understanding faces. She recalled what Ernie had said just minutes earlier about everybody having been there. A chill chased itself up her back and forced a gusher of tears to burst from her reddened eyes, "and, I'm an alcoholic," she whimpered, and then buried her head in her hands.

Myles sprang to his feet and wrapped an arm around her shoulder as the chorus in the background repeated their obligatory line. "Hi, Jean."

"You don't have to say anything else if you don't want to," Myles reassured her.

The comforting tone in their collective voices gave Jean pause. She had to be honest for a change. No more misleading. No more half-truths, no more denial. She sniffled. "Thank you, but I've got to do this." She let Myles go and addressed the others. "I'm a single mom, with a wonderful son who has forgiven my drunken behavior more times than I can count. I've done everything wrong, but most of all I deeply regret what I've done to Stump, the one person I could always count on. On top of everything else, I've lost my driver's license and spent a month in jail. But today was the worst day of them all. My wonderful son got in a stupid fight because of me. Because I embarrassed us both. Again. Now I don't think he'll ever be able to forgive me. I'm so, so sorry for what I did to my sister and my precious son. They're the only people I have, but I've disappointed them over and over again." She shook her head visciously. "But not anymore. Not anymore." She buried her face in her hands and eased back into her chair. She pulled a crumpled-up hanky from her purse. "Not anymore."

Myles scooted closer and patted her arm. "It will get better," he whispered.

CHAPTER 39

"Why bother? I'm fed up with her crap."

Aunt Gerry rolled her eyes like she always did when Stump employed colorful language. He was fed up with that too, but this wasn't the time to fight that battle.

The previous night, after providing a tasty Stump dinner to a riverful of mosquitoes, Stump waggled his battered self over to Cousin Willie's place. After he got cleaned up, Aunt Gerry wanted to take him to get stitches in his lip, but he refused. Refused to go home too, and school in the morning. They would just expel him anyway.

Uncle Dirk pulled into the driveway with Stump's mom in the car. Obviously, neither of them went to work either. Stump glared at his aunt. She must have set him up.

"I apologize, Honey. I know you're upset, but you and your mother need to talk things out."

"No way. She's a liar."

"We won't be back for a couple of hours," Aunt Gerry said, as she patted Stump on the back. "Give her another chance."

"Don't matter to me none," Stump said. "I ain't talking to her no more."

Outside, after a brief powwow, his aunt and uncle drove off. His mom stepped inside and sat across from him in the living room. "I know you don't believe me, but I've changed."

Yeah, right. He went into the bathroom and hung around for a while before she knocked. "Honey, we really need to talk." He returned to the living room but said nothing.

"I went to an Alcoholics Anonymous meeting last night." He yawned.

"Would it help if I told you about your dad?"

No matter the topic, her explaining and excuses held no more value to him than one giant burp. He blew over to the other side of the room and out the front door. Didn't care what she said or if she tried to follow. There was no way she could keep up. He'd go back to the ditch until school let out.

* * *

"Dude. Your lip looks like shit," Richard said.

"It's worse on the inside." Stump rubbed his cheek.

"Everybody's talking about you. Pretty damn tough considering Phillip is older and bigger."

"Screw 'em all. I don't care what they think." He ran his tongue over the swollen gash inside his mouth. Damn thing hurt. "Thanks for helping out," he said. "I couldn't breathe or fight anymore."

"What about your mom? You talk to her?"

"I'm done with her, too. I threw Phillip's phone at her." He licked his wound again. "Thanks for getting that phone for me."

"No sweat. Everybody will get bored with the pictures and be talking about something else in no time."

"I may not have been able to stop everybody from forwarding those pictures but at least a few people learned there are consequences when they do shit like that."

"Hey, my old man is out of town. Why don't you stay over here, tonight? My mom won't care."

Stump shrugged. "I guess so. At least that will give Mom something to think about."

"We could lift weights or invite Terry Devine over. I hear she's easy. We might both get laid."

"Naw. That wouldn't be right."

"Why not? You want to get laid, don't you?"

"Not like that."

"Oh, I get it. You're saving yourself for your wife or something noble like that, huh?"

"Not really. It's just that I was thinking about going to a meeting. You remember that guy at the drug store? He's talking about motorcycles at the school in a little while."

"Oh yeah, I remember him," Richard said nodding his head. "He was alright."

This time, they could walk the whole way. They hadn't known each other real long but Richard had already become Stump's first best friend—other than Willie, but Willie was forced on him and probably wouldn't be a friend at all if it weren't for that—and not in the shallow way the girls threw around the BFF label. Richard's friendship was real. They stuck up for each other. They went places together, like motorcycle meetings.

A bunch of older guys were already at the meeting when they arrived. The biker shook their hands. "I thought I might see you guys here." He pointed at Stump's lip. "A girl hit ya?"

Stump would've rather avoided the conversation, but Richard leaned in. "He got in a fight."

Stump glared at Richard, then back to the biker. "Should I call you Mac or something else?"

"You guys are my friends. Call me Mac."

"What are we going to talk about?" Richard probed.

"I had some old pictures converted into a power point presentation. I thought we'd talk about them."

"Is Annie in there?" Stump asked.

Mac grinned. "You remember my bike's name. I'm impressed. Actually, I've had several Annies over the years. Most of them indigo."

"A rainbow color," Stump said.

Mac smiled. "Did you know that all rainbows have the exact same colors in the exact same order?"

"Yeah. I knew it."

"I call b.s.," Richard said. "You didn't know that."

Stump rolled his eyes. "Roy G. Biv, Dude. Red, orange, yellow, green, blue, indigo and violet. Don't you pay any attention in art class?"

"I'll be talking about quite a few bikes," Mac said. "Not just mine. They're all awesome." He pointed toward the seating area. "Let's get started."

As Stump and Richard slid in a row, Mac took to the front of the room. "Before we begin," he said, "I promised I'd mention the upcoming football game. As you know, our Bulldogs need to win. I hope to see all of you there."

Somebody behind Stump tapped him on the shoulder. "Way to go." Stump nodded. The respect was welcome, but he'd gladly trade it for a normal family.

An hour later, after the meeting, he and Richard filed out with the others. He was glad to have had something else to think about besides his mom. "That wasn't bad," Richard said as they walked back to his place. "I'd like to ride the open road like that someday."

"It seemed kinda lonely to me."

"Lonely? That guy's met tons of people."

"But they were all strangers. He didn't have any good friends."

"Everybody is a stranger until you get to know them."

"If you're always leaving people behind and looking for new people, you never really have a permanent friend—like you and me."

Richard's lip curled up. "I see what you mean. Hey, I've got some Red Bull and some Viagra that I stole from my grandpa."

Stump chuckled and smacked Richard's arm. "Boner pills? Why'd you do that?"

"Would you rather be a Little Richard or a Big Dick?" A monster grin filled his face.

Stump shook his head. "You're a Big Dick, alright. I know what we can do." He reached inside his shirt and retrieved a bottle of vodka. "Get drunk."

CHAPTER 40

The sky may have been bright and clear but Jean's spirits were dark and muddied. She lit a cigarette and sucked the first drag deep into her lungs. Having just left work she wished she hadn't agreed to meet Myles, but there he was, out in the parking lot waiting for her just like he said he'd be.

He seemed nice enough at the AA meeting the previous night, and his offer to lend her a non-judgmental ear was comforting at the time, but now that the moment for their get-together had arrived she realized she really didn't know anything about him and that was the same way a fair number of her previous problems had begun.

But one thing was different. Myles said he knew where they could get a great slice of pie and that was a lot safer than going to a bar. She hesitantly proceeded in his direction.

Second thoughts, third thoughts and fourth ones filled her head as she drew closer. She would have changed her mind entirely if it weren't for Ernie Evers's special endorsement of Myles. She sucked in another drag from her cig. "Stupid. Stupid. Stupid," she said as she blew it out.

"Rough day?" Myles asked while she was still ten feet away.

"Awful, but I don't want to dump my problems on you."

Not surprisingly Myles opened her car door. Before piling into the cab she flipped her cig onto the pavement, which was yet another reminder of Stump. He was constantly on her back about her smoking.

While Jean buckled up, Myles scooted around to the other side of the truck and climbed in. "I'm glad you came. A lot of alcoholics can never face their demons."

"I have to do something different. Everything's going wrong. My son won't talk to me. I'm too distracted to help my sister with her marriage. I can't concentrate on my work. Can't afford to take any more days off. And I'm smoking more than ever. How's that for starters?"

"That's a pretty good list, alright," he said nodding his head, "but I'm betting that a piece of pie will make you feel better."

"Doubt it." She turned her head toward the rider's window. "I'm just a damn loser."

"If you don't mind my saying so, Jean, I think you might be too close to the forest to see the trees." His tone was soft and understanding.

"Stump has never ignored me like this before."

"Well, I don't know exactly what prompted him to fight for you, but I'm guessing he was so upset he had to do something that matched his frustration level."

"He must be so ashamed," she said, holding back a fresh batch of tears.

A couple of quiet minutes passed before they reached a cute little café. After they were seated Myles ordered them each a cup of coffee and a slice of Xtra-Flakey Dutch Apple pie. That done, he examined his fork. "I know how you feel. Believe me. I've been there too. It's painful for both of you, but I think he'll forgive you if he sees progress that he can rely upon."

She spun her head back and forth. "Not this time. He's reached his limit."

"It won't be easy, but I think he'll come around."

"What makes you say that? You haven't even met him."

"Don't need to. Didn't you say the fight was at school?"

"Yeah? So?"

"There had to be lots of older kids around. Friends of the other guy. If Stump didn't care about you any longer, why would he subject himself to the danger of their ganging up on him?"

Jean tilted her head.

"He still loves you. I'm sure of it. He's just frustrated because he can't help." Myles sawed off a forkful of his new slice of pie. "He obviously thought you were worth fighting for. Is the feeling mutual? Do you think a son who would do all of that for his troubled mom is worth fighting for, too?"

It was just a rhetorical question, but he made a good point. She'd die for Stump if she had to.

"Then you've got to get everything out in the open. Be one-hundred percent honest with both yourself and with him. Show him that you understand what the problem is and that you're beating down your demons one at a time. Show him that you're determined to change your life forever, for both of your sakes. Once you do that, and prove it's a long-term commitment, he'll be back. I'm sure of it."

Myles's clear head was exactly what she needed. "Is that what you did with your family?"

"Should have," he said, shaking his head. "I was married to a sweet woman and I let bourbon ruin everything. I had a very bad habit of dropping by the neighborhood bar and getting wasted and buying everybody a round. I blew way too much money that I should have used to create a family. I said hurtful things. Even blamed her for my drinking. It was all my fault."

The fact that he took full responsibility for destroying his marriage made it easy to believe him. If she approached her own situation the same way, maybe Stump would believe her. "Apparently you made a nice recovery. What do you do, now? For work I mean."

Myles chuckled. "Sorry. I guess I never really told you who I am. I'm a detective; I specialize in burglaries and fraud, and counterfeit items. I work out of L.A."

"Forty minutes each way? That must get old."

"Not really. It gives me time to myself."

"Why not work in Palmdale? We must have detectives here, too."

"Size matters," he said. "L.A. has a lot more resources. Pays better too. Don't get me wrong—small towns have their benefits, especially in the twilight years when we want to take it slower, but for now I like the bigger department."

"You must have a girlfriend?"

"Not really, but just to get the other questions out of the way," he said, grinning, "I'm thirty-seven. I moved to Palmdale six years ago to get a fresh start. I like the 49ers, and of course," he pointed his fork at his plate, "apple pie."

Jean smiled. "Sorry. I didn't mean to give you the third degree."

"No problem. I use the club to keep me busy in the evenings, when I'm more likely to feel temptation. I've never felt better."

"I hope I can get my act together like that."

"You're not alone. There are twenty million alcoholics in the country; at least five million are women. The good news is you're one of the few who found a way to do something about it."

Myles's comments made Jean feel like she wasn't such a horrible person after all.

"One thing that most of the more successful members have in common is that we realized we had to face the whole truth. Confess everything. Admit we needed help. You're in the same boat. Now you've got a chance to save a sinking ship. It'll probably be tough for a while. You just have to be honest about what your problem is. Prove to your boy that you're both worth the effort. He'll get the message."

Jean grinned.

"What's so amusing?"

"Your comment about Stump and messages. He's got this amazing ability to decipher them. It's like a foreign language. When he looks at license plates, as an example, he sees both the numbers and the respective letters they represent on a phone pad. Sometimes those letters make up cute sayings."

"Smart kid."

"I can't afford to lose him, Myles. He's all I've got. What should I do next?"

"I'm no psychologist," he said, poking at some piecrust, "but I'd say as long as he's safe, give him a little space. In the meantime, keep attending the meetings and in a few days, when he's calmed down, you can talk with him. When that time comes, I can join you, if you'd like."

"You'd do that for us?"

"If you're willing to give it a chance, I am too. In addition, you might want to find a symbol that will constantly remind you of your new commitment." He reached into his pocket, retrieved a brass token and set in on the table. "Are you familiar with these?"

She took it and looked it over. "Is this what you talked about last night?"

"Yep. Six years sober. Whenever I get tempted to do something stupid, these silly little coins remind me of what I've been through. They don't look very important to anybody else but they've saved me a couple of times, especially in the beginning."

"Do they have one that says three days?"

Myles grinned, "I don't think so but you can come up with something else that serves the same purpose."

"I'm not very creative."

"Many people don't need reminders but if it helps you, I recommend you identify something unique and personal that you can draw on for inspiration. For instance, you might simply go for a walk at the same time every day. Or, keep your meds in a coffee can so that you're regularly reminded that you have the 'grounds' to stay sober. I know it's corny, but that's the point. You'll remember why you're doing it. One guy wore his underwear inside out for two years because it made him smile every morning."

Jean bit her lip, looked around the room, then reached in her purse. "I know what I'm going to do," she said as she pulled out her pack of cigarettes. "Stump hates these. I'm going to quit smoking."

Myles's jaw tightened. "I don't know about that, Jean. From what I understand nicotine is just as difficult to overcome as alcohol."

"That's what makes it perfect for me. The urges will be intense but continuous. Every time I want to plop a cigarette on my lip, I'll think of Stump's bloody lip after the fight and that he got it because I couldn't control myself."

"Are you sure? I've never heard of anybody trying to quit both addictions at the same time. As you saw at the meeting, lots of recovering alcoholics smoke."

"It's like you said about Stump. He had to act out to the same degree as his frustration. I have to do the same thing. I have to do something drastic to prove to him I mean business." She crumbled up the half empty pack of cigs. "I hate what I did to my son and he hates the smoking. It will work, Myles. I know it will."

"You know something? I can hear the determination in your voice."

"Another thing. When I get to that meeting tonight, I'm going to confess to everything—not for you or the other people—but for Stump."

CHAPTER 41

Just days after Rachel took the pregnancy test she advised Mac that she'd started her period, which prompted a conversation between him and Miranda. They noted that it had been three months since Rachel's last period, and that her phrasing suggested the event was newsworthy to her as opposed to a simple process of nature, all of which essentially confirmed that she indeed wanted to have a baby. But, more importantly, if the same three-month cycle were to repeat itself, the stage was set for the most important phase of the con.

Now another month had passed and Mac had been slipping sleeping pills to Rachel, both so he could spend more hours with Miranda and because drowsiness was a frequent early symptom of pregnancy.

On this particular day, Rachel was still asleep and the not-yet-warm sun lingered in the eastern sky as Mac made his way downstairs. He put on a fresh pot of gourmet coffee and threw a few strips of bacon in a frying pan. That done, he snuck out to the garage and secured a couple hand-tools and a dusty old pink phone.

Back inside, he slid into the living room and plugged the phone into the outlet between the recliner and the end table, after which he returned to the kitchen where he removed the hardline wall phone and disconnected one of the wires.

That done, he dropped a pill from Dr. Gravely into Rachel's cup.

As he waited for Rachel, he would have liked to talk to Miranda, but that wasn't possible. Instead he mentally rehearsed the plan they had devised. Timing would be critical, but if it worked, they would have paved a direct path to the trust.

Finally, he heard Rachel moving around. He scooted toward the kitchen and filled her cup. "Wow, it smells great in here," she said as she descended the stairs. "Is that new coffee?"

"Good nose," Mac said, handing her the spiked cup. "Here you go."

"How nice." She sipped at her drink, then gestured toward the wall phone now lying on the counter. "What's going on?"

He sighed. "It's bad enough our cells don't get a decent signal in this valley, but now the damn hardline is screwed up too." He pointed toward the living room. "The pink one from the garage is over there. It's got a short cord, but it'll do until we can get something better."

She twisted her head toward the cord. "I'm glad you're so handy."

After Mac made some toast and scrambled some eggs they finished off their breakfast, then Rachel went upstairs while he cleaned up and once again, he waited.

A little later when his hands were immersed in dishwater, she returned. The creases in her forehead indicated her discomfort. "You okay?" Mac asked, knowing that her nausea was a result of Gravely's pill.

"Just a little queasy. Might be the eggs."

"Don't think so," Mac replied. "We ate the same thing and I feel fine. Why don't you have a seat in the family room and read a magazine until you feel better?"

"I just hope it's not the flu," she said. She grabbed a magazine and plopped into the recliner.

"You know what they say about nausea."

She lifted her head.

"You could be pregnant."

She snickered. "Did you forget about my surgery?"

"You said they told you it's not impossible."

"They were just trying to make me feel better, but I remember the negativity in the doctor's tone."

"Tone? You can't go by that. There's only one way to be absolutely certain."

Rachel sighed. "Not that again."

"I know you don't like to get your hopes up, Rachel, but nausea is a real symptom. So is drowsiness and you've been awfully tired lately." He pointed toward the stairs. "I'm getting one of those tests, just to be sure."

She shook her head. "It's a waste of time."

A moment later, he returned with the orange box they'd opened the previous month and smiled. "I'm not going to take no for an answer," he said, "so you might as well make this easy on both of us."

She rolled her eyes. "After all you've done this morning, I guess you deserve that much. Give me the damn box."

Rachel sighed and eased toward the bathroom and pushed the door mostly closed. This was Mac's chance. He slipped toward the corner of the kitchen and speed-dialed Miranda. Just as they'd previously discussed he waited for one ring and hung up.

Almost instantly the pink phone rang back. The timing was impeccable. "I'll get it," Mac said loudly. "Hello." He paused, then said, "Do you mean Rachel?"

Another short delay. "What kind of accident?"

Then, "Oh no. Is she going to be okay?"

Mac observed Rachel's shadow move under the bathroom door. "Wait a minute," he said to his caller. "I'll go get her." He set the handset on the recliner, dashed toward the bathroom. "Rachel. You'd better hurry. There may be something wrong with Granny."

As expected, Rachel made a quick exit and rushed toward the short-corded receiver. While she was practically tied to her chair, Mac quickly slipped inside the restroom. Rachel had filled the cup with urine and dipped one of the strips in it as required. He replaced her urine with some that Gravely had given Miranda and dunked a different strip into it. Then he set both where Rachel's had been and quickly hid the other cup and strip under the sink.

Rachel was leaning forward in the recliner and listening intently to the caller when he returned just a minute later. She wrinkled her brow. "Are you certain we're talking about the same woman?" she asked.

Mac moved closer to Rachel. "What's going on?" he asked rather loudly.

Rachel shrugged at Mac and returned her attention to the caller. "I think you might have the wrong number." Following a brief pause, she said, "Hello? Are you there?"

She sighed as she held up the receiver. "She hung up."

Mac twisted his head and squinted. "That's strange. You'd better call Granny, just to be certain."

Rachel's fingers jackhammered the buttons on the receiver. Then she said, "Thank God. Granny? You okay?"

Mac sat close by while Rachel satisfied herself that her grandmother was fine. After she hung up he hesitated and then lifted his head. "The test," he said excitedly. "We forgot about the test."

Rachel grabbed one of her magazines. "You can check it out if you want to."

Mac measured his pace. Once in the bathroom he examined the substitute strip. Two lines. Perfect. His pulse quickened. He hurried toward Rachel. "Take a look at this. What'd I tell you?"

A combination of disbelief and hope filled Rachel's eyes. She checked the strip and looked up.

Mac smiled broadly and waved the strip at her. "I knew it. I knew it. I knew it." He grabbed her hand, coaxed her to her feet and gave her a big bear hug. "Sleepiness and nausea. I knew it."

Rachel just stood there, obviously stunned. She looked at

the strip again and then plopped back into the recliner. "It must be a mistake."

"Why don't we try again, just to be sure?" He stepped into the bathroom, grabbed the cup and the last strip from the box. Then right before Rachel's eyes, he dunked the last strip in the liquid gold and placed it on the magazine beside her. This time she paid attention. Then, there they were again. Two magical lines. "Hot damn," Mac yelled.

Rachel's eyes filled with tears.

*　*　*

Some five minutes later, across town Miranda answered her burner on the first ring.

"A home run," Mac said. *"She's taking a shower now, so I don't have long."*

"Fantastic. I wish I could have been there." Miranda lowered her voice. "Now listen. She'll want to call the doctor's office so as soon as she sets an appointment you call me back so I can give Dr. Gravely a heads up. He'll want to move her appointment up."

"Why do we need to do that?"

"She might want to test herself again. You've got to keep her preoccupied every minute so she doesn't have that opportunity."

"No problem. We're going to Granny's after a while. That ought to do it."

"Good. Now, another thing. You need to convince her not to tell anybody, including Granny. There's no telling what will happen from here on out, so the fewer people who know what's going on the better."

"Never thought of that."

"Shouldn't be too tough. Most women keep it to themselves for a few months anyway, until they're certain. But by then, we'll be out of the picture. I love you, Sweets."

"I love you, too."

CHAPTER 42

Miranda got up early, changed her sheets and sprayed the air with perfume before she took the familiar 10-mile drive to the prison; only this Thursday was different. Don was to be released at precisely 10:00 a.m.

She arrived early and made her way to the gate where she anxiously waited out the last moments of his three-year sentence. Minutes later she heard them coming. The guards escorted Don out of the final security gate right on time. She rushed to him and wrapped her arms around him, and then their lips met and they hugged and kissed again.

When the clanging bars closed behind him for the final time, Don turned around and waved his middle finger in the air. "Fuck you, shithole." He grabbed Miranda's hand and they hurried off to her SUV. As soon as they hopped in, her burner went off. "Dammit. Why is your brother calling me? I told him I had a dentist appointment and I'd call him when I was done." She hit the off button.

"Good," Don said, "'cause we've got some serious catching up to do."

* * *

"What's that supposed to mean?" Don probed while he and Miranda were still lying in her bed.

"It's not that big of a deal, Donnie. It was just a suggestion."

"Is that what my brother does? Take his time?"

As a matter of fact, it was, but it wasn't really fair to expect Don to approach the matter the same way as Mac did, especially considering their timing restraints lately. "For crying out loud, Donnie, this has nothing to do with him. I just asked you to slow down and enjoy the moment, because we've had to rush through everything recently, that's all."

He punched his pillow. "You must think I'm stupid. We lived together before I got thrown in the shithole and you never complained until after you'd been with him. Now all of a sudden, I'm not good enough to satisfy you."

She sighed, took his hand. "You're reading too much into this. You're a much better man than he is—or anybody else for that matter. You're smart and loyal and you figured out a way to provide for Mickey."

"Yeah. I'm wonderful, except in the sack."

She shook her head. "You're every bit as good, but you've been in a lousy situation." She rolled over, rubbed his forehead with the palm of her hand. "I'm sorry I brought it up. That wasn't fair. We both have to give you a little time to normalize."

He pushed her hands away. "Alright then. I still think we should kill the bastard when we're done with him—and that lady principal too."

Before she could answer, Miranda overheard the familiar rumble of a motorcycle coming from up the street. She sat up. "It can't be." But the bike kept getting closer until the engine stopped at her home.

Don sat up too. "I thought you told him—"

She grabbed her robe. "He's got a key." She jammed her feet into her slippers. "You stay here. I'll get rid of him." She closed the bedroom door behind her and heard his key wiggle in the lock. She rushed to the door, just as it inched inward and Mac stepped inside. "Sweets," she said as she raised her hand to her jaw, trying to sound sick. "I'm sorry I didn't call you, but I feel like crap from the novocaine. Can we just meet tomorrow?"

He glanced over her shoulder and around the room. Fortunately, there wasn't any sign that Don was there. "I thought your phone was broken."

"I just didn't answer it 'cause of my tooth."

"Oh," he said, lifting a gentle knuckle to her chin. "I can stay with you if you'd like."

CHAPTER 43

The next evening, Mac was at Rachel's, looking through a magazine in her living room when she descended the stairs. "What did I tell you?" she said in a dejected tone.

A quick glance in her direction revealed both disappointment in her eyes and an applicator from a typical pregnancy test in her hand. She'd obviously tested herself. A chill danced up Mac's spine. When did she have time to buy a pregnancy test of her own? He'd been with her practically every minute lately. She held up the stick. "It's negative. I knew it."

She was scheduled to see Dr. Gravely the next morning. Why couldn't she have just left well enough alone until then? He rose. "Can I take a closer look?"

"I shouldn't have gotten my hopes up," she said, dropping her head slightly. It was negative all right. His pulse quickened.

He wished he could discuss the matter with Miranda, but he was on his own. "I'm so sorry," he said, as she stepped toward him and held out her arms.

Her body was limp, except for her arms, which clung tightly around his neck. "I'll have to cancel my doctor's appointment," she mumbled.

Another chill, stronger than the first, wrapped around his back. That would be a disaster. He had to calm her down before she became hysterical or derailed everything that he and Miranda had been working towards for months. "Where'd you get that test?" he probed. "Maybe, it's wrong."

She sniffled. "It was in the closet. I've had it for a long time."

That was something to cling to. "Well, there you go. The darn thing probably expired."

"Expired? Those things wouldn't expire."

"Well, how long have you had it?"

"I don't know," she sighed. "I had a relationship about four years ago, but it didn't last."

"That's a long time ago. I'm betting it's no good. Either way, you said you've always had lady-problems. We both know that your doctor will still want to see you just to be sure. If it will help, I'll take tomorrow off and go with you."

Rachel sniffed again and pulled back slightly. "I'd like that."

"Sure," he said, pointing to her stomach. "That's my baby too, you know."

*　*　*

"Does the father want to come with you?" Dr. Gravely's receptionist asked Rachel after she turned in a urine sample. Shoulders rounded, Rachel turned toward Mac.

"If it's okay," he said.

Thanks to last night's late conversation with Miranda, they figured he'd better stay close by Rachel until Dr. Gravely got her back on track.

Almost immediately after they were seated in the exam room, a nurse joined them. "Hi. I'm Paula," she said. "I need a blood sample."

Rachel nodded solemnly extended her arm. Minutes later, Paula had taken the blood, asked a series of routine questions and added the information to Rachel's file. "That's all for me right now," Paula said. "I'll tell Doctor you're ready."

"You've got to cheer up," Mac said when they were alone.

"I'm sorry. It's just so frustrating."

"I'm sure it is, but try not to flip out, at least until you know the facts."

A gentle tap came from the other side of the door. "Hello, Rachel. Looks like it's been nearly a year."

"Thanks for squeezing me in."

He turned to Mac. "I'm Dr. Gravely. You must be the father?"

"Yeah. Name's Mac Evans." They shook hands and Gravely took a seat on a stool in the corner. He looked at the file again. "When I saw why you came in," he said to Rachel, "I was pleasantly surprised."

"I was too," she said softly, "but after last night, I'm not so sure what to think."

"Last night?" Gravely said, twisting his head. "Why? What happened?" He was so smooth.

"The first time we tested," Rachel explained, "I used one of those cup and strip pregnancy tests. It came out positive twice. But then last night I tried one of the normal tests—the applicator-type—just to be certain. It came out negative."

"It was an old one, Doctor," Mac added. "I told her it had probably expired."

"I see." Gravely returned his attention to Rachel. "I wouldn't worry about it too much. There are plenty of false negatives but never a false positive. If you did everything correctly on the first test, that's the one we care about."

Rachel lifted her head. Mac thought he saw a hint of color in her face. "See. I told you," he said.

"One of my staff members is currently testing the urine sample you just gave us. Let's see how that one comes out before we get too upset. Do either of you have any other questions," Gravely asked, "before we do the rest of the exam?"

Rachel nodded. "Shouldn't I have some spotting or sore breasts?"

"Not necessarily. Every woman is different. There are even differences among pregnancies in the same woman. For now, you should count your blessings. You might have plenty of both of those symptoms before your baby comes."

Mac shifted his feet. "I have a question. How long does she have to put up with morning sickness?"

"Hard to say, exactly. Sometimes it lasts a couple months. Sometimes just a few days. Some women never get it at all." He looked at Rachel and tapped her file. "In your case, it came a little early, but your cycles have always been off just a bit, so I wouldn't give it another thought." Gravely checked his watch. "You guys wait here for a moment while I check on that specimen."

As he closed the door behind him, Mac grabbed Rachel's hand and squeezed. "I can see why you like this guy. Good bedside manner. How long have you been coming here?"

"I don't remember. Seven or eight years I suppose." She was perkier but didn't sound convinced.

"That explains why he's so good."

A knock and Gravely returned. He instantly showed them a pencil-sized applicator. "I thought you'd want to know right away," he said. "Congratulations."

Mac smiled and turned toward Rachel, whose face glowed. "Are you certain?" she asked.

Gravely showed Rachel the lines. "See for yourself. Like I said, there's never a false positive. There's no doubt."

Rachel's hands shot to her face and covered her mouth. "I can't believe this," she mumbled, excitedly through her fingers.

"See. I told you."

"We'll get the blood reports back from the lab in a few days," Gravely said while smiling at Rachel, "but it's safe to say you've got cause to celebrate."

"Oh, my God," she muttered.

Gravely's foot pressed the trashcan pedal and he dropped the applicator inside. He sat down and looked Rachel square in the eyes. "In a case like yours, when a woman has had reasons to doubt her fertility there's a tendency to want to retake the store-bought pregnancy tests over and over just to be certain; but those tests are not as reliable as ours. They can make both of you worry too much and you don't need that."

Rachel's fingers shook as she nodded. "No problem. I'm convinced"

"I'll make sure she remembers that," Mac said.

Gravely calmly rose and moved toward the sink. "Why don't you schedule a follow-up appointment with my receptionist for three weeks from now. We'll monitor you closely."

Rachel nodded.

"Should she rest a lot?" Mac asked.

"As long as you don't do anything overly strenuous," he said to Rachel, "you can keep to your daily routine. Is there anything else before I let you folks celebrate?"

Minutes later giddy Rachel and Mac entered the elevator. Rachel hopped up and down and hugged Mac. "I can't believe it. This is wonderful."

Mac smiled. It must have been easy for Gravely to get an applicator that had a positive reading. Now the ball was back in Mac's court. "You know something?" he said. "I just had a wild idea."

Rachel was still grinning. "I'm not sure I can take any more excitement today."

"That doctor was correct. We need to celebrate. Why don't we drive out to Vegas for a few days?"

Rachel turned toward him. "Are you serious?"

"I'm very serious." He looked right at her. "C'mon. You're usually very guarded and under control, but this is a super-special moment in our lives. The spontaneity will make the whole weekend unique and memorable forever."

"You really do mean it, don't you?"

"Sure I do. My work is slow and you have a bunch of personal days built up. There's no reason not to. We can even catch a show."

"I don't know. It's so impulsive."

"That's what makes it so perfect."

She thought it over a few seconds and then turned toward him. "I've heard there are some giant fountains and a lovely indoor flower garden at the Bellagio."

CHAPTER 44

Mac and Rachel slept in. He got up first and plugged in the courtesy coffee pot. Within moments it was dripping away. He enjoyed a long hot shower and toweled off, then stepped into his boxers and joined Rachel in the bigger room. She was on her cell phone.

While she was distracted, Mac laid out two coffee cups just like he had been doing every morning. He plopped half of a nausea-inducing pill that Miranda got from the doctor into Rachel's cup and then filled them both with coffee. Moments later, Rachel hung up. "Was that Granny?" he asked before taking a sip from his cup.

Rachel grinned. "Yes. She's so excited."

"You didn't say anything about the baby, did you?"

Rachel shook her head. "No. You were right about that. It's better to keep it between us for a while. But after I told her that we got married last night she was so excited I just let her ramble. She wanted to know how you proposed, and about the little roadside chapel—everything. I promised her we'd have a bigger, full ceremony a little later." She took a sip of coffee. "Granny asked if we can stop by after we get home for a bite to eat. I hope you won't mind, but she said something about a surprise."

Mac grinned.

CHAPTER 45

Mac's furtive attempts to call Miranda about the goings on at the gynecologist's office, as well as the trip to Vegas and Granny's surprise for Rachel all went unanswered. About all he could do was assume her phone was turned off and stick with their plan, which led him to Granny's home with Rachel.

A class full of school children couldn't have been more giddy than he and Rachel when they entered Granny's home. They'd barely made it past her front door before the elderly woman's wide eyes inspected Rachel's rings—rings that Miranda paid for with her line of credit. "They're lovely," she said. "Come on in. I want to hear all about your little trip."

"I didn't even see it coming," Rachel said, grinning from ear to ear. "Then, he just sprang it on me." She grabbed Mac's hand. "It was wonderful."

"I love you," he whispered.

Granny smiled at Mac. "How romantic."

"It was," Rachel said. "But I felt guilty cause you couldn't be there—for the wedding, I mean."

"Oh, baloney. It was special just the way it was. You'll always remember how surprised you were."

"Like I said on the phone, we're still going to have another, more formal wedding, when we can invite our friends and take some time for a real honeymoon."

"Probably to Hawaii," Mac added.

"Next time I want you right in the middle of all the planning and everything."

"Except the honeymoon," Mac said.

Granny laughed, "Oh, why not? I like Hawaii, too."

"So, you're not mad at me?"

"Heck no. I'll call Anderson Powell at the *Herald*. He'll want to announce your wedding in his newspaper."

"I remember him." Rachel turned toward Mac. "He's one of Pappy's old friends."

Granny rose. "I might as well get your surprise. Why don't you two have a seat in the dining room."

"Maybe it's my mom's wedding ring," Rachel whispered to Mac as they took seats. "I never knew what happened to it."

"That'd be nice," he whispered back, his own heart thumping. He and Miranda would be a lot happier if the surprise were a million bucks or so.

Granny returned with a manila folder and a grin worthy of a picture. She sat at the head of the table, laid the folder down and crossed her arms on top of it. "Rachel, sweetheart. I have something very exciting to tell you."

"So mysterious," Rachel said, smiling. Mac's pulse quickened as he stared at the envelope.

Granny slowly inhaled. "I can hardly believe this time has finally come. Before Pappy died, he arranged for a wonderful wedding gift for you."

Mac's heart pounded and Rachel's eyes widened. "A wedding gift from Pappy? But he's been gone for a long time."

Granny grinned. "You know how quirky he was."

Rachel looked Mac's way. "That was one of the things we loved about Pappy."

A million would do.

"After he sold our Silicon Valley ranch, he set up a trust for you."

Rachel's hands cupped her mouth. "What kind of trust?"

Kathump, Kathump.

"We never told you about it because we believed that when people get too much money, too quickly and too easily, it spoils them. Pappy wanted you to get married for the right reasons, not because of the money." Granny looked at Mac, then back to her granddaughter. "Pappy would be very pleased that you picked Mac. He's a very nice young man and you guys obviously love each other. That's just what Pappy wanted." She laid her hand on the envelope. "This is for both of you."

A half-million would be enough.

Both Rachel and Mac were dead silent as Granny slowly, teasingly, opened the weathered manila packet. Then she slowly pulled out a short stack of papers.

Hurry woman, you're killing me.

Granny turned the papers face-up and slid them across the table toward her precious granddaughter.

Mac struggled for a glimpse at the number, but before he could find it, Rachel's hands shot to the side of her head. "Oh, my God!" she squealed and slid the paper over to Mac, "If you move the last comma over, the numbers are the same as my birthday." She jumped up and rushed for Granny.

Huh? Mac pulled the papers his way. There it was. Mid-page. $11,241,974. His jaw dropped. "Holy shit!"

"Plus about a half-million in interest," Granny said, beaming.

"It's the same as my birthday," Rachel said again. "November 24, 1974."

Mac grinned crazily. He, too, stood, and the trio twirled around in circles, each one thrilled for a different reason.

Finally they calmed down and returned to the living room. "I wonder if I should quit my job?" Rachel asked.

Uh-oh. That would mean Mac would have to spend more time with Rachel and even less with Miranda. "Not right away," he offered. "Pappy said when people get too much money, too fast, it usually changes them. He wouldn't want that."

Rachel shook her head. "You're right. I have to be smarter than that. Now that I think about it, I should work at least the rest of the school year."

"Now you're talking," Mac said. "I think we should keep this to ourselves for a while, too."

* * *

Miranda had ignored Mac's calls long enough. This time she and Don had finished their dinner in a local restaurant and were waiting for their bill. "Hi, Sweets," she said into her burner, trying not to sound too affectionate. "Where have you been?"

"*Me?*" he asked loudly. "*I've been wondering the same about you.*"

"I hope you've got some good news?"

"*I guess you could say that,*" he said. "*But all I'm going to say for now is, the trust is real.*"

She damn near stopped breathing as she gave Don a thumbs up. "That's fantastic. I knew you could do it, Sweets. How much is it?"

"I ain't saying right now. I'm on my way to your place. I'll tell you when I get there."

She gulped. "But aren't you with Rachel?"

"Hell, no. I wanted to see you so I slipped her a sleeping pill. She'll be out all night."

Oh crap. Don wouldn't stand for that right now. "But, I'm at the grocery store," she blurted for lack of something better to say.

"At ten-thirty? Which store? I'll come and help you."

"No. I'm going to get gas, too. Can't you just tell me now, and I'll see you in the morning?"

"That's not good enough. I haven't been with you for three days and we've got some celebrating to do. I want to spend the night. I'll just use my key and wait for you. How soon can you get here?"

It wouldn't look right to put him off when he was so juiced up. "I guess it'll be a half-hour or so."

Don wasn't going to like what she had to do. After hanging up she slammed her drink on the table. "Your brother is such a dumbass." She got up and tugged his arm. "We've got to go right now."

"What about the trust?"

"It's real," she said pulling his sleeve, "but he wants to tell me the amount in person. Now, let's go."

"Oh, for Christ's sake," Don said. "Why didn't you insist he tell you over the phone?"

She faced him, raised her voice. "Dammit, Donnie. You heard me. I tried to, but he was too stoked and wouldn't cooperate."

"Alright then," Don said. He threw forty bucks on the table. "But what's the big damn rush?" he said to the back of her head as she moved away.

She turned. "He's already at my house. He'll be inside any minute."

"What? Why the hell'd you give him a key?"

She raised her voice. "He's supposed to think he's my boyfriend. Remember?" Miranda's SUV was just outside the door. She took the driver's side and blew out of there. "I gotta drop you off at your motel, then grab some items at a grocery store. I just hope I'm not too late."

"I hate that son-of-a-bitch."

"I know you do. You tell me all the time."

A moment later he asked, "How long will you be?"

Miranda sighed. "I hate to tell you this, Donnie, but he wants to stay overnight."

"No way," he snapped. "You already spend the days with him. The nights are for me."

"He hasn't seen me for a couple days and he gave Rachel a sleeping pill. I couldn't tell him that his brother had other plans."

While Miranda hurried, Don sat silent for a half-minute. Then, "Didn't sound to me like you put up much resistance."

Miranda lowered her voice to a near-whisper, "What the hell's that supposed to mean?"

"Simple," he said. "I think you're in a hurry cause you genuinely like fucking him."

She widened her eyes and raised her voice. "That's ridiculous. We talked about this from day one. You knew things would have to get steamy between him and me. You said you understood that. So don't pull this crap on me now. I've got enough to worry about without your going off the deep end."

"So you really do enjoy it?"

She waved her arms wildly. "Well I can't just lay there like a damn bump on a log, can I?"

"I just want to hear you admit it. We both know you like fucking him. So admit it."

Miranda sighed, rolled her eyes and pulled her SUV to the curb, and stared right at him. "Yes, Donnie. If it will make you feel any better, I enjoy fucking your brother. I have to. Alright? It's all part of the plan. *Your* plan, remember? You said you understood that." She pointed in his face. "If you can't deal with it anymore, you can call it quits. I'll finish up with Mac and see if I can help my brother on my own."

Don nodded. "At least now we're being honest with each other."

CHAPTER 46

Miranda clutched the steering wheel to conceal her shaking hands from Don. How did he figure out that she actually had stronger feelings for Mac than she was supposed to? Feelings that provoked still other feelings such as guilt and shame. That wasn't supposed to happen. Now she was stuck trying to deal with a green-eyed monster.

She held back a sigh. "I know you don't like staying in a motel, Donnie, but it can't be helped," she said.

"You think that makes me feel any better?"

"Of course not, but I'll get back as soon as I can. I promise."

"It ain't just the time apart that pisses me off. After what I've been through, I could spend the night standing on one foot. But that motel is just like the shithole, only there's even less to do."

"I know it doesn't help much, but there's a liquor store up the street. Why don't you get a six-pack and watch some TV? We can get a nicer motel tomorrow."

"I never expected my asshole brother would want to sneak out at night. Or worse, that you'd let him stay with you that much." He turned his head away. "I don't give a shit no more."

"Of course you do. He'll have to leave early in the morning and by then we'll know just how big the trust is. If there's enough to help Mickey, we can hang in there. But if it's too small, I'll dump him and you and I can finally catch up on all the time we've lost."

"Don't matter no more."

They pulled into the motel's parking lot. "I'd come in with you for a few minutes," she said, "but I'm already late."

"No problem," he said in a calmer voice. He opened the door and turned his head. "But I've changed my mind. When this is all over, I still want us to kill both of them." He closed the door and walked toward his room.

Regardless of whether Don really meant what he said Miranda didn't have time to argue. As far as killing people was concerned, she couldn't do that, especially not Mac, now that she owed him so much and had all these new feelings for him. And certainly not Don. She owed him even more. If she had to choose—stop that! She couldn't eliminate either one. She'd changed Don's mind about killing Rachel and Mac before. She'd just have to do it again.

She turned the final corner and headed home. Mac was parked in her driveway and appeared to be talking to his bike. As she pulled in, he smiled, then opened her car door. It was another small example of what she appreciated about him.

Once she was on her feet, he drew her to him. "I'm glad to see you," he whispered.

The feeling was mutual. "Me too, Sweets. Let's go inside."

"I'll get your bags."

Bags? Oh, crap. "Uh-oh. I can't believe what I did." She twirled a finger near her temple. "I was so excited about seeing you, I forgot to put them in my car."

He grinned. "Glad to hear I have that effect on you. We can go back and get them."

"Nah. Somebody probably got them by now. Besides, I'd rather be alone with you. Let's just go inside."

Mac draped his arm across her shoulder. "Fine with me. You smell wonderful."

He was always noticing the small things, but Don rarely

made comments like that. Safely inside and hidden from nosy neighbors, Mac immediately turned Miranda toward him. He gazed into her eyes and whispered, "God, you're beautiful."

"Thank you," she murmured faintly.

He gently took her head in his steady hands and drew her closer. She welcomed the slower pace and the tenderness when their lips met. Her eyes drifted upwards while her eyelids came sinking down. Her legs were numb. She quietly lowered her purse to the floor. For the time being she only had one thing in mind and it wasn't the trust.

CHAPTER 47

Five a.m.

Mac had gone home to Rachel, and the moonless sky had laid a shadowy blanket over the streets as if to tuck the city in one last time before sun-up. Meanwhile, Miranda had grabbed a shower and now she was just about the only one on the road.

"I had to do it," she said out loud. "It's just part of the plan, Don's plan," she scoffed. Truth was, no matter how many times she tried to convince herself otherwise, she enjoyed Mac's company too much and couldn't snuff out the guilt pangs that accompanied those feelings.

Off in the distance, the flickering neon sign of Don's motel came into view. If she were lucky, he'd be asleep or at least more concerned about Rachel's trust than the fact that she had just spent the night with his brother. She pulled in and quickly scanned the shadowy areas. Nobody was lurking.

A long cement catwalk that reminded her of her conjugal visits led her to unit 118. Don immediately let her in, revealing a room dark enough for bats. The TV was off. No radio. No bathroom light. Don turned away, said nothing. Somehow, she knew he'd not gotten any sleep. "Hi, Donnie. Mind if I turn on the light?"

"Don't care."

The flicked switch revealed a partly crumpled paper sack at

the side of the only chair. On the counter, a line of empty beer cans stood side-by-side like lazy tin soldiers. "You okay?"

Don didn't speak, or nod, or ask about the trust. She sat on the corner of the bed closest to him. "You got an extra beer?" she asked, looking for any way to melt the veil of ice between them.

A single warm one remained. She popped the tab and glanced around the room. "I'm sorry you have to spend so much time in here."

"Seen worse."

"Yeah, I know. Three years behind bars for protecting me." She dragged her foot across the matted carpet. "And this is how you get repaid."

"Not your fault."

She reached out, lifted his chin. "Well, I'll never forget what you did for me."

Don gently pushed her hand away. "Enjoy yourself?"

"I couldn't stop thinking about you."

"Bullshit."

"It's true. You're the one I love."

"Then why'd it take you so long to get back here?"

"I couldn't tell Mac that his brother was waiting for me, could I?"

"You coulda made up a good lie if you wanted to."

"Would it help if I said I had some good news?"

He raised his head.

"You were right. Rachel didn't know anything about the trust. But you were wrong about something else. And you're gonna be very glad you were."

He raised his chin. "Oh, yeah. Just how glad am I going to be?"

She took another slow but teasing sip of her beer. "There's going to be enough for Mickey, and a little more if you still want it."

"After what we've been through, damn right I want it. How much?"

She rose and set her beer can in line with the others, then she slowly twisted them so they all faced the same direction.

"What do donuts, astrological signs and months of the year all have in common?"

Don's eyes popped. "They all come in twelves." He sprung to his feet. "Twelve million?"

She let her happy eyes answer his question.

"Twelve effing million? No shit?" his voice was much louder now and a smile replaced the previous frown.

Miranda put her finger to her lips, "Shhhh."

"I knew it. I knew it. I knew it," he shouted as he jumped into the air.

"Donnie, be quiet," She scolded. "You'll wake the neighbors."

"Screw 'em," he screamed out. "I knew it. I knew it!" He grabbed Miranda and threw her on the bed. It cracked and one side fell to the floor, causing them to roll downhill into a pile, with Miranda more or less on top. Don broke out in hysterical laughter. Miranda tried to shush him again, but his out-of-control enthusiasm was both welcomed and contagious. She giggled too.

Don rolled over on top of her and their eyes met. He gently collapsed upon her and their lips found each other—just as somebody banged on the wall.

Miranda pushed him back slightly, smiled, whispered. "See. I told you."

"I'm the one who told you," he boasted, as he banged on the wall too. "Let's get outta here. Go get some breakfast or something."

Relieved, Miranda squeezed his hand and looked him up and down seductively. "Don't you want to finish what we started?"

He shook his head. "Too stoked. We can do that later."

*   *   *

Nearly a full hour had elapsed since daylight had erased the night. Mercifully, Don was so excited he hadn't mentioned Mac again.

Miranda wiped some toast crumbs from their table, peeking at her watch. "Ten after seven. I'm going to need some sleep pretty soon."

"Yeah, me too, but I'm still a little pumped up." Don threw a few bucks on the table for a tip and grabbed the check. "Let's get outta here."

"I'm going to the restroom while you pay the bill." A minute later, alone and settled into the stall, Miranda reflected on the chain of events since the twin convention. How had everything gotten so damn complicated? At the moment she was particularly concerned about Don's living arrangements. It was almost as if he were still in prison. If there were only some way she could spice things up for him so that he didn't spend so much time fretting over the time she had to spend with Mac.

When she re-entered the hallway, she could see Don up ahead in the lobby. Just a few minutes earlier he'd implied he wasn't quite ready to go to the motel. Couldn't blame him for that. Too much like the shithole.

"I know what we can do," she said as they pushed the doors open. "You've never seen Vivian's office. Why don't I show you how it came out?"

"Why would I care about that place?"

"We had to pay for the full three months, so you might as well see it." She tugged his hand. "C'mon. It'll help us wind down."

"All right." He stuffed the breakfast receipt in his jeans.

They slowly walked to Miranda's SUV. "You drive," Miranda said. After she buckled up, she placed her palms on her eyelids and gently massaged away the scratchiness.

"I meant what I said, you know," Don said in a firm voice, "about killing that woman—and my brother too."

He might as well have jolted her with a stun gun. "No. No. No, Donnie," she said shaking her head wildly. "We already settled this."

"Things have changed. That big chick is smart and she can afford to hire a slew of investigators."

"But we're clean, Donnie. I made sure Mac never left any clues."

"I don't trust him. He's been living with that cow for several months. He could easily decide he'd rather stick with her and her pot of gold than share it with you."

Miranda dug her fingernails into her palms. Taking Rachel's money was one thing, but taking lives was altogether different.

"We gotta off her first and we gotta do it pretty soon, before she has another period and screws everything up."

"But I can't do that, Donnie. I don't think Mac could either."

"Fuck him. He's a pussy. I don't give a shit about him. That's why he's gotta go, too."

Don turned the SUV into the driveway of the midwife's building. A few cars sprinkled the lot. "I wouldn't mind offing both of them today, right now," he said.

Now he was just being insane. Miranda placed her hand on his arm. "You know I'm on your side, but I think we ought to wait to make plans until we're sure Mac has access to the trust. They're seeing an attorney in a few days. We should know more after that."

Don parked. "Good. Then we agree."

She ignored the comment for the time being and nothing more was said until a few minutes later when they arrived at suite 303.

CHAPTER 48

There it was again. That God-awful piercing scream. Mac begged it to go away, but it refused. Motionless, and unable to concentrate, he felt something on his arm. "C'mon husband. Get up. Time to go to work."

Easy for Rachel to say. Thanks to a sleeping pill, she had gotten a good night's sleep, but he'd spent the bulk of the night with Miranda and a couple hours of real sleep wasn't enough. "Hit the snooze," he muttered as he packed his pillow around his ears.

Rachel lifted the corner and said, "I've put on some coffee."

Mac hated this part of his life. The make-believe. Getting up before he was ready. Nevertheless, he had to maintain his image: that of an electrician at NASA. Mickey and Miranda were counting on him and for once in his life he was determined to complete a significant good deed.

His feet found the floor, his elbows found his knees and his head found refuge in his palms. A little later, his coffee and oatmeal were followed by a ritual shit, shower and shave, during which he scowled at a red-eyed idiot in the mirror.

Routine completed, he and Rachel made their way to the garage, where he jiggled Annie off the kickstand. This was when he usually went to see Miranda, but she said she wouldn't be available before noon. This sucked. Maybe he should circle around the block and come back to snag some more Z's. Nah. Nosy neighbors might see him and blow his cover. He kicked Annie into low gear and hit the remote. Might as well get gas.

"You look like crap," he imagined Annie saying.

"No shit. I'm fed up with alarm clocks and stupid clothes. Always trying to stay in character. Four months of that'll just about kill a guy."

"Can't you just go sleep at Miranda's?"

Mac snickered. "Sometimes that chick's really weird, too. Everything comes with strings, especially lately. She used to see me pretty much any time I wanted. Except on Thursday mornings, of course. But, for some reason, that's no longer important to her. Instead, she only wants to see me when Rachel's at work or I set an appointment, like she's some damn attorney or something."

They stopped at a light, across from the midwife's office building. He smiled. Miranda's creativity when they had "played doctor" trumped all of her little quirks.

The light turned green. When he got up a little further he glanced toward the midwife's parking lot. "Hey. That looks like Miranda's SUV."

CHAPTER 49

Don was halfway to the elevator when Miranda locked the door. She hurried to catch up but wasn't sure what to say. The bell pinged and the doors opened.

Miranda had hoped that some adult recreation would distract Don from all his murderous ideas. She even pointed at the same padded table with the stirrups and asked him essentially the same question she'd asked of Mac about "playing doctor," only this time, it sounded stupid. Based on what didn't happen, Don must have thought so, too.

"Don't worry about it," she said as she pushed the button. "It happens to all men."

"First time for me."

"You'll be fine after we get some sleep."

Don turned and faced her. "I bet you did my brother in that office?"

No use denying it. She'd already admitted she liked having sex with Mac. She simply turned her head away.

Nothing else was said until they reached the lobby where Miranda heard a not-so-distant rumble of a motorcycle. She clutched Don's elbow. "I hope that's not who I think it is. Wait here."

"That asshole."

She quickly eased to the building's front entrance and peeked out the glass doors. "Crap. It's him alright."

"Did he see you?"

"Don't think so," she whispered. "He was looking inside my car."

She bent down slightly and peeked again. "Damn it. He's parking." She turned to Don. "You have to get out of here."

"Get rid of him," he said, backing up. "I'll meet you back here in a half-hour." He hurried off toward the back of the building.

Miranda fluffed her hair, waited until she saw Mac's shadow approaching and stepped outside. She raised her eyebrows and stopped abruptly. "Sweets," she said trying to sound innocent as possible. "What are you doing here?"

Mac stopped abruptly. "I was going to ask you the same thing."

"Me?" She tapped her bag. "I was looking for this."

"Your purse?"

"Last night, after you left, I couldn't find it," she said. "Then I realized it was probably over here."

Mac looked down the hallway toward the elevators. "Why would it be here?"

Miranda rolled her eyes. "It's so embarrassing. When I was coming home from the store last night I had to use the bathroom real bad, but I don't like that store. Since I had to drive right past here on my way home anyway. . ."

"You came here, forgot your purse and realized it this morning?"

She shrugged, "It's dumb, but it made me nervous so I had to come get it."

He wrinkled his brow. "But that was hours ago. You should have been back home by now."

She sighed. "I know but there was an article in one of the magazines that I'd been wanting to read. I got into it, then I needed to rest my eyes for just a minute. You know what happened after that."

He smiled. "You fell to sleep on that leather couch?"

"Yeah," She rubbed her neck. "If you want to call it sleep."

Mac grunted. "I know what you mean. I only got a couple hours myself. Why don't we go back to your place and get caught up?"

She shook her head. "We'd just get distracted and I'm too tired."

"Just to sleep." He held up two fingers. "Scout's honor."

"No. I told you I have other things I need to do."

Mac gently grabbed her shoulders. "What's going on? You've never been like this."

She glanced away. "I don't have to explain anything to you."

"I know that, but we both need some sleep and your place is close by. Let's go there for a few hours."

"I said no."

"How about tonight, after Rachel goes to sleep? I can slip her a pill and sneak over around midnight for a few hours."

She exhaled. "You're not listening to me. I said no and I meant it. I need a break and I don't want to see you again until tomorrow morning."

Mac's shoulders slumped and he stepped backwards. "Okay. I get it. You don't want me around." He threw his hands up. "If that's what you want, that's the way it'll be." He turned and walked off.

"Things will be better in the morning," she insisted to his back. "I'll make it worth your while." She lowered her voice to a whisper. "I love you. Please don't be mad."

Tears tracked down her cheeks as Mac drove off. A swishing sound came from behind her as the doors opened and Don rejoined her. "How'd it go?"

Startled, Miranda sniffled and turned away. "Oh, hi. I chased him off."

Don turned her to the side. "You're crying."

"Me? No. I'm just real tired. That's all."

"Bullshit. It's obvious that you love him. That's why we have to rip his heart out. Let him see how it feels."

She covered her ears and ran toward her SUV.

CHAPTER 50

Stump and Richard started out lifting weights in between shots of vodka, with Stump choking down the first shot and an extra two as they finished off the bottle. They ended up with Stump puking all over the bathroom.

The next morning both of Richard's parents went to work and Richard was able to get to school, leaving Stump alone to recover and clean up his mess. The smell of day-old vodka puke made him do it again. After that he buried his pulsating head in a pillow until noon when he went down by the riverbed and nursed and cursed both the hurricane in his gut and the earthquake between his ears.

After wasting a couple hours wondering why his mom would subject herself to the torturous after-effects of booze for something as stupid as a short-term head-buzz he went to Aunt Gerry's house and pretended that he'd just gotten home from school.

The following morning was his first day back in class since the fight. He slithered into his seat and acted as nonchalant as possible, but the peace only lasted a half-hour. A messenger came to say the assistant principal, Ms. Johnson, wanted to see him.

As Stump meandered down the hall, he wondered which of his misdeeds had caught up to him: fighting, getting drunk or cutting class?

He entered the office where a man he didn't know sat in

the waiting area. "I'm Neal Randolph," Stump said to the office lady. "I was told that Ms. Johnson wants to see me."

"Go on in," she said, pointing off to the side. "They're waiting for you."

They? He tapped the door and pushed it open. Off to the right, his mother was seated at a round table with Ms. Johnson. He'd been ambushed again. "Hello, Honey."

Ms. Johnson pointed across the table. "Have a seat."

It was the first time Stump had seen or spoken with his mom since he ran out on her a couple of days earlier. She probably didn't care about that either. He said nothing as he took a seat off to her side so he didn't have to look at her.

Ms. Johnson opened a file, then addressed Stump's mom. "It says here you're Neal's contact person. Is there a Mr. Randolph?"

Stump scoffed.

"It's just me," his mom said softly.

"Okay then, we might as well proceed." Ms. Johnson reached in a drawer and pulled out a cell phone. She looked at Stump. "I have a video of you fighting with another student."

That answered one of Stump's questions.

Ms. Johnson pivoted her head toward Stump's mom. "Unfortunately, there are also some other unpleasant pictures in here."

Out of the corner of Stump's eye it appeared as if his mom lowered her head.

"You guys obviously have some serious issues. If you'd like to tell me what's going on, I might be able to get you some professional help."

A waste of time and money. He could tell anybody what's wrong: His mom drank too much. Simple as that. They didn't need no voodoo doctor poking around in their heads. "I'm the one who got in a fight," he said. "And I'm the one who makes her do those things, so leave her alone." He rose and held out his wrists. "You can take me to jail if you want to."

His mom tugged him back toward his chair. "Don't listen to him, Ms. Johnson. He's just covering for me. He's always done that. To be honest, a lot of the time he's been the parent and I've been the child. That's a big part of the problem. I'm supposed to be the leader, but I'm afraid I haven't done a very good job in that regard. We all know this is all my fault. He was just standing up for me." She turned to her son. "You can't know how proud that makes me. But when I saw your injuries I sincerely hated myself for what I did to you. This time I finally did something constructive about it."

He turned his head toward the window to avoid scoffing in her face. He'd heard every possible variation of "I've-learned-my-lesson" before. If she wanted to believe that bullshit, it was up to her, but her history told him all he needed to know. She'd be a drunk until the day she died.

"The last few days," his mom persisted, "I've attended AA meetings. I haven't touched a drop and I even quit smoking."

Stump turned his head slightly. She'd never done that before. Oh, well. It was just another opportunity to fail. Before long she'd have a cigarette in her face and say that the tooth fairy made her do it.

"I have a sponsor. He's a detective and he knows what I'm going through. He's helped lots of people before me." She pointed to the door. "He's out in the sitting area right now. I can go get him if you'd like to meet him."

"Not necessary," Ms. Johnson said. "I'm just glad you're working on it. If you decide you need support from somebody else, don't hesitate to call me." She glanced at Stump, then back to Jean. "I'm afraid we still have a problem on our hands. We have a zero tolerance policy for fighting and I can't ignore the damage that Neal and Phillip did to each other. I almost called the police, but I've already spoken to Phillip's parents. They apologized for what their son did. Up until now he has had a clean record and they'd like to keep it that way. I'm assuming you do, too?"

"Police? Just because my son was defending me? If anybody should go to jail, it's me. I'm the one who could have ruined both of their lives."

"What about you, Neal? What did you learn from all of this?"

"I dunno. I guess we all did something wrong. Mom, Phillip, me, the guys who pass that shit around."

Ms. Johnson raised a finger. "I don't allow that kind of language, Neal."

"Sorry, but I bet if it was your mom, you'd be pissed off, too."

"Your language is not earning you any points, Neal."

He folded his arms across his chest.

"I've decided both students will be suspended from school for a full week beginning right now. Neal may not return to class until next Friday. Is that understood?"

Less school? That was a bonus, not a punishment.

"You're lucky I'm not calling in the police. Do you understand that, Neal?"

"I don't really care and I doubt my mom does either. She's been in court, in the hospital, and in jail. I've found her passed out at home." His mom bit her lip. "She's lied to everybody, especially me. She'll just tell them what they want to hear like she always does. She never cares about other people. If she doesn't care, why should I?"

"He's right," Jean said. "I've done all of that, and more. But, this time, I'm really doing something about it and I really do care what happens to both of us." She scooted forward in her chair. "I'd appreciate it if you'd give us a chance to work this out, Ms. Johnson. I promise if you'll leave the police out if it, I'll prove to my son that I care and he should too. He doesn't need a police record because of what I did."

"Alright then. We've got an understanding." Ms. Johnson turned her head toward Stump. "Right, Neal?"

He shrugged. "Whatever."

CHAPTER 51

Life wasn't fair. Stump's mom was the one who lost control and embarrassed both of them, yet he was the one who got punished. Nine-thirty at night, and essentially imprisoned in his room, he bounced back and forth between the Internet and some boring homework. He saw the headlights coming. The white pick-up meant she'd been out with that same guy who brought him home from the principal's office—another damn alcoholic.

Theoretically they'd gone to a meeting, but that was probably just a cover. That dude was even more likely than the rest of her boyfriends to get her drunk and then pounce on her before disappearing into obscurity. Stump shook his head, vowing to himself that he was done saving her ass. A second later he smirked, knowing that he'd made that same stupid promise to himself before. That pissed him off, too. He couldn't even rely upon himself to be firm when she screwed up.

As the truck pulled up, Stump watched closely to see if his mom would stumble over the curb or if the guy would dump her on the lawn like had happened once before.

Both truck doors flung open. Stump raised one brow. At least this guy got out of the truck—probably to help her stagger to the door. But his mom gracefully slid out and appeared to be steady. He smirked as he noted a paper sack in her hand. They undoubtedly planned to send him to his room and finish off a bottle before slipping into her bedroom.

They joined hands and walked up to the front step. Surprisingly, there was no loose swaying, no boisterous talk. This dude must have taught her how to hide her drunkenness.

He moved into the living room and waited for the door to pop open and his mom to fall across the threshold. He'd have to put her in bed again. As he waited, he could hear them talking, but not loud enough to make out the words. Several minutes passed before he heard the truck start up at just about the same time that the door swung inward. "Hi, Honey," she said in a surprisingly steady voice. "I brought you a piece of peach pie."

Huh? Weird. She was sober. He heard the truck drive off. "Gee. Thanks."

"I'm glad you're up," she said as she removed her shoes. "Before you eat your pie, I have something I want to talk to you about."

At least she was safe. He shrugged and they moved toward the kitchen. Stump pulled his pie out of the bag while his mom got him a plate. "My friend, Myles, would like to take us to the high school football game on Friday night."

"Friday? Can't. My mommy said I'm grounded cause I got expelled. Remember?"

"I know I said that, but Myles convinced me I was too harsh, considering I played a major role in the matter."

"Major role?" he scoffed. "That's an understatement. You caused it all."

She shook her head. "I admit I started it, but that doesn't mean you had to get in a fight. We both screwed up. I've taken responsibility for my mistakes and you have to take responsibility for yours. You know that, right?"

"Not fair. I was just defending you."

"That's why I was thinking I might suspend your punishment a little early. So how about it? Myles would like us to go to the game together." She poured him a glass of milk.

"Doesn't this Myles dude have any friends?"

"Sure he does, but he would just like to get to know you better. That's all."

"That's gay."

"Now you're being ridiculous."

"He sounds lame to me."

"He's not lame. He's a nice guy who'll probably pay your way."

"Do I have to sit with you guys?"

Jean chuckled. "Would your world come to an end if you were seen in public with a couple of adults?"

"Yep. If one of them is my mommy."

"Okay, I get it," she said. "I'll tell you what. If you'll go along and be nice to him, you don't have to sit with us. C'mon. Give him a chance. You'll probably like him."

He gulped down a big chunk of peach, chewed it thoughtfully, then said, "Alright. I guess it would be okay. Richard might be there."

CHAPTER 52

By the time the football game rolled around Stump's mother and Myles had been seeing each other every evening for several weeks. Stump had to admit that Myles had a positive influence on his mom. Namely, she was both sober and happy; but the part of him where haunting memories resided knew that her previous alcohol-free periods had ended with ugly drama of one sort or another.

All of this made it impossible for Stump to overlook the fact that Myles was an alcoholic, too. Hell, they could fall off the wagon together. Another reason Stump was apprehensive about Myles was he kept asking nosy questions about school and Stump's hobbies. Then he'd grill Stump with detective-like, follow-up questions. There was no way the dude really gave a shit about algebra, video games or lifting weights. Overall Stump felt he couldn't trust either his mom or Myles.

It was a half-hour before kick-off when they parked and moved toward the stadium. Stump's mom and Myles held hands. "Your mom tells me you'd rather not sit with us old people," Myles said as they reached the ticket window. "I wouldn't either."

"I'm supposed to meet Richard."

"Ah, yes. The weightlifter. You guys have a good time. We'll just meet you back here after the game. In the meantime we will try to find seats near mid-field so you can find us if you want to."

"I'm not a little kid. I won't need you."

A few minutes later Myles bought the tickets. "Here's four bucks," he said to Stump as they approached the gate. "Buy a hot dog or something."

That was sorta cool. The kind of thing real dads did. "Thanks," he said, being certain not to use up all the words in his vocabulary. He turned to his mom. "I'm going to look for Richard."

"Are you sure you don't want to sit with us?"

"He's not a little kid, Honey. Remember?" Myles winked at Stump, who shook his head.

While the ancient ones headed for their seats, Stump scoped out the area behind the bleachers where he and Richard had agreed to meet.

All of the fans sat on the same side of the field with Palmdale fans on the near end and the visitors at the other end. Twin refreshment areas with black, white and green awnings flanked each end of the stadium. The restrooms were in between. As Stump headed for the other end of the stadium an announcer introduced the home team players.

Stump glanced around and saw familiar faces but no Richard. He walked slowly past the first refreshment area, which had lots of late-arrivers in line. Eventually he made his way past the restrooms and to the visitor's end where he noted their refreshment stand was less crowded. He peeked around the side of the bleachers and observed the players lining up for the opening kickoff. He figured he'd grab a drink with the money Myles gave him before resuming his hunt for Richard.

While he waited in a short line he glanced back toward the restrooms and saw Ms. Johnson and the cool biker he'd met a couple of times coming his way.

"How you doin,' kid?" the biker asked as he and Ms. Johnson settled behind Stump.

"I'm fine. I'm surprised you remember me."

Ms. Johnson smiled at the biker. "How do you know Neal?"

"He came to my meeting." The biker turned to Stump. "I remember you have a unique nickname, but I don't remember what it is?"

"It's Stump."

"Oh, yeah, the sturdy part of the tree." The motorcycle guy held out his hand. "Good to see you again."

The guy's rough knuckles reminded Stump that he'd said he crashed one of his motorcycles. Stump looked at Ms. Johnson. She didn't seem so threatening out here. "Are you Annie, Ms. Johnson?"

Both adults chuckled. "No, she's not Annie."

"Uh-oh. I hope I didn't say anything wrong."

Ms. Johnson chimed in "No, but I'm not Annie. I hope you're staying out of trouble."

"I'm trying to."

A couple minutes later, they reached the cash register and a loud whistle from the field-area signaled the opening kickoff. Just seconds after that the crowd on the Palmdale end of the stadium roared and stomped their feet on the bleachers.

"Touchdown!" the announcer decreed. The Bulldogs must have run the kickoff back all the way. Would have been nice to see. Stump wondered where Richard was. Maybe he'd decided not to come.

"I'll get that," Mac said to the cashier, referring to Stump's Pepsi. Cool. He'd still have his four bucks.

Just then, an eerie scream came from directly overhead. Stump looked skyward just as a falling male body crashed into the awning at the other side of the concession stand, collapsing the framework and ripping the fabric just before he careened into the trashcans and bounced onto the asphalt. The low groan was so gruesome Stump cringed. The fall was some thirty feet.

Additional shrieks instantly filled the evening air as Ms.

Johnson, Mac and Stump hurried toward the fallen body. Chaos ensued, both in the bleachers above and on the ground, as other people hurried over to see what happened.

"Somebody call 911," Ms. Johnson yelled out before Stump got his first look at the body.

Stump pointed to the end of the field. "There's an ambulance over there."

Other kids ran for it as Stump reached the body. Blood was already pooling underneath him. He moaned and barely moved, but at least he was alive. Stump got closer.

Oh, crap. It was Richard.

CHAPTER 53

The game stopped until another ambulance could fill in, but many fans, including Stump, his mom and Myles, lost interest and migrated toward the gates. For Stump there was a lot more to worry about than simply making an exit. He couldn't forget Richard's mangled face, his vacant eyes, or his God-awful moan.

"You going to be okay, Honey?" his mom asked. "We can stay with you or we can all go get a piece of pie. That might take your mind off it for a while."

"I don't feel like doing anything. You guys do whatever you want."

"I understand. We'll drop you off at the house and bring you back something a little later."

After his mom and Myles left, Stump's gut felt as if a horse had kicked him. If he hurried, he could get something for it at the drugstore. Although his mom didn't say anything about him no longer being grounded it was kinda, sorta, maybe, almost implied.

After jogging the first block, he slowed. If he was so damn good at picking out simple messages in license plates and phone numbers, why was he so frigging clueless when it came to reading people? Richard had said he liked to sit in the opposing fan's section and mouth off when something bad happened to their team. Messages didn't get any clearer than that. They were both dumb shits.

Another few run/walk cycles and Stump reached the edge of the drugstore parking lot. His stomach still hurt but at least he understood more completely why his mom drank so much—to numb her pain. That was exactly what he needed to do: to numb his pain. He'd try bourbon this time.

If he had had enough money, he would have asked somebody older to buy it for him, but as usual he was alone, left to his own devices.

Inside, he scoped out the place. The only cashier had a short line of customers. She'd be preoccupied. A white-coated guy in the pharmacy posed no threat. There were no other visible workers and only a few customers in the entire store.

He eased over to the magazine rack and glanced at the liquor displays that were just a few feet away. Most of the smaller bottles were on shelves next to the wall. He looked for a brownish-gold color. He thumbed through a motorcycle magazine and watched out of the corner of his eye until nobody was in sight. Finally the only customer in that area, a tall man with a baseball cap, walked toward the cash register.

Stump swiftly sidestepped a few feet, seized a bottle and hid it inside his magazine without anybody seeing him. He took another nonchalant look around. All clear. He stuffed the glass flask in his shorts. It was all remarkably simple.

His liquid gold safely stored, he traded the magazine for a cheaper one about bodybuilding and meandered innocently to the front, where he took a position in line behind the tall man with a baseball cap. As he waited his turn he noted an article about steroids. It reminded him of Richard. Then it was his turn. He plopped the magazine on the counter and paid for it with the money Myles gave him and stepped toward the exit. A quick push of the door and a couple baby steps later he'd made it outside—just as the man in the baseball hat and another guy whom he hadn't seen backed him against the wall between them and a soda machine. "Sorry, kid. You ain't going anywhere."

Stump gulped. His eyes shot glances up the street and back to the big guys. Running off was out of the question. They had him outflanked, cornered and nearly screwed to the wall. His chin dropped to his chest. "Back inside," the hatted one said.

The term *dumb shit* had become way too familiar lately.

Upstairs, in a manager's office there was a two-way mirror that overlooked the store. On the sidewall there were four monitors: two for the inside of the store, and one each for the front and back of the lot. Somehow it never occurred to Stump that somebody could be spying on customers from the manager's nest at night.

A dark-haired and pudgy uniformed lady of the security team held a cell phone as she pointed to a wooden chair in front of the monitors. "Sit over there." Stump did as requested, which left him more or less in the middle of the room with his back to her. She stepped around from behind with her phone to her ear. "Give me officer Benoin. It's Betsy McCracken—from the drug store, again."

The police? That's all Stump needed. One of the monitors flickered and a recorded image of Stump, near the magazines, came on. The lady pushed a button on a remote and the image began to move. Stump curled a lip of frustration as he watched himself snag a bottle of booze and ultimately work his way outside.

"Don't you guys ever learn?" the lady quizzed, as if Stump had been there before.

What could he say? Blame it on Richard? He'd just get lectured about how that's no excuse for what he did. The video started over, apparently on a loop.

"Officer Benoin," she said into her cell. "Betsy McCracken here. I've got another one." It was like something right off a TV show. *Bad boy. Bad boy. Whatcha gonna do?* Only this time Stump was the stupid one.

"Okay, see you in fifteen." She hung up and returned her attention to Stump. "What's your name?"

"Neal Randolph," Stump said, hanging his head.

"How old are you, Mr. Randolph?"

He scuffed his nearly worn out tennis shoes across the floor. "Thirteen."

She clicked her tongue. "Thirteen, huh? You young guys are all the same. Out to impress your buddies. Don't think about the consequences. Don't care who you hurt, just so long as you get your thrills. We'll see if your friends are still impressed when you get hauled out of here in handcuffs."

He thought about telling her that he was alone, but that wouldn't make any difference. The underlying message was still the same. He screwed up.

"Stealing anything is bad enough, but stealing liquor at your age is even more serious. I don't know where your parents are but you can take my word for one thing. We're all going to make an example out of you."

CHAPTER 54

Stump had been in the police building when his mom was in trouble, but the giant double-hung doors were much more intimidating when he was the one who was handcuffed.

"Over there," a deputy said, while nudging him toward a dirty-looking wooden table.

"I'd like to call my mom," Stump said, noting the irony. Here he was pretending to be a big shot, but the first person he wanted to call was his mommy.

"In a minute," the deputy said. "Hold out your right hand, palm up." Stump did as he was told and the deputy grabbed his index finger. "Roll it across the inkpad."

"Huh?"

The deputy used both hands to guide Stump's finger onto the pad, dousing it in ink. Then he rolled the finger over a precise spot on a thick official fingerprint card. "Next finger," he said, seizing the middle finger. Under other conditions the procedure might have been interesting, but not at this moment. He and the deputy quickly found a rhythm as they progressed through the rest of his fingers.

"Here," the deputy said handing Stump a quart-sized container of wipes. "After you clean up, the phone is on the desk behind you."

A little later Stump was locked in a small room with a single table and four folding chairs. The only window was in the door to the hallway. If he were to run away, where would he go? They already knew who he was and where he lived. All he could do for now was wait and hope that his mom would cut him a break—just like he did for her all the times when she was in trouble. He scoffed. Fat chance. At least he didn't have to worry about an angry dad who'd want to kick his ass.

Ten minutes passed, then twenty. Finally, just after ten, a beefy desk cop, who looked as if he'd just gotten out of college, popped his head in the room. "Your mom and dad are here," he said in a stern, business-like monotone.

Dad?

The cop-kid stepped aside so Myles and Stump's mom could get into the little room. Her face looked as rigid as the dead presidents on Mount Rushmore. "Hi, Mom. Sorry."

She raised a hand like she wanted to hit him, but didn't swing. "What the hell's the matter with you?"

Myles lightly clasped her elbow. "Why don't we have a seat until we find out what happened?"

Stump's mom sat next to him. "What made you do such a stupid thing?"

"You both do the same thing."

"We sure as hell don't steal things that don't belong to us."

"Well maybe if I had a dad, he'd give me an allowance and I wouldn't have to steal things either."

"This isn't about an allowance or even stealing. It's about responsibility. I thought if we took you to that game you'd be grateful, but you don't appreciate anything."

Myles shifted. "If you guys don't mind me butting in, I think we'd all be better off if we find out what's up before we yell at each other."

"That's easy for you to say," she snapped. "You aren't the one who has to get an attorney." To Stump, "How am I supposed to pay for that? Huh? Did you even bother to think of that?"

"You can just get one of your friends to do it for free, like you always do."

She shook her head and raised her voice. "I can't afford to ask for more favors. I'm already in too damn much trouble."

"Calm down," Myles insisted. "You've got the cart in front of the horse. Let's just see how things play out."

At least now they were talking about his mom and not him. He looked straight ahead for what seemed like fifteen minutes while his mom ranted and Myles tried to be supportive. Then the cop who arrested Stump joined the room. "I'm Officer Benoin," he said. "You folks Neal's parents?"

Myles rose and extended a hand. "I'm Myles Cooper. Detective. LAPD. Friend of the family." He swept his arm toward Stump's mom. "This is Ms. Randolph."

Benoin shook hands with both Myles and Stump's mom before taking a seat at the head of the table. "First, I want you all to know that if things go as expected, you'll all get out of here tonight."

Myles nodded as if to say, "See. I told you so."

"A few weeks ago, the drugstore took inventory and discovered they were missing a lot of items, including some alcohol. They set up a security system, and decided to make an example of whoever was the first person they busted. That person turned out to be Neal. I tried to talk them out of pressing charges, but the manager's mind was made up."

"What will happen to him?" Jean asked.

"If the drugstore won't back down, he'll have to attend a hearing and either admit or deny the charges. If he admits them, the procedure is fairly swift. There will be a disposition hearing and a judge will impose some penalty. In the worst case he will be sent to juvenile hall, but probation is more likely."

Stump's mom shook her head and sighed. "Probation? Juvenile hall? I can't believe this."

"If Neal wants to deny the charges," Benoin continued, "there will be a pretrial hearing and other formal legal proceedings will follow."

"Not going to do that," Stump said. "That would be lying."

Myles nodded.

"You can decide what to do on Monday morning at the hearing, but for now, let's just get you folks out of here."

CHAPTER 55

"It's him," Miranda said to Don. She tilted the phone so that he could listen in. "Hi, Sweets," she said, trying not to sound too lovey-dovey. "I'm sorry about our last meeting. I hope we can put it behind us."

"I'd like that, too. I guess everybody has to have their little quarrels sooner or later."

"I'm just glad it's over. We were both awfully tired from too much celebrating."

Mac chuckled. *"Too much celebrating? Impossible."*

"Well, we sure tested the limits, anyway. I hope I'm going to see you today?"

"Rachel's getting ready for work now, but I can come right after that. We visited her attorney."

"I hope it's good news?"

"The good news is that the bad news isn't as bad as it first sounds. So don't get shook up when I tell you that part."

Don rolled his eyes. "Do you have access to the money or not?" Miranda asked.

"This estate stuff doesn't work like we thought. Rachel doesn't get a big check or anything like that."

"But, we get the money somehow, don't we?"

"Not yet. Most of it is tied up in CDs, mutual funds, bonds. Shit like that."

"Huh? Is that the bad news or the good news?"

"It's just a starting point. After we got married, Rachel became the beneficiary of the trust. She can sell off the investments and take the money out if she wants to but when she does that, it gets taxed, so people in her situation tend to leave most of the money in there and buy big things like houses and cars in the trust's name."

"But we don't care about all that legal gibberish. We just need to know if we can get what we need."

"We can't just reach in a cash register and grab whatever we want. There are certain limits and procedures."

"How much can we get right now?"

"Not very much 'cause I'm not a beneficiary. We're going to set up a joint checking account. Maybe put fifty K in it. I can probably get to some of it. Kinda like an allowance."

Don bolted to his feet and kicked his flimsy chair over, while a previous discussion slipped into Miranda's mind. "Would you get it all after she's gone?"

Don perked up and tapped his ear, indicating he wanted to listen again.

"Great minds think alike," Mac said. *"I was wondering that too. That Pappy dude was pretty smart. He set it up so that if Rachel croaks, the money goes to her kids. I think that makes them the next beneficiaries or something like that."*

Miranda's pulse surged. "Please tell me she didn't say anything about being pregnant 'cause—"

"Don't worry about it. We covered that a long time ago. It's all under wraps for now. She hasn't even told Granny."

"Okay then, what if she doesn't have any kids when she dies?" Miranda said quickly, *"It goes to you. Right?"*

"Now, calm down. I told you this works out."

Miranda breathed heavily into the phone. "I hope so, 'cause I haven't heard any good news yet."

"It's not as easy as you want it to be, that's all. If she dies, and doesn't have any kids, and if we leave things as they are now, then it all goes back to Granny."

"For crying out loud," Miranda bellowed, "that's even worse."

"I know. But cool your cookies for a minute while I finish the story."

"Pleeeeze," she said rolling her anxious eyes while Don mouthed the word "dumbass."

"I was just as bummed out as you are. Then the attorney asked me to leave the room so that he could talk to Rachel in private. It was torture, sitting in his lobby pretending to read a magazine while they were discussing all that money."

"I feel the same way. Would you please tell me the good part before I come through the line and strangle you?"

"Turns out she has the option to change the subsequent beneficiary from Granny to anybody she wants."

Don poked Miranda gently in the ribs. She smiled and pushed his hand aside. "Okay," she said to Mac. "That's better."

"It was beautiful. Rachel told the attorney that Granny said the money was for both her and me."

Miranda grinned at Don. "I'm beginning to like this again," she said.

"I told you. They decided that if anything happens to Rachel, I would automatically get half of the trust and her kids would get the other half. Then I'd be their guardian until they're old enough to manage their share by themselves."

"But, there won't be any kids."

"Yeah, I know, and you're going to love this part. If that happens, I get that half too."

Miranda squealed and blew out a deep breath. "I love that old woman," she said, while Don flopped backwards onto the bed and kicked his feet in the air.

"If it wasn't for Granny saying the money was for both Rachel and me, I don't know what Rachel would have done."

"Perfect," Miranda said, while Don held two thumps up.

"Not quite. There are still two hurdles."

"Hurdles? I hate hurdles."

"First, Rachel can change her mind anytime she wants to. Even after everything is finalized."

"That doesn't seem right. Once she gives the money to you, she shouldn't be allowed to take it back. She'd always have you by the balls. You couldn't make a move without her threatening to remove your name."

"No shit," Mac said. *"The other thing is the attorney has to draw up some papers, making me the co-beneficiary or something like that. Nothing is official until Rachel signs it."*

"When's that?

"Monday. Then it's official."

"So all we have to do is make sure Rachel signs that paper on Monday, then you can get to the trust?"

"Not right away, but I'd be next in line, instead of it going back to Granny."

"Wow. You've gotta kiss Rachel's ass this whole weekend. Take her places. Tell her you love her. Do anything she wants." Don pretended to spit.

"Nothing to it," Mac said. *"Compared to what we've been through, that should be easy beans. Now all we gotta do is hope she doesn't have a period. That could screw up everything."*

"Don't even think like that. You just concentrate on keeping her calm and happy until those papers are signed."

"Alright. Now, I did my part. When can I come over? I need you."

"Just give me 45 minutes to get a few things cleaned up."

Miranda no more than tapped the off button when Don broke in. "I've always loved my brother."

She playfully slapped his arm. "You're a lying sack of shit."

"Maybe so, but I'm a rich sack of shit."

Miranda wrapped her arms around him. They hugged and kissed and hugged again before she pulled back slightly. "You do realize I have to go be with him for a while?"

Don hesitated and then shrugged. "I guess he deserves a reward after putting up with that cow."

She kissed him again. "Thank you for making all this possible, Donnie," she whispered." I know this hasn't been easy for either of us, but I'm feeling way better now that I know there's enough money for everybody."

Don stroked her hair with a tenderness he hadn't shown for ages. "But you forgot one thing," he said.

"Oh, yeah? What's that?" Miranda asked, her eyes half-closed.

"My brother said he can only get to fifty grand at a time, and that cow ain't gonna let him pull that off more than once before she changes the rules. If you really want to take care of Mickey we've got to kill her. Then Mac gets control of the entire trust and we can grab it all at once."

Miranda's face went pale and she covered her mouth. "Oh my God, Donnie, I was so excited I didn't put that together."

Don looked into her eyes. "It's taken us four months to get this far. I think we should go through with it, for Mickey's sake."

Just then her burner rang again. The caller's number was unfamiliar.

CHAPTER 56

"Before he cheats..."

Miranda scoffed. Usually when she was alone in her SUV she welcomed the poignant lyrics of Ms. Underwood's songs, but not this time. She turned the music off. If only her situation were that simple.

Neither Don nor Mac would go along with dragging this mess out. That meant the whole scam pretty much boiled down to an "all or nothing" situation. If she stopped the con right now, she'd lose the money she gave the gynecologist and Mickey would be doomed to spend his remaining days in crowded and substandard government facilities—sometimes doped up—and always with little hope of ever getting better. That would amount to her passing a death sentence on her own brother. She certainly couldn't pull that trigger.

The only other option wasn't much better: Rachel had to be killed so that the entire trust would revert to Mac. That would take care of Mickey, but Rachel didn't deserve to die any more than Mickey did.

It would all be so much easier if she didn't inject her feelings into everything and everybody. When she approached it without the jumbled emotions, she agreed with Don: The least bad choice was to eliminate Rachel. But even if she were to go along with such a repulsive idea, Mac would have to be in on it. How in the world was she going to get him to kill the mother of his imaginary child?

Then, yesterday, just when she thought things couldn't get any more complicated, she'd gotten an unexpected call from Dr. Gravely. He wanted to see her first thing this morning. It was not yet seven-thirty when she met him in his office.

"I don't have much time," he said, without saying hello or sitting down, "so where are we?"

"Well," she said, fussing with a strand of hair. "The trust is real but everything got complica—"

"Don't care. I want the rest of the money you owe me and I want it within forty-eight hours."

Her heart rate jumped. "But I thought the money I gave you was enough."

"Enough to buy you a little time, that's all. Now the time is up and I want the rest."

"But we don't have it and we don't have access to the account numbers yet."

"Your problem, not mine. You shorted me last time. Now I want what you owe me."

"But—"

"But nothing." He looked at her over his clipboard. "Cops love conspiracies, you know. Gets them lots of headlines."

"But, you'd be in the middle of it, too."

"Not really," he said, adjusting his stethoscope. "Since you paid me with cash, there's no evidence of our previous arrangement. Ask yourself who those nice police officers would believe: an upright doctor in the community, such as myself, or a drifter, a con man and a gold-digger such as yourself who's never had her own source of income?" He paused and glared at her. "I've done a little checking on my own. You're nothing but a high-priced whore." Then he gracefully spun around and disappeared like a ghost in the wind.

*   *   *

The only good thing to come out of Miranda's ultra-brief encounter with Dr. Gravely was it left her enough time to get back to the motel to advise Don of the newest blackmail before hooking up with Mac for one of their routine morning rendezvous.

Don was watching the *Godfather* movie on Pay-Per-View when she barged in. He hit the pause button. "You're back. What's up?"

He listened carefully as Miranda fought back tears and apprised him of Gravely's demand. Eventually, she said, "I can't take this anymore, Donnie. Maybe we should just move across the country while we still can?"

"We can't give up just because we hit a couple bumps in the road."

"Bumps in the road?" she said, nearly crying. "More like giant craters. We could all get arrested before we get any of the money."

"Calm down. That isn't helping anything. You just worry about Mac, like we talked about. Find out if he's hot or cold about Rachel. If you can convince him that she has got to go away, then all we have to worry about is the doctor, and I can take care of him."

"Even if Mac should agree about Rachel, how are you going to get the doctor to back off? If he doesn't get his money he's going to turn us all in."

"He's not going to the cops as long as he still thinks he's going to get his share." Don pointed his jaw toward the frozen image of the godfather on his TV. "In a worst case scenario, we just gotta make him an offer he can't refuse."

CHAPTER 57

"**B**ad news, Sweets," Miranda said after her initial embrace with Mac.

"You're not kicking me to the curb again, are you?" he asked, smiling.

"Rachel's gynecologist called me last night and I had to go see him this morning. He wants twenty thousand more."

"You want me to go talk with him? Maybe I can talk some sense into him."

That was basically what Don had said, only Don's language was more colorful and his threat more menacing. "It won't do any good. Since I got him a big chunk of money last time, he thinks I can do it again. I was hoping you could get to Rachel's accounts a little sooner than we talked about."

"Not a good idea. I think we'd better hang in there for just a little while and see if there's some way we can make one big hit and then get the hell out of California."

"But he said he'd turn us in."

Mac placed his hands on her waist. "Relax. He has to say that, but I don't buy it. He wouldn't have gone along with this whole idea in the first place if he didn't need a big payday just as badly as you do."

Once again Mac's thoughts ran down parallel tracks to Don's. If they both thought that way, maybe she should go along with them. She should stay focused and find out what Mac thought about wiping out Rachel. "Maybe you're right," she said. "But there's something else that's even more troubling."

"Oh yeah, like what?"

"When you were telling me about the trust, you said there are only two ways to get to the bulk of it. One way is to get Rachel to change the conditions, so you can both get to the whole thing or at least a lot of it anytime you want to."

Mac shook his head. "She's too smart to fall for that."

"But that only leaves one other way," she said, tapping her fingers nervously. "You know what that is, don't you?"

"Sure. It's obvious."

"But we'd have to get rid of her."

"Why are you acting so surprised? I thought you understood that. We're going to have to eliminate her so that I'm in charge. Then I can get us all the money we want."

Miranda couldn't believe her ears. Mac was so casual it was as if they were discussing a minor chore. "Are you sure you're okay with it, 'cause it scares the hell out of me?"

Mac grabbed her shoulders and brought her to him. "Look. I've never seen anybody as devoted to a brother as you are. His situation is dire. If we can't help him, who can? The way I see it, it's a numbers issue. Either take care of one person or take care of all three of us. Mickey, you and me."

Miranda's skin tingled. She had underestimated Mac's commitment to her and Mickey. Her mind raced for excuses to a problem she didn't really want to solve. She was the only one who wasn't completely on board with killing Rachel. "But how would we do it?"

"We still have plenty of time before Rachel gets out of work. Why don't we go see Mickey and talk about it along the way?"

$$* \quad * \quad *$$

Miranda was apprehensive about taking the motorcycle to see Mickey, but Mac insisted that her brother would love a ride. Now that they were at the front curb of The Broadhouse, she was both more nervous and more excited than before.

Mickey wore both his sunglasses and a baseball hat. "Here ya go, Mick. Try this on," Mac said as he casually handed Mickey the rider's helmet. "We have to stay safe."

If one picture is worth a thousand words, then one grin was worth a thousand pictures. Miranda grabbed her cell and snagged a video as her special brother took the helmet and tried to figure out what to do with his baseball hat. "No problem," Mac said. "I think we can wear them both." He turned Mickey's baseball cap around. "That ought to do it."

Miranda nearly laughed out loud as Mickey pulled his helmet over his hat. Mac double-checked the job and then helped Mickey with his chinstrap, thereby framing that contagious smile Miranda had always loved.

"Thank you, Mac," Mickey said with his hands, checking out the ear holes.

"Alright, now. I gotta get on first," Mac said while Mickey paid very close attention. "Then you climb on right behind me. Okay?"

Mickey hesitated then, nodded excitedly.

Mac swung his foot over Annie's seat and slid forward noticeably more than he usually would. "Okay, buddy. It's your turn."

As Mickey grabbed hold of Mac's shoulder, Miranda felt like a proud mother at the Olympics who was watching her child get ready to perform for the entire world. It was both terrifying and thrilling.

Mickey held Mac tightly as he lifted his leg and rested it on the seat and in front of the roll bar. Then he paused. It was obvious he was having trouble figuring out how to get up on top.

Still grinning, Miranda rested her hands on Mickey's shoulders. "Come back down, Honey. I'll hold you. Then, you can put your foot on here," she said, pointing to the footpeg. "Then, just step up and over like it is a horse."

"Okay, Miranda."

It took three tries but Mickey figured it out and eventually took his place in the bitch seat where he grinned proudly at Miranda. He looked like a happy emperor with a goofy crown. Miranda raised her cell. Click, click, click.

Minutes later, Mac escorted his special rider all around the parking lot in big loops. Mickey ignored Mac's coaching about hanging on to his belt loops and opted instead to wrap his arms all the way around Mac like he might get away.

Each time they made their loop they came back in front of Miranda, who enjoyed the experience more than anybody. Mickey couldn't get enough of the ride and Miranda couldn't get enough of Mickey's smile. A steady drip of happy tears chased each other down her cheeks as she realized she'd done the right thing by moving Mickey into The Broadhouse.

That single simple message couldn't have been any clearer than right near the end when she and Mac were about to head home. Mickey hugged them both, then, "I love you, Mac."

Miranda knew love, too.

*　*　*

Two hours later they returned to Miranda's for a little private time before Mac had to rejoin Rachel. Conflicted, Miranda put her coat away while Mac turned on the TV. "Mickey was happier than I've ever seen him," she said.

Mac pulled her to him. "In some ways he's the luckiest guy in the world to have somebody who loves him so much."

She let Mac draw her in. "I get your point," she said. "There's no real way for both Rachel and Mickey to live a full life, but I hate to think of what that means for Rachel."

"That's why I have to be with you on the platform,"

Mac said, referring to the viewing area over The Devil's Punchbowl. "If we're going to push her over, we have to make sure it's quick and nothing goes wrong."

"I don't like that, Sweets," she said, slipping her hand around his waist and partway down the back of his jeans. "You're the first person the cops will look at. You have to have a perfect alibi." She nudged him toward the bedroom.

Mac turned to his side, leaving her with the opportunity she wanted. She instantly bent down and lunged with all her force at his knees. He grunted and buckled over. His head bounced off the wall and he fell to his back. "What the hell was that all about?" he snapped.

"I told you I could do it," she said, hands on her hips. "It's all about the element of surprise. Like at the World Trade Center. An airplane can knock over a tall building if it hits it just right."

Mac rose, rubbing the back of his head. He untucked his shirt, lifted the shirttail above his belt, and revealed a swollen welt. "Okay. I guess you proved your point."

"If we decide to kill Rachel, you don't have to be there," she said, gently touching his reddened area. "I can handle her. I promise. And this way you can concentrate on your alibi."

He snapped his fingers. "Come to think of it, I might need a large screwdriver, but mine aren't stout enough. Do you have any?"

"My ex left some big ones out in the garage. You can look at them before you leave."

He pointed at the TV. "Hey, look at that." He turned up the volume as a young female reporter addressed the camera.

"Channel Five News has just learned that local doctor, Gregory Gravely, was found dead outside his office about ninety minutes ago. A police spokesman said it appears the doctor was strangled. Police are asking anybody with information about the murder to come forward. Now back to our programming."

"Holy shit," Mac said as he hit the mute button. "It looks like our other problem just got solved."

Miranda's flesh grew a complete gaggle of goose bumps. She knew exactly who did it and if she was correct she and her lovers had just passed the point of no return. Two deaths were no worse than one. Like it or not, Rachel was next.

CHAPTER 58

During the next few days, Lydia drove Jean to her office and Gerry brought her home. One morning, Jean made a pot of coffee as usual before Frederic Gann, one of the partners, asked to see her.

"I'm sorry to tell you this," he said, as soon as she sat down, "but the partners have decided we're going to have to let you go."

Jean bowed her head. It wasn't particularly a surprise, but that didn't blunt the disappointment. "If it's because of my drinking—"

"It's not about any particular incident," he said, shaking his head. "We all know that nobody's perfect. It's more about the cumulative effect of several things."

"But I really have quit. I've got witnesses."

"We've had to cover for you too many times. When our lawyers are in court working on your case they can't be working on the cases that bring money into the firm."

Her fingers shook. "Can't you just put me on probation or something? I really need this job, Mr. Gann."

"Sorry, Jean, but when your personal problems endanger our relationship with our biggest client, we have to make a decision. Clifford says he's innocent so this could drag out a while."

"That's ridiculous. I was raped. I can show you hospital records."

"It's not just that. It would be too awkward to have you both here at the same time—it's a conflict of interest."

"But he might be going to jail. Then he may not have enough money to pay you."

"You'd think so, but his sales are actually up. Being in the news is like getting free advertising. I shouldn't tell you this, but he actually wants to drag out the case as long as he can. If it does end up in court, he thinks all the public support will work in his favor."

"But he can't win. There are medical records and everything."

"Stranger things have happened and that's not the point right now."

"Oh my God," she said. "It isn't right to fire somebody because she got raped. That's blaming the victim and rewarding the rapist."

"I'm sorry, Jean, but he's forcing our hand. It's either him or you and he's a huge client. You can see that, can't you?"

"And I'm just a lowly receptionist, right? This isn't fair. I work harder than anybody."

"The partners have agreed to give you two months' salary as a severance package and if anybody should call for a reference we'll restrict our comments to how you did at the office and leave your personal problems out of it."

"Isn't there anything I say to change your minds, Mr. Gann? I need this job."

"Sorry."

*   *   *

That evening after the usual AA meeting, Jean and Myles went out for ice cream. Jean stabbed at her sundae with her spoon. She'd spent the afternoon crying. "Sorry, I'm just not in the mood for ice cream—or much of anything."

"I understand. I just wanted you to have a chance to talk things out."

"Thanks for being so sympathetic, Myles. You're the only person who has any faith in me."

"You made me incredibly proud, you know?"

"Proud of me? Are you nuts? I've shamed my son. I can't control him and I got fired. How can anybody be proud of a record like that?"

"You turned to ice cream this time, instead of alcohol," he said, smiling. "That's the underlying bonus, here. You're a big winner. As long as you make choices like that, everything else will get better. Trust me. I've seen this type of fork in the road many times. And you took the right one."

"Too much ice cream will just make me fat," she said, fishing for a little more support. "Then you'll probably dump me."

"No way. I love you more now than ever. And I don't care about your weight. That's superficial. It's what's inside you that counts. That's where you shine. You have true integrity. True character. I love that about you."

She dragged a tiny dip of chocolate off the top of her ice cream. "I damn near bought some cigarettes, you know."

"But you didn't. To tell you the truth, I'm glad this happened."

"Glad I got fired? That doesn't sound like you."

"You bet. You needed a fresh start." He dug his spoon into his bowl.

She stared in his eyes. "You mean someplace where I don't have a reputation."

"Stop being so hard on yourself. I thought you needed someplace where the cards aren't stacked against you."

"Why didn't you say anything before now?"

"I figured you'd rather work it out on your own."

"Lydia was always good to me."

He raised his spoon. "But the others are petty."

She tilted her head. "Maybe you're right. But it's not going to be easy to find something else in this economy, especially without a driver's license."

"It will all work out. You might even enjoy taking a couple weeks off before looking for a job."

"I can't afford that."

"You can get unemployment insurance and if that isn't enough, I'll loan you some money to help you get by."

"I can't take money from you. Wouldn't be right. I don't think I want unemployment either. I should be able to find something."

"It's up to you. Just think it over. You know I'll support you no matter what you decide."

"Me, too," she said, scooping up a peanut.

"You too, what?"

"Earlier you said you love me more than ever. I love you more than ever, too."

Myles grinned. "See. We've both got a lot going for us. Now that we have that straightened out, there's something else I want to ask you about. How's Stump doing lately?"

She sighed. "He still doesn't believe that I've quit drinking. He's disrespectful. Doesn't care about much of anything, not even his shoplifting case. That scares me. He said when he goes back for his hearing, he's just going to lie his way out of it, like I've done."

Myles scoffed. "I think he's just trying to shock you. Are you open to a weird idea?"

"I dunno. What is it?"

"There is an air-show near L.A. tomorrow. I'd like to take him—just him and me."

"What? How can I possibly rationalize that after grounding him?"

"I know how you feel, but I have an idea that might help him get back on track."

"What is it?"

He hesitated. "I'd rather not say right now. I'd just like you to trust me."

"I don't know. It doesn't seem right to send mixed signals."

"We both know he's not a criminal. Do you remember in the

meeting when he said he wouldn't lie? He's just a confused kid, who loves his mom so much that he'll even self-destruct to prove it. I'd really like a chance to talk with him—man to man—not like a kid."

"Well, he has been asking a lot of questions about his biological father lately."

"There ya go. See what I mean. He's thinking about the adult world. Speaking of his dad, would it hurt you to tell him who the guy is?"

Jean looked at her bowl. The melted ice cream looked like chocolate-covered potato soup. "I don't want to talk about him," she said.

CHAPTER 59

"Neal Joseph Randolph."

Stump nearly bolted to the front of the room.

The grey-haired judge looked up from his file. "Are you Mr. Randolph?"

"Yes, sir," Stump said anxiously.

"Looks like you have a birthday next month. How old will you be?"

"Fourteen, Your Honor."

"I see. Are your parents here?"

Stump pointed behind him. "My mom is right back there."

"Ma'am, would you mind joining your son?"

Jean did as requested. "Well, Mr. Randolph, you've been charged with shoplifting alcohol. Is that correct?"

"Yes, sir. My friend almost died and I made a dumb mistake."

"I see. It's a good thing you weren't near a school. That would make your problems even worse. Do you admit to or deny the charges?"

Stump nearly interrupted, "I admit it. I stole it, sir. And I'm sorry."

Jean's head turned. She raised her eyebrows.

"Do you understand," the judge said to Stump's mom, "that your son's answer can prevent him from employing certain other legal defenses that might be available to him?"

Stump stood motionless as his mom turned toward Myles, who nodded. She turned back to the judge. "We understand."

"You'll both have to come before me again for sentencing. Do you realize there's a very real chance that Neal will be sent to juvenile hall?"

She hesitated. Then, "Yes, sir, I understand," she said through trembling lips.

"Can you be back here on Wednesday at one-thirty?"

"Yes. I'm unemployed."

"Let the record show that we'll hold a disposition hearing at one-thirty p.m. this Wednesday afternoon." He gently tapped his gavel on his desk.

CHAPTER 60

Friday night, after their AA meeting, Myles and Jean went to his apartment. While he poured pink lemonade, Jean rested her hand on his upper arm. "A quiet evening on the couch will be a nice change of pace."

He smiled. "I can't believe I got tired of both pie and ice cream." He slid the pitcher back into the fridge. "Before we settle in, can we talk about Stump?"

"I thought we were going to talk about my job options."

"We can do that too, but I've been meaning to get to this other thing, if it's okay."

"Did he do something else wrong again, because if he did—"

He waved her off. "Last week when we went to the air show, we talked about family and honesty with our loved ones."

"Oh. He and I are not always tactful, but we do seem to get the cards on the table."

"Yeah. Well. That's the point. He asked me to talk to you about his father."

She pursed her lips. "That again. I just wish he'd forget about it."

"Not likely, Jean. He's at an age where you can't distract him and hope he forgets the topic. He'll just come back to it later."

"No kidding. He's like a boomerang."

"He's doing it for you. He thinks the guy might be able to

kick in some money and make things better for the both of you. That's pretty unselfish for a kid his age."

Jean smiled. "Sometimes I forget that about him." She sipped at her lemonade. "I've considered it, but I'm stuck. I can't tell him the truth and I won't lie to him."

"What could possibly be so troubling? He's already proved he can accept just about anything. He knows about unplanned pregnancies, things like that. Is the father somebody he knows?"

"No. I told him I don't know who it is and that's the truth."

"Oh I see. A college prank? Did you pass out or something? It just can't be that bad."

She bit her upper lip and rubbed her neck. Then, "Look, I didn't want to tell you either because you're in law enforcement. But I did something very bad. Illegal even. I'm not proud of it, and I don't want to lose you."

"Is that it? You can tell me anything. I promise not to tell anybody. You're a good mother now, and that's all that matters."

Jean nervously sipped at her lemonade, turned the glass around and sipped at the other side. "This would be much easier if I simply got knocked up. Stump would accept that, but it's worse. Back in Wisconsin, when I was nineteen I moved into my first apartment building. The neighbor was a single woman, a little younger than me, who already had a cute little baby boy." Jean's hands began to shake. She looked in Myles eyes. "This is not easy. I'm so ashamed."

"It's okay. Go on."

A couple deep breaths later, "She had quite a few 'boyfriends,' if you know what I mean. They drank a lot and smoked marijuana. But the worst part was she ignored her baby. The little guy cried and cried, sometimes for hours without her doing anything about it. One night, after he was asleep, I heard her door close and looked through my peephole. She snuck off with two guys somewhere, probably to a bar. I was concerned so I paid attention. They came back drunk a couple hours later. I almost called the cops, but I couldn't be sure what all happened."

"So the little guy was Stump?"

Jean shook her head and sipped lightly at her drink. "The next day I told her if she ever had to do that again, I would watch her baby. After that, I watched him a few times before it became a pattern. I watched him nearly every night while she went out and had her fun. That's when I found out she was pregnant again."

"Uh-oh. I think I see where this is going."

"She couldn't handle one baby, Myles. How was she going to handle two?" Myles rubbed his chin, but said nothing. "We had a heart-to-heart," Jean went on. "She told me how hard it was to be a mom. I must have scoffed because she asked me if I thought I could do any better. Without even thinking I said I could do better than she was doing. She must have hoped that was what I was going to say, because she asked me if I was just a big talker."

"What did you say?"

"She told me I could have the new baby, if I'd make a deal with her. I was stunned that she'd even think of such a thing. It was as if she was tired of a TV program and just wanted to change the channel."

"Did you tell her that?"

"I tried to talk her into giving it up, but she said she had to keep it—not because she'd love it, mind you—but because it would enable her to get more money from the government." Jean ran her finger around the rim of her glass and sighed. Her eyes filled with tears. "It was either her or me. One of us was going to be its mother. If I didn't take that baby, it was going to be neglected."

"Wow," Myles said standing up to get her a tissue. "No wonder you kept it quiet."

She sniffled. "I knew I only wanted one child, but I was young, and just as naïve as she was."

"So you agreed to take the baby?"

"I had to. She couldn't take care of one baby; how was she going to take care of two?"

"How'd you explain it to your family?"

"I said I was pregnant. But if I had stayed there, they would have seen that I never got bigger. Several months later, I lied again and said I was moving away." Jean lowered her head. "I didn't want to lie to them but I had to. They all hated me for leaving and having my baby on my own."

"But that's not what you really did?"

"No. I stayed in that apartment and watched my neighbor get bigger and bigger until she had the baby—my precious Neal. He lived with me in my apartment until she got all her papers in order and her first check came in. Then we really did leave. I took him to Michigan. I waited until he was walking before I went back home. That's when my sister came up with his nickname. Nobody knew any different. Not even her. I've never told anybody else."

Myles tweaked his head sideways. "What about medical records and that other woman? Didn't she need to have the baby around to carry on her scheme?"

"I don't know about her. I didn't care. Didn't tell her where I went either. I just got out of there to protect that baby, my baby, and I never looked back."

"What about the medical records and birth certificates and the like?"

"It wasn't a problem. I told a new doctor that I just came to the U.S. from England and didn't have any records in this country yet."

Myles rose, walked to the kitchen and poured out his glass. "This is more serious than I thought. We're talking big crimes here, like conspiracy. Kidnapping. Fraud. Child endangerment. And I don't know what else a DA might dream up."

Jean gasped. "But it wasn't kidnapping or endangerment because the mom wanted it that way—and Stump was safer with me than he was with her."

Myles shook his head. "I'm sure that's what you thought at the time, but that didn't mean it was okay to take him away. What if that mother had a change of heart? What if some other family could have given him a better situation? Did you think of those things?"

"I just wanted to protect that baby. Nobody would love him more than me, Myles. I had to keep it a secret. It's also why I drank so much in the beginning. To hide from what I did."

"It's definitely conspiracy, and defrauding the government to get the financial aid."

Jean lowered her head into her hands and wept. "Are you going to turn me in?"

Myles hesitated, then rose. "Well, I can't just overlook it. That would be wrong and you're always a stickler for doing the right thing."

"Oh my God, Myles." she said, crying. "What are you going to do?"

"The only thing that makes sense. I'm going to blackmail you."

"Blackmail? What do you mean? I don't have anything I can give you."

"Oh, yes, you do." He walked toward his bedroom. "You stay right here."

"Are you going to turn me in or not? I gotta know."

"You'll see. Just wait a minute. I'll be right back."

Jean shivered, her lip quivered and tears rolled down her cheeks. How could she expect a cop to keep a secret like that?

Myles returned. "Did you know that spouses can't be forced to testify against each other?"

She looked up, tears flowing down her cheeks.

He knelt and held out an engagement ring. "I was planning on doing this anyway, but as wrong as your deed was in the law's eyes, it was so incredibly noble and loving, it just confirms everything I've come to think about you. If you'll marry me I'll keep your secret forever."

"What? Oh my God, Myles. That's it? This is unbelievable. Of course I'll marry you."

"Good. To tell you the truth, I would have kept the secret even if you said no."

She shook her head and grabbed the back of his hand. "How could I say no to such an incredibly understanding man?"

"And you're a wonderful mom. Thinking back on what you did, you only had two other options and they were both lousy. If that lady had kept Stump, he'd be far worse off. If the state tried to find him a home, they would have never found anybody who'd love him any more than you do. What good would it do to stir up a hornet's nest, now? None. He's already got a good situation."

She rolled up in Myles's arms. "And now it gets even better."

"And you don't have to work if you don't want to."

CHAPTER 61

Mac had already dropped by the sporting goods store to pick up a spool of ultra-fine fishing line and grabbed a *Gazette* from the newspaper stand. Now he was at a burger joint and gathering his last-minute thoughts. On page three there was a story about some traveling salesman named Kevin Lapport who had been decapitated when his car crashed into the back of a dump truck on the interstate.

Others might scan the article and note words like "bloody," "senseless," and "tragic," but Mac zeroed in on words such as "single," "age 38," and "no known family."

He went outside, tossed the paper into Annie's saddlebag and placed the most important phone call he'd made in years.

"*Rachel Johnson.*"

"Hi there. How's it going?"

She sighed. "*Can't get to my work. Everybody wants to congratulate me for getting married.*"

"You didn't mention the other things, did you?"

"*It's tempting, but the baby hasn't even moved yet, and I want to be more certain before I make any announcements.*"

"What about the inheritance?"

"*Same thing. Pappy wouldn't want me to make a big deal out of it. I wish you could have met him. How 'bout you? How's your day going?*"

"I'm glad you asked. After talking with your attorney and

signing all those papers, I got to thinking about families, kids, stuff like that." He paused. "I've put an ad on Craigslist to sell Annie."

"What? Why? You love that bike."

"A daddy-to-be shouldn't own a dangerous motorcycle."

"Wow! That's very noble, but it seems awfully sudden."

"I might get a truck or an SUV."

"If that's what you want, it's fine with me. I always thought it was a little too dangerous anyway."

"I still have one more thing I want to do, before I let her go. I was hoping that you'd help me get a few pictures of me and her. Might want to look back someday."

"Pictures? Sure."

"If you wouldn't mind, I'd like to meet after work, at that viewing platform I told you about, at the Punchbowl. Then you can snap a few of me and Annie with the sunset and panorama behind us—and I can get some of you too, before you start swelling up. You know, capture this phase of our lives."

"Tonight?"

"It shouldn't be crowded and I thought you said you don't have any after-school activities today."

"I'll have to stop by the house and change clothes first. Can we go to dinner after that?"

Mac chuckled. "That's the least I could do. Do you remember how to get there?"

"Yeah, it's up that canyon about forty-five minutes from here."

"Great. I'll bring the digital. Let's say four-thirty. There'll be lots of orange sky by then."

"Should be lovely."

After the call Mac took a final look in Annie's saddlebags for tools and supplies. Satisfied that he had everything he needed, he mounted his two-wheeled helper and headed for the Devil's Punchbowl.

There was only one piece to the strategy that still made Mac nervous. It was one of those perspective issues. While he still harbored doubts as to Miranda's ability to handle Rachel on her own, she had so much self-confidence he had to reluctantly trust her and instead remained focused on his alibi.

As he and Annie neared the park entrance, Mac took a gander in his rearview mirror. Nobody was back there for at least a half-mile. Ahead, a gradual hill hosted some gentle curves that seemed to have been placed there solely for his and Annie's amusement. Just before entering the canyon the speed limit dropped to forty and a yellow sign announced an S-shaped curve. Annie loved those little challenges. She dug down into third gear.

Mac and Annie made their way through the initial stages of the canyon where the walls grew taller and the midday sun cast intermittent shadows across the slithering road as if a child were overhead, playing with a light switch.

Ten minutes in, just after the halfway point, they had ascended to the top rim of the canyon. The view was astounding. Mac nodded his approval. "Nobody up here," he said to Annie.

"Looks like all the homework paid off," he thought he heard her say. He and Annie danced gracefully over the remaining hills and around the final few bends until they pulled into the small parking area near the platform. Mac dropped the kickstand, jiggled it into place and turned off the engine. No traffic for the moment. He opened Annie's saddlebag and grabbed what he needed.

A groomed trail led him to the platform, where he went to the back corner that jutted out a full two feet beyond the canyon ledge. Even though he'd thought about this moment countless times, he leaned over the rail and confirmed his previous findings. They were at least fifteen stories above ground. Satisfied, he reached in his pocket for the eight-foot stretch of one-inch nylon strap he'd gotten from a hardware store. He tied one end to the bottom of the corner post and the other end to the bottom edge of the adjoining fence section and dropped the slack over the edge.

The bad-ass screwdriver that he got from Miranda's garage loosened, but didn't remove, the huge screws that attached the fence section to its upright posts. His eyes glimpsed movement off to the side. He grinned. Below, a pair of red-tailed hawks were playing in the updraft.

He reached in his pocket for the spool of transparent fishing line he'd picked up earlier. He wound a couple of loops around both the post in the corner and the upper part of the fence section. Then he did the same thing on the other end of the section. With the post and fence section barely held together, he took one of several yellow pencils from his pocket and broke it in half. He removed the lowest screw from the post and replaced it with a piece of the pencil. Slowly he replaced the remaining screws, one by one, being certain to continually test the strength of his makeshift pencil plugs against the weight of the aluminum section. Then he set the screws by one of the side posts on the ground. With the weight of the fencing held up by pencil plugs and the whole section attached to the upright posts with fine fishing line, he nodded. "Oughta be good enough for a few hours," he said into the mild breeze. He moved swiftly back down the path to the parking lot and within a half-hour, he and Annie had eased their way out of the canyon.

* * *

Back in the city, Mac and Annie parked several blocks away from Palmdale High, off the primary route. A quick walk delivered him to a large palm tree, which provided sufficient cover, yet allowed a view of the parking lots.

The bell went off at 3:10 as expected, and the first wave of students hit the doors. Mac smiled. He'd never liked school much either. He watched patiently as most of the students dispersed into buses, the parking lot and the bike racks while a few others walked up the side streets or scooted along on skateboards.

Moments later, the adults migrated toward the lot where Mac had introduced himself to Rachel some six months earlier. Rachel was one of the last ones out. Alone, she made her way toward her vehicle. Mac watched intently as she drove off. All he could see was the back of her head.

He put on a pair of surgical gloves while he waited calmly for a few more minutes, making sure nearly everybody was out of the building. It was time to make his move while the doors were still propped open. Once inside he went through a set of double doors that led to the teacher's lounge along with a conference room and several offices, including Rachel's. He snagged a copy of her key that he'd made a couple weekends earlier without her knowing.

Inside Rachel's office, he dropped the *Gazette* on her desk and opened it to the article about Kevin Lapport's accident. He grabbed a nearby book and set it on the paper in a haphazard fashion to discourage the janitor from throwing the newspaper out.

He took a seat behind Rachel's desk, booted her computer and logged in using her usual password of *Nov24*, for her birthday. He brought up the computer's notepad and typed a very brief message, before closing the computer back down, and returning to his indigo friend.

Five minutes later he and Annie were far away from the school at a Safeway parking lot. Mac dumped the surgical gloves and approached the ATM to make his first withdrawal from Rachel's account. His next stop was the Lucky Strike Bowling Alley.

Inside, only a few lanes were being used and several employees were getting ready for the league play that would begin at six. Mac made his way to the bar area where the only other customer was on a stool, near the far corner. Mac slid onto another stool, just a few seats away and checked the time on his cellphone. "Ten to four," he said to the stranger. "Looks like we missed *Oprah*."

"Damn," the man replied as the big door behind the bar

opened and Cecil the bartender wheeled out a dolly full of beer cases. "Be right with you," he said to Mac.

Cecil leaned the stack upright near the beer chest. "Back again, huh?"

"Yeah," said Mac. "I'll have a Bud when you get a chance." Mac gently pointed to the other customer. "Give my pal one too...on me."

"No problem." Cecil said. He reached in the case, grabbed two bottles, removed the caps and plopped them on napkins. "Eight bucks," he said.

Mac dropped a twenty on the bar, and the other customer picked up his free beer, tipping it toward Mac. "Thanks."

"Sure," Mac said. "My wife's supposed to meet me here a little later, but it ain't no fun drinking alone." He extended his hand. "Name's Mac. Yours?"

"Barry," the fellow said. He reached to complete the handshake.

Cecil returned with Mac's change and a receipt. Mac checked the slip. The transaction was completed at 3:54 p.m. He nodded ever so slightly, and slid it in his shirt pocket. He looked at Barry. "What do you do?"

"I sell industrial products," Barry said. He tilted his head toward the lanes. "Floor finishes for bowling alleys, gymnasiums...floors like that."

"Oh, really? You got a card?" Mac asked. "My wife's the assistant principal at the high school. I think they're going to redo their floors during Christmas break."

"Sure thing." Barry had one in his shirt pocket. "What about you?"

Mac tucked the business card safely away with the register receipt.

CHAPTER 62

Don parked Miranda's SUV and together they hurried up the trail toward the viewing platform. From thirty feet away, Don snapped, "That asshole better not have fucked this up."

"Calm down," Miranda replied. "I told you he took care of it."

A few more paces and they reached the outer corner of the platform. Miranda pointed at the bottom of the post. "Down there. A small strap. See it?"

Don focused. "Okay. Let's check the rest of it."

Miranda tapped the thin fishing line that Mac used to hold the fence section to the upright posts. "Look at this."

Don moved in, examined the job. "Excellent," he said. He leaned out and over the adjoining section to get a better look at the backside of Mac's work. "Ah, yes. I see what he did."

She saw one of the homemade plugs on which all the weight of the fence section rested. "Looks awfully delicate."

Don glanced out over the canyon and back. "I just hope the wind doesn't come up. Those pencils ain't gonna last forever."

"Shouldn't be much longer." She reached through the railing to the base of another nearby post. "Here's the screws. I'll put them in my purse."

"Good. We're all set. What time you got?"

She looked at her watch. "Four-twenty."

"Shhh." Don heard it first. Then Miranda heard it too. Off in the distance, toward the canyon, a vehicle was approaching.

"This should be it," Don said.

Miranda took a deep breath. It was either Rachel or Mickey. "Good luck, Donnie."

"We deserve that money," he said, pulling her close. Miranda closed her eyes as his lips found hers. Her heart banged for a few seconds but there was no more time to spare. "I love you," she whispered, meaning every word of it.

"Yeah, me too," he said, his tone devoid of affection.

Rachel's car rounded the final turn—right on time.

"It's her alright," Don said. "Get right next to me and up close to the rail." He turned his back to the road.

Some two hundred feet away, Rachel pulled into the dirt parking lot and turned off her engine, but didn't get out. Don and Miranda remained at their post, with their backs toward the trail. "You think I should go drag her ass down here?" Don asked.

"You won't have to do that." Miranda said. "She just drove a long way to have her picture taken on this platform. She's not going to give up without a little effort. Just stay where she can see that there's another woman out here."

Don did as suggested. "Just act natural," he said, resting his arm on Miranda's shoulder.

While they waited for Rachel to approach, they snuggled and pretended to lean on the railing. It didn't take long before they heard the sound they wanted. Rachel's car door opened, then closed again.

Miranda squeezed Don's hand. "See, I told you," she whispered.

"We gotta ignore her as long as possible," Don said. "We need her to come fairly close."

A minute later, a floorboard on the other end of the platform gently creaked. Then another. Miranda's heart pounded in unison with each of Rachel's footsteps. One after the other, they drew closer.

"Excuse me," Rachel said from a few feet behind them, but they held steady for two more steps. "Excuse me." She was louder this time, off to their left and close behind them.

Without speaking Don and Miranda took a short step backwards and away from Rachel who stepped closer to the newly opened space. "Have you seen a motorcycle?"

The duo took yet another step backwards and away, opening up the space between them and the railing still more.

Rachel leaned slightly toward the opened area. "I'm supposed to meet my hus—"

Don took one more step back and they had Rachel essentially where they needed her—closer to the rail than they were. Don turned to face Rachel and Miranda focused on Rachel's face as Rachel got her first glimpse of Mac's identical twin. Rachel's head twisted from Don to Miranda and back to Don as her eyes raced for answers to questions not yet asked. Her brow wrinkled. "What's going—?"

In that split second Don lowered his shoulder and charged Rachel with the force of a raging bull. Upon impact, her eyes widened and a painful grunt escaped her lungs. Shoulder down, Don drove into her like a linebacker. She desperately reached backwards for the support of the handrail, just as Don let go and momentum finished the job. The lightweight tippet snapped and the railing gave way and slid off the pencil pieces.

Miranda saw the horror in Rachel's eyes as her foot went off the back end of the platform and the fence section led her over the edge. But unlike Rachel, the fence section quickly reached the end of the nylon strap that saved its life. Then, in an instant, it was over. Rachel had reached the canyon floor and the fence section dangled below the platform.

Don looked down the canyon wall towards the body. "She ain't moving," he said, as he pulled up the fence section. "Let's get this back together as fast as we can."

Miranda barely heard him. She couldn't forget the look on Rachel's face when she took her final step. "I'm surprised she didn't scream."

"I think I knocked the wind out of her."

"Poor thing. That must have been awful."

"Doesn't matter now. Hand me those screws."

Within a few minutes, Don put all the screws back and the fence puzzle looked as before. He cut the strap from the post and shoved it in his pocket and they jogged to Miranda's SUV. As they descended the canyon road, neither said a word. Part of Miranda was pleased that two men loved her enough to help her get much closer to the money Mickey so desperately needed but deep down in the pit of her soul it wasn't going to be easy to get over what they did.

At the bottom of the canyon road and still numb, Miranda pulled her burner from her purse. "I gotta call Mac," she said stoically, "to tell him it's over." It was eight minutes past five.

* * *

After Miranda confirmed Rachel's death, Mac returned to his barstool. He too was numb, partly because he was impressed by Miranda's ability to pull off such a dastardly deed on her own and partly because she didn't sound as happy or relieved as he expected. Nonetheless he still had some work to do.

Barry had left, but he'd already served his purpose. Mac ordered himself another Bud and waited for Cecil to bring it before he used his primary cell phone to place a call to Rachel's cell. He waited awhile and then disconnected. "Damn," he said to Cecil. "Can't find my wife. She should've been here by now."

"She's probably close by," Cecil said, "and just didn't answer cause she'll be here in a minute or two."

"Hope so," said Mac. He took a sip of his beer.

Another half-hour, another beer and another failed phone call. "I'm getting a little worried," Mac said to his bar-keeping ally. "If she doesn't show up pretty soon, I'm gonna have to go look for her."

"I wouldn't get too shook up," Cecil said. "Her phone's probably dead or something."

"Yeah, I guess she might have forgot we were supposed to meet and went shopping instead." Mac looked at his phone. "Geez, it's already seven-twenty," he said.

Mac shot the breeze with a couple other bar customers while he stalled another half-hour and washed down another beer. He ordered a shot of bourbon and acted like he took it all in one gulp but slipped off to the restroom where he spit it out. When back he began to slur his words. "Know something?" he finally said to Cecil, "I better go home. Look for my wife."

"We've got a couple guys washing dishes in the back. I'll get one of them to take you home."

Not long thereafter, Mac and Juan Pacheco, the dishwasher, drove by Rachel's school, ostensibly to see if her car was there. A while later, they pulled into Mac's driveway. Mac asked Juan to stay put while he went to get the kid a tip. He swayed as he walked away.

A couple moments later he opened the large garage door and brought a five spot to his driver. When he was sure Juan saw him, he stumbled slightly, approached Juan with the tip money and pointed to the empty garage, "Wife's car ain't here. Dunno where the hell she is," he said. "Guess I'd better lie down awhile and wait."

Juan took the money. "If you're okay, I better get back to work."

"Yeah, I guess so," Mac said. "You go wash dishes."

CHAPTER 63

After a couple days of serious soul searching, Stump was ready to face the judge for sentencing. Richard was improving slowly and Stump's world wasn't quite as dire as it seemed after the football game. He wished he hadn't stolen the booze, but the fact of the matter was that he did indeed do it. If Juvenile Hall was the outcome, well, he'd just have to make the best of it.

Myles and Jean picked him up at school and drove him to the sentencing with very little conversation between them. Even his mom had calmed down and stopped lecturing him. At 1:30, the court clerk called out, "All rise," and the dozen people in attendance did as told. "Neal Joseph Randolph" was first.

Stump and his mother took their position at the lectern while Myles remained in the primary seating area behind a sturdy wooden rail.

"Is there anything either one of you want to say before I pass sentence?"

Jean shook her head while Stump softly spoke into the microphone. "Yes, sir. I just want to say I'm sorry, sir. I know what I did was wrong, sir."

"Duly noted," the judge said. He pointed toward the back of the courtroom. "I see Detective Myles Cooper back there. Would you please come up here and join the proceedings, sir?"

Befuddled, Stump and his mom turned toward Myles as he advanced to the lectern.

"Please state your name for the record."

"I'm Myles Cooper, Your Honor."

"Mr. Cooper, per our discussion earlier in my chambers, are you still willing to act as a friend of the court in this matter?"

"Yes, sir. I am."

While Stump stood motionless facing the judge, Jean stared at Myles.

"In view of Mr. Cooper's commitment in this matter, the court orders Neal Joseph Randolph to perform eighteen hours of community service. He will work three consecutive Saturdays, for six hours each. Mr. Randolph will remove graffiti from government properties, under the supervision of the Police Department. If he fulfills that obligation, and does not come before this court again within six months, his record shall be expunged."

The judge then spoke directly to Stump. "Young man, I want you to know that I was prepared to be much harsher on you, but Mr. Cooper visited me in my chambers this morning and told me that you are capable of being a very fine citizen. This court has learned it can rely upon the judgments of Mr. Cooper, and if he has faith in you, so do I. But, let me make one thing perfectly clear. I had better not see you in here again. That would be a slap in Mr. Cooper's face and make me very unhappy. Do you understand me?"

Smiling wide, Neal Joseph Randolph responded, "Yes, sir. Thank you, sir."

The judge shifted his attention to Jean, "Ms. Randolph, do you know how lucky you are to have a man of Mr. Cooper's character vouch for your son?"

If Stump's mom's grin were any bigger, her face would surely have broken. The obviously amazed mother glanced into Myles's eyes and then addressed the judge, "Yes, sir, I surely do."

The judge dropped his gavel.

The trio had barely stepped outside the courtroom before Jean asked Myles, "Would you mind telling me what happened in there?"

"Well, it all started in that meeting room right after he was arrested, when he said it wouldn't be right to lie. It's the kind of character his mother has. Then, on the day of the air show I told him it was important to build strong character by taking on responsibility, especially when circumstances are the most difficult. Later, when he was so quick to admit his guilt at the first hearing, I knew he had the courage to face his problems, head-on, and he was worth fighting for."

Jean paused in her tracks, turned Myles toward her and kissed him on the mouth.

"Gross," Stump said.

CHAPTER 64

Understandably, Don wanted to celebrate but Miranda was on a different page in a different book in a different library.

His comments about taking a step backwards before you could go forward, or what Rachel's death would mean to Mickey, rang hollow. Finally, in the very early morning, he nudged her. "Why don't we go to San Francisco?" he said. "To get our minds on something else."

Anything else was exactly what Miranda needed. Now, halfway to their destination, she felt a chill that even two thick sweatshirts couldn't insulate her from. She reached for the heater knob and turned it up another notch.

"You keep doing that and I'm going to have to open the window," Don complained.

"Sorry, but I keep getting shudders. Do you think we're doing the right thing—by leaving town, I mean?"

"Oh yeah. Your boyfriend is going to be occupied for a while. It's best if you're way out of the picture."

She sighed. "Stop calling him that." Thus far Don had been correct about how to carry out the con, but she could do without his callousness. She twisted the heater knob again, this time to full on. Even if she could get over what they did to Rachel, she still had other life-and-death matters to consider. What would happen from here? To Mickey? To her? To Mac?

If she could figure out a way for Don and Mac to reconcile they could all live together like a small commune. She'd gladly allow either one or both of them to take on a girlfriend if they wanted. She rolled her eyes and looked out the side window. Why was she lying to herself? She despised cheating, even when she was the one doing it. The answer was always the same. She was going to have to choose one or the other.

A ringtone came from inside her purse. "It's Mac," she said to Don. "I'd better get it."

"Remember what we talked about."

"Hi, Sweets." she said, trying to sound friendly to Mac without drawing Don's ire.

"I gotta hurry," Mac said. *"It's gonna be a crazy day."*

"You can handle it, Sweets. Just focus on being a grieving husband—like we talked about."

"I'll try. What are you doing today?"

"To tell you the truth, since we can't get together for a while, I thought I'd drive to L.A."

"L.A. What for?"

"I'm going to visit with an old friend, Gloria, just to keep my mind busy." It was difficult to concentrate with Don listening to every word.

"What if I need you?"

"I'll still have my cell. But you can only call me when nobody can see you."

"Yeah. If they did and there's no record of the call on my main cell, they'd know I had two phones."

"I want to thank you again—for both Mickey and me."

"Had to. You needed me. I probably ought to get going. I've got a lot to do. I love you."

The words were bittersweet. "I love you, too," she said.

She hung up and tossed the phone into her purse. "Sorry, Donnie. I had to say it."

"You know you're just like a black widow, don't you?"

"Huh?"

"They kill their lovers when they're done with them." He

looked right at her. "We gotta get rid of 'Sweets,'" he said, making air quotes.

In the beginning she was so desperate to help Mickey, she tricked herself into believing they could pull off the con without anybody suffering any long-term damage, but now it was clear that Don's only certain path to the cash was just as he had said in the beginning: to dispose of his brother entirely. Otherwise he would be at Mac's mercy to share the money. It was all or nothing for both of them.

Regardless of how they got to that point, two people were dead and it was imminently clear that the black widow comment was Miranda's not-so-subtle notice that Don expected her to help him with the third—his brother.

Her entire body felt cold. Her love for Mac was every bit as strong as her love for Don. She couldn't kill either one of them—but she had to—but she couldn't—but she had to.

A road sign said they still had 80 miles to go.

CHAPTER 65

After Mac called for a cab, he placed the call that he genuinely dreaded more than any other he'd ever made.

"Hello?"

"Hi, Granny. It's me, Mac."

"Yes dear? Is everything okay?"

"To tell you the truth. I'm pretty worried about Rachel."

"Why, what's wrong?" she said quickly.

"We were supposed to meet at the bowling alley last night, but she didn't show up, or come home all night. I was hoping you've heard from her."

"Oh, dear! No, I haven't. I hope she's okay." The pain in her voice grated on his ears like screeching tires at an intersection just before an accident.

"Me, too. I guess I'll check to see if she made it to work this morning. If not, I'm going to call the police."

"Okay, and please be sure to let me know as soon as you hear anything. If I don't answer, keep trying."

"I will. Bye." It was excruciating. The best way to escape his guilt was to go on. He speed-dialed Rachel's work number.

"Palmdale High School. Ms. Place speaking."

"Hello, Angela. Mac Evans here. Rachel didn't come home last night. Have you seen her this morning?"

"No, I haven't seen her, Mac. I'll check around, just in case she's

in the teacher's lounge or talking to somebody in the hallway. Where can I reach you?"

"Do you have my cell?"

His last call was right into the belly of the beast: the police station. *"Missing Persons."*

"Hello. My name's Mac Evans. My wife didn't come home last night. I need you to find her."

"When was the last time anybody saw her or spoke with her, sir?"

"Yesterday afternoon."

"I'm sorry, Mr. Evans, but we can't do anything until she's been missing for a full 24 hours."

"But she's never done this before. Can't you make an exception?"

"Sorry. Call back after she's been missing for 24 hours. Then we'll see what we can do."

"That's ridiculous," he bellowed, releasing some of his own inner tension. "It's already been eighteen hours. A few more hours isn't gonna make any difference."

"I can't help it, sir. I don't make the rules."

Mac's cab was still a half-block away from the Lucky Strike Bowling Alley when he breathed a sigh of relief. His indigo pal was the kind of bike that thieves preyed upon, but fortunately she was patiently waiting for him right where he'd left her.

As the cabbie pulled away Mac jiggled Annie's kickstand into place. It was almost like being home. "Morning, Annie. I'm glad you're okay."

"So, the proverbial shit's hit the fan?" he imagined her saying.

"Yeah. It's getting hairy now. I just hope we haven't forgotten anything." He inserted his key and started her up. "I gotta convince some pretty smart people that Rachel committed suicide."

"But Miranda's skipped off again, just when you need her most?"

"To be fair, she had a good point. People might be watching me for a while so we can't really get together anyway. All we can do is talk on the burners when nobody is watching." He shifted her into gear and pulled away.

"*Where we headed?*"

"Safeway. I need a couple onions and they've got an ATM. After that we'll get a late breakfast, then buzz over to the Missing Persons Bureau."

CHAPTER 66

A dark sedan pulled in front of Rachel's home a little sooner than Mac expected. His eyes already stinging, he made a quick trip to the fridge where a baggie contained an onion that he'd cut in half a few hours earlier. He patted the onion's wound with the ring finger from each hand.

At the door stood a stocky white guy in his fifties who looked like he'd enjoyed more than a few raised-glazed donuts; and a young, golden-skinned Hispanic woman, both in plain clothes. Mac spoke softly. "Is this about Rachel?"

The fellow held up a badge. "Sergeant Byrdswain." He tilted his head toward his female partner. "This is Detective Sanchez. Can we come in?"

"Where's Rachel? What's going on?"

"We'd prefer to come inside if you don't mind."

Age-wise, Sanchez could have passed for Byrdswain's granddaughter. She was no taller than five-three, thin, with a tiny hint of bluish-grey eye shadow that belied child-like eyes as dark as her plush, medium-length hair.

Mac stepped back, let them in and pointed to his couch. Byrdswain took a seat, but Sanchez waved off the offer and meandered across the living room. She glanced down the hallway, then back toward the kitchen before she returned her attention to Mac.

"I wish we had better news," Byrdswain said, breaking the silence.

Mac straightened and glared at the old-timer. "Oh, no. Tell me it's not real bad."

"The Park Service discovered your wife's car a few hours ago, in a canyon, about thirty miles out of town."

In that split second, Mac knew that four well-trained eyes were drinking in his every move and gesture. He frowned and feigned a fearful look. "A canyon? What would she be doing up in a canyon?"

"There's a viewing station up there," the sergeant said, softly. "They found her on the canyon floor. It appears she may have jumped. We're sorry for your loss, sir."

Mac scowled. "Loss? Are you saying—"

Byrdswain nodded. "We just came from there, sir. It's a very long fall."

"Oh my God!" Mac buried his face in his palms and tapped his onion-coated fingers to the corner of his eyes. The sting was immediate. "This has to be a mistake."

"No sir. It's not a mistake," Byrdswain said. "They found her car."

"And her purse," Sanchez added. "It was inside the car. Women don't usually leave their purses lying around like that."

He raised his head as the first onion-tear rolled down his cheek. "I can't believe this."

"She's not the first one," Sanchez said. "We don't think she suffered."

Mac wiped away the early tears and caught the corner of his eyes again, sobbing. "This just can't be."

"Are you going to be okay, Mr. Evans?" Sanchez quizzed. "Do you have somebody you can call?"

Mac shook his head. "Just her grandmother." He lifted his head. "Oh, no. What am I gonna tell Granny?"

"Granny?"

"Rachel's only relative."

"I see. Where does Granny live?"

Mac waved his hand dismissively. "Glendale."

Byrdswain pulled a small notebook from his pocket. "I know this is a bad time, sir. But, we have to ask you a few more questions."

Eyes burning, Mac looked briefly at the sergeant, then at Sanchez.

Sanchez pointed down the hall. "Would you mind if I look around, Mr. Evans? To see if there's anything that can help us."

"Go ahead," he said softly.

Sanchez disappeared down the narrow corridor and into the main bathroom. "Did Mrs. Evans work outside the home?" Byrdswain quizzed.

"She's an assistant principal at the high school. I guess I'm going to have to call them, too."

"When was the last time you spoke with her?"

"Yesterday. I called her just before school let out." He allowed another onion-tear to glide to his jaw before wiping it away.

"Was there anything unusual about your conversation? Did she sound okay?"

"Now that you mention it," he said before sniffing, "she seemed a little gloomy."

Byrdswain tilted his head. "How so?"

"Short sentences, almost whispering, like something was on her mind. I asked her if she was okay, but she said I'd find out later. I just figured it had something to do with one of the students."

Sanchez returned, moved into the kitchen and out into the garage.

"What happened next?" Byrdswain asked.

Mac hesitated. "I suggested we meet at the bowling alley, around dinner time. Maybe grab a couple burgers. I thought all the activity might cheer her up."

"What did she say?"

"Said she had something to do first, so I told her I'd have a couple beers while I waited."

"Is that all she said?" Byrdswain asked. "Did she agree to meet you?"

"Yes, but she stays late sometimes. Helps kids. Talks with their parents. I just assumed it was something like that."

"Anything else about that call that might help us?"

"I dunno," Mac said. "I guess she seemed distant when we said goodbye."

"Distant?"

Mac sniffed, wiped his eyes again. "She whispered that she was sorry. I assumed it had something to do with her staying late or whatever she was doing."

"What did you do after your phone call?"

Mac paused. "I took a shower, then dropped by the ATM to get some cash before going to the bowling alley."

"What time was that?"

"I dunno. Must have been at the ATM about four o'clock. At the Lucky Strike about fifteen minutes later."

"Will somebody there remember you?"

He looked directly at the sergeant, displaying his red eyes. "What's that got to do with anything?"

"I'm sorry, sir. Nothing personal, but we have to check everything out. Just to be sure. You must have spoken with somebody?"

He dipped his head just once. "The bartender, and a salesman. I got his business card for Rachel." He lowered his head. "She won't be needing it now."

"How long did you stay at the bowling alley?"

"I guess I was there until eight-thirty or nine."

"Weren't you worried about Mrs. Evans while you were drinking those beers and waiting?"

"Not at first. She's stayed late before. But after a while I tried to call her plenty of times, but she didn't answer. I just thought she was tied up with some other people or her phone was dead, so I just waited. Eventually, I had too many beers, so Cecil had some kid take me home."

"I see. What do you do for a living, Mr. Evans?"

"I've been trying to find some construction work, but the economy's so bad nobody's hiring. Then I met Rachel."

"I see."

Sanchez returned and Byrdswain twisted his head toward her. "We're just about done here. You got any questions?"

"Just a few," she said, turning toward Mac. "Were you and Mrs. Evans getting along okay?"

"Yes, of course. We loved each other." He rubbed his eyes again. "I shoulda known it was all too good to be true."

"What was?" asked Sanchez.

"We just met about seven months ago. Hit it off great. Then a few weeks back we went to Vegas and got married. When we returned Granny sprang this trust on us."

"Trust? What kind of trust?"

Mac and Miranda had already agreed that it would look better if the cops heard about the trust from him rather than stumble upon it on their own. "Apparently when Pappy was alive, he and Granny set a lot of money aside for Rachel that nobody knew about until after we got married."

Sanchez looked at Byrdswain and they both looked at Mac. Byrdswain spoke again. "Just how big was this trust?"

"Over eleven million dollars. They got it from selling their ranch in Silicon Valley."

"But that was the first time you heard of this trust?"

Mac nodded, wiped his eyes again. "Neither one of us knew anything about it until after we got married. Pappy wanted Rachel to get married before they told anybody about it."

"That's a lot of money, Mr. Evans. Are you sure you didn't know about this trust until after you got married?"

Mac shook his head. "Nobody knew until that night."

"What happens to all this money, now that your wife has passed away?" Sanchez asked.

"Huh? I don't know. I guess I'd get it, but I don't want to think about that. I'd rather have my wife back."

"I'm sure you would, sir. Would you mind if we borrow

your computer for a couple days? It might have some useful information in it."

"Go ahead," he said, his eyes still smarting.

A moment of awkward silence filled the air before Byrdswain stood. "Okay," he said. "That's about it for now. We'll do some checking around and get back to you when we know more. I'm going to need your cell phone number, along with the receipt from the ATM machine if you still have it, and that business card you mentioned. Oh, and the grandmother's name and address."

"Sure. Can I go talk to Rachel's grandmother? She's going to be devastated."

"Go ahead. We've got a couple other stops we can make."

Mac dropped his head into his hands. "How'm I going to tell that sweet woman that her only grandchild is dead?" A real tear formed in his eye.

CHAPTER 67

Over the next few weeks Stump fulfilled his community service and was doing better in school, but he was still worried about Dogg. One lazy day right after school, he stepped out back with a bowl of food for his four-legged pal, who was curled up in the shade of the house. It took a couple of "Here, boy's" before Dogg lifted his head and came over to investigate. Stump lifted Dogg's ears.

"How do they look?" Stump's mom asked from behind his shoulder.

"Better, but he still doesn't hear too good."

"If it weren't for my severance package I couldn't have afforded his pills," she said just as the doorbell rang. "That's Myles. I'll get it."

Stump sat down on a lounge chair and petted Dogg while he ate. A minute later, the adults came out back. "Sweetie, Myles would like to talk to you so I'm going to take Dogg for a walk."

Myles sat on a folding chair next to Stump. "I hear congratulations are in order for finishing your community service. How'd it go?"

Stump picked a small rock off the ground and tossed it toward the center of the yard. "I could tell some of the guys had been in trouble before. One guy's mom picked him up in her Cadillac."

Myles nodded. "That's what we said at the air show. Some

people have it made but don't even realize it. That reminds me, how's Richard doing?"

"He's home but spends most of his time in bed or a wheelchair, rehabilitating."

"He's another good example of what I'm talking about. He may have more material things than you do, but I bet he'd trade his problems for yours. That makes you the wealthier one." Myles smiled and put his hand on Stump's shoulder. "You just keep taking responsibility for your future and you'll do fine."

"I guess so."

"I'm not sure if your mom told you but we've been talking about getting married. I was hoping you'd give us your blessing and be my best man."

"Why you asking me? If I say no, you can do it anyway."

"True, but it wouldn't be as nice for your mother. I was hoping you'd be excited about it."

"Well, I'm not. I'd rather find my dad."

Myles nodded. "I can understand that, but you may never find him and your mom and I love each other. That's what really counts, isn't it?"

"You're okay I guess, but right now I just want to find out about my dad. See who he is and if we can be a family."

"I know I'm not your dad but I'd be like a dad. I can show you a few things about discipline and help you make something of yourself. You could even go to college some day. How does that sound?"

"Like a commercial to join the Army."

Myles smirked, "Yeah, I guess it did. Sorry. Let me try again. We get along well, don't we?"

"You're nice enough but what happens if you fall off the wagon and make mom start drinking again? That would make things worse. I'd have two drunks on my hands."

Myles reached in his pocket and showed Stump his token. "See the six on here? That means it's been six years since I've had a single drink. Not many people can say that."

"That's because they don't have a problem with it. I still think mom and me would be better off with my real dad."

*   *   *

The front door slammed. "Damn idiots," Stump's mom said loudly. She came through the house and into the back yard where Stump and Myles were still sitting in the shade. "This neighborhood needs a doggie park," she said as Dogg rushed towards Stump as if they'd been apart for an eternity.

Stump petted their pal. "Why? What's wrong?"

"First off, we were just up the street and the Kline's mutt charged us. I thought the two of them were going to chew the hell out of each other." She shrugged her shoulders. "Fortunately we got out of there okay. Then on the way home, a squirrel bolted across the road. You know how Dogg is. He went after it, but I couldn't hold him back. He damn near got run over. If we had a doggie park, Dogg could run around with some dogs with better social skills. Nobody would worry about their pets getting killed."

"And they could sniff each other's butts."

"Yeah, that too," Jean said, shaking her head. "How'd you guys do? Did you have a nice talk?"

Myles stood. "Stump's not sure it's a good idea for us to get married."

She spun her head toward Stump and back to Myles. "Did you tell him he'd be the best man?" Back to Stump. "You ought to be honored."

"It's not my fault I told him the truth."

"What truth? Myles is the nicest man I've ever met and I love him. What's the problem?"

Myles took a step toward Stump's mom and kissed her on the cheek. "He wants to find his dad. I can understand that. I'd want to know such a thing like that too—if it were possible."

"Oh, that again. Well, it's not possible. I've told him that before."

"I think I'd better leave you two alone. Maybe you can work things out if I'm not in the middle of everything."

Jean sighed. "Okay. Give us a little time and I'll call you later."

"See what I mean?" Stump said to Myles. "It doesn't matter what I think. You guys are going to do whatever you want anyway."

After Myles left, Jean sat in the chair next to Stump. "Honey, can't you let this father thing go? It's very uncomfortable for me."

"No. This is important to me. He might be rich and drive a nice car, not a dumb pickup truck."

She stared right at him. "Would it make any difference if I said I'm ashamed to talk about it?"

"I bet you told Myles."

She let out a long low sigh and her chin fell to her chest. "Alright," she said, lifting her head back up. "If I tell you what happened, do you promise never to bring it up again?"

"Depends."

"Okay then. It's against my better judgment, but here goes." He leaned forward.

"I've told you the truth all along," she said, putting a hand on his knee. "I really don't know who he is. When I was in school I suffered from low self-esteem, like lots of girls do. Then, the summer after I graduated I had my first romantic encounter. I don't have to tell you what I mean by that, do I?"

Stump shook his head. "Who was it?"

"That's not relevant to what you want to know. Anyway, I was flattered that anybody would want me. It made me feel attractive for the first time. After that I did the same thing with somebody else and somebody else after that. Then one time I went to a college party. There were lots of college–aged people drinking and going up to the bedrooms. They just kept saying NQA, NQA."

"What's that?"

She shook her head, "'No Questions Asked.' It was supposed to be exciting to do it with somebody you didn't even know."

Stump twisted his head. "Did you do that?"

His mom sighed. "I was young and stupid—and way too drunk. Some older guy I didn't even know asked me to go upstairs with him and I went along because that's what everybody else was doing. They just kept saying NQA, NQA. I was so drunk I barely knew what was going on."

"Isn't that rape? Didn't you turn them in?"

"I couldn't turn them in, Honey. Everybody knew what was going on upstairs in those bedrooms. They'd just say that I wanted to be like everybody else. They'd stick together and I couldn't prove otherwise."

"But don't you know who he was? Couldn't you find out?"

"Not really. That's what I've tried to tell you over and over. I didn't know any of them, the college guys or their guests. I doubt if anybody knew everybody who was there. When I found out I was pregnant I was too humiliated to ask questions. Now, those people probably have their own families. Even if I could find out who they are, I wouldn't want to risk ruining their families. I'm ashamed of it, for both of us. But I thank God it brought you into my life. You're the most important thing that's ever happened to me. More than Myles, more than Grandma and Grandpa, more than Aunt Gerry. More than all of them put together. Now can you understand why I had to keep it from you? It's painful enough without dragging you into it."

"What took him so long?"

"Who? What?"

"Myles. What took him so long to ask you? I could see you loved each other a long time ago."

Happy tears joined Jean's fresh new grin. "Does that mean you're okay with us getting married?"

"Love goes both ways, Mom. Now that I know what happened, I have to show respect."

CHAPTER 68

ater that night, and right after their AA meeting, Myles and Jean went to his place. "How'd it go?" he asked.

She backed up a full step. It was the kind of question that used to make her light a cigarette. "I hated it. I finally realized he wasn't going to drop the topic until he got a believable story out of me so I made up a watered-down version of the truth."

"What did you say?" he asked, leading her into the kitchen.

"It was bad enough admitting I did something stupid, but I didn't see any benefit in telling him that his mother was a criminal."

"Understandable," Myles said looking through the fridge. "Sometimes we have to tell little white lies to protect the people we love."

"I think he believes the important part—that I really don't know who the father is."

He pulled out a couple Cokes. "I think he'll be fine. He's dealt with tougher situations."

Jean opened the upper cabinet and produced two small glasses. "I hope so because something else came up that's going to be just as tough on him. Earlier today, my sister called. She and Dirk are moving to Texas."

Myles's poured the soda. "Oh, really? Why Texas?"

"Work. They were hurting financially because of the economy, but he found a job outside of Houston, so he took it."

"A double-edged sword for you, I'd guess."

"Right. I'm happy for them, but I'm not sure how Stump's going to deal with it. He can't remember a time when Willie wasn't in our lives." She rinsed out a dishrag and cleaned a few drops off the countertop that Myles spilled. "Gerry invited him to spend the night and then go with Dirk in the morning to get a few things out of his office. Stump will make a little money."

"So you're alone for the night?" Myles asked with a naughty grin.

"It was either clean out our own grossly over-stuffed shelves in the catch-all room for free or go with his cousin for a few hours and do essentially the same thing in a cool air-conditioned building for money. What could I say?"

"Good point. Sounds like he's not going to have that many more opportunities to be with them anyway. When are they moving?"

"Six weeks. They have to sell their house. Thankfully they'll still be here for the wedding. Gerry can help me plan it all—flowers, food, decorations. She likes those things." Jean looked around the room. "God knows I can use the help. Tomorrow a neighborhood kid is coming by around eight to start painting."

"Neighbor kid? Does he know what he's doing? I might be able to help."

"I think he'll be okay. He's young, but he's painted a few places around the area. And he's affordable. Anyway, Stump got out of cleaning out our pig sty once again."

CHAPTER 69

Dark clouds were slow-dancing in the skies when Uncle Dirk dropped Stump off with a fresh twenty bucks in his jeans. "Whew," Stump said, crumpling up his nose when he stepped inside. A couple towel racks and the light fixture from the central bathroom were on the living room floor and a bunch of painting supplies had gathered on a drop cloth in the hall.

A young adult stuck his head out of the bathroom. "Hi. You must be Stump. I'm Jason."

"What stinks?"

Jason raised a paintbrush. "Oil-based primer. We put it in bathrooms because it doesn't blister with the moisture."

"Where's my mom?"

"Shopping, I think. She should be back shortly."

Stump wiggled into his own room, tired from a morning of tugging furniture and boxes around. He would have liked to plop on the bed and read a muscle magazine, but the shower curtain beat him to the spot. He sighed and put on some cruddy old jeans and went looking for a plastic bag to use to clean up the back yard. Just then he heard a car door slam in the driveway. A moment later his mom poked her head in the door. "Hi, son. Could you help me and Aunt Gerry bring in some things?"

His eyes nearly popped when he got his first look in the back seat. "Good God. You guys must have bought everything the store had." He grabbed a giant package of paper towels.

"There's more in the trunk."

In the laundry room he placed the towels on the only available space—on top of the dryer.

"When we get these items unloaded," his mom said, "Aunt Gerry and I have more to do. I'd like you to pick up all the dog poop before it rains, and then clean out the laundry room so Jason can paint it."

"But I'm tired. Can't I do some of it later?"

"You've already put it off too many times, Stump. I want you to put a big dent in it. At least get those old puzzle magazines of yours out of there."

"But I was planning on looking through them again."

"Yeah, right. They've been in there for three years and you haven't even touched them."

"I can't help it if I'm too busy."

"You poor boy," she said sarcastically. "I'll meet you back here later. Myles might take me to a movie tonight. You might be able to go with us if you want to."

"Gross. I think I'd rather hang out and play video games or something."

"Suit yourself. Just get as much done as possible so Jason can paint. Okay?"

After his mom left Stump took another gander at the combination laundry/catch-all room. He set a few paper bags full of other paper bags on the floor and opened an old dusty box, which contained some of his puzzle magazines. Oh, yeah. He was reviewing a brainteaser when the phone rang. Richard wanted him to come over. Why not? The laundry room could wait.

He scooted down the hall to the main bathroom. "Hey, Jason. How long will it be before you get to the laundry room?"

Jason rubbed some paint on his coveralls. "I still have to finish the bathrooms, then do the kitchen. I won't be in there for a couple days."

"Good enough, I can still clean this place out tomorrow. I'll leave a note for my mom."

* * *

Although Stump and Richard had spoken on the phone quite a few times while Richard was in the hospital, Richard had only been home a few days and this was the first time they'd gotten together in weeks. Anxious to see The Big Dick (as Stump had begun calling his buddy), he employed his run/walk technique to get there a little quicker. They'd have plenty to talk about.

Slightly winded when he arrived, Stump sucked in a few deep breaths as he entered Richard's home. The unpleasant blend of antiseptic, yesterday's chicken soup and bathroom reek was more unpleasant than the paint fumes at his own house. Stump had to breathe through his mouth as he made his way toward Richard's room.

A hinged hospital bed dominated the room. The drapes were drawn and the lights were low. The air was as heavy as in an underground fort. A bag of clear fluid was dripping into Richard's arm and a larger tube was coming from under the covers and draining a nasty fluid into a bag beside his bed.

Stump's first glance at his buddy revealed that Richard more closely resembled a shriveled after-shower penis than a Big Dick, but he resisted the urge to say so. "It's hot in here, Dude. You want me to open a window?"

"You can turn up the air conditioning if you want to."

Stump waved his hand in front of his face. "Gotta do something, Dude. Can't you smell anything?"

"You get used to it," he said, sounding defeated.

Stump made a fist and tapped Richard on the arm. "Welcome back. For a while there, I wasn't sure you'd make it. Good thing that awning broke your fall."

Richard wiggled from side to side and scooted up a few inches." If I ever get a chance to get even, those guys are going to wish I would have died. I'll run over them in a car if I have to." He motioned to the side table. "Hand me that water bottle, would ya?"

Stump handed it over. "*The Dark Knight* just came out on DVD. Have you heard about it?"

"Not much. It's Batman, isn't it?"

"And the Joker. Everybody says it kicks ass."

"You got a copy? It sounds like a good way to get my mind off all the shit I gotta deal with."

"No, but they're at the store. Where are your folks? If they'll take me I can show them what to get."

"They ain't here. It's the first time I've been alone since the fall. My dad's at a lawyer's office and my mom had to go to the drug store. But they wouldn't buy those things anyway. They're dead broke from all the hospital bills and everything. They're always fighting about money."

"No shit. I thought my mom and me were the only ones who did that. But now I find out Cousin Willie—you remember him—and his family have to move to Texas 'cause they're having a tough time too."

"What about you? Any luck finding your old man?"

"Naw. Turns out my mom was telling me the truth. She doesn't know who he is." He smiled. "But she is getting married and I get to be the best man. Myles seems alright, so this could work out okay after all."

"I hope so."

"I've got an idea. I just got a few bucks for working and didn't really have anything in particular to buy with my money. Why don't I run home and get it, then I can buy a copy of *The Dark Knight*? *Iron Man* is out, too. I could come back here and we could watch it together."

Richard smiled. "Would you?" He lifted himself as best he could. "I'd really appreciate it."

Stump grinned. "Dude. When you just sat up it was like The Big Dick just got a hard-on."

CHAPTER 70

Lightning ricocheted off the clouds when Gerry and Jean returned home from shopping. They each grabbed as many paper sacks and plastic bags full of goodies as they could and ducked inside. Jean flicked on a light, causing Dogg to whimper a happy welcome-home greeting from the back yard. Paint fumes suggested that progress had been made down the hall, but neither Jason nor Stump were around. Jean shook her head. What else could she expect?

She observed a drop cloth in the hallway with paint supplies stacked on top. She sighed. She couldn't let Dogg in with those things in the way, but before she could move them she first had to finish unloading Gerry's car.

After the sisters made a couple more trips between the car and the house Gerry hurried off. Alone, Jean cracked open the kitchen window to encourage the paint fumes to trade places with the more pleasant breeze from the outdoors. There was a note on the fridge: Stump was at Richard's and would clean out the laundry room tomorrow. Figures. Always tomorrow.

A fresh bowl of dog food kept Dogg busy while Jean checked out the hall. The bathroom was full of ladders and tools, but the laundry room, which was even messier than before, had a little room on the floor. It would have to do for now.

She returned to the kitchen and put away the groceries and other items before she crammed a new collection of plastic and paper sacks onto the already overcrowded laundry room shelves. Now she could open up that hallway.

She jammed the drop cloth and paint supplies onto the limited space on the floor and carefully put the paint thinner can and brushes on top of the mess. The door wouldn't quite close but it was good enough for one night. A faint smile visited her lips. In the old days such moments led her to cigarettes and screwdrivers.

Back in the kitchen, Jean let Dogg in just as the phone rang. She smiled. "Hi, Myles. I was just thinking about you. I've been running around all day and I'm too exhausted to go to our meeting tonight. I just want to grab a hot bath and wind down."

"You should have thought of all that before you agreed to marry me," he teased.

"I still would have said the same thing."

"Don't worry about it. I understand. I'll check with you tomorrow. You'll feel better by then."

"Thanks for understanding, Honey. I love you."

"I love you, too."

Free for the evening, Jean retreated to her private bathroom, threw a capful of bubble bath in the tub and turned on the hot water. She hit the play button on the CD player and placed lighted candles in their designated places. After she closed both her bedroom and bathroom doors she turned off the overhead light, disrobed and settled gently into her glorious pool of luxury. Already soothed, she gently rested her head on the back of the tub and closed her tired eyes. She needed this.

For the next forty minutes Jean's favorite songs floated in and out of her sleepy mind while she welcomed a collection of happy thoughts about the rewards of sobriety and Myles and finally finding true love. She appreciated the aroma, the warmth of the water. The peace. Everybody had forgiven her past. She didn't need cigarettes or screwdrivers. It was the closest she'd been to heaven on earth since the day she rescued Stump from a horrible fate with his biological mother.

Eventually, she came out of a deep calm. She smelled smoke. Startled, she opened her eyes to a light haze and sat up. The smoke was stronger than she first thought. One of her neighbors must have lit a fireplace and it was blowing her way. She had to close her windows.

Standing up, the campfire smell was worse. She coughed, quickly put on her robe and struggled to breathe. Something was wrong. A tug on the bathroom door revealed a blanket of dark smoke had engulfed her bedroom. Still-darker smoke curled in from under the door to the hallway. What the hell was going on?

She cracked the door to the hall, but was overwhelmed by smoke before she could see what the problem was. Her lungs forced a cough as she wiped her stinging eyes and rushed back to the bathroom for better air.

There, she closed the door. Think. Think. She dunked a hand towel in bath water, held it to her mouth and sucked in two deep breaths. Had to try again. Make a run for it. She swung the door open for a second time. The bedroom was still darker. Black smoke burned her eyes and the overpowering odor of burning wood filled her lungs. The sting forbade her from gasping in horror.

Anxious to escape, she hurried along the bedroom wall, fighting her urge to take a breath. Her heart pounded a loud warning signal in her chest. She quickly seized the bedroom knob and pulled it inward so she could get to the living room, but a roiling mass of floor-to-ceiling fire bolts filled the hallway and chased her back. Lord. No exit here. A flood of adrenalin rushed through her veins as she slammed the door. What to do? She had to get back into the bathroom where it was slightly easier to breathe.

There, she sucked eagerly through her towel for partially filtered air, but it too was smoky. She coughed and sucked and coughed again. Her throat was on fire. If she didn't quit coughing, her stinging lungs would explode. She fell to the floor. Time was running out. Her brain throbbed and raced for an alternative. Anything was better than this. The windows were her only hope.

She hurried into the blackened bedroom yet again, and grabbed a large candle off the dresser. With all her strength she threw it at the window, breaking the glass. Both she and a room full of dark smoke rushed for the opening. Oh, God! She'd forgotten the bars.

CHAPTER 71

Unfriendly clouds spit a befitting drizzle on Stump as he drew closer to his neighborhood, carrying the barely watched DVD. The visit with Richard had been a bust. Richard's dad had come home and told Richard they were going to have to file for bankruptcy and move away in a few months because of the medical bills. Then he and Richard tried to watch *The Dark Knight* but The Big Dick had petered out.

Stump kicked at a stick. Everybody he cared about was moving away. He got a whiff of smoke, probably coming from a restaurant or somebody burning leaves. Some small ashes landed on his arm. The smoke odor got stronger. He kept going.

Up the street he saw people standing in the drizzle and pointing down the block toward his home. Overhead, smoke billowed in the sky. It was coming from one of the houses very close to his own. Stump jogged quickly, hoped nobody was hurt.

The last corner revealed the horror of horrors. Flames shot through the roof and windows of his own home. His heart pounded. Where was his Mom? He dropped his DVD and ran. "Mom. Mom." Others were in the street, but he couldn't see her among them.

He sprinted past the last few houses as large dark smoke clouds ballooned out his mother's bedroom window.

A neighbor was tugging on the bars. Stump slowed for a split second as he realized what that could mean. "Hang on lady," the guy said loudly. "They're coming."

"Mom. Mom," Stump screamed as loudly as he could as a series of sirens shrilled from a few blocks away.

Stump and two other men ran to the window. The earlier guy was now coughing and wiping his eyes. "Is my mom in there?"

"I think so," the guy said between gasps, "but I couldn't get her to answer."

"Let's all yank on these bars," another neighbor said excitedly.

Everybody grabbed hold. Crackling wood snapped continuously from deeper inside the home. "Mom. Mom. Hang on. I can hear the fire trucks coming."

"One. Two, Three." Stump and the others all yanked simultaneously, but the bars wouldn't budge.

"Again. One, two, three." No luck. "Again. One, two three."

The emergency equipment rounded the corner and a large fire truck sped to their home. A bunch of uniforms scurried around like angry ants. "Over here. Over here," Stump pleaded as he coughed and tugged on the window one more time.

Then from inside the window a weak hand inched its way over the top of the sill. Stump's heart pounded with hope. "Mom." Her head barely got to the sill. Her hair and face were black except for scribbles of tear tracks on her cheeks. She opened cherry-red eyes and withdrew a ragged towel from her lips. With horror in her eyes, she gasped but couldn't speak. She mouthed "I love you" at Stump before she slipped back down and out of sight as water from the fire hoses rained down on Stump's head.

"Mommmm!"

Somebody grabbed him. "Get back, son. You're in the way," said a fireman. He resisted but they were stronger. He coughed and gagged and rubbed his burning eyes. "Hurry. That's my mother in there," he cried desperately. "Please help her."

While hose-water rivered down, masked firemen threw axes at the bolts holding the bars to the wall while a smaller fire truck backed up as close to the house as possible. One guy tied a rope to both the truck and one of the bars on the window. "Get back," he yelped as he jumped in the cab and pulled with the truck, but the bars were too strong. The rope quickly snapped. "Double it up," somebody said.

"It won't be long enough."

Stump dropped to his knees. "God help her," he coughed out. "Please help her. I'll do anything."

Another fireman, an elderly one, touched Stump's shoulder while the others pecked impotently at the bars on the window. "Come with me, son. We need to get you to the hospital."

Stump shook his head. "I can't leave my mom. She needs me," he sniveled through a raw sore throat.

"You have to get treatment, son. We'll do the best we can and call you as soon as we know anything."

"No. No. I can't leave," he said, then coughed up blood.

Emergency personnel with an ambulance gurney charged toward him. "It won't help your mom if you choke to death," one of them said.

"But, that's my mom."

CHAPTER 72

Aunt Gerry was beside Stump in his hospital room when the late-night call came in. She immediately broke down and eventually sobbed her way through the bad news.

It was as if a grenade had exploded in Stump's stomach. He never knew anybody who died. He'd never cried like that either. They gave him some pills so he could sleep.

The next morning was no better. The residual stinging in his eyes and throat paled compared to the agony in his heart. He couldn't escape that shocking final image of his mom or the last words he saw her say. They'd said them to each other countless times, but this time they represented the most powerful message of his lifetime. She loved him. Love. He understood that word much better now. He knew to the marrow of his bones that he loved her, too. The tears returned. So did the sobs. The runny nose. Such pain! He needed her back.

By late morning he was examined and given clearance to leave. Shortly thereafter Uncle Dirk arrived. "I'm really sorry, Stump," he said as a nurse wheeled him towards the main entrance. "Your mom was a good woman, and she turned her life around."

Was? Sorry? Those words meant more now too. His shoulders and head sagged. Nobody could be sorrier than he was.

When they arrived at Aunt Gerry's house Stump could

see Willie looking out the window. Aunt Gerry had probably called school for both of them. Stump's lips trembled. He wiped away his freshest tears and wished that he was tougher.

Willie opened the door revealing a roomful of people, presumably neighbors. Stump sniffled, wiping his nose with his wrist. Dammit. Don't cry.

He barely joined the room when Aunt Gerry hurried to embrace him. Her nose and cheeks were red and blotchy. He took a deep breath and tried to control himself, but he dropped his head onto her shoulder and wept again. "I miss my mom," he sobbed. Sympathetic faces in the room were awash in tears of their own.

"Is there any word about what happened?" Uncle Dirk asked nobody in particular.

"Yes," Aunt Gerry said, finally withdrawing from her embrace with Stump. She patted her eyes with tissue. "They called a little while ago. They found her in the bathtub. She died from gas and smoke inhalation."

"Thank God," one of the visitors said. "At least the poor thing didn't suffer from the fire itself."

"But what happened?" Dirk persisted. "What started the fire?"

Stump wanted to know the same thing. He looked at Aunt Gerry and waited until she wiped her eyes. "They don't know yet. They said they have to make sure the property is safe before they can do an investigation. They're expecting to do that later this morning."

Stump's throat was dry and his lungs stung. If he hurt this badly, he didn't want to imagine what his mom went through. Not knowing what else to do, he sat there with watery eyes while conversations shifted from mortuaries to funeral services and to relatives whom Stump had never met. Would he have to go live with those people? Would he go to an orphanage? Texas with Willie? He paused. His eyes opened wide. "Dogg?" he yelped. "What about Dogg?"

Uncle Dirk turned his way. "Dogs have good instincts, Stump. He probably got away. We'll look for him a little later."

Probably? Probably wasn't good enough. "What about Myles? Why isn't he here?"

"He was here last night until late," Aunt Gerry said. "I suspect he had a long night too." She put her hand on Stump's shoulder. "You can stay in Willie's room, Honey. We'll get you some clothes, too."

He hadn't thought about his clothes or anything else he owned. None of it could have survived that fire. All he knew for certain was he would gladly accept any version of his mother if given the chance. Even if she was mangled up like Richard; even if she drank; even if they were poorer than before. Anything would be better than losing her.

CHAPTER 73

For the moment Stump was alone on Aunt Gerry's couch. Her voice quivered as she explained to a caller the tragic story about Stump's mom. Stump felt sorry for her. Thought about the word love again. Obviously Aunt Gerry loved his mom, which was remarkable considering all the years his mom leaned on her. He appreciated her more now, too. Just then a car pulled up.

Stump looked out the window. It didn't look good. Nothing looked good lately. Earlier Uncle Dirk went out to look for Dogg, but Stump wasn't allowed to go. The absence of a positive sign from Uncle Dirk as he walked up the sidewalk said it all. When he stepped inside, he simply glanced at Stump and slowly shook his head. "I gotta go," Aunt Gerry said to her caller from behind Stump.

She hurried to Stump's side and wrapped her arms around him. "I'm so sorry, Honey."

Amazingly they both had more tears to shed. Stump sniffled. "I'm all alone, Aunt Gerry."

"You're not alone, Honey," she said solemnly. "You've got all of us."

Uncle Dirk rested a hand on Stump's shoulder. "They found Dogg pressed against the back door. Couldn't get out. They said the gases got him."

Emptiness, worse than that which Stump felt when Richard fell, filled him. He whimpered.

"Any word from Myles?" Uncle Dirk asked.

Aunt Gerry looked up through red, watery eyes. "Not since last night. Didn't answer his phone. Do you suppose you two could look for him?"

When Stump saw Myles's truck, his whole body trembled with relief. It took several loud knocks before Uncle Dirk tried the knob. Inside, obnoxious body odor overpowered the unmistakable smell of bourbon. Myles lay shirtless, belly up on the couch. He raised his head, moaned, and dropped back onto a small red silk pillow. "Whew," Uncle Dirk said. "Let's open a window."

That done, Stump looked toward the kitchen. The booze bottle, nearly empty, sat upright on the counter. Its bag and a soggy receipt were crumpled on the floor.

"It looks like you had a pretty rough night," Uncle Dirk said to Myles.

Myles mumbled something inaudible and then sat up. He placed his elbows on his knees and lowered his head into his hands. He sobbed for a moment and then raised his head. "Why would God take her away from us, just when she finally got her life together?"

Once again Stump knew how somebody else felt. A stomach monster had been bombarding him with the identical question. He joined his mother's fiancé on the couch.

"I'm sorry, Stumpster," Myles slurred with bourbon breath, "I got drunk. It's the one thing your mother wouldn't want me to do. You were right. It was just a matter of time."

Stump instinctively laid his hand on his elder friend's knee. "It's okay, Myles. I understand your pain. You get a pass this time."

"Thanks, Stumpster. You're a good kid. I'm done drinkin' now." Then, he lay back down and seemed to pass out.

Dirk held his finger to his lips, then whispered to Stump,

"Go get me a better pillow. We'll turn him around, and lay him down." Stump nodded.

After they got Myles straightened out, Stump poured out the remainder of the bourbon. "He's done with this," he said, having already forgiven Myles.

CHAPTER 74

It was late afternoon when Detective Sanchez and Sergeant Byrdswain pulled up to Mrs. Ellerbe's home. "It's strange," Byrdswain said, interrupting the younger one's thoughts. "Our little two-man shop has been open for business nearly sixteen months and never had a real homicide—"

"And now we might have two of them," Sanchez added, thinking they might be connected. "Should we call in the county office?"

"Not yet. We may have a lot fewer resources than they do but our shoes are just as good as theirs."

"Good, 'cause they'd probably just brush me aside since I look like I'm young enough to be a Girl Scout."

Byrdswain sniggered. "It's not quite that bad, but you have a good point. We'll just leave them out of it if we can." He pulled up to the curb. "You take the lead. She'll like you." Grateful for the opportunity, Sanchez nodded.

An elderly woman, puffy-faced and red-eyed, cracked the door slightly. "Yes?" Her voice was barely audible.

"Mrs. Ellerbe?" I'm Detective Sanchez. "This is Sergeant Byrdswain. We called earlier to discuss your granddaughter."

"Just a minute." Mrs. Ellerbe closed the door and unlocked two different chains before she reopened it and slowly led the detectives to the living room. There, she sat on one end of an old but solid-looking sofa. A basket of just-used tissues lay at her feet. Sanchez couldn't help but notice that the room was hot and smelled like damp cement.

She knelt at Mrs. Ellerbe's feet and placed her hand on the closest knee. "We're very sorry about your loss, ma'am, but we need to ask you a few questions."

Granny put her hand on top of Sanchez's. "Go ahead. I'll try." Her voice was soft and meek.

"Thank you, ma'am. We won't be long. Would it be okay with you if I refer to your granddaughter by her first name?"

"It's Rachel, and I like to be called Granny."

"Yes, ma'am. Thank you, Granny." Sanchez rose and moved around to sit at Granny's side. She took the elder woman's hand. "Did Mr. Evans drop by to speak with you earlier?"

Granny nodded.

"What did he say?"

Granny sniffled; her lip trembled. "He said they found her body at the bottom of a ravine, but it's too early to know how she got there." She looked straight into Sanchez's eyes. "Do you think Rachel killed herself?"

"That's what we're trying to find out, ma'am. Would you say she was depressed?"

"She's been a lot happier since she met Mac."

"What about before that?"

"She's struggled ever since her parents were killed in that accident." Granny lowered her head. "We both have."

Sanchez rubbed the old woman's hand and arm. "Take a deep breath. That usually helps." Granny sighed and the couch cushions seemed to swallow her up.

"We've been told that you're Rachel's only relative. Is that true?"

"She was my daughter's daughter," Granny whispered. "All I had."

"If you don't mind my asking, what happened to your daughter?"

"Boating accident. She drowned. Her husband, too."

Sanchez shook her head. "What kinds of things made Rachel sad?"

"Her job. Mostly the kids. Some of them have it pretty rough."

"What about men? Did she have any serious relationships?"

"She dated a few of them, but nothing worked out, until Mac."

"Did Rachel ever mention the name Kevin Lapport?"

Granny paused. "Don't think so. Is he one of Mac's friends?"

"We're not sure. Are you certain Rachel hasn't mentioned him?"

Granny grabbed another tissue and wiped her nose. "My memory isn't as good as it use to be. I can't be sure of anything."

"Do you think Rachel was the kind of person who would take her own life?"

"I don't think so, but I guess you never know what's going on in a person's mind."

"What about enemies? Was there anybody who would want to hurt her?"

"Not that I know of. She had to discipline some tough students from time to time, but I don't think she ever feared any of them."

"How about Mr. Evans. Did he always treat her well?"

Granny nodded. "Mac would never hurt Rachel. That's what made him so special."

"How did Mr. Evans appear to you tonight? Was he upset or more matter-of-fact?"

"Heartbroken, just like me."

"I see," said Sanchez. "How long have you known Mr. Evans?"

Granny paused. "It's been nearly a year."

"What does he do for a living?"

"He's an electrician at NASA, near their home."

Byrdswain made a note while Sanchez continued. "Do you know where he comes from? His home town, I mean?"

"The Midwest I think, but he never talked about that very much."

"Have you met any of his friends or family?"

She shook her head. "He said he lost touch with them years ago."

Sanchez took a deep breath. "You're doing fine, Granny. I just have a few more questions. I understand that Rachel just received a large trust?"

"My husband set it up for her."

"When did she first learn about the trust?"

"Just a couple weeks ago, when she and Mac got back from Las Vegas, after they got married."

"What about Mr. Evans? When did he find out about it?"

"The same night Rachel did. I told them both myself." A weak smile visited Granny wrinkled lips. "We danced and danced. It was a wonderful evening, just like Pappy planned."

"Are you certain that neither of them knew about it earlier than that?"

"No, definitely not. None of my friends. Nobody. My husband wanted to keep it a secret until Rachel got married, so I was real careful to honor his wishes."

"We understand it was eleven million dollars?"

"Before interest. It's twelve million now."

Byrdswain made a brief note on his pad, then joined the interview. "Just to be clear, you don't have any problem with this fellow, who you only knew for less than a year, getting a lot of your money?"

"No, of course not. The trust money was set aside just for Rachel and whoever she married. It just turned out to be Mac, and he's always been nice to both of us, even before he knew of the trust."

Byrdswain hesitated, nodded. "Okay, thank you, Mrs. Ellerbe. I think that'll be all for now."

Sanchez patted Granny's hand, then rose. "Thank you, Granny. You've been very helpful. We'll get back to you as soon as we know anything."

Back in the car, Byrdswain asked his young partner, "What do you think, detective? Did Evans do it?"

"I don't see how. He was pretty shook up this morning and his alibi is solid. We've seen the victim's suicide note on her computer, and learned from her own grandmother that she wasn't particularly stable, so suicide makes sense. Plus we verified that he just learned of the trust a short time ago. Everything checks out. He seems clean."

"I'm not so sure. It's awfully convenient."

"Convenient? He lived with the victim for the better part of a year before they got married. That doesn't sound very convenient to me."

Byrdswain nodded. "Alright. Convenient may not be the correct word, but what if he suddenly decided that a rich guy has a lot of new options in life, and his wife was holding him back?"

"But he couldn't have killed her. We already verified that there was only forty minutes between the time Rachel was seen at school and when he bought a beer at the bowling alley. He'd have to drive thirty-five miles to the scene, then kill her, then drive all the way back in that time, plus stop at an ATM. Not even remotely possible."

Byrdswain pursed his lips. "He could have done it right after Rachel got out of work; then he could have stashed her body somewhere while he went to the bowling alley to set up his alibi. Maybe he took her body up there and dumped it after that dishwasher took him home."

"Possible," Sanchez said, "But how? We would have seen evidence somewhere, like strangle marks on her neck, or blood at their home or in her car. And how would he get home? We know he didn't have his motorcycle because the security guard said it was at the bowling alley all night."

"He could have drugged her, or gotten her drunk, then thrown her over. Could have had some other bike or car up there or even an accomplice."

Sanchez tilted her head. "The M.E. might find something,

but I doubt it. I looked in the medicine cabinet, and their drawers, and the kitchen, even in his motorcycle. No heavy-duty drugs anywhere."

"Well then, maybe they went up there together, after the dishwasher took Evans home, then had a fight and Evans threw her over the edge."

"That would be after nine o'clock," Sanchez said. "The M.E. ought to be able to tell us if that was near the time of death; but even if it is, we'd have to figure out how he got home."

"He could have walked or hitchhiked."

Sanchez shook her head. "Don't think so. Way too far to walk, and people don't pick up hitchhikers much, especially in the middle of the night. Even if he did hitchhike, how would we find whoever picked him up?"

"I dunno. I'm just thinking out loud. What about an accomplice?"

"I thought about that too," Sanchez replied. "But that doesn't make much sense either. Evans just learned of the trust a couple weeks ago. He'd have to have a big change of heart about his brand-new marriage and then know somebody heartless at his fingertips who he could count on to help him pull off the murder—all on extremely short notice—and do all of that for money that was half his already. Then there's the timing issue."

"Timing?"

"If he did have such an accomplice, what's the rush? They could have taken their time and done it when it was less suspicious."

"Could be," Byrdswain said. "We might learn more about his acquaintances in the morning after we get some background information. But just in case, I want to ask his neighbors if they've seen him hanging around with any new people lately."

Sanchez nodded. "So, what do we do next?"

"First off, I want to compliment you for the way you handled yourself back there. You're coming along nicely."

"Why do I think there's a qualifier coming?"

He cracked his window. "Just don't get too soft-hearted. It can cloud your thinking. There's not much more we can do tonight. Let's get some sleep and get back at it in the morning.

"I'll check their email and phone records, and find out if there's anything interesting on the computer."

"Good. I'm going to put a tail on him for a few days, just in case there's an accomplice lurking in the shadows. I want to see if this guy really did fall into a pot of gold."

"It happens," Sanchez said. "One guy just hit the Powerball for seventy million."

"But nobody died."

They arrived at the station and pulled into their parking spot. Sanchez turned to her partner. "What about the law firm that set up the trust? There had to be a couple people over there who knew about it. At least the attorney who drew up the documents."

Byrdswain nodded. "Now, that's another good point, detective. We'll visit them tomorrow."

CHAPTER 75

"We'll be brief, Mr. Fritz," Sergeant Byrdswain said after they were all seated. "We know your time is valuable."

"Call me Fritz," said the dark-haired late fifties attorney. He pushed a button on his phone. "Sharolyn. Would you mind joining us in here for a minute?"

Detective Sanchez glanced around. Save for a legal pad and a picture of Fritz's family on the corner of his desk, the room was devoid of clutter. Everything was organized and "ship-shape," as the sergeant liked to call it.

Almost instantly, Sharolyn joined the room. Roughly the same age as Fritz, she wore a light-blue button-down blouse and a black skirt that covered enough of her thighs to remain tasteful but not so much as to hide her slender knees. Her short brown hair was beauty parlor perfect. "Yes?" she said in an all-business tone.

"Have a seat," said Fritz. "Sergeant Byrdswain and Detective Sanchez want to ask us a few questions."

"Thank you both." Byrdswain said. He turned to Sharolyn. "We're trying to get some information regarding the Ellerbe trust. Do you remember them?"

"Oh, sure," she said. "Mr. Ellerbe was an interesting gentleman, and we met with his granddaughter just a couple weeks ago."

"That's another reason we're here. The granddaughter, Rachel, died recently."

"Oh no," Sharolyn said. She turned toward Sanchez. "What happened?"

Sanchez shrugged. "Looks like suicide. But that's what we're trying to figure out."

Sharolyn sighed. "How can I help?"

Byrdswain began. "I'd like you to think back to the very first time that you helped prepare the original trust."

She paused a moment. "That would have been over 20 years ago—so long I don't really recall the first meeting."

"Understandable, but let's see if we can reconstruct what would have happened to that file. Were you and Fritz the only ones who worked here then?"

"I'd say we had about six different attorneys and I did the clerical work for all of them."

"Anybody else work for the company?"

"Just a receptionist at the front desk. I think her name was Debbie. She answered phones too. But that's about it."

"I see. So how did a typical file get set up? Did you sit in on the meetings with a legal pad and take notes, or was there some other technique?"

"The attorneys usually met with the clients in private. Then, they made copies of their notes and put instructions in my in-basket."

"From there, what did you do?"

"We were doing a few things on the computer by then, but we still made hard copies of everything, so I got a file folder from the supply closet and labeled it. Then I made a first draft on the computer, printed it out and gave the file to the attorney for review."

"So if you had to guess you'd say this is how you and Fritz handled the Ellerbe trust?"

"That was our normal policy up 'til about fifteen years ago, when we were all linked together on the same network, and we could send copies back and forth a lot easier."

"Okay. What did you typically do with a file like the Ellerbe's after that?"

"The lawyers made any revisions and we passed the file back and forth until we got the final version. From there, they'd meet with the clients again—to sign the papers."

"And each time you revised the document, you made hard copies for the file?"

"It seems inefficient now, but we didn't have our networks set up or flash drives or anything like that."

"What did you do with the earlier drafts as you created newer, modified ones?"

"I kept them until I knew I was done with the file; then I returned all of the attorney's papers to him and threw my working copies away."

Byrdswain scrunched his brow. "You threw your copies away?"

"We still had the attorney's original notes and computer copies of all the drafts, so I got rid of the superfluous papers."

"Could any of the hard copies have gotten out of this office or gotten in somebody else's hands—like maybe another attorney or the janitors at night?"

"Don't know why they'd do that," Sharolyn said. "But it's definitely possible."

Byrdswain raised his eyebrows. "Possible? How?"

Sharolyn looked at Fritz, then back to Byrdswain. "Once in a while one of the attorneys would visit my in-basket to add something to their project or modify a comment or even take their files home. They might have gotten a few papers mixed up when they did stuff like that."

"Did anybody else have access to your computer?"

"Only if I wasn't here, like maybe after hours or on weekends." She grinned. "But they usually had to call me first—to figure out my system."

Byrdswain faced Fritz. "What about a master file? Are there any other copies of the finished documents in some other place where different people could get to them?"

Fitz nodded. "We keep a set of original documents in the file room, and each of the attorneys keeps another set of originals in our personal files."

"So it's possible that somebody else, like another attorney within the firm, could review a file without you knowing it?"

"I've never seen anybody doing anything like that—unless one attorney is covering for another one who is in court or on vacation, but it's pretty rare."

Byrdswain turned back to Sharolyn. "Do you know if anybody else ever reviewed the Ellerbe file?"

"Trusts like that can sit around for years or decades before they're needed or even touched. Just not much reason for anybody to look at it."

Byrdswain returned his attention to Fritz. "Has anybody ever gone through or breached any of those files?"

"Not that I know of," said Fritz.

"Can either one of you think of any reason why somebody would sneak into the Ellerbe file in particular, or what might make it special or different from the rest?"

Fritz shook his head. "Not really. It's a little more money than most of the trusts that we've set up, but not the biggest one. Mostly it's just like the others."

Byrdswain paused. "So, let me be certain I understand this. You set up the Ellerbe trust around twenty years ago and it's possible that other attorneys or janitors or maybe even other clients could have seen some of your computer-work or secret papers somewhere along the way, but there's no particular incentive to do so?"

Fritz nodded. "It's possible," Sergeant. "But, we're very careful to protect the privacy of our clients—just like a police station."

Byrdswain took another glance around the private office; then he looked at Sanchez, then back to Fritz. He smiled. "To tell you the truth, Fritz, it sounds like you do a better job of guarding private information than I do." He stood.

"I think that'll be all for now. Again, I want to thank both of you for your time."

*   *   *

Later that afternoon and across town a shadow moved on the sidewalk. A closer look indicated that Detective Sanchez had just visited one of Mac's neighbors. He hurried off to the kitchen, dabbed his fingers on his onion and waited. The knock came minutes later.

Red eyes awash, Mac greeted the detectives and let them in. Byrdswain went right to the living room while Sanchez delayed just a moment. Mac caught a whiff of her body lotion and gestured toward the sofa. "Actually," she said, "I'd like to have a look around again."

"Go ahead," said Mac softly.

"As a matter of fact," she said, "I want to examine your shoes."

"My shoes? What for?"

"There were some shoe prints on the viewing platform. We just want to be certain you weren't out there."

Visions of the path and platform swished through Mac's head. He couldn't remember any mud or loose dirt that he might have stepped in. Either they were bluffing or it was old dirt from somebody else. "It's okay with me, but I already told you where I was the night it happened. Didn't you check it out?"

Sanchez smiled. "We like to be thorough."

"I thought we were talking about a suicide, but if it will make you feel any better, go ahead."

"Thank you," she said, "I'm going to check the garage first." He wiped his eye and waved his approval.

Byrdswain interrupted. "You told us you're unemployed, but Mrs. Ellerbe said you work at NASA. Where would she get an idea like that?"

Mac tilted his head and pursed his lips. "It was Rachel's

idea. She wanted everybody to think I was an electrician until I got a job. She even liked me to dress up most mornings and act like I was driving to work. I just went along with her."

"Didn't you find that strange?"

"Sure, but it was important to her. And it got me moving, so it was okay."

"Something else has come up. Did you hear about the gynecologist who was strangled last week?"

"No. Why would I?"

"We did a little checking. It seems he's the same one your wife used to go to. Did she say anything about his death?"

"Rachel's gynecologist? That's horrible."

"Don't you find it interesting that two deaths in such a short time were people who knew each other?"

Play if cool, Dude. "Well, I wouldn't know about things like that, Sergeant, but Palmdale's a small town. There are probably lots of locals who go to that doctor."

"Where were you a week ago Wednesday?"

Mac's mind raced to the newscast he and Miranda saw the day they visited Mickey. They got back late that afternoon and the reporter said the doctor died just a little earlier. That would mean around three-thirty. "Not sure but that might have been the afternoon Rachel and I drove to Santa Barbara to watch the sunset."

"Anybody who can vouch for you?"

Mac would have liked to say something like, "I'm not the one who has to prove anything, you are," but Miranda had warned him about being belligerent. "Not really. I can't even remember what we did."

"I want you to know we're going to check it out," Byrdswain warned while looking him in the eye.

Stay calm. "I'm sure you know what you're doing."

"On another matter, you said you came here about a year ago. Is that right?"

Mac sniffed. "A little less than that, but yes."

"Had you ever been in the area before that?"

"No. Why?"

"What about your parents and family? Did any of them have relatives back here?"

"Not that I know of. My mom's family came from Missouri, and my dad's roots were in North Dakota."

"How'd you meet your wife, Mr. Evans?"

"I was driving my motorcycle past the high school and pulled over to watch some guys on the football field. Her car was there, she had a flat and I helped her fix it."

Byrdswain nodded, reached inside his jacket, laid out the copy of the *Gazette* that Mac left at Rachel's computer. "Did you see this newspaper?"

Mac reached out to take a closer look. Then, "Yeah, we subscribe to it. I glanced through it a couple days ago. What of it?"

"Did your wife see it?"

"I don't know. Why?"

Byrdswain pointed to the article on page three. "Do you know Kevin Lapport?"

"Who?" Mac looked closer, wiped his eyes. "Oh. The dead guy. Never heard of him. Why?"

"It appears your wife knew him pretty well."

"Really? That's strange." He looked back at the newspaper. "She never mentioned him, but I've only known her for a year. She hasn't told me about everybody she's met in her life. Did he work at the school too?"

Byrdswain pulled a folded white sheet of paper out of his pocket and handed it to Mac. "See for yourself."

"What's this?"

"It appears to be your wife's suicide note."

Mac wrinkled his brow, "Suicide note?" He grabbed at the paper, unfolded it. "Where'd you get this?"

"Her computer, at the school. They let us print a copy."

Mac examined the paper and whispered the note out loud.

K-Lap's gone.
God's punishing us.
so ashamed
forgive me.

He slowly lifted his head, his lip twitching. "Are you telling me she was having an affair with this guy?"

"Looks like it." Byrdswain said.

"Can't be. Not Rachel."

"We think you might have found out about the affair, got angry, and pushed your wife off the platform."

"That's ridiculous. This is the first time I've heard of it." Mac lowered his head into his hand, wiped his eyes, and the onion did its thing. "This is unbelievable."

On their way to their car Sanchez looked over her shoulder and addressed her partner. "Why did you ask him about the gynecologist? We already checked that out and nothing was unusual, just a routine exam."

"I just wanted to see how he'd react if he knew we were going there."

"What did you think?"

"Not much there, really. I'm beginning to think you might be correct. He could be telling us the truth."

Detective Sanchez nodded. "Looks like it."

CHAPTER 76

Miranda's burner sang out. By this time, she had convinced Don she should treat Mac better or risk chasing him off—perhaps with all of their money. "Hello, Sweets," she said, this time not sharing the phone with Don. "It's good to hear from you. Everything okay?"

"I'm scared shitless."

"Why? Where are you?"

"Rachel's. The cops were just here, asking a bunch of questions. They think the two murders are connected."

Even though Mac had no idea it was Don who killed the gynecologist, Miranda and Don had already covered that base between themselves. "Don't worry about it. They're just fishing. Even if they do snoop around, the doctor told me he was going to keep her file sterile so there wouldn't be anything suspicious about it."

"Thank God. I wish you would have told me that."

"I'm sorry, Sweets. It didn't seem relevant at the time, but it doesn't matter. It's a small town and he had almost a thousand patients, so it's no surprise that she went to him."

"Whew. I said something similar."

"It's a dead end. That ought to be good enough for them to back off. Everything else go okay?"

"I'm more nervous than I expected. I want to see you. Hold you. Sleep with you."

"You know I want to, Sweets, but we have to be very careful. Anybody sees us together, it would arouse suspicion. That's why I came out to L.A. so we wouldn't be tempted to do something stupid."

"Your head is always way ahead of me."

"I've had extra time to think out the details, when you've been with her. There've been some lonely nights and weekends for me too, you know?"

"If not now, when?"

"I've been reading up on things like this. As I understand it, if there's no sign of a crime, they try to wrap these things up fairly early so the family can grieve and begin to move on. Once they declare it a suicide, they won't pay attention any longer. You have to be the grieving husband, go to the mortuary, attend the services, do what any other husband would do."

"Mortuaries give me the creeps."

As usually was the case, Miranda felt easiness when talking with Mac. There was give and take. He listened to her. Empathized with her, even when he was the one who was living in a pit of drama. "Ick. I know what you mean," she said, "but you can handle it. Just do a closed casket service. They're less suspicious and you won't have to look at her."

"Alright, but I still need to see you."

"Not for a few more days, Sweets, but there's something else I think you should do. I need you to get some money."

"Is that a good idea?"

She shook her head as if he could see. "No problem. A rich guy in your position would need some operating capital. As long as you don't do anything wild it'll all appear to be normal."

"Okay, I can stop by the bank. How much do you need?"

"A couple hundred to buy some things for Mickey and several thousand so you can rent a nicer place."

"A new place? I'd love to get out of this home, but why don't I just move in with you?"

"Too soon. We wouldn't want anybody to think you have a full-time girlfriend already. You should move to someplace more befitting a stud muffin of your means. Something bigger, maybe with a little land and no reminders of a dead wife."

"Great idea. Let's do it."

Impressed but not surprised, Miranda thought about how unselfish Mac was. He didn't hesitate at all about the money that would help her brother to have a few extras for the first time in years. *If Don weren't there, she'd be the first to say I love you.* Instead she simply enjoyed the moment.

"Are you crying?"

How could he read her so well? "I don't know how I can ever repay you."

* * *

Mac adjusted Annie's kickstand and immediately began a conversation. "Good morning, friend," he said while turning the key.

The quick start was as if she'd been waiting. *"Welcome back."*

He sniffed his finger and wrapped his hand around the throttle handle. "Can you smell the onion?"

"Not really. What gives?"

"You wouldn't believe what I've been going through."

"After your girlfriend offed your wife?"

"Dealing with Rachel's death is bad enough but I really feel sorry for Granny. She's a nice old lady. Too bad she had to get hurt."

"Didn't you say she'd get over it?"

"That was before I got to know her." He shifted into cruising gear, shook his head.

"It's too late to worry about that now, isn't it?"

"Spilled milk, I guess, but right now, I gotta get Miranda some money. Later they're going to release Rachel's car. Then I'm meeting Granny at the mortuary. That'll be rough. After that we gotta figure out what to do with Rachel's house and all her things."

"*That's a load.*"

"No shit. I wish you and I could just blow this town."

"*I'm game.*"

"Don't tempt me. I ain't seen whites in my eyes for days. To top things off, there's a couple detectives snooping around." He glanced in the right-side mirror. The closest car, a gray late-model station wagon, was a half-block back. He gently dipped into the turn lane, coasted to the intersection and caught the light. He turned right and accelerated. A long block ahead, the bank was across the street. Before he dipped Annie into the turn lane, he checked her mirror and then raised his eyebrows. The wagon had made the same turn and was way back there, moving slowly. "I'll be damned," he muttered.

CHAPTER 77

The first whiff of Aunt Gerry's cooking jarred Stump awake. Unfortunately, as soon as his brain reminded him of his mother and Dogg, the stomach monster stole away his appetite all over again. He wanted to go back to sleep where he could forget it all. He wanted his old life back. He wanted his mom.

The bedroom door opened. "Come eat a pancake," Uncle Dirk said. A lazy glance to Willie's bed revealed that he'd gone off to school where all he'd have to worry about was taking tests and getting laughed at in gym class. Stump scoffed at the false importance his peers lent to such activities.

Aunt Gerry's hair was drawn back in a ponytail. As before, her eyes were bloodshot, her robe untidy. Somehow, some cinnamon pancakes made their way to the table. "Morning," was all he could think of to say.

"Good morning, Honey," she repeated, then gave him a hug.

He halfheartedly forked a pancake, doused it in margarine and poured a quarter-bottle of syrup all over it. In a previous time, Aunt Gerry might have reprimanded him for being so wasteful, but she simply slid him a cup of hot tea as she'd been doing since he was released from the hospital. "How's your throat?"

"You know something, Aunt Gerry?" he said, softly. "I owe you an apology."

"Why? For what?"

"Until mom died, I never really understood how much you guys love me and Willie. You've helped me a whole bunch of times, but I just took everything for granted. I thought you were silly for making me use good grammar and not wanting me to cuss and everything. I'm sorry for all of that. I should have appreciated you more. I promise to try harder."

"Oh, my goodness. Now you're going to make me cry again." She bent and wrapped her arms around his neck. "That's one of the sweetest things anybody's ever said to me, Stump. Anybody. Ever."

Some other time Stump would have thought the tears that swam their way into his eyes were corny. "I just want to say thank you and I love you."

Aunt Gerry squeezed his neck just as the doorbell rang. Stump followed her to the living room, hot tea in hand. It was the elder fireman who had escorted Stump to the ambulance a few days earlier. "I'm sorry I look a fright," Aunt Gerry said. "Things haven't been easy around here lately."

"I understand, ma'am." He turned to Stump. "How are you holding up?"

"I guess I'm okay. My throat still hurts a little, but that's about it."

"I'm so sorry about your mom. That's one of the most difficult things about my job."

"I never knew you guys had to be so brave."

The chief nodded. "We finished our investigation and thought you'd like to know what we found out."

"Yes. Please," Aunt Gerry said. "Please come in. Sit down."

"We've seen this kind of thing before," he began. "It happens too often, especially in some of the older neighborhoods."

Stump swallowed some tea and rubbed his throat as he listened carefully.

"It appears there were quite a few highly flammable items in the center of the home where the washer and dryer and hot water heater were."

Stump clenched his teeth, thinking about all his magazines and the tax returns and the Christmas wrapping paper.

"Near as we can tell, sometime during the storm some paper sacks must have fallen off the top shelves." Stump recalled all the paper that he and Willie stuffed around the metal box when they looked for a birth certificate. He set down his tea.

"There was some paint thinner in a can and some paint brushes. When the items from the shelves hit the can, it must have tipped over, spilling the thinner and spreading fumes everywhere."

Aunt Gerry lifted her hands to her mouth "Oh, no," she said.

Stump's stomach monster bit him.

"By that time, Ms. Randolph had begun a bath, which caused the hot water heater to kick on and the whole place ignited. All the rising heat brought down anything else that was loose on the shelves. There were lots of magazines and other combustibles."

"And she didn't hear any of it because she likes to play her music when she bathes," Gerry added, whimpering.

"That's probably right. We also found some open windows. Throw in wooden doors and poisonous, pitch-black smoke from burning carpets and it just takes a few minutes for a fire to close off the entire house."

Another gusher of tears flooded Stump's eyes. "This is all my fault," he cried between gasps. "Mom asked me over and over to clean out that room. But I made excuse after excuse. If I'd done what she asked me—"

"That's part of it, son," the fireman said, cutting Stump off. He sat forward, raised a hand. "The bigger issue was those bars. They appear to have been installed before there were building codes. That's one of the problems with the older neighborhoods. These days, when consumers install bars like that they have to pull a permit and have safety latches that operate from the inside—precisely to prevent situations like this."

"Why didn't anybody say anything?" Aunt Gerry asked through her own flowing tears.

"Grandfather clauses. When they change the codes it's only for new construction and remodels. Not anybody else."

Stump shook his head. "I don't care about any of that shit. If I would have done what my mom asked me to do, she'd still be alive today." He wept wildly. "I killed my mom. I killed my mom."

With tear-filled eyes, Aunt Gerry sprung to his side and pulled him to her. "It was an accident, Honey."

"No it wasn't, Aunt Gerry. I killed her."

"I'm very sorry for all of you," the fireman said. "It's not really anybody's fault. It's the combination of a few bad things that happened all at once. As I said, these things sometimes happen in the older areas."

CHAPTER 78

As much as the thought terrified and sickened her, Miranda resigned herself to the inevitable fact that she was destined to play a role in the demise of either Mac or Don. At the moment, she and Don were at the Pier Market Restaurant on Fisherman's Wharf, where there were candles and flowers on the tables and soft background music. Miranda slipped her right foot out of her pumps and rubbed it on Don's leg as they waited for an after-dinner glass of tawny port.

"We gotta get more cash," Don said.

Miranda reached her fingers out and touched Don's lips. "We said we were going to forget about things like that for tonight."

The waiter arrived with their wine, slowly removed the cork and offered it to Don. "No thanks," Don said.

Undeterred, the waiter poured the port into a crystal glass and passed it gracefully to Don. Without examining the contents he sniffed at the edge of the glass, as if he wanted to get the exercise over with.

Miranda reached her hand nearly half-way across the table. "Thank you for making all of this possible, Donnie." She slowly withdrew her hand, hoping Don would hold it like he did on visitor's day.

"You know something," he said, missing the hint. Sometimes I forget what a beautiful woman you are."

She raised her eyebrows, rubbed her bare foot on his leg again. "How nice. What made you say that?"

"I dunno. I guess I finally had a moment to pay attention."

"You'll have to do that more often. I like it when you take the time to appreciate me."

"Yeah. I know I could do better, but—" He looked at his watch. "We've already been here long enough. What would you say to us heading back to our room?"

"What's the rush?" she asked softly, trying to get him to enjoy the moment. "We haven't even finished dinner yet."

"I know, but you make me horny."

"I'm glad to hear that, but we have all night. I'm looking forward to some port and dessert."

Don pursed his lips. "Okay, but you're looking so good, I don't know how long I can wait." He may have been a little too direct, but it was nice to hear that he was paying attention to her as a woman.

As soon as they ate their dessert, he pushed his plate back. "I gotta get out of here. Let's at least go for a walk or something."

Outside, the brisk salt air filled their lungs. Miranda took Don's hand, and they crossed the street to the boardwalk overlooking the Pacific. Once there, a wooden handrail was all that separated them from the relentless waves that played tag under the moonlight. A handful of pigeons nervously pecked at the boardwalk for crumbs while a lone gull with a mangled foot limped along as if to escort them to the best spot before it flew off. They leaned up against the rail and gazed over the water toward the far-off lights of small boats bobbing up and down. Miranda leaned gently into Don's side. "Put your arm around me, Donnie."

Don did, then he tapped the top of the handrail. "What does this remind you of?"

She cringed, knowing precisely what he meant. She considered admonishing him, but chose discretion instead. "You know what?" she whispered. "I've got a surprise for you."

"Oh, yeah? What's that?"

She lifted her purse slightly. "It's in here. Close your eyes."

Don grinned. "Okay. Cool." He did as requested.

"Do you know why I'm a lot colder than you are right now?"

He tilted his head. "Colder? Not really."

"Keep your eyes closed," she reminded him as she pulled a pair of white lacey panties from her purse. "See if you can guess what I'm rubbing on your face?" She lightly draped the delicate undies across his forehead and slowly, teasingly, guided them up and down and from side to side and then rubbed them gently on his cheeks and eyes and lips.

With his eyes still closed, Don tapped a lone finger across the silky material and a wide toothy smile washed across his face. "Oooh, you naughty girl."

"I didn't think I'd need to wear them tonight," she said. "Now you have to take a two-part test." She placed the panties in his hand and lifted his arms slightly before she leaned into him. They wrapped themselves tightly together and slowly, slowly, slowly enjoyed each other's lips and tongues. Miranda moaned softly. Moments later she gently pulled away and whispered, "Congratulations. You passed the oral part of the exam."

"The oral part?" he murmured as he opened his eyes.

She touched his lips with her index finger. "The second half of the test has to be taken back at the hotel."

"I'm in." Don held up her bikinis. "What do I do with these?"

She smiled and moved his hands toward the rail. "Leave them right here."

In their car, and on their way back to their hotel, Miranda knelt on the seat and teasingly played with his hair and kissed his ears and neck. She ran her hand around his thigh. He reached for her, but she quickly placed his hand back on the steering wheel. "Not while you're driving. That would be unsafe."

When they got to the elevator, Miranda leaned into Don, encouraging him to put his arm around her, but it seemed as if he was simply going through the motions. They arrived at their floor and he quickly scooted her toward their room. Barely inside, he grabbed at her clothes. "What's the rush?" she whispered. "We have plenty of time."

But it was no use. She'd seen that look in his eyes plenty of times. He was too revved up to play slow-down games. A half-hour later, they'd both cleaned up and Don was fast asleep. He just needed a little more time.

*   *   *

Two mornings later, north of San Francisco, with giant redwoods all around them, Miranda and Don pulled out of the gas station and headed for home. Don drove, which gave her an opportunity to lay her head back. As far as she was concerned Don blew a good opportunity.

It wasn't necessarily his relatively sophomoric performance in the bedroom that bothered her as much as his general lack of intimacy in the day-to-day life. If it weren't for his other qualities such as excitement, loyalty and his calmness under pressure, she'd already know which brother to spare. And then there was the fairness issue. He was still getting used to life out of prison.

"I've bit my tongue long enough," Don said, abruptly. "It's time to talk about eliminating that prick brother of mine."

She sucked some air between her teeth. She either had to argue or agree. "I know you're right, Donnie. We have to do something but I'm still hoping we can find some way to patch things up between you two and split the money."

"Screw that," he snapped. "While I was in the shithole taking a crap in front of other dudes, he was screwing you and that other cow. Now we've got millions and it's my turn to enjoy the goodies."

"Calm down," she said turning toward him. "I still like the idea of renting a house in a quiet neighborhood and away from anybody who knows us. Then, when we're certain we've got the account numbers in the trust, we can decide what's next."

"We both know damn well what's next. We're both going to off him."

Inwardly Miranda recoiled, but she let her silence do the talking.

"I guess you're right for now," Don said. "In the meantime, you still have to get pictures of his tats, when he's asleep, so I can duplicate them."

"Will do," she said just as her burner rang out. "It's him. I'd better get it."

Don nodded.

"Hi, Sweets. How are you?"

"Overwhelmed and I miss you."

"I know. Me, too. But is everything okay?"

"Sucks. I feel sorry for Granny, and everything else is morbid." Miranda squinted. Mac did it again, illustrated another excellent example of contrasts. While Don was methodically plotting a third murder, Mac was feeling compassion for an elderly woman he barely knew.

"I know how you feel, Sweets, but you can't afford to get sentimental. Are you going to be alright?"

"It'd be a hell of a lot easier if the cops weren't following me."

"Oh, no." She tapped Don's elbow. "The cops? How do you know?"

"They must think I'm stupid."

"Well, you're not stupid. You're smart. But don't worry. I think they're just covering their bases."

"I hope so, but it makes me nervous. I need to see you."

"We have to wait a little longer, until they give up."

"No. I don't want to wait. I can ditch them."

She didn't need this. "If it looks like you're trying to ditch them, they'll think you have something to hide. I think we need to play it safe and lay low a little longer."

"I ain't doing that. I know exactly what to do. But it has to be during rush hour. How about tonight?"

"No, no, no, Sweets. It's not safe yet."

"Yes, yes, yes it is. You have to trust me on this."

She sighed. "Even if I want to, I can't tonight. I'm still on the coast."

"Then we're doing it tomorrow night." His voice was strong, inflexible. *"Five o'clock. Your place. Have your garage door open."* He hung up.

CHAPTER 79

It was late afternoon when Mac and Granny returned from the mortuary after making Rachel's burial arrangements. Granny gave him a hug. "Thank you for driving, Mac. I couldn't have done it."

"No problem," he said, struggling to look her in the eye. "Do you need a ride to the services on Friday?"

"Why don't you call me later; I might have my neighbor take me."

That would make it a lot easier on him, but he still felt an obligation to help her if he could. "Sure. I'll check in with you later." He returned to Annie and pulled away from the curb, hoping she'd eventually get over losing Rachel. Previously, Mac had derived a certain amount of comfort from knowing that Granny had lived so well all those years without Rachel's trust money, but now her heartbreak was so complete, his own comfort had dissipated.

He made a left and joined the traffic. Then he saw it. Off to the right. The gray station wagon—at the 7-Eleven, with two men inside.

A half-mile later, he and Annie joined the northbound bumper-to-bumper insanity of the California rush hour. Mac examined Annie's left mirror. The wagon followed about five cars back. Perfect. He casually pointed to the ground and took the next lane to his left. The wagon turned on its blinker and lost some ground before it too could change lanes. "That's right, assholes," he said. "Let's do it again."

He and Annie inched along in the center of their lane for a few hundred yards or so, while brake lights flashed on and off like strings of red lights.

"*You're setting them up, aren't you?*" Mac imagined Annie saying.

"Yep," he said, inching over yet again. "Another mile ought to be about right. It gets very congested up here."

"*I'll be glad when we can go for some cross-country rides again.*"

"Me too, Annie," he said as he moved another lane to the left. Back at least ten cars the wagon turned on its blinker. The taillights up ahead began to glow. Everybody was slowing down. "Miranda said she'd be willing to go to Sturgis. I'd like to show her off."

Another dip to the left and Mac had made it next to the high occupancy lane. He glanced at the overhead road sign. "Two miles 'til our exit, Annie. We've got 'em where we want 'em."

"*Good, I'm tired of this slowpoke pace. I'm ready to haul ass.*"

Mac snickered. "Not this time, Annie, we're going to crawl our way out." Usually red lights meant stop but when the next snake of taillights flashed as if in unison, it meant the opposite to Mac and indigo Annie. "This ought to be funny." He slowly dipped onto the white lines that separated his lane from the one next to it. Even if somebody let the wagon inch over, they were going to have to pick one lane or the other and all the lanes were at a near standstill.

"This is too easy," Mac said, grinning. He and Annie proceeded ever so casually up the lines, between the lanes, and slowly but methodically passed a couple dozen unmoving vehicles. Then they nonchalantly dipped in front of one of the cars on their right and slid on over to the next set of lines. Mac laughed in the breeze. In what surely must have been the slowest get-away chase in the history of California highways,

Mac and Annie made sluggish but steady progress up the broken lines. He checked the mirror again. The wagon was so far back there, he couldn't see it. They'd ditched it without going more than ten miles an hour. Miranda's home was just a few miles away. The next exit and a few side roads would take them the remainder of the way.

*　*　*

While Miranda prepared for her visit with Mac, she reflected on the San Francisco trip. It proved that Don would never be the lover that she hoped for. At one point he said, "You're responsible for your orgasms and I'm responsible for mine." It sounded like a comment he'd picked up in prison.

His quick climaxes were ordinarily followed by a nap or a good night's sleep, while leaving her feeling empty and abandoned. When it came to intimacy, they'd become water and oil. Now she held legitimate doubts if she could live an entire lifetime with a man like that.

On the other hand, nobody ever understood her needs better than Mac did. In that regard, they were soul mates.

Nearly ready, all she needed to do was put on her shoes and open the garage door as Mac had requested. She turned toward the closet just as she heard a car pull up.

She moved toward the window to take a peek. A cab? She slid her foot into her shoe as the back door of the cab swung open. She recognized the yellow shirt. Couldn't believe her popping eyes. What the hell was Don doing here?

She bolted downstairs to meet him. Her heart pounded as the cab drove off and he approached her front door. She flung it open. "Dammit, Don. What are you doing? You know your brother's going to be here any minute."

Don forced himself inside and looked her up and down. "You sure got dolled up. How come you never do that for me?"

Miranda sighed, couldn't believe her ears. "I wore this same outfit for you, in San Francisco, but you didn't say a word."

"Bullshit. If you'd dressed like that, I would have noticed."

"Well I did, but it was cold. I wore a jacket too. We don't have time for this right now. You've got to get out of here. Take my car—anything—just go away before you ruin everything."

He brushed her hands away. "Oh, I ain't going nowhere."

"What? If Mac sees you, everything's over. Twelve million flushed down the toilet."

"I'm going to be hiding out upstairs, in the bedroom next to yours, so I can hear everything you guys do."

She rose nervously and said, "You can't do that, Donnie. How'm I supposed to act natural, knowing you're right in the next room?"

"Oh, you've got plenty of experience. I got a feeling you'll do just fine."

Exasperated, Miranda raised her arms. "Well, then I just won't bring him upstairs."

Don shrugged. "That's up to you, but if you don't, I'll get real curious and be forced to sneak downstairs to look for you. You wouldn't want that, would you? Then you'd be the one who ruins everything. I can get by without that money, but what about Mickey? If you screw this up, he could be the one who gets the shaft."

She turned completely around. "Oh my God, Donnie. This is crazy."

"Serves you right. Every time you run off with him, you stay too long. Drives me nuts. It's about time you deal with some of the drama for a change." He pinched the end of her sleeve. "Besides, I just might learn something. I bet you'd like that."

Miranda heard Mac's motorcycle coming from down the street. "It's him," she said, shaking. "Quick, hide."

Don stood firm. "What's the rush? He ain't in the garage yet." He held up his index finger. "Remember. One hour." He sounded like Officer Jackson on conjugal visit day.

"But I can't cut him off too soon, Donnie. We're supposed to be in love. How would that look?"

"About the same way it looks when you cut me off, but you don't seem to have a problem doing it to me."

The rumbling reached the driveway.

"But the trust money is still in his name, not ours. If we piss him off and he dumps me, we lose everything."

"Then chase him the hell away right after he enjoys your services, just like you do to me."

The rumble stopped. Brief seconds were all she had left before Mac would be inside. She shook her head. "I can't believe this."

Don pointed in her face and whispered, "One hour from the first second he walks in the door." He turned and headed up the stairs toward the bedrooms.

Miranda grabbed her head, looked toward the kitchen, then back at Don climbing the steps. The knob of the kitchen door turned. She took a deep breath and scooted toward the door as it swung her way. Mac entered and handed her a single long-stemmed red rose. "You don't know how much I missed you," he whispered.

Miranda smiled nervously, quickly filled a vase with water and plunked the rose into it. She tried to control her harried breathing. "Me, too." She closed her eyes. If only she could tell him how stressed out she was.

They held each other in silence. Longer. Tighter. Longer still, while she gathered her wits. Their lips gently blended together but the kiss only lasted a few seconds before Mac backed away slightly. "Something wrong? You don't seem like yourself."

It had taken mere seconds for Mac to read her. "I was just worried about you. That's all," she said softly. At least Don couldn't hear their conversation from upstairs. "Are you sure nobody followed you?"

Mac grinned. "Nah. Dotted lines make it easy."

"Clever, but what if they get another biker to follow you next time?" She visited her music center and hid her shaking hands while she selected a playlist.

"That would be even more obvious than the station wagon."

"Just don't act suspicious; they'll get bored and give up before much longer." She wondered where Don was, exactly.

"I hope so. You know something," Mac said, changing the subject, "I'm kinda hungry. I feel like a burger at a drive-through. How's that sound?"

Her pulse quickened. She couldn't take that much time. "No, I have another idea."

"Oh yeah, what's that?"

She twisted her head and flashed him a smile. "Well, sometimes being apart makes getting back together all that much more exciting."

"True that. I've been climbing the walls."

"See what I mean? Think how horny we both are. It would be fun to get it on right now, without messing around. Down and dirty for a change, but with one more twist."

Mac smiled, "Okay, I guess we could do that. What's the twist?"

"That's where my idea gets interesting," she said, leading him upstairs. "You'll have to leave as soon as we're done. Not even talk about it. Like two mystery lovers who have only minutes to do what they can in secret, and then end up wanting each other just as badly the next time."

Mac frowned. He shook his head. "I don't need to make up ways to want you. I already miss you whenever we're apart. You're my island of sanity in this sea of craziness."

They reached the landing. Thank God Don had closed the door to the small bedroom next to hers. "But that's the fun of it, Sweets," she said. "It'll make us crave each other even more."

"But you're the one who keeps saying how risky it is to get together in the first place," he said as they entered her room. "Wouldn't it be better to spend the time together now, while we have the chance? I was hoping to spend the night."

Miranda locked the door behind them. "You just leave everything to me."

Mac grinned. "You've never closed that door before, let alone locked it. You must have something extra special in mind."

Miranda held her index finger to her lips. "Shhh. No more talking." She pulled him onto the bed.

CHAPTER 80

Detective Sanchez and Sergeant Byrdswain rendezvoused at the police building for an early morning meeting. "I know you're a little dubious," she said tactfully, "but it's been a couple of weeks. Don't you think we owe Mrs. Ellerbe an explanation of what happened to her granddaughter?"

"You too, huh? Just yesterday the Mayor asked me the same thing."

"So what are you thinking?"

"This one has always bothered me and we can't afford to be cavalier."

"Cavalier? We've gone over everything again and again."

"Yeah, I know. But let's go over it again in case there's a flaw in the logic or something we overlooked. Why don't you give me a synopsis of how you see it."

"Alright then," she said, honored. She took a deep breath. "The Medical Examiner's report confirmed that Mrs. Evans died from the fall somewhere close to four-thirty. There's no sign of foul play and she left a credible suicide note. The husband is the only person we know of with a motive, but he's got no rap sheet, and an iron-clad alibi. There was nothing fishy in his phone records or his computer and there's no sign of an accomplice."

Byrdswain nodded. "Not much room for doubt, is there?"

"You're the one who's always saying things are usually just as they appear. I think it's suicide. It happens."

"I don't know. Most people work all of their lives and never even dream of that kind of wealth. But right out of the blue, a drifter meets a rich woman, hits it big. It just doesn't seem right."

"But people meet each other all the time. I know I do. And, Mrs. Ellerbe said Evans didn't know the victim was rich until after he married her. Somebody had to fall into the pot of gold. Just happened to be him."

"Maybe, but what are the chances that the rich woman would die within a month or so of receiving the trust?"

"Coincidences do happen. We can't hold up Mrs. Ellerbe just because there's a single coincidence in the wind."

"What about the supposed affair? If our victim was messing around with that Lapport fellow, we should have found some phone records, emails, love letters. Something. But we came up empty. How could that happen?"

"Are you kidding? There are all sorts of reasons that people want to keep their relationships quiet. Religion. Shame. Racial or economic differences. You never know. She might have just liked having a mystery lover."

"Mystery lover? You're single and only twenty-two. What do you know about mystery lovers?"

"Don't you ever read romance novels? Happens all the time. Boy meets girl at a bar or party and they have an instant fling—no questions asked—it's exciting because they don't know anything about each other. It's so mysterious they do it again and again. Probably the same time and place every week or once a month."

"Go on."

Sanchez smiled, pleased that her boss wanted to hear her out. "Somewhere along the line the victim meets Evans. But she hasn't had a lot of men in her life and figures either one of the guys could skip out at any time, so she strings them both along. Eventually she finds out Evans wants to get more serious but Lapport never really declares either way. So she focuses on Evans, keeps Lapport on the sidelines just in case Evans doesn't work out.

"Seems far-fetched."

"You're living in the old days, but lots of women play the field, now. It's more fun."

"Alright. Suppose you're correct," Byrdswain said. "Wouldn't she break it off with Lapport once she got married?"

"Maybe she was about to, or felt important by playing them both for a while. Whatever her reasons, an assistant principal would be smart enough to cover her tracks if she wanted to."

"If that's the case, she'd be relieved that her lover died, rather than kill herself over it."

"Who's to say? Her own grandmother said she was unstable from time to time. Maybe she loved Lapport more than Evans all along and couldn't deal with a broken heart or all that guilt."

Byrdswain tilted his head. "Maybe this is why I ended up divorced. I never understood what pushes women's buttons."

"You're always asking me for my opinion and I think it's just what it looks like: suicide. Mrs. Ellerbe, herself, said she trusted Evans, and wanted him to have the money. Not to mention it was half his already anyway."

"I have to admit, that's always been a good point."

"We can't hold that poor woman off forever."

Byrdswain paused. "Okay, you're breaking my heart. I'm going to wrap it up, just so that woman can have some closure, but we're going to check in on this Evans guy from time to time."

* * *

A week had elapsed since the yellow shirt day. Come to find out, Don didn't stay in her bedroom after all. He slipped out the back window and left her to stew in her juices.

In some regards his performance amounted to psychological abuse but it made another point, too. Don's point. She had let her emotions run away with her even though they'd hammered and hammered on how dangerous that was.

It may not have been the best way to make a statement but he was correct. She had become mushy-headed over Mac and it was screwing everything up. After all, Don was the one who was exciting and fun and dared to put together the strategy that saved Mickey from a merciless plight, when all Mac really brought to the table was the ability to make her melt. It was as if she was the candle and he was the flame that made it come to life. But when it came right down to it Mac was rather shallow compared to Don, and their high schoolish passion could easily wear off just as it had between her and her ex after they got married

Then, when Don found out how badly he frightened her he apologized for messing with her head. He admitted he was frustrated and promised to keep his act together. She heard the genuine regret in his tone. If she was fair about it, she had to acknowledge that Don had a tender side, too. He just didn't wear it on his sleeve like Mac did. Then there was the fact that Mac tended to focus on all the problems, while Don was the one who always had solutions. Negative vs. positive. That was in Don's favor too.

She was just as confused as ever and still had a horrible decision lingering in her future.

Meanwhile Rachel's death had been classified a suicide and it was time to advance Mac's image. Miranda took him to the million-dollar home she rented for him in Moon Shadow Hills. "Wow, this is nice," he said, as they entered the foyer.

She took his hand. "I told you, Sweets. It's a former model home. Nobody has ever lived here. The appliances are still in crates in the garage. How do you like the furniture?"

"I've never had stuff like this."

She wrapped her arms around him. "Get used to it."

Mac kissed her, then scanned the kitchen and dining area. "I can't believe this place. How'd you pull this off?"

"Easy. I told them that most of the trust papers were about to be put in your name and you might be willing to buy it a little later if they'd cut you a good deal now. They called the attorney's office and verified it all. No sweat." She pointed across the large living room toward the back of the home. "Wait 'til you see the sunken hot tub."

"I can hardly wait."

She grabbed his hand. "Later today, we can go pick up your new BMW. It's pearl white and has a hard top convertible."

Mac stopped cold. "What the heck are you talking about? Isn't it a little early to start spending money like a drunken sailor?"

"No way. The cops closed the case. You're a millionaire now. You deserve a reward for all you've done."

He grinned and shook his head. "A BMW, huh? I hope Annie won't get jealous. Does this mean we can finally spend the night together?"

"We still want to be cautious, but nobody's been tailing you, so I think we can go to dinner tonight, like a date, and then come back after that and jump in the hot tub. One night can't hurt."

"Why don't you just move in?"

She'd expected to hear something like that. "That might be too much. We can't go crazy. Let's just play it by ear. You want to go outside and see the garden area?"

"I'd like to see that hot tub first. How long do you think we need to keep this up?"

"I don't know. At least a month, then maybe we can leave town. Spend a week or so somewhere."

"I'd like that."

"Before we do anything else, we should move some of the money into a mutual fund, just to verify that you have control of it."

Mac stalled. "I guess we could. How much you got in mind?"

"At least a quarter million or so," she said.

His eyes widened.

Miranda grinned and tapped his nose. "If you want to play with the big dogs, you can't pee-pee like a puppy."

Mac laughed and drew her in. "God, how I love you. Okay, let's do it."

By the end of the evening they had successfully transferred two million bucks into a handful of different mutual funds. Each time they set up a new account, they used the password *Annie5*.

CHAPTER 81

"You'll set him up. I'll finish him off," Don said.

Miranda swallowed hard. Don had mentioned killing Mac repeatedly, but up to this point it was mostly just idle talk. But Don's patience had run out and the end was approaching her like the ground to a skydiver whose chute had failed to open.

"Can't we wait for a couple weeks?" she probed, knowing full well Don would nix the idea.

"Waiting will only make it harder. We have to do it before anybody in the neighborhood gets to know him."

Miranda's mouth went silent, but her heart screamed.

"Here's how we do it," Don said. "After a long day, you'll bring him back to his new place and settle in near the hot tub. You'll have a glass of wine and in a moment of poetic justice, you'll slip him a few of the sleeping pills from the same batch he fed to that cow."

"You mean Rachel," she insisted. "Her name was Rachel."

Don grinned. "You gettin' soft on me?"

"It's just that we ought to have a little respect for the dead. That's all."

"Screw that. We've got other things to worry about."

Miranda's jaw tightened. She wished she could desensitize too.

"When you see him getting drowsy—"

Miranda stared at Don's face. His eyes were glazed. A faint smile indicated he was enjoying himself. She wanted him to stop, but he didn't.

"Let him sleep for about an hour before you call me. Got it so far?"

Her lips moved, but no words came out.

"Are you following me or not?"

"I understand," she murmured.

"Good. You can get any last-minute pictures of his tats if you don't have them by then. When he's zonked out and weak, I'll sneak into the room and strangle him." He made the appropriate gesture.

Miranda's hands shot to her neck and she swallowed.

"You'll be standing by his head with a short-handled sledgehammer." Goose bumps rose along her arms and legs. "If anything goes wrong," he said in a slower and softer manner, "you'll hit him so hard, it will knock him into a faraway galaxy."

Her entire body went cold. She envisioned Mac lying on his back and her holding the sledgehammer overhead. She squirmed. Wouldn't Don's head be in reach, too? But if she took out Don, what would she do with his body? She couldn't recruit Mac without revealing she'd been lying to him from day one. She thought about a knife and shivered. She sure as hell couldn't cut Don up into manageable parts either. "I don't want to watch him die," she pleaded. "Couldn't you just do it by yourself?"

"No way. I want you to see him suffer. Teach you why you should have trusted me when I warned you not to get so lovey-dovey with him."

The vision of a black widow flashed in her mind. "But he hasn't done anything."

Don stiffened. "The hell he hasn't. While I've been forced to live in sewers, the two of you have been fucking like a couple of spider monkeys." He extended his index finger to within an inch of her nose. "I did a lot of this for you and your brother, so am I going to be able to count on you or not?"

For the first time ever Miranda was genuinely afraid of Don. She knew he'd always hated the trysts she shared with Mac, but now she understood how badly he wanted to watch his brother die—even more than he wanted to acquire Rachel's money. That was his real motive all along. How could she have missed it? "No," she said, trying to keep her voice from shaking. "We don't have a problem. I love you, Donnie. I'll be right by you, as you said."

"Good. Then, call him right now and set it up for tomorrow."

The force in her jaw sent shooting pain to her temples.

CHAPTER 82

His mother's funeral was yet another heart-rending experience for Stump. He broke down repeatedly and continued to blame himself for her passing. Other than Aunt Gerry, nobody was more supportive than Myles. He dropped by each night after Stump got out of school. Sometimes they went to dinner, other times they went to Myles's apartment. It didn't really matter, but Stump appreciated the effort.

The following Saturday, Myles picked up Stump to watch *Iron Man* on DVD. Stump turned down the volume during the pre-movie crap. "Do you really like this kind of picture?" he asked.

"You never know unless you try."

"What would we see if you were picking? A detective movie?"

"They're okay, but I tend to see the flaws."

"Like what?"

"Oh, I don't know. They might show an interrogation or a court scene and do it all wrong. It's hard to overlook."

"So what do you like then?"

"Mostly comedies. They don't have to be realistic."

"I like Jim Carey."

"Me, too."

Stump glanced at the screen. Still crap. "Can I ask you something else? What did the people at your meeting say when . . . well, you know?"

Myles turned his head Stump's way. "It's okay to say it, Stump. What did they say *when I drank?*"

"Yeah. They must have been disappointed in you."

Myles tilted his head. "That's not how it works. We don't shoot our wounded. We help each other get back on our feet. It's very supportive."

"I wish I treated Mom like that."

Myles raised his finger. "You had to endure some very difficult situations. Your mother was extremely proud of how you stood up to bullies for her sake. That's way more support than a lot of us get."

"They should just make alcohol illegal. That would be easier on everybody."

"You're right—it would solve a lot of problems. Some people can drink in moderation. For other people alcoholism is a disease, not a choice. It's like somebody who has pneumonia. They can't just quit. They need medication and therapy. Speaking of therapy, what's it like, living with Uncle Dirk and Aunt Gerry?"

"Not very good. I heard them talking the other night, when I was in bed."

The promos were nearly over. "What'd they say?"

"Uncle Dirk said they have to cut back on a lot of things just to pay for me and to move and everything."

"Oh, I see."

"There is a lot more work for Aunt Gerry too. She tries to pack boxes for our move but ends up crying. They argue a lot. Willie gets mad because I have to share his room." He lowered his head. "I make it worse for all of them."

"Now wait a minute," Myles insisted. "Nobody blames you. You didn't cause the fire. And you certainly weren't responsible for those bars. Any one of us should have been able to see they were unsafe."

"I guess so, but I never realized how much trouble I am. I'm always in the way. It would be worse if Dogg had lived." Stump turned his head Myles's way. "Do you think I can get a job when I get to Texas?"

                    *   *   *

After the movie, Myles took Stump back to Aunt Gerry's and offered to buy pizza for everybody. While the boys were busy in Willie's room the adults waited for pizza downstairs. Lemonade in hand, Myles glanced at the stairway and then addressed Gerry. "Did you hear yesterday's news?"

"Not really. We've been awfully busy."

"It's about that Clifton guy—the car dealer. A friend of mine says they're essentially going to drop the charges."

Gerry cupped her hands over her mouth. "That bastard."

Dirk turned her way. "I can't remember the last time I heard you say anything like that."

"Without the key witness," Myles continued, "all they have is Stump's testimony. There's no way to prove whether Jean gave consent or not."

"Consent?" Gerry said. "That's absurd. She was given a roofie! Why don't they just ask us?"

"The problem is that guy has a lot of money and can drag things out in court for a long time. They don't like to tie up a lot of time and money unless they're sure they're going to get a big-time conviction; but he could say she agreed to it, and all it takes is one juror to think there's a *reasonable doubt* and Clifton walks. They offered to let him off with a misdemeanor."

"That bastard."

Dirk looked at her again and then back to Myles. "Should we tell Stump?"

"I think I can do it. It would probably be better if there wasn't a long drawn-out media circus anyway." Myles set down his drink. "That wasn't why I came here. I've got something else I'd to ask you two." They looked at each other and nodded.

"You guys already have lots of responsibilities—raising your own son, the upcoming move, a job change. Now, Stump is thrown into the mix."

"It's tougher alright," Gerry said. "But Stump is family."

"You're both wonderful to him. He tells me so. That brings me to my question." Myles paused and looked at Gerry. "If it's okay with you, I'd like to adopt Stump, that is, if he's up for it."

Dirk leaned back and Gerry looked deep into Myles eyes. "Wow. I don't know, Myles. That's awfully generous, but—"

"I was thinking about doing it before Jean died, but now it makes more sense. I can afford him, we get along well and we share a common loss." Myles held up his finger. "The last thing she said to each of us was 'I love you.' We need each other."

"I like the idea," Dirk said.

Gerry waved him off and returned her attention to Myles. "Where would you live?"

"At first, I'd have to get a bigger apartment, closer to his school. Maybe later I could buy a house. They're pretty cheap these days."

She frowned. "But you're talking about him staying here in California. I don't want to break up the only family he's ever had."

Myles nodded. "But he and I can make a good family too. California is his home. He needs to be around his friends. It would be even harder for him to adapt to Texas. It would give us all good places to go on vacations."

"Has he ever been on a vacation?" Dirk asked.

"What would happen if you met another woman?" Gerry ignored Dirk's question. "Down the road, I mean. What if you wanted to get married? He'd be in the way all over again, especially if this new woman wanted to have her own family. Then what?"

Myles shook his head. "I don't see anything like that happening for a long time, if ever. Even if it does, Stump and I would be a package deal. Any woman who couldn't accept that wouldn't be right for me anyway."

"What about your drinking problem?"

"Geeze, Gerry." Dirk said, "Give the guy a break. He's had one relapse in six years. Hell, you drink more than he does."

Myles made a gratuitous nod toward Dirk. "I admit I got drunk, Gerry, and I'm very sorry about that, but as soon as I was with Stump again, I realized I didn't want any more of the bottle. And I'd been sober six years before that."

"We like you a lot, Myles, and so does Stump, but this is a huge decision. Can you give us a few days to think it over, perhaps talk it over with him?"

"Well, it makes sense to me," Dirk said, seconds before the doorbell rang.

CHAPTER 83

When Don made it clear that the time to eliminate Mac had come, all Miranda could do was agree, but it wasn't anywhere near as easy as that. If she followed his plan she and Mickey and Don would be intact with enough money for all of them. But that would mean Mac would die and she'd still have to deal with Don's faults.

She considered running off with Mac and leaving Don behind, but if she betrayed Don in any way, he'd want revenge. He wouldn't care if he went to prison. All of that would happen without Mac knowing that he would forever wear a target on his back—she might have one too.

She also considered cutting a deal with Don: She could peel off enough money to take care of Mickey and leave all the rest to him in exchange for his forgetting all about her and Mac; but the number one thing Don hated about his brother was the fact that Mac was always beating him in everything they did. No matter how much money Don got, he'd always know that his brother had bested him again, this time in the game of love, without Mac even realizing he was in a competition. Sooner or later Don's humiliation and ego would get the best of him. He'd have all the resources he'd need to find some way to destroy Mac. And how would she explain to Mac her sudden willingness to forget the money?

Try though she did, there just wasn't any way to escape

the inevitable fact that one of them had to die, and based on
Don's strategy, she was probably going to be able to pick
which one.

* * *

Mac began to stir around eight. The hole in Miranda's heart
spoke loudly. She looked at him, innocently sleeping, and
wondered if this really would be his last day alive. It just didn't
seem possible. She hoped a shower would help clear her head,
but it didn't. She stared into the mirror at her bloodshot eyes
and tried to fathom what she should do, whom she should
save, but that didn't help either. Nothing did.

By the time her hair was done and her makeup was in place,
Mac had joined her. "Your eyes are bloodshot. Something
wrong?"

"Didn't sleep too well," she said. Maybe she could
pretend she was an actress in a play, like when she was
in high school. Just go through the motions and imagine
it was all just make-believe. The final act. Then when the
right moment came, she'd let her instincts take over and
determine who her life partner would be. It would all just
happen naturally.

"I gotta go to the store," she said, sticking with Don's plan,
"but after I get back, I'm going to show you how much I
appreciate everything you've done for Mickey and me. How
would you like to be treated like a king for the entire day?"

He smiled and pulled her to him. "Just being with you goes
a long way toward doing that." He kissed her; she sensed his
passion, but had to stay in character, like an actress would. It
was all just a charade. The grocery store was waiting.

A half-hour later, Miranda had selected a well-marbled
porterhouse, mushrooms, and fresh strawberries and
sherbet. Finally she aimed for the liquor department where
she picked up two bottles of expensive wine before checking
out and returning to Mac's new home.

"What's in the bags?" he asked. "The king demands the best, you know?"

"I bought the best of everything. Dinner. Wine. Dessert. The whole works."

Mac shook his head. "I'm not sure I deserve this."

"Sure you do. You've been stressed out for months." She pointed toward the garage. "Let's begin by taking the Beemer to Santa Barbara. Later I'll put together a nice cozy dinner and we can jump in the hot tub." She rubbed his forearm. "I bet you can guess what comes after that."

Mac grinned. "I think I have a pretty good idea."

In Santa Barbara, they took a very long walk on East Beach, holding hands. Eventually, they passed a little sidewalk café where they decided to get a foot-long hotdog and some fries. As they waited in a short line, Mac slipped his arm around Miranda's shoulder and pulled her close. He kissed her cheek, then whispered, "Can I ask you something?"

"Of course."

"I was going to wait for later," he said as he reached into his pocket, "but I just can't wait." He kneeled. "Miranda. You are so beautiful, and I love you more than you could ever know. I always have. I'm empty when we're apart. The flowers lose their color. The birds don't sing, and the sun isn't bright. But whenever I'm with you everything comes to life; even visiting a hotdog stand is fun. I want you at my side every day from here on out. Will you'll marry me?" He snagged an incredible diamond ring from his pocket. It glistened like a second sun.

Miranda's knees grew wobbly. Ever since she was a little girl she'd imagined a moment like this. The right setting. The right time. The right man. Mac was the only one she'd ever known who could make a hotdog seem special.

The warm sun, the sandy beach, the crashing waves and the whiff of hot dogs on the grill all contributed to the mood. It was the moment she needed. She knew exactly who she wanted to spend the rest of her life with. A smile washed across her face as she murmured her approval.

Mac rose and slid the ring on her finger. They looked in each other's eyes as he pulled her toward him. She welcomed his embrace. His arms. His lips. And, in that instant, the anxiety that she'd been carrying for months blew away in the ocean's breeze. Together they swayed in harmony like the palm trees overhead.

A few strangers in line in front of them who had already turned around applauded. Miranda grinned as a couple of the women said nice things to her. She'd never been so happy. She took Mac's hand and they kissed again, briefly.

"Hey, you two . . ." A gruff voice from behind the ordering window butted in. "Are you guys going to order, or spend all day playing kissy face?"

They had reached the front of the line. While Mac ordered a foot-long frank, Miranda accepted compliments and warm wishes from the strangers who'd played a minor role in her special day. It was a moment she'd never forget.

Miranda and her new fiancé pulled into his driveway around 6:30. For the time being, she had to remain focused on Don's primary plan because hidden in the details was her opportunity to take out Don instead of Mac. If she were correct, there would be a moment when Mac was zonked out and Don would straddle him to get a grip on his neck. She'd have to hold the sledgehammer high in the air as if she was ready to hit Mac if Don needed her, but instead, there should be a brief moment when the back of Don's head would be exposed. She'd just have to figure out what to do with Don's body.

"Would you mind turning on some jazz and lighting some candles?" she asked of Mac.

"Sure, but if we make this day anymore romantic, I might have to bypass dinner."

Miranda kissed him on the cheek. "There will be plenty of time for that, my love. First, you have to let me pamper you like I promised."

Shortly thereafter, Miranda began the king's feast with

a delicious lemon-avocado salad sprinkled with fresh shredded coconut. She ended her future husband's meal with a very small dish of lime sherbet covered with strawberries. Afterwards she handed him a bottle of after-dinner wine. "Before we slip into the hot tub, would you open this? I'd like to pour my king's drink and serve it to him on a silver platter."

Mac grinned. "I could get used to this."

When he turned his back, she added a sleeping pill to his glass before she delivered his drink and joined him, naked, in the hot tub.

Before long, both the sleeping pill and the soothing jets were doing their job. Mac yawned. "The king appears ready for bed," Miranda said. "Wouldst thou allow this maiden to join him?"

An hour later, Miranda called Don to tell him Mac was ready to be finished off.

CHAPTER 84

While Miranda waited for Don, she removed her engagement ring and retrieved the short-handled sledgehammer from the garage. She stared at the grotesque weapon and recalled Don's plan. How could he be so vicious?

She returned to the bedroom to check on Mac. He was lying in the fetal position, on the right side of the bed, facing the edge. She imagined him lying on his back, and mentally rehearsed the moment she'd finish off Don. If she were lucky, he'd fall to the floor without touching Mac and maybe without bleeding. She shrugged. Even if Mac were awakened he would be too groggy to know what was going on.

Satisfied, Miranda stood back a couple of feet from her lover and wondered what it would be like to live without Don. She replayed the day she first met him, and the time he defended her in the bar fight. She recalled his smile when she made her weekly visits to the prison, especially on conjugal visit days. Then there was the sparkle in his eye when he told her how he could make them both millionaires.

As she anticipated how things would play out she heard a car stop outside. She took a deep breath and went to meet Don. She crossed her fingers, ready to enter the stage. She reminded herself it was all make-believe. That would make it easier.

Don had a small satchel in his hand when she let him in. "Everything okay?" he asked quietly.

She nodded. "He's been asleep for at least an hour."

"Perfect. Are you ready?"

"The hammer's in the kitchen."

Unexpectedly, Don grabbed her and forcefully pulled her toward him. His lips attacked hers. She found a certain eroticism in his determination. Don pulled back. "Go check on him one more time, while I get ready."

Miranda's heart pounded mercilessly as she tiptoed to the bedroom that was destined to become a killing chamber in her little play. Mac had rolled over to his other side, closer to the center of the bed, but he was still in a very deep slumber, and vulnerable, just as Don wanted. She frowned as she noted that Don would be a little further away than she would have liked.

When she rejoined Don in the kitchen, he had a sinister, intense look in his eye, like a boxer just before a title bout. There was something shiny in his hand. A large carving knife. Her eyes widened. "There's been a slight change of plans," he said. "I'm gonna wake him up just long enough for him to watch me slit his throat."

Her mind flashed to the day he'd done the same thing to a dog. "God, no, Donnie," she whispered. "Too bloody. We have to stick with our earlier idea."

Don looked her in the eyes and paused for a fairly long time before he finally nodded and set down the knife. "All right then. You just stay close by, in case I need you."

She took a deep breath and exhaled. "You know I will."

"Let's do this."

Miranda bobbed her head in approval and grabbed the sledge. It seemed heavier now.

As they moved toward the bedroom, her heart thumped against her ribs. Within minutes she would carry out a slightly different version of the scheme they'd been planning for months. The anxiety of her ambivalence was finally going to end.

Her fingers trembled. That familiar doubt that she'd felt so many times before returned to the deep recesses of her mind.

Go away. Her lower lip quivered. If only it were merely stage fright.

A few steps more and her hands shook and her knees had gone weak. She glanced at Don. He appeared calm and confident. If only she shared his ease. He took her hand in his and gently squeezed. "Relax," he whispered.

That was one of the things she'd always liked about Don. Whenever things got the stickiest, whenever they had to make a tough choice, whenever the stakes were the highest, he always knew what to do. In some ways, he deserved to live, too. No, stop it. There was no more room for second-guessing. She'd already made up her mind how this was going to end.

Don tugged on her hand. When they were a single pace from the bedroom, he paused and whispered, "Open the door and step aside. I'll take the position I want. You stand right next to the edge of the bed by his head, in case I need you."

By his head? "But wouldn't it be better if I stood right next to you," she whispered, "so I can get a better swing?"

"No. I need you to see me, so I can signal you without waking him."

"But I can see better if I'm back by your side."

Don glared at her like he did the day he scared her. She'd have to do it his way, even though his head would be a little farther away. She'd just have to reach a little further. Extend her arms all the way.

She nodded, slowly opened the door. Mac remained in the exact same position, near the center of the bed. Don quietly slid past her and into the room. He stopped and stared at the body in the bed. Miranda knew it was the first time he'd seen Mac up close in nearly ten years. With the stealth of a combat solider, Don slowly and cautiously moved around to the other side of the bed. Oh, my God. Stay calm. It's a play. Make-believe. Watch for an opening to his head. Any opening.

Don inched onto the other side of the bed and moved closer and closer to Mac. Miranda dug her knees into her side of the mattress to get a fraction of an inch closer to where Don's head should be when he pounced on Mac and went for his throat. She gripped the sledgehammer tightly, rested it on her shoulder and waited for him to move closer.

Slowly Don progressed across the bed, to within a foot of Mac's body and stopped. If he didn't come closer, there was no way Miranda could get to him, but he would still need to lean forward and reach out. She needed him to come closer. She needed a little luck. He held up his hands to signal he was ready. Miranda stalled. He wasn't close enough. Don mouthed for her to hurry. She stalled again, hoping he'd lunge closer, but he didn't. Saliva oozed from the corners of his mouth. He waved his arms wildly and mouthed "C'mon." She couldn't delay much more. She raised the hammer. The adrenalin in her system made it lighter than before. Lean in. She needed him to lean in. Her heart pounded.

Don moved the final foot, extended his hands slowly toward his brother, but he remained to the far side of Mac's body. Too far away. Lean in. LEAN IN. Her eyes darted around the room and back. Lean in. Get closer.

Don's powerful, determined hands shot forward with the precision of a rattler's strike. "Asshole," he screamed as he took the grip on Mac's neck. Oh my God, he was too far away. Mac's hands instinctively rose to his throat, but he was too slow and too weak to put up a good fight. Don stayed back out of the reach of Mac's flailing arms, and more importantly, out of Miranda's reach. Don thrust his thumbs deep into Mac's throat. Groggy and helpless, Mac gurgled. His eyes opened slightly. She raised a knee to the top of the bed but it was too high to get up there without putting the sledge down.

"Goodbye, brother," Don screamed, saliva dripping down his chin.

All of Miranda's nerve endings drew her into the moment. The play. The incredible drama. Her eyes bounced back and forth between the brothers like crazed windshield wipers. These were the final seconds of her moment onstage. She entered a trance, no longer driven by logic or past plans. No longer connected to the men in the room. They, too, were play actors.

"This will teach you, you asshole," the standing-up actor yelled. "You always thought you were better than me—but not this time, you son-of a bitch. Not this time."

The lying-down actor's face was deep red. His desperate eyes searched the darkened room until he found Miranda. He played his role perfectly. She watched closely and without emotion as the swollen veins rose in his temples and he made another weak attempt to shake loose. Then the standing-up man glanced at Miranda. "Hit him," he screamed. "Hit him."

Miranda looked at the lying-down actor. She'd rehearsed her role plenty of times but all she could remember was that she had to hit somebody.

"Hit him, Baby. Hit him."

Dazed, she turned her head to the standing-up actor.

"Do it! Do it! Do it!"

Her eyes dropped to the lying-down man. His head had to be a prop. She raised the sledgehammer as high as she could. "Do it! Do it! Do it!"

With all the force she could muster, she pulled the handle down and slammed the now lighter sledge into the waiting head below her. Its skull cracked and the forehead caved a half-inch. A gusher of red instantly shot out its nostrils as its body went limp.

The standing-up actor stepped back. "Hit him again. Again."

She raised the hammer just as high as before. This time she aimed for the offensive nostrils that gushed red stuff everywhere. Three pounds of deadly cold steel exploded into the mannequin-like head once again. This time a deep grunt and a swoosh of air escaped the lying-down man's body and more red liquid splattered all over the stage. She felt an orgasmic surge of power. Her legs were strong, her breaths deep and hard like those of an Olympic sprinter.

The standing-up actor grabbed her, picked her up off her feet, and spun her around. The sledgehammer dropped to the floor, just as it did in rehearsal. The standing-up actor squeezed her and her benumbed brain began to tingle, to focus, to return to the present. It was as if she'd just driven a dozen miles in a fog without remembering any of it. She slowly recollected where she was, who she was with, what they were doing. She glared at the pool of redness that was spread all around her.

Without understanding how it all happened, she'd finally arrived at the crossroads of Excitement Street and Romance Boulevard and somehow decided which road to take. Mac was no more—and she was the recipient of Don's one-man standing ovation.

CHAPTER 85

The man who became the new Mac marched back and forth across the room. His hands flailed wildly. "You did it, Baby, you did it. That was the greatest thing I've ever seen. I'll never doubt you again."

Miranda looked his way. As she was still not completely out of her trance, his words weren't much more than background noise. Devoid of emotion, she noted the sledge-gnarled skull on the lifeless body before her. She scowled and twisted her head. Her mind tried to put some of the pieces together, but it was as if part of her brain had shorted out.

New Mac wrapped her in his arms and kissed her.

At first, her arms dangled limply at her sides, but the passion in his kiss was an unexpected elixir. Her hands rose mechanically to his shoulders and then around them. She closed her eyes. The embrace felt good.

New Mac grinned, "Why don't I cut him into pieces and bury him out back, like an old dog?"

She shook her head, reached down and nonchalantly pulled the sheet over the mangled man on the bed. "No, the body would be too easy to find," she said in a matter-of-fact monotone. "We have to get rid of him altogether. I know where there is a dumpster, near the edge of town."

"Okay. But, that won't be as much fun for me."

"I'll open the back of my vehicle. You get one of the

wooden appliance crates from the garage and line it with plastic."

New Mac completed his task and laid the crate on its side in the back of the SUV. Then together, they pulled Mac's corpse toward the edge of the bed and let it fall on top of a throw rug as if he never mattered at all. They dragged him to the garage and together lifted his body into the crate.

Back in the bedroom, Miranda pointed at the blood splatters on New Mac's shirt and pants. She unbuttoned her blouse. "We have to get rid of our clothes," she said. She calmly bent over and grabbed the blood-drenched bedding. "This stuff, too." They both stripped naked and New Mac moved toward the closet.

"No clothes, yet," she said as she motioned toward the wall where blood and bits of Mac's skin speckled the headboard. "We have to clean all of this up first. You pack the bedding and clothes around the body, I'll get a bucket and sponge."

"You okay, Baby? You're like a robot."

"Let's just do what we have to do."

Very little was said as the nude couple went about their work. Miranda wiped away carnage while New Mac stuffed the other messy items, the burner phones and the sledgehammer into Mac's makeshift coffin, thereby putting all the evidence into one single place. When done New Mac nailed the top back on the crate.

An hour later they had cleaned up, and were on their way toward the main drag. New Mac looked Miranda's way. "I didn't think you could do it. Hit him like that, I mean."

Less benumbed than earlier, Miranda turned toward him. "Why not? I told you I could."

"I know, but I thought when it came right down to it, you'd chicken out."

Off to the left, a convenience store came into view. She pointed. "It's over there."

New Mac slowed, surveyed the situation. Several customers were using the front gas pumps and other vehicles were near the entrance of the store. "There are people all over the place."

"They'll keep the clerks busy. Take the side driveway. The trash area is in the back."

New Mac hesitated. Then, "Okay, but we've got to hurry." He turned onto the side lot, pulled slightly past the dumpster. He parked and Miranda looked in her mirror.

A white pickup truck had taken a position at one of the pumps on the side of the building facing their SUV. Almost instantly, the driver got out of the cab and marched toward the store.

"Wait 'til he's out of sight," Miranda suggested. "With all those people in there, he'll be inside awhile."

They waited before New Mac flung open the tailgate and took hold of the crate. "Give me a hand, will you?"

Together, they tugged the wooden container to the back edge of the SUV and let it fall to the ground.

"Let's do this," New Mac said, his voice filled with determination.

Her mind still partially deadened, Miranda squatted and attempted to reach her arms around the box but it was bigger than she expected.

"Okay. Lift," he said.

New Mac elevated his end a half-foot, but Miranda immediately lost her grip and dropped the crate to the ground. "It's too heavy. I can't do it."

"Well, we can't leave it here. Let's try again."

"I can't."

At that moment, the door to the rider's side of the white pickup truck swung open and a young teenager headed their way. "You guys need some help?" he asked. He looked at Miranda, then at New Mac. "Hey. Hi. How you doing?"

New Mac ignored the comment. "Help me lift this."

The boy nodded and they stooped down to get their hands underneath the lower end of the crate. "Lift with your knees," New Mac said. "One, two, three. " They both strained as the crate rose a foot off the ground, then two, then the top leaned over the edge of the large container and a couple seconds later a crate full of Mac and other bloody items settled in the bowels of the dumpster.

New Mac rested his hands on his knees to catch his breath. "Thanks, kid. I appreciate it."

Miranda noticed the youngster staring at New Mac. "We gotta go."

"Don't you remember me?" the lad said. "We've met a couple of times."

"I don't know you," New Mac said, as he took another deep breath.

"Yeah, you do. I'm Stump. I came to your meeting and talked to you at the football game before the accident."

New Mac hesitated. "Oh, yeah. I almost forgot. When you've seen one wreck, you've seen them all. Sorry, but we gotta go. Thanks again."

As Miranda and New Mac drove away some of the vacantness in her mind had dissipated.

CHAPTER 86

"How you doing, Baby?"

It had been five days since Miranda and New Mac had disposed of Mac's body. In that time her thought process slowly returned to something resembling normal, but her feelings and emotions took a little longer. At first nothing mattered. Not even Mickey. For the most part she went along with whatever New Mac wanted. She knew that Mac was gone but didn't recall the gory moments of the murder. "I'm okay," she replied.

Then, she and New Mac transferred a small amount of money from each of Mac's mutual fund accounts into his checking account to verify that they could move the trust money around at will. Everything worked perfectly. The millions they'd worked so hard to capture were indeed theirs. At New Mac's suggestion she mailed a check for a hundred thousand dollars to The Broadhouse, but there wasn't much gratification in it. It was as if she were paying a utility bill.

After that she and New Mac flew to Hawaii to get their minds off the past and into the future, as he referred to it.

While there, New Mac practiced his brother's signature. They used Mac's credit cards over and over without incident. By the time they went to a fancy dinner on the final night, she had just about come to grips with her new paradigm. She was with New Mac and would be forever. "I'm sorry," she said to New Mac. "But it's harder to get used to what we did than I expected."

He shrugged. "You can feel sorry for those other two, but my brother got what he deserved."

She slumped in her chair. "I think I loved him."

"Yeah, I know. But I told you to watch out for him. Sooner or later he would have stabbed you in the back."

"You're always so confident, so under control, but the only way I could do my part was to play a role."

He placed his hand on hers. "I'm sure it was hard, but you were great. You even convinced me for a while—and I knew it was all play-acting."

"I'm glad you understand."

"Sure I do. When you have to pretend like that for so long, you actually become the person you're portraying. Otherwise everybody can see right through you. I hear it happens to professional actors, too."

"I need you to bear with me. It may take me a while. Okay?"

Fortunately, Hawaii was good for that. Don handed her a paper sack in which there was an engagement ring.

CHAPTER 87

County restrictions forbade the unnecessary running of water, so Miranda turned off the hose as soon as she gave her SUV a good soaking. It was the third time she had washed the vehicle in three days, trying to wash away all traces of their sins. Don wanted her to trade in the SUV, but she wavered. It was a link to the past, a time when Mac still lived. By this time when she spoke of her partner she had trained herself to refer to *him* as Mac, but in her own mind he was still Don.

"Son-of-a-bitch." She turned toward the profanity. New Mac was back near the garage and trying to figure out that purplish motorcycle they'd inherited. He kept swearing at it. Miranda could get by without that damn bike too.

As she dipped a sponge in her bucket of water she noticed an unfamiliar car approaching. She splashed a sponge full of water on her bumper as the vehicle came to a stop right behind her SUV. She wasn't expecting anybody. A closer look revealed a man and a woman. Too old to be cops. Probably husband and wife. What the hell did they want? She looked over her shoulder toward Don, but he was squatted down, with his back toward her and dealing with the bike.

The couple exited their car and came directly toward Miranda. "Hello. Are you Mac's wife?" the woman asked.

Up until that moment Miranda and Don had played their new roles in safe settings, but this smelled like something more threatening.

In their mid to late fifties the couple had less tanned skin than most everybody else around there. Probably from out of town. "Er, no. I'm just a friend. Who are you?"

The woman looked over Miranda's shoulder. "Oh, that must be him," she said. "He always liked motorcycles." The woman walked right past Miranda toward Don with her partner in tow. Miranda didn't like this. The lady was too friendly.

"Mac? Is that you?" the woman asked. She pointed at the bike. "Oh, of course, it is. You've got another Annie."

"Huh?" Don turned around. His eyes widened, but the remainder of his body seemed to freeze in place. "What the hell are you doing here?"

"What's going on?" Miranda asked. "Who are you people?"

"My name's Bonnie. I'm his mother." The woman glanced back at Don, stared for a moment. "Hey. Wait a minute. You're not Mac. You're Donald." She smiled. "Now I'm the one who doesn't know what's going on."

Uh-oh. This wasn't good.

The woman's partner extended his hand to Don. "I'm Arnold. Your mom found your brother's name on the Internet—something about him getting married. Is he close by too?"

Don declined the handshake. "You're wrong. I'm Mac and I don't want to talk to you."

The woman took a step toward Don. "I don't mean to be difficult, but a mother knows these things. I see that little mole on your neck. You're my Donald."

Miranda's jaw tightened. She looked rapidly up and down the street. This had to end before too many questions were asked and suspicions were sparked. "We don't want you people around here," she snapped.

"She's right," Don said. "We didn't invite you."

His mother tilted her head. "Why are you so unfriendly? Have you and your brother been in touch? He lives in the area."

"We don't have to explain anything to you," Miranda said. "Just get out of here before we call the cops."

The woman hesitated, traded glances with her partner.

"Who the hell do you think you are?" Don snapped at his mom. "I haven't seen you in fifteen years. You were a lousy mother, now you show up out of the blue and have the nerve to start asking questions."

The man stepped forward. "You don't have to be so rude. She tried to call but couldn't find a number. Se we flew all the way across the country. The least you can do is be civil."

"Screw you, old man. I said to get out of here and I mean it." He grabbed a large wrench like he was prepared to use it as a weapon.

The woman shrugged, shook her head. "Okay, Okay. I get it. I'm a lousy mom and you don't want to be bothered. We'll leave, but I can tell that you're Donald and don't try to tell me differently."

Miranda pointed at their car. "You're nuts, woman. Now get out of here and don't come back."

*　*　*

"Weird that they would show up now," Miranda said, as she and Don watched his mom and her partner drive away. Up a little further a FedEx truck was coming from the opposite direction. "I hope that's the last we see of them."

Don waved his hand in the air. "I doubt she'll be in any hurry to come back."

"Well, I don't want to see her again," Miranda said as the FedEx truck reached their house and pulled over. "Now what?" she said, maddened. "I'll see what this guy wants."

Don nodded and turned his attention back toward the downed motorcycle. "I want to see if I can figure out that damn kickstand."

A moment later Miranda had signed for an envelope and was checking the label when Don looked her way from behind the bike. "What is it?"

"It's from that bowling alley your brother used to go to. A letter." She tore open the envelope and reviewed the single sheet of paper inside. She gasped. "Oh, my God. Listen to this." Don looked over her shoulder as she began to read out loud.

My beautiful Miranda,

I asked a friend to send this to you if I didn't show up for a weekly meeting that we've been having, which would mean that somehow you and my brother have killed me. Yes, I know all about the two of you.

I figured it out after I opened that toolbox in your garage and saw an old pocketknife in there. It looked like one we had as kids, so I looked closer and saw his initials carved in it.

I followed you that night and saw you together. From that time on, I knew whenever you weren't with me, you were with him. I thought I might be able to win you over anyway, but I guess I wasn't man enough. Too bad, because I genuinely loved you.

Bottom line is, I don't want to be on this earth without you, so I'll be waiting for you in hell.

Love, Sweets

p.s. Tell my brother that since you are such a special treasure, he won't be needing my money. I guess that means you won't get it either. My apologies to Mickey.

Stunned, Miranda lifted her head and looked at New Mac. He threw the motorcycle onto its side and they dashed into the house and to the computer.

Within an instant, Don was hovering over Miranda's shoulder as she pulled up the home page of their Vanguard

Mutual Fund account. She hyperventilated as she typed in the password. "At least that still works."

"Check the account balance."

One click and Miranda's brow jumped. She gasped as a horrible chill danced across her neck. "One dollar?"

Don's arms thrashed wildly in the air. "That asshole."

Miranda shook her head, murmuring, "There was almost three million dollars in there."

"That son-of-a-bitch." Don yanked the toaster from the wall and threw it at the refrigerator. "Asshole, cocksucker, mother fucker."

Miranda quickly pecked at the keyboard. "I'll try T. Rowe Price." Her heart sank further. A lone dollar was all that was in the account. Likewise Janus, Strong, Barclays and the savings account. Somehow, Mac had gotten to every one of them from beyond the grave. "Oh, my God," she said as she slouched down into her chair. "He must have set the accounts up to transfer funds on a specific time and day. As long as he was alive he could get back into the account and extend the date as many times as he wanted, but if he never changed the instructions the transfer would go through."

An endless string of Don's profanities pierced the air as Miranda lifted her hands and covered her face. "Twelve million. Gone. All of it."

"Well, I'm not giving up that easy," Don snapped. "What's the eight-hundred number for that first one?"

While Don made the call, Miranda sat there, gawking at the astonishing information on the computer screen. Then she shook her head and smiled. "You were right, Donnie. Sooner or later he was going to turn on us. Face it. He beat both of us. Just like you said he would."

CHAPTER 88

After giving it some thought, everybody agreed to Myles's adoption idea. In addition to getting the paperwork going, they had to move some furniture around and get Stump some clothes along with other necessities. The days were long but Stump and Myles enjoyed the diversion.

Neither of them was a great cook so they ate a combination of delivery food, drive-through, frozen dinners and restaurant meals. This particular evening Myles gave his name to the hostess at a sit-down place and went to the restroom—leaving Stump behind in the lobby.

While standing there, Stump rubbed his head, realized he needed a haircut. "They're twins," one of the ladies standing in line said to another customer. "I haven't heard from either one in nearly twenty years but I found one on Google, so we flew out to surprise him."

"He must have been shocked," the other woman replied.

"It was strange. It turns out we found the other one. I was confused at first because he was trying to get his brother's motorcycle to stand up. But when I got a good look I knew right away which one he was. He and his girlfriend, or wife— we never did find out—kept pretending he was his brother, but how dumb do they think I am? A mother can tell her kids apart, even after all these years. When I told him he wasn't fooling me, he chased me away."

"That'll be eighteen-eighty," the cashier said to the petite woman. "Anyway," she said, going through her purse, "They were totally rude to me. I decided it was their loss and we left. Now we've got a plane to catch."

"Cooper. Party of two?" the hostess asked Stump.

"Yes. My dad will be here in a minute," he said. He followed the hostess and planned to order a cheeseburger and fries.

After being seated, Stump grabbed his napkin and thought about the petite woman and how kids of all ages constantly disappoint their parents—even full-grown adult-aged kids with motorcycles. Motorcycles. He knew a guy with a motorcycle that had trouble standing up. Could that woman have been talking about the same guy? His mind flipped into puzzle-solving mode.

When he was at the 7-11 he had assumed he saw that same biker again, only the guy was strange and didn't even recognize him at first. Then there was that crate. He clicked his fingers and glanced toward the lobby. The petite woman had left, but couldn't be far. He stood and raced outside. She and her husband were in their car at the exit and ready to enter traffic. He ran after them, but they made their turn and got away. Frustrated, he hurried back to the restaurant where Myles had found their table.

"Where were you?" Myles asked.

"You know something, Myles?" Stump said, half out of breath. "I think there was a murder."

"A murder? On TV? A movie? What?"

"No. In real life. Right here in Palmdale. I think I know the guy who got killed."

Myles drew back. "Who?"

"A biker guy. He married Ms. Johnson from my school. The one who passed away about the same time as Mom did."

Myles set down his coffee spoon. "That's a pretty wild accusation. What makes you think so?"

"While you were in the restroom I overheard a lady in the

lobby say she had twin sons and came out here to see one of them, but instead she saw the other one."

"So?"

"The second one had the first one's motorcycle."

"You're not making much sense, Stump."

"I think I met them both. Mac was the first one. I met him a few times including the night Richard got pushed out of the football stadium."

"I don't follow."

"Don't you see? The second one was pretending to be the bike rider. I met him too, only I didn't know it at the time." Stump sucked in a deep breath. He was excited for the first time in quite a while. "Remember that night we went to get gas, and I helped a guy throw a big wooden appliance box into the trash container?"

"Yeah, I remember that."

"That was the second guy, the twin, but he didn't remember me or Richard's accident. How could anybody forget an accident like that?"

"They couldn't. Go on," Myles said, cell phone in hand.

"Now that I think about it, I don't remember seeing the scar on his hand either. Scars don't just disappear."

"No, they don't."

"I've been lifting weights lately and that box was heavy as hell," Stump said, talking faster. "I think I helped the second brother and his girlfriend throw away the biker's body. Considering the death of Ms. Johnson and that woman's comments about twins and motorcycles, I'm pretty sure of it."

Myles punched at the face of his cell. "That's a darn good string of circumstantial evidence. I'm calling the detective who's been on that case. If they can find that crate at the landfill, that biker's body should be in there."

Stump grinned. "Tell them the girlfriend drives a black SUV and I know her license plate number."

Myles beamed and shot Stump a respectful "thumbs up."

CHAPTER 89

A chilly drizzle washed Miranda's face as she stuffed the computer behind the passenger's seat of her SUV, which was packed to the rim with anything of value that might later be pawned. Exhausted from having pulled an all-nighter, she wiped her forehead on the back of her arm. All that was left to retrieve was a final armload of clothes and a thermos of coffee that would last until Phoenix.

Inside, she peed one last time, washed up and looked at her watch again. Six-thirty. Pre-rush hour. She grabbed the last stack of clothes, all pantsuits, and flicked off the switches on the way out.

Outdoors, Don was behind the garage. A hint of daylight glistened off Mac's motorcycle, which still lay on its side. A lightning bolt flashed in the distance and a deep belch of thunder followed. She piled her things on top of the computer, closed the door and started her SUV. She buckled up and adjusted her rear-view mirror just as a dark sedan pulled into the driveway behind her.

She watched as a mature man and a younger woman swiftly approached her SUV. The fellow came up on the driver's side, while the woman went the other way. Possibly cops. Adrenalin began to swirl inside her. Her eyes flashed toward the garage. Don wasn't coming. She was on her own. She dropped one hand to her stomach and lowered her window. "Can I help you?" It sounded stupid.

"Yes ma'am," the fellow said, flashing a badge, just as two other police cars and a white pick-up pulled to her curb. "I'm Sergeant Byrdswain. Palmdale Police Department. That's Detective Sanchez. We have to ask you some questions. Can we step inside?"

Freaked out and fingers shaking, Miranda sneaked another peek out back but there was no sign of Don. Maybe they wouldn't find him. "I'd rather not. I already locked up," she said, trying to keep her voice from quivering.

The sergeant held up a folded sheet of paper. "It's a search warrant, ma'am. I'm afraid you don't have any choice." This was looking really, really bad. She began to breathe deeply.

Detective Sanchez whispered something to Byrdswain, then motioned for two uniformed officers by the street to join him, while she remained outdoors.

Inside, Byrdswain gazed around. "Anybody else in here?" he asked Miranda.

"We're alone," she replied, her throat dry, thickened from rapid breathing.

He gestured toward a love seat. "Have a seat right there, ma'am." He stood in front of her and motioned for the officers to search the home. "You know why we're here, don't you?"

"No, why?" she said softly, while she stuffed trembling fingers under her thighs.

"Alright. Let me make this a little easier on you." His eyes pierced hers. "We have a witness who says he saw your vehicle in town, behind the convenience store at a trash container."

"There are lots of vehicles like mine."

"True, but the witness said there were two people there —one of them was a woman who matches your description. He said he helped them load a big wooden box into the dumpster."

Her heart pounded in her chest with all the force of a freight train. "Well, it wasn't me. It's just a coincidence."

"Don't think so." Byrdswain pulled a small notebook out of his pocket, opened it and showed a page to Miranda. "See, right here. He got your license plate number."

Her stomach tightened, but she didn't move.

"You'll never guess what he suspected."

A powerful thunderclap rumbled overhead, as if to warn her to remain silent.

"He thought there might have been a murder. He was a pretty smart young man so we thought we'd better check it out. It took a while but the people at the landfill found the wooden box, ma'am, just like the witness suspected. We knew that victim. His name was Mac Evans. My partner threw up when she saw what happened to that poor man's face."

For the first time since Miranda hit Mac, her mind flashed to an image of his mangled skull. Her hands flew to her mouth and she nearly barfed.

"We checked with the post office and found out Mr. Evans had just filed a change of address to this location. We know his death relates to another one, that of the assistant principal at the high school. Might have something to do with the death of a doctor, too. If so, we'll find the connection before too long. Do I need to go on, ma'am?"

Busted, Miranda lowered her head and sobbed. "No."

"The only other thing we don't know is the whereabouts of your other partner. Mr. Evans's twin—the ex-con?"

Just then Detective Sanchez entered the home, damp from the drizzle. "He's behind the garage, Sergeant, in a brand-new grave, covered with manure." Sanchez turned to Miranda. "That's him, isn't it?"

CHAPTER 90

After Detective Sanchez's discovery, she read Miranda her rights. Then the detectives spoke privately while two uniformed cops guarded Miranda. When done, Byrdswain spoke to Miranda. "My partner's going to take it from here. If I were you, I'd pay close attention to what she has to say."

Miranda lifted her head. The young detective could have passed for a teenager.

Detective Sanchez waited until Byrdswain was outside to speak. "We know this wasn't your idea. Your boyfriend was a fast talker and you were in love. I know how that can be. I had a boyfriend like that in college."

Miranda sighed. "I loved both of them."

"That happens sometimes."

"Mac didn't know about Don, but Don suffered more because he knew what Mac and I were up to. I should have known better. The world will be a better place without any of us."

"You left a lot of destruction behind. Not just your lovers, but Rachel Johnson and her grandmother."

"Yeah, I'm really sorry about her. Mac was, too. He said she was a very charming and trusting woman." Miranda shook her head. "I can't believe I let Don talk me into killing anybody."

Sanchez leaned forward. "Nobody deserves to be treated like that, especially frail seniors, but I'm going to let you in

394

on a secret. We want to give that woman full closure and help her get her money back as quickly as possible, so after you get booked and get an attorney, if you'll help us make that easy for her I might be able to do something for you."

Miranda looked in the young detective's eyes. "What could you possibly do for me? I'm going to be behind bars the rest of my life."

"But which bars? There's a big difference between Valley State Prison and Central California Women's Facility. It's newer, less crowded, not many gang members, more things to do. In this case, sooner is better for everybody. It's up to you."

Miranda lowered her hand to her stomach. "Will they let me keep my baby?"

Sanchez's back straightened. She stared at Miranda. "You're pregnant?"

"Just found out yesterday, I don't know which one is the father."

Sanchez held out a steady hand. "I'm sorry, but prison is no place for babies. Do you have somebody else who can raise the baby?"

Miranda shook her head. "Not really, but Mickey would have made a wonderful uncle."

*　*　*

Considering Stump played a key role in breaking the case and that Myles was a detective who knew the workings of an investigation, Byrdswain had allowed them to go along for the arrest.

After what seemed like an entire school year the sergeant came outside and indicated to Myles and Stump that he'd be right back. He went behind the garage for a few minutes before he approached Myles's side of the truck.

"Stump was right," Byrdswain said. "Looks like a two-fer," Brydswain said. He flipped a thumb toward the garage. "A second one's out back—in a crude grave."

"Can we go back there?" Stump asked with the same glee as a kid who was about to go on his first adult ride at Disneyland.

Myles shook his head as Byrdswain gave the answer. "The county boys have to take the body out of here and do an investigation before we do anything else." He held up a small plastic bag. "This case is still unfolding. Got two engagement rings in here."

"Did the woman confess?" Myles asked.

"Pretty much. My partner's wrapping it up with her now."

Just then the house door opened and Detective Sanchez led the woman Stump had seen at the convenience store parking lot, now handcuffed, to the first cop car and helped her get into the back seat. Sanchez gave a thumb's up to Byrdswain, who tipped his head in return. "I can tell you one thing," he said turning to Myles. "Some of these young people are pretty impressive." He pointed at Stump. "That includes this one. He'd make a good detective some day."

"That's my son," Myles said. "I couldn't be prouder."

A peaceful warmth filled Stump. A biological dad couldn't be any better than this.

CHAPTER 91

Over the weeks that followed the arrest, Miranda Munchak revealed the entire story in exchange for being sent to Central California Women's Facility. All of the relevant parties including Myles and Stump were advised of the outcome.

After hearing what happened to Stump's mom, Ms. Johnson's grandmother wanted to meet the young man who had been through as much as she had, yet ultimately proved that her granddaughter didn't commit suicide after all. A buffet dinner was scheduled in Stump's honor. Everybody agreed to keep the event upbeat and not to dwell on either death.

When the evening came, Stump was the most relaxed he'd been in weeks. Just blocks from the elderly woman's home, Stump leaned forward. "Ironic isn't it, Myles?"

Myles glanced his way. "What's that?"

"A while back, all I wanted was for my mom to help me find my dad, but instead she introduced me to you. Now you're my dad. I like that, because I always knew whoever my dad was, he would be somebody special."

Myles grinned, tuned the corner. "Thanks, Stumpster. You're pretty special, too."

When they arrived, they were told to refer to the grandmother as Granny. They were introduced to a handful of Granny's friends, along with Anderson Powell, an elderly reporter from the local newspaper, and Powell's photographer.

Myles and Stump were seated next to Mr. Powell and an old-fashioned tape recorder. Within seconds, various people probed Stump for the details of how he solved the case. Did he have any help? Did his dad really do it and just give him the credit? What did he learn from the experience? But, thankfully nobody asked about his mom.

Finally Powell asked a question of his own. "I understand you memorized the bad guys' license plates before you knew anything about them. Is that right?"

Stump shook his head. "I don't really memorize them, but sometimes I see patterns or messages. That plate was *prime*."

"Prime for what?" Powell asked.

"Just prime. It was a zero followed by REO and then the number one hundred seven."

"What's so special about that?"

"Easy. When you see zero and REO together it looks like Oreo. Everybody likes Oreos. They're sorta *prime* cookies."

"Is that it? Cookies?"

"Not all of it. One hundred seven is the first three-digit prime number that is also a prime number when you read it backwards. So when you turn it around you get seven hundred one. Either way, you get a prime number. Once you group those two 'prime' things together," he said, making air quotes, "you couldn't forget it if you wanted to."

"What the heck is a prime number?" Granny's next-door neighbor asked. "I know we talked about them when I was in school but that was sixty years ago."

Stump smiled. "It's a whole number that is only divisible by the number one and itself."

"Huh? That's still too complicated for this old gal. Thank goodness I still know what Oreos are. Do we have any of those?"

Everybody laughed and then Granny spoke. "You know something, Stump. You remind me of Pappy. He was always good with numbers and puzzles too." Stump blushed. It was nice to be near-normal again.

Eventually they ate their dinner and coffee was served, after which Granny tapped a spoon on a glass. "Can I have everybody's attention please? I have something I want to say." She took a plain white envelope out of a nearby hutch. "I want you all to know I am so grateful to young Stump here, I have decided to give him a reward."

What? Stump glanced at Myles, who smiled while a smattering of applause sounded.

"There's a check in this envelope for three percent of the trust money that my husband and I once earmarked for our precious granddaughter, Rachel."

More cheers and applause wafted as Stump nervously accepted the envelope. "Really?"

"Yes, really. Open it," Granny said. "It's all yours. You deserve it."

Stump's hand trembled slightly as he smiled and opened the envelope slowly like he would a birthday card from his mom that might contain a five-dollar bill. He reached in and pulled out a pristine cashier's check in the incredible sum of $338,459.22. He jumped up. "Fantastic." Then he handed it to Myles and rushed toward his elderly benefactor. Granny welcomed the hug from the boy she knew had gone through a similar hell to her own.

"Pass it around the room," Granny said to Myles, "so everybody can see it." There was an endless chain of "ooh's" and "aah's" as Stump's check circled the room.

Finally, Powell asked, "What are you going to do with all that money?"

Stump looked at Myles, who was grinning as much as Stump was. "Well, first I want to buy my own laptop. Then some video games, and my own phone, maybe a big screen TV and some weights."

"What about college?" Myles asked in a mood-killing, fatherly tone.

"He's right," Anderson Powell added. "A young fellow like you is certainly college material."

Stump cocked his head and placed a finger to his chin. "I know. I'll set half of it aside for college, but I want to use the rest to make a doggie park and name it after both Ms. Johnson and my mom. I want to put in lots of lilac bushes because they were my mom's favorite flowers."

Myles patted Stump on the back and the guests indicated their approval with still more applause. Several women were shocked that Stump knew which flower was his mother's favorite, let alone that he wanted to do something unselfish with the money.

Granny had tears in her eyes when she clinked the glass again. "A park like that," she said to Stump, "is going to cost a lot of money, maybe even more than your check. I've got a vacant lot on the edge of town. I've never done anything with it. I will give that to you too, and that can be your park. All you have to do is finish it off the way you want. And you'll still have enough left over for college someday."

There was a standing ovation and for one incredible moment, the *Stumpster* was back.

ABOUT THE AUTHOR

Like most Americans I liked my career of several decades but I have to admit that I didn't always approach the mornings with wild enthusiasm.

But then, I retired and discovered something I never would have guessed: When the day is mine, I love to get up even earlier. Now I'm the guy who wakes up the rooster. I still work as much as I ever did, only I now work on things that bring me a different form of compensation. Like writing books.

Some have asked me where I get my ideas, but it's no mystery. I had a storied youth with six sisters and a wild family. When I wasn't engulfed in that world, I spent a fair amount of my time wandering the alleys and streets of our neighborhood. A fellow learns a lot from all of those people even before he arrives for his first day of school. If he has the ability to recall the characters and the activities in which they engaged, and blend that with a dash of make-believe, there's a goldmine full of fodder from which to draw his inspiration.

BOOKS BY THIS AUTHOR

NON-FICTION

Instant Experience for Real Estate Agents
(Multiple Award Winner)

Stop Flushing Your Money Down the Drain
(Multiple Award Winner)

FICTION

Three Deadly Twins
(Now Available on Amazon)

Monday's Revenge
(To be Released Winter 2015)

Grandma's BFF Does Coke
(This one is beginning to boil)

Zero Degree Murder
(*Zero* is dying to get off the back burner)

All books available in paperback or ebooks

Books may be ordered from
www.bookcrafters.net
Amazon or other online bookstores